T0274627

# Dear Wendy

# Dear Wendy

## Ann Zhao

FEIWEL AND FRIENDS

New York

Readers, please be advised that *Dear Wendy* contains depictions of aphobia (discrimination against asexual and aromantic individuals) and mild anxiety, as well as other issues. For a detailed list, visit **annzhao.com/dear-wendy.**

A FEIWEL AND FRIENDS BOOK

An imprint of Macmillan Publishing Group, LLC

120 Broadway, New York, NY 10271 • fiercereads.com

Our books may be purchased in bulk for promotional, educational, or business use. Please contact your local bookseller or the Macmillan Corporate and Premium Sales Department at (800) 221-7945 ext. 5442 or by email at MacmillanSpecialMarkets@macmillan.com.

Library of Congress Cataloging-in-Publication Data

Names: Zhao, Ann, author.
Title: Dear Wendy / Ann Zhao.
Description: First edition. | New York : Feiwel and Friends, 2024. | Audience: Ages 13 and up. | Audience: Grades 10–12. | Summary: Aromantic and asexual students Sophie and Jo, engaged in an online feud as the creators of popular relationship advice accounts "Dear Wendy" and "Sincerely Wanda," unwittingly become real-life friends and navigate their shared aroace identities as they face the challenges of college life.
Identifiers: LCCN 2023028050 | ISBN 9781250885005 (hardcover)
Subjects: CYAC: Universities and colleges—Fiction. | Online social networks—Fiction. | Advice columnists—Fiction. | Friendship—Fiction. | Asexual people—Fiction. | LCGFT: Novels.
Classification: LCC PZ7.1.Z5127 De 2024 | DDC [Fic]—dc23
LC record available at https://lccn.loc.gov/2023028050

First edition, 2024
Book design by Julia Bianchi
Feiwel and Friends logo designed by Filomena Tuosto
Printed in the United States of America

ISBN 978-1-250-88500-5

10  9  8  7  6  5  4  3  2  1

To the real-life Wendys and Wandas who brought me joy during my time as a Wellesley student.

And to the people who are about to realize they're asexual and/or aromantic after reading this book. (You never know. It could be you.)

# Dear reader,

I'm going to be fully honest with you: *Dear Wendy* was first and foremost written to entertain myself while stuck in my room doing Zoom class. And it achieved that purpose! But secondly, it was written out of love for many things: Wellesley College, the asexual and aromantic community, and queer people of color.

This novel is a fictionalized and at times idealized portrayal of the college I attended. The Wellesley of *Dear Wendy* is a perfect place for Sophie and Jo to be (did COVID even happen in the DW universe? Who's to say!), but the real Wellesley, like any institution, is not perfect. Nevertheless, there are many things that I have found to love about it, and I'm happy to have had an overall positive experience as a student. I hope that this story can immerse you in all the most fun, quirky, and admirable parts of campus life.

Although this is *not* a semiautobiographical novel, the discussions of aromanticism and asexuality in this book, as well as many other aspects of identity, are largely informed by my own experience. Jo and Sophie, as well as all their friends, reflect the knowledge that I have, based on my life and the lives of those around me. One book cannot reflect every single a-spec experience and all of its intersections with other identity markers—my goal with *Dear Wendy* was to add to the a-spec literary canon, not to encompass it. I hope, though, that at least some parts of this book will resonate with readers who are looking for familiarity. I know that *Dear Wendy* certainly would have helped me when I was a teenager. It still helps me now.

Finally, all my love goes to the queer kids (or adults!) of color who have picked up this book. Sophie has been living in my head since I was thirteen and desperate for my life to be represented on a page, and I'm endlessly glad that I finally found a place for her in the form of this story. If you see parts of yourself in Sophie or any of the other QPOC characters in this book and you're not sure what comes next, please know that you are not alone, that there are many of us out there, and that you will find your community one day—if you haven't already.

On a lighter note, I'm, like, such a Wendy for writing this author's note. I promise the book itself is not this serious. I wrote it just for funsies, after all.

Sincerely,
Ann

# CHAPTER 1

## *Sincerely*

### SOPHIE

Giving love advice to the chronically heartsick students of Wellesley College is practically a full-time job.

When I started Dear Wendy last semester, I already expected it to take up a lot of my time. But in the months that I've been on Instagram anonymously answering my peers' questions about how to navigate their love lives, I've devoted more and more time to this endeavor. Day after day, my mind is occupied with thoughts of how to advise dozens of strangers on their personal lives. I've even had a dream or two about it.

I'm crafting a response to my latest question when my roommate, Priya, says, "Hey, Sophie, look at this."

Priya is still in her pajamas—a maroon T-shirt from high school that reads JOHNS CREEK GLADIATORS and a pair of checkered fleece pants. Her long, wavy hair is a mess, but her brown skin is annoyingly clear despite her total lack of a skin care routine. She looks absolutely indignant.

She hands me her cell phone, open to Instagram, on a profile page with three posts, all slideshows in Comic Sans.

I frown. "What am I looking at?"

"The profile," Priya says, pointing at the username. "Look at the posts."

I take it all in. The username is @wandawellesley69. The profile picture is the Wellesley *W* logo but distorted and discolored. The display name says, "sincerely, wanda," the bio reads "dm your submissions!!!", and the account has just over a hundred followers. I grab Priya's phone from her hand, muttering, "Let me see," and open the first post.

**anon**: my boyfriend keeps ignoring me every time i tell him that the way he talks to me makes me feel insecure. how do i tell him to stop???

And on the next picture in the photoset:

**answer**: omg dump his ass!!!!!!!!!! get a partner who can treat you right!!!!! life is too short for you to be dealing with dickheads!!!!!! 🖤 🖤 🖤

The other two posts look pretty similar: an anonymous person asks a question, and the person presumably behind the account answers.

"Okay . . . well, this is weird," I say.

"It looks just like your account," Priya says. "Like, besides the aesthetic and the general attitude."

She's right.

Priya is the only person at my school who knows my secret. I won't lie, it's wonderful to know that so much of Wellesley pays attention to my advice. I'm used to telling people what to do—I am, after all, an eldest daughter—but with Dear Wendy, I think people actually listen because I'm a disembodied wall of text instead of a petite Chinese girl who sounds shrill if she tries to raise her voice.

This account looks like what would happen if someone with absolutely no sense of professionalism decided to try being me.

Aside from the fact that they're calling themself "Sincerely, Wanda," thereby making it very obvious who they're trying to imitate—Wendy and Wanda are our college's jargon for type A and type B personalities—@wandawellesley69 offends me because they seriously have no style. There isn't much worse than Comic Sans on a blank white background.

"Oh my god," I say, not really knowing how I feel about all this just yet. "Um. Yeah, that's definitely like me. That's—that's so rude of them." I glance at the clock in the corner of my computer screen. "Hey, it's almost 2:15. Go to class."

"I still have time," she insists as she takes back her phone from me. "And besides, this is important. We need to know: Who's Wanda?"

I roll my eyes at her. "Dear Wendy has over a *thousand* followers who don't know her identity, so why don't you put this aside for later and try not to be late to class on the second week of the semester?"

Priya sighs. "Fine. But we're coming back to this."

While Priya pulls on an acceptable outfit for her 2:20 P.M. English class, I turn back to my computer, to the response I'm supposed to be typing. This is an easy enough question to answer—just another person hesitating over whether their crush likes them or not. I start typing: *I'll admit, the line between platonic and romantic relationships can be pretty confusing—*

"Hey, I'm going now," Priya says, snapping me out of my thoughts.

She's standing by the door, all bundled up in a winter coat that's far too long and bulky for the late January weather. (Thanks, climate change.) Her hair pokes out from under a hand-knit beanie—I think her girlfriend, Izzy, gave it to her. She has a tote bag slung over her shoulder.

"Have fun," I say. "Wait, are we doing dinner tonight?"

"Yeah, I'll text you."

She leaves and closes the door.

As soon as I look back at my screen, at the mess of words I just typed, I know I can't focus. Sincerely, Wanda is on my mind.

I get up and walk across my room. After moving three potted plants out of the way—African violet Fernando, cactus Janet, and crocodile fern Ted—I have enough space to sit down at our window seat. Priya and I accumulated these plants over the course of fall semester, and it's a miracle they survived in the care of our neighbors during winter break while we were hundreds of miles away—me in Illinois, her in Georgia.

I pull out my phone and look up the username. @wandawellesley69—how very creative and mature. I look through the account, reading the posts over and over again and trying to find some indication of what all this is about. Sincerely, Wanda is definitely trying to be ... well ... something like me.

I don't want to start anything, but what exactly is going on?

# CHAPTER 2

# Dear God, I Really Don't Want to Answer a Sex Thing

## JO

Wendy Wellesley is a state of being. A mindset. The archetype of the perfect Wellesley student—a high-achieving, no-nonsense young adult of the twenty-first century.

That student who always gets called on by the professor? A Wendy. The one who actually eats three meals a day? A Wendy. Someone who reads nonfiction for fun? Definitely a Wendy.

So, you know . . . not me.

If anything, I'm a Wanda Wellesley: just trying my best to have fun and relax (most of the time). So that's what I named the Instagram account I created a few days ago. Everyone knows about the Wendy/Wanda dichotomy, so everyone is going to know exactly what I'm trying to do here.

Funny that I'm getting followers now—lots of questions too—when it was originally supposed to be just one post.

It was all because my roommate Katy Murphy had the shittiest boyfriend to ever exist: Jason Wilmington-Montgomery.

Look: I always hate it when my friends date people. I hated it in high school, the way it made my friendships fluctuate endlessly. I hated it in middle school, when relationships barely count as such yet, because it simply made me uncomfortable. But when I say I hated Katy's relationship with Jason, I mean it.

You can't trust MIT frat boys, you can't trust guys with *J*-names, and you definitely can't trust guys with pretentious old-money last names (two of them, at that). Katy met him on Tinder in December. They became official just before winter break and dated through almost all of it—as it turned out, the two of them live two towns away from each other in New York.

The few weeks that they were together were torturous. For Katy, for me, and for Lianne, the third roommate in our triple-occupancy dorm room. We weren't even on campus. Lianne and I experienced all of it through Katy's frantic texts.

How do you describe a guy like Jason?

Frankly, he's an asshole.

When Katy brought up her bisexuality, Jason insisted she was straight but "wanted attention." After Katy pushed back against that, he started saying that it was "kind of hot" that she liked girls. He tried to pressure Katy to have sex when she didn't want to yet. Every now and then, he made some vaguely racist comments, expecting Katy, who's also white, to agree with him, and when she challenged them, he got mad.

She tried telling him that the way he treated her made her feel insecure and generally terrible, and he ignored her. After two weeks of dating him, Katy went back to her high school therapist for an emergency session.

Good on Katy for having her life together; I would've just wallowed in despair if I were in that situation. Not that I'd ever be, since I have no interest in dating, but all the same.

With help from her therapist, Katy was already making plans to break up with Jason when I came up with my Instagram idea last week, after we'd all come back to campus for spring semester. She never asked Dear Wendy for help since she'd gone straight to counseling, but I didn't want her to miss out on the already-iconic Wellesley experience of getting advice from some random person who we all decided has the authority to tell us what to do.

It was easy to fashion a simple Q&A template. I made the two slides, created an account on Instagram, posted the images, and DMed them to Katy, saying "You're welcome" and adding a silly set of emojis.

When she saw it, she rolled her eyes and said, "Thank you, I think." I also showed it to Lianne, who responded, "You're literally the worst. Do one for me."

Katy broke up with Jason the next day. It's been nearly a week now, and all is right in room STO-202.

I did end up making a post for Lianne as well, just so she wouldn't miss out.

**anon:** i think i am extremely cool and sexy, so why don't i have a girlfriend? pls help

**answer:** it's funny how everybody at this school complains about being single, sees each other complaining about being single, and then you all remain single anyway!

It was funny. It made Lianne laugh, at least. But then Katy shared it to her story, and she has a lot of friends here, so the followers came streaming in.

My school is very different from most other colleges in America. Different, even, from most other liberal arts colleges. It's part of the historically women's college charm. (Not just a women's college. We're not all women here, despite what our administration often says.) Being in an environment where none of your peers are cisgender men really compels you to be your most authentic self, including on social media. Actually, especially on social media.

Sure, there are many official Wellesley Instagram accounts run by offices of the college. Most of our clubs and organizations have accounts too. But we also have a ton of weird anonymous ones. The one that tells you what ice cream is at what dining hall. The one that posts pictures of various patches of grass. Dear Wendy, the love advice account that only just popped up this year, is the one I modeled my account after.

At this school, as soon as you make an account, people find you. All it takes is one or two students following you to cause a massive ripple effect as the algorithm suggests you to anyone even tangentially affiliated with the college, which is magnified when you follow them back, which, of course, I always do, because that's just basic internet etiquette.

Since then, I've been getting a lot of DMs asking for my take on people's problems.

I talked it out with Katy and Lianne, and I guess I'm doing this. I'm going to run an advice account. I don't want people to think of me as a replacement for Dear Wendy. More like . . . an alternative. A second opinion. Someone fun and honest instead of dead serious and oddly chipper. Someone who's as much of a disaster as they are, instead of the poster child for the light academia aesthetic, which is outdated and uncool anyway.

I'm making a fourth post to put up. Someone asked me a sex thing, and dear god, I really don't want to answer a sex thing, but I've already replied to their DM saying I'll give it my best shot.

Except what are you *supposed* to say when a person tells you their boyfriend doesn't want to wear condoms? I sure don't know. I've never experienced sexual attraction, and I've certainly never experienced sexual intercourse.

There's only one person I know who's had sex with a guy before.

I look over at Katy. She's sitting on our beanbag chair in the corner of the room, sketching on her iPad. Her headphones rest perfectly over her long, straight hair, a few shades darker brown than my curls, and she's wearing a floral maxi dress that drapes loosely over her curves.

She looks so serene and comfy. I almost don't want to bother her.

I do anyway. "Katy?"

No answer. Either the music is incredibly loud, or those headphones cancel noise better than I thought.

"Katy!" I say again, waving at her.

She looks up, alarmed, and removes her headphones.

"Everything okay?" she asks.

"I have a question," I say.

She raises her eyebrows. "What is it?"

I take a breath. I don't know how to start this lightly. "So, you've had sex with a cisgender man before."

What a great way to start a conversation, Joanna. Isn't it fun to talk about your roommate's sex life? I love having the knowledge that Katy has had other people's parts touching her parts. Very cool. Very awesome. Couldn't be me! I would not like my vagina to be seen in any context except medical.

Thankfully, Katy doesn't seem too fazed. "Uh . . . not since high school, but yeah. Why?"

"Um." I shake my head. "What would you do if he refused to use protection?"

She considers this for a moment. "I mean, I just wouldn't have sex with him. I didn't do it with Jason, right?"

"Mm. Yeah, that makes sense."

"Why do you ask, is this for your Instagram?"

"Yeah, I don't know what to tell them."

Katy shrugs. "Unless this person is fine with going on birth control *and* insisting they both get tested for STIs *and* trusts that their partner won't cheat—"

We're interrupted by our door opening to reveal Lianne coming back from class. She's wearing a silk-lined knit beanie that completely covers her closely cropped hair, and her leather jacket has little drops of water on it from the rain outside. Despite this, her dark brown concealer, which I know is covering a few acne scars, looks entirely undisturbed.

Comparatively, Lianne is a bit more of a mystery to me than Katy. We didn't get along super well when we started living together—we had such different living habits and schedules—but now she's the only person I know who can match my energy at any moment.

Case in point: She takes one look at me and Katy and says, "Am I interrupting something? 'Cause you two look way too serious."

"We're talking about condoms," Katy replies, totally nonchalantly.

Lianne's eyes grow wide. "You're—*what?* Why?"

To be fair, there's pretty much no serious reason why Katy and I would talk about condoms. I'm not going to need to procure one anytime soon. Or probably ever.

"Someone DMed me asking what to do if their boyfriend refuses to wear condoms," I explain.

Lianne scoffs. "Break up, obviously. Would they rather get chlamydia? Or . . . uh . . . pregnant?"

"Well, wait," Katy says. "Maybe they can negotiate somehow. Not every guy is a total piece of garbage."

"Yeah, I do feel like I shouldn't say *dump them* for every question I get," I add.

Lianne shrugs. "Say what you want. It's your account."

Oh yeah. I *can* say whatever I want.

Except no, I can't, because if I say something wrong, everyone will hate me, and I would very much like not to be publicly canceled by all the chronically online students at this college before I finish my first year.

"Anyway," Katy says, "Lianne, how was class?"

Their voices fade out from my mind as I unlock my phone, where I have . . . six messages on Instagram from @dearwendywellesley.

Huh.

This is much more interesting than hypothetical social media shame.

I should've known Dear Wendy would find me. But I didn't realize it'd be so soon.

**@dearwendywellesley:**
Hi! My name is Wendy, I'm the person who runs this account
(I mean, that's not my real name, of course)
(Or maybe it is! Who knows!)
I found your account today and it's very funny!

And I just wanted to welcome you to the Wellesley
Instagram community
I'm sure you'll have a lot of cool things to contribute :)

What kind of passive-aggressive bullshit is this? A smiley face?
Seriously?

**@wandawellesley69:**
oh
hello
thanks? glad to be here lol??

I can't tell what this person is up to. Do they want me to take down my
Instagram? No, right? Because they're welcoming me.

**@dearwendywellesley:**
Glad to have you!
I just wanted to know, if this wasn't too much to ask . . .
Is your account supposed to be a parody of mine or
something??
It's cool if it is :) but I was curious

Again with the smiley face.

**@wandawellesley69:**
oh uh . . . not really???
more of
a mockery of my friends
that turned into giving actual advice to wellesley
people, sort of
i'm not trying to tread on your territory though!
just wanted to do something fun

---

If I were truly altruistic, I would offer to shut down my account now that my initial goal has been achieved. But I was consistently given a check-minus on my elementary school report cards for being "considerate and kind to others," so naturally, I don't say anything else.

And it honestly works in my favor.

**@dearwendywellesley:**
Ah totally fine!!
I wanted to make sure haha
Might be cool to have another advice-giver on board

Interesting. I can't tell what their motive here is.

I send off a reply that I think is adequately passive-aggressive—*super cool :)*—and a couple seconds later, I see they've liked my message. And that's it.

Should I be intimidated or something?

Dear Wendy,

I have a crush on one of my friends, but I can't tell if she likes me back. We've been spending a lot of time together lately; sometimes, I come over to study, but then we end up watching Netflix on her laptop. One time, we decided to meet up for lunch, and she replied, "It's a date!" but I don't know if she meant that in a friend way or a romantic way. She likes to hug me a lot when we see each other, but I'm not sure if she's a touchy person with everyone or if it's just me. How do I talk to her about it?

Best,
Confused and Gay (she/her)

Dear Confused,

I'll admit, the line between platonic and romantic relationships can be pretty confusing. We all sort of flirt with each other in a platonic way, even the straight girls. (*Especially* the straight girls, if I'm being honest, but let's not unpack that today.) Some questions to ask yourself: Does she spend as much time with other friends as she does with you? Is she as physically affectionate with others? Does she have a habit of flirting with all her friends? If the answers to all those questions are no, then maybe she likes you back, and even if the answers are yes, it's still possible for her to be open to dating you (unless she's straight, of course, but I'm assuming you've already considered that).

The next time you're together, pay attention to the way she acts around you. Look for signs of attraction—lingering eye contact, leaning toward you, blushing. And in return, adjust your own body language so she can tell you like her.

If playing this waiting game feels a little slow for you, though, then tell her how you feel! Look at my post from January 22 for tips on how to tell someone you like them; the most important thing is to make it clear that you respect their boundaries and will only pursue a type of relationship that you're both comfortable with.

Sincerely yours,
Wendy Wellesley

**priyachakrabarti05 9h**
ah the eternal gay struggle
3 likes Reply

**floresalicia214 8h**
absolutely losing my mind at "especially the straight girls, if i'm being honest, but let's not unpack that today"
7 likes Reply

**wandawellesley69 10h**
lol just make out already
4 likes Reply

> **dearwendywellesley 9h**
> Or they could handle the situation like a mature adult??
> 1 like Reply

> **wandawellesley69 4h**
> someone tell wendy that adults do, in fact, kiss
> 2 likes Reply

# CHAPTER 3

## Services

### SOPHIE

I'm hunched over, my right ankle delicately balanced across my left leg, listening to ABBA on blast, when Priya calls my name.

"Sophie! Hello?"

My eyes snap upward, and I take my earbud out of my left ear. Priya, tucked under a massive pile of blankets on the bed across the room, is glaring at me. We just woke up and are doing our usual morning routine (Priya groggily checking her notifications while I put on my workout clothes and stretch before a run).

"Huh?" I say.

Priya laughs. "Did you even hear me at all?"

"Oh. Sorry." I stand up straight. "What's going on?"

"I was asking if Izzy can come over tomorrow."

Priya's girlfriend—and my only remaining friend from high school—is a freshman at Brown University, which is just close enough to us that the two of them visit each other every couple of weeks. They are disgustingly cute together.

"Oh, yeah," I say.

I never deny Priya (or myself) the opportunity to see Izzy. I've been friends with Izzy since one fateful school lunch period where we bonded over being queer Chinese American former-gifted-kids who spent all our free time on our high school extracurriculars (me in yearbook, her in a politics club).

"Is it fine if she gets here at, like, 1:00?" Priya says.

"Go for it."

"Cool," Priya says. She smiles. "I can't wait to see her."

"Ew," I say jokingly.

"*Ew* yourself," she retorts.

This is a frequent exchange of ours. Priya says something cute about Izzy; I mock her.

It's all in good fun. Izzy is the reason Priya and I live together. They'd been friends for a couple of years because of their politics club and had been dating for just a little while when I got into Wellesley.

I was scared at first to get to know Izzy's girlfriend. High school relationships don't tend to last, and this wouldn't be the first time that I'd be friends with two people who were dating each other. But luckily, I didn't have to worry. Priya and I immediately hit it off when I messaged her, and I quickly realized after a few conversations with both of them that their relationship was more than just a high school fling.

It's a breath of fresh air to be friends with a couple that doesn't shove me to the side, which has happened to me before. Izzy talks to me as much as ever, and the two of them always consider my feelings when they make plans. For that, I am eternally grateful.

I exit my room to take the elevator down to our basement; there's a treadmill in Claflin Hall's ugliest common room. While I'm descending in the elevator, I check my phone, where I see that Wanda has replied very rudely to me. Of *course* I know adults kiss.

I shake my head and send them a DM.

**@dearwendywellesley:**
Are you going to be putting sassy comments on all of my posts from now on?
Would've appreciated a heads-up lol

The thing is, I don't really mind these comments, but it does feel a little weird for this account that just popped up to be suddenly antagonizing me, even as a joke. I work too hard for this.

I turn on the treadmill and start running in the empty, echoing room, trying to put Wanda—and my own account—out of my mind. But my mind will not cooperate.

Dear Wendy started because Priya asked me a question last November. A pretty simple one, at that.

We were sitting around a table in our crowded, poorly lit dining hall eating brunch with our next-door neighbor, Alicia. Alicia, as a vegan, hates weekend brunch because she can never eat anything except a salad or a poorly constructed sandwich. I, however, love weekend brunch, in that I also hate it, but it's an opportunity to send my dad—a home cook—a picture of what I'm eating so that he can share my disgust for mass-produced scrambled eggs.

That day, I sent him a picture of my eggs with some off-brand sriracha on them. I thought I was being fancy. He promptly sent me some money on Zelle to buy a carton of real eggs, which I sent back because I don't have a skillet, a spatula, or the patience to wait for my dorm kitchen's incredibly slow burner to heat up.

Anyway, while I was taking a bite of these gross eggs, Priya spoke out of nowhere.

"If I haven't seen Izzy for a couple of weeks, and I *don't* really, really miss her, is that bad?" she asked.

My immediate thought was, *Of course not, your relationship is the most stable one I've ever encountered, what are you talking about?*

That would be a little rude to say outright, though, so I took another bite of eggs and said, "Well, I think you're just out of the honeymoon phase."

"Imagine being with someone long enough to move out of the honeymoon phase," Alicia said, which earned a laugh from me and a pout from Priya.

"But I don't want to," Priya whined. "It's fun being in the honeymoon phase. It's how I know we're still in love."

I laughed. "I never said you didn't love each other. But these days, you're used to being a couple, and you're used to being far away, so it doesn't hurt as much when you're apart. That's all. And besides, it's only been two weeks since you last saw her. You spent senior year hundreds of miles apart."

I'm still in awe that they managed to do long-distance like that, with Izzy in Chicago and Priya in Atlanta. I guess that's what happens when you meet the love of your life by doing remote work as high school club leaders.

Priya seemed to consider this, and then she let out a breath. "Yeah, you're probably right. I don't know. I just feel bad because, like, what if Izzy still misses me a lot?"

"Then . . . she misses you a lot," I said. "It doesn't mean you love her less; it just means her brain's taking a little longer to slow down its release of happy hormones. And you call each other, like, every day. Also, let me reiterate: It's been *two weeks.*"

"It's technically been less than two weeks," Priya admitted, which was true; she'd taken the train down to Providence on a Sunday, and the day we were talking was a Saturday.

"And you're still super happy every time you see her, right?" Alicia said.

Priya sighed. "You're right. I'm overthinking. How are you so good at this?"

I kicked my foot up and crossed my legs dramatically. "This is all a hundred percent from personal experience."

We all burst into giggles. I'm aromantic and asexual; I had, and still have, no experience whatsoever. My relationship knowledge at the time came almost exclusively from reading romance novels, though that would soon change.

"Really, though, you should capitalize off your relationship advice," Alicia said.

I gave little thought to that sentence for the rest of our conversation, but later that day, I suddenly remembered it. Maybe she was onto something.

I thought of a few ways I might be able to offer my services to the Wellesley community, and one thing led to another. I found myself coming up with some designs and making an Instagram account. I checked out a couple of self-help books from the library to do research. I created a Google Form for people to anonymously submit their relationship questions and confessions. I followed all the Wellesley students that I knew of.

I started getting submissions just days after that conversation with Priya and Alicia. And thus, Dear Wendy was born. Ever since then, I've been spending my free time fielding questions and restoring balance in people's lives as a neutral third-party observer.

It's one of my favorite parts of my day.

# CHAPTER 4

# A Slowly Dying Art

## JO

'm so glad it's the weekend.

I manage to sleep in a bit—always difficult when you have two roommates—and when I wake up, I find out that I have fifteen new followers (oh my god?) and two new questions for my Instagram alter ego. I then respond to a rude DM from Dear Wendy; dude, I don't need to give you a heads-up for my own comments.

After I eat a quick brunch with Lianne, I head over to my main commitment of the day: my radio show.

College radio stations are a dying art, but my college is nothing if not stubborn. I trained to be a DJ last semester for WZLY Wellesley, and now I host a weekly show on Sunday mornings.

Not many people listen to it. My roommates play the internet stream, and a few other people from my dorm might listen if I remind them in our group chat. A couple other students might tune in just for fun. My moms tune in every week because, as my moms, they will support anything that I do, and as local residents, they listen to the college radio anyway. That's about it; I don't really have any friends outside Wellesley that I can bully into listening.

I walk inside Billings Hall and down the stairs to the radio station. The white cinder-block walls of the lounge are covered with notes and scribbles from DJs past. It's mostly heartfelt messages from people who've graduated, but there's also a circle where someone traced their boob, song lyrics, and a few confessions from people who've had sex here.

I try not to think about that whenever I'm in this room.

Down another small flight of stairs are the actual studios. I wait for a couple of minutes for the last hour's DJ to finish, and then I walk inside Studio A, hearing pop music playing softly through the speakers as I set down my bag and take off my winter coat.

Playing my music is pretty straightforward. On the computer in the studio, I search my username on Spotify to find the playlist I made last night, and then I reach over to the soundboard, fade out our auto-player, and turn on the mic.

"You're listening to WZLY Wellesley, 91.5 FM," I say. "My name is Jo Ephron, no relation to *High School Musical* star Zac Efron. You'll note our names are pronounced slightly differently. We're going to start off with one of my all-time favorites; this is 'Oh No!' by MARINA from her album *The Family Jewels*."

Turn off the mic, click play on Spotify, fade in the music. All that's left to do is sit back and listen while the next three songs play.

I've gotten into a routine with this. Sometimes, I text my friends about my song choices. Sometimes, I have a dance party. Sometimes, if I'm pressed for time, I'll do homework.

Today, I'm answering questions from Instagram.

I pull out my positively ancient laptop from my bag. It's closer in age to my younger brother than to my phone, but I won't part from this computer until it refuses to turn on.

It takes a moment for my browser to open up so I can make my posts. I've been using Google Slides to do it, which I think is pretty ingenious of me but Katy thinks is deeply uncool.

If she were here, she would say something like, *You should really use Illustrator for these kinds of things.* Ha. Like my computer can house Adobe Illustrator without crashing for good.

Google Slides finally loads, and I get to work. I have a question from Jessica Nguyen, a fellow resident of my dorm.

**@jessie.nguyen14**
Hi! I have a submission for you if that's ok
Someone else at W who's never talked to me before
liked a bunch of my Instagram posts out of nowhere
Does this mean we're married now or???

Ah, Wellesley. Never change.

For a few moments, I consider what I can say in response and then type up her question and my answer.

*lmao pls,,, i know people are desperate for love but this probably means they don't understand proper instagram etiquette. (esp if they have a weird following/follower ratio, y'know??) pls chill sdklfjklsffjldks*

That'll suffice.

Right? Well, maybe not. I don't know. I think this is fine. This is funny enough. And it's not really that mean.

Okay. Yes. This looks great.

As "Oh No!" comes to a close and "Love Me More" by Mitski starts playing, I download my slides onto my phone and put them on Instagram. Easy peasy. Wendy seems to take this advice-giving stuff very seriously, but I'm having a good, fun time.

Right as my post uploads, I get a text message. It's Jessica, complimenting my choice of music. She must be listening to the stream.

I was just answering her Instagram question, and she has no idea.

This is fun.

# CHAPTER 5

# At the End of the Day, What Is Gender?

## JO

"**W**hat the hell did she say?" I whisper.

The person next to me shakes her head and shrugs.

Most of the professors here are extremely smart. That's, like, a baseline requirement for being a college professor, right? But being smart doesn't mean you have to be all pretentious about the way you speak, and my professor in WGST 110 (an intro-level class in women's and gender studies) doesn't seem to know that she can talk to us like we're normal people.

I'm pretty sure Dr. Lisa Fineman is talking about toxic masculinity. She keeps on using words like "hegemonic" and "juxtaposition" and "pervasive." Do I know what these words mean? Technically, yes. Do I know how to understand them when they're used together in a sentence along with a dozen other big words? Absolutely not.

You'd think that a 100-level class would be a little easier to comprehend. But I'm on week three of this class, and I have yet to figure out what's going on.

"Now, I'd like you all to turn to the person next to you for a few minutes and talk really quickly about the readings you did for today," Professor Fineman says. "And come up with at least two key takeaways that you might be able to share with the class."

I turn to my neighbor again. She's an East Asian girl with long hair held in a high ponytail, wisps of it tucked behind her Wayfarer glasses. She is positively swimming in her oversized mustard-yellow turtleneck sweater.

"Okay," she says, giving me a small smile. "Hi."

"Hey!" I say. "Uh, sorry, what's your name?"

I still don't know everyone's names, which I guess is okay because it's only the fifth time this class has met. It doesn't help that people constantly switch where they sit. But it looks like she doesn't know my name yet either, based on the way her shoulders lose their tension.

"I'm Sophie," she says. "She/her."

"Cool," I reply. "Jo, she/they."

Pronouns are second nature in introductions at our college, which is a fantastic improvement over high school. "She" and "they" both feel right to me, so I tell people to use both, and they don't question my femme appearance or pry about the precise nuances of my gender identity.

Which, to be honest, I don't even know myself. I'm a girl, but I'm sort of not a girl? Maybe? At the end of the day, what is gender?

That's actually the title of our class: "What Is Gender?" Ha.

Sophie seems unfazed. "Nice to meet you, Jo."

I nod. "Same to you."

We look at each other blankly. Class has been like this: Fineman tells us to talk, but none of us know each other that well, so we sit there not sure what to say for five minutes straight.

Best to begin by being relatable.

"Okay," I say, "before we talk about the reading, am I the only one who's fully lost whenever Fineman says *anything*?"

Sophie's eyes widen. "Oh, no, I can't figure it out either. It's like, I can tell she's saying things, and I know what all the words mean on their own, but together, they make no sense."

The sigh of relief I emit!

"I thought I was the only one," I say.

"You are definitely not."

That little icebreaker is enough to get us talking about our reading, which was actually pretty interesting. It's an essay about ways that the gender studies field has become more inclusive over time. Sophie notes, though, that most of the field is still super privileged: cishet, white, affluent, nondisabled, et cetera, et cetera.

"Mm," I say, a blank smile spreading on my face. "Disgusting!"

Sophie chuckles. "Yeah, there's still a lot of work to do."

After our class reconvenes and shares thoughts on the reading, Fineman reminds us that we're going to start doing group presentations next week.

"Please do not overexert yourself on this assignment," Fineman says. "You're leading a discussion on a reading, like what I do during class. You can use a slideshow, give handouts, or simply stand up here and talk. Your groups can have two to six people. The assignment is designed to be flexible."

She puts up a link to a Google Doc so we can sign up for a day to present.

I look around and make eye contact with Sophie. She raises her eyebrows hopefully. I've only known her for a few minutes, but . . . I guess we can work together.

I shrug and say, "Sure. Why not. Um, what day should we sign up for?"

Sophie frowns and scrolls through the document. Already, people are starting to sign up for slots. The only one still completely empty of names is the first possible day to present.

"Hmm." Sophie clicks her tongue. "The first day? The reading is about TERFs."

Trans-exclusionary radical feminists, the bane of my existence.

"Oh, perfect," I say. "Great way to let out some pent-up rage."

"I can't wait to slander some celebrities," Sophie says.

"It's not slander if it's true," I counter.

"You make a good point."

We decide to meet up tomorrow to start planning since we have such a quick turnaround time. After class is over, we exchange phone numbers and head off in opposite directions.

When I settle down in the library, hoping to get work done, I want to do anything but our reading, so I check Instagram and find a new DM for Wanda.

**@coldsoymilk:**
hello i have a submission for you (anon pls)
this guy from my high school keeps texting me all the time
and i never want to respond bc like i REALLY don't like him
how do i tell him to stop???
i literally haven't seen him in like two years??

Imagine having people from high school who actually try to talk to you. All my high school friends have moved on. Or I've moved on from them, I don't know.

This is too simple of a question. I already know how to respond. I open Google Slides and begin typing.

lmao i've been there. just fucking,,, don't respond to him??
if you don't like someone there's no reason why you should
keep talking to them. muting is magic, blocking is bliss <3

I save the question and answer onto my phone and upload them.

Inevitably, I end up scrolling through Instagram since I'm already on the app. On my feed for my personal account, I get a row of suggested accounts to follow. The first one is @sophiachi_. Sophie from WGST.

I tap on her profile. Her display name says "Sophie Chi 池乐水," the latter half of which I assume is her name in another language. I google "chi last name" out of curiosity, and it looks like it's Chinese since the

Korean spelling of it looks really different. Wait, do Chinese and Korean people have a lot of the same last names? Do they mean the same thing? Okay, no, I can't get into this. Back to Instagram. Sophie's icon is a picture of her smiling in a field of sunflowers, her hair in two pigtail braids. Her account is on private, but her bio simply says "Chicago → Wellesley."

I request to follow her. I hope she won't judge my profile too harshly. My icon is from three years ago, and though I haven't changed much in appearance—same long, curly brown hair, same round face, same sunburn-prone skin—I should probably update it soon.

Not twenty seconds later, I get a notification that Sophie accepted my follow request and has requested to follow me back. Looks like she's on her phone a lot; that alone tells me we should get along great.

Now I've got to do some Instagram stalking.

Is this only furthering my procrastination? Yes. But is it necessary? Also yes.

I check who she's following, and . . . she's not following Wanda. Damn. But . . . she's not following Wendy either.

Maybe she's just not into love advice.

My phone buzzes with a text. Speak of the devil.

Sophie (5:07 PM)

Hey were you able to find the TERF reading??

I think Prof. Fineman might have forgotten to upload it or something

Great, I have to look for it now. Which means if I find it, I need to get started.

I could pretend I didn't see Sophie's text yet, but I've only just met her, and I don't need her to think I'm the one who slacks off in a group project.

I force myself to put away my phone and open my computer

to check our course website. Sure enough, I can't find our reading anywhere.

I shoot a text to Sophie telling her this.

Sophie (5:12 PM)

Well that's lovely

I'll send her an email in a few minutes, just have to finish up something first

Me (5:12 PM)

cool thanks!!

Right when I think I might finally be ready to do something productive, my phone buzzes with a notification from Instagram on my Wanda account. It's a comment on my most recent post.

**dearwendywellesley 1m**
Good call! There's a certain Instagram account I've been meaning to block myself. They keep making these horrible comments on my posts . . .
Reply

Jesus.

Who the hell is Wendy, and why do they think this is a normal way to behave on the internet?

Dear Wendy,

I've been with my boyfriend since freshman year of high school. I love him beyond words, and I'm pretty sure we're going to be in this for the long haul. But lately, I've been feeling like our relationship is kind of . . . well, kind of boring. The most exciting things we do together are, like, going grocery shopping. How do I bring back a sense of excitement?

Sincerely,
B.

Dear B.,

I think you should have a conversation with your boyfriend about how you're feeling. You're probably past that initial phase of newness and excitement, so it's normal for things to stagnate (you've been together for years, after all!). But it's important for you to be clear with each other about your feelings. Maybe he feels the same way, and you can brainstorm ways to keep things fresh. Think about what brought you joy in the early years of your relationship, and see if there's a way to replicate that. Even in a years-long relationship, communication is still key!

In case you come up short, here are a few things I might suggest you try on your next date. Go to a new restaurant that neither of you have tried; ask each other the 36 questions that make you fall in love; cook or craft together, even if it ends disastrously. If you're sexually active, try something new in your sex life.

My last piece of advice for you is to not devalue domesticity. Who's to say that running errands can't also be fun and exciting? Personally, I think my personality is best expressed when I'm in a near-empty Target with my friends or family. It's good to find excitement in little things.

Best wishes,
Wendy

**wandawellesley69** 3h
you heard it here first, sibs, getting groceries at roche bros IS a date after all
4 likes Reply

> **floresalicia214** 2h
> tell that to @chen.sue.122
> 1 like Reply

> **chen.sue.122** 2h
> @floresalicia214 LSKDFJLSKDFLK don't call me out like this
> Reply

> **dearwendywellesley** 41m
> If both of you agree it's a date, then yes, it is a date. Otherwise, it is simply running errands
> Reply

> **wandawellesley69** 11m
> @dearwendywellesley booooooooooooooooo
> Reply

# CHAPTER 6

## Easier

### SOPHIE

I meet up with Jo at the library to hammer out as much of our presentation as possible. We're sitting on the couches on the ground floor, right by the huge windows looking out at the walkways, comparing notes and making a short Google Slides presentation. But as tends to happen anytime you're working with someone, it doesn't take long for our conversation to devolve.

"So," I say. "TERFs."

"The scum of society," Jo replies. "Hey, are you worried about if someone in our class . . . *is* one?"

"Hopefully, they'll keep their mouth shut after reading this."

College is definitely the most progressive environment I've ever been in, though I'm not quite sure if it's actually *that* progressive here or if I just have a poor frame of reference. Back at home, I—a cisgender woman, at that—never would've been comfortable giving a presentation about transphobia in front of a class. Some of the kids in my hometown held horrible opinions; others just hated *me* specifically. Here, though, the bigots are in the minority, and I'm far from being the most annoying person in class, so expressing my beliefs feels a bit safer.

Jo scoffs. "Wish the TERFs at my high school would've shut up."

"Yeah?" I say. "What was your school like?"

I realize as soon as I ask this that Jo is probably going to ask me in turn about my high school experience, which I'm not sure that I want to divulge just yet. High school wasn't bad, per se, but I think Jo would get a bad impression if they learned that I was widely known as being aloof and bitchy and too much of a teacher's pet, even if half the students at our college are also aloof, bitchy teacher's pets.

Jo shrugs. "Typical suburban public school, I guess. Most people understand basic human rights, but there's always a few creeps."

"Where are you from?"

Jo wrinkles their nose. "Natick."

Only one town over from Wellesley. The border is within walking distance.

"Whoa," I say.

"Yeah, I can literally bike home," Jo says. "A lot of my high school friends were like, 'Jo, you should get out of here and be independent,' but . . . I guess Wellesley just seemed right."

"Is it weird being this close to home? Why do you even live on campus if your family's so close by?"

"It's a little weird," Jo says. "But it's a whole different place here, you know? The culture is so different. My parents were worried that if I lived at home, I wouldn't make any friends. Also, because of how financial aid works, we pay the same amount regardless."

I laugh. "I guess I am friends with a lot of people because of dorm living."

"Yeah." Jo tilts their head. "Where are you from?"

"The suburbs of Chicago."

Jo's face lights up. "Oh, hey! My mom's from there. Do you know Schaumburg?"

"I do," I say. "It's a half-hour drive away from where I live."

"Small world," Jo says. "How'd you find out about Wellesley? There aren't as many Midwesterners here."

"My eighth-grade English teacher went to Smith." Another Seven Sisters college.

"Nice," Jo says. "My aunt went to Mount Holyoke." Word of mouth is so powerful. "Why did you decide to come here?"

I'm relieved not to have to dive into my high school's culture. The inevitable *why Wellesley* question is far preferable. I've been asked this enough times that I practically have a canned response. "Well, the academics are great, there's a big alum network, and I wanted to be somewhere that I wasn't afraid to be my most authentic self." I sound like an advertisement. Jo narrows their eyes. "Why did you *really* choose Wellesley?"

They've caught me. "I . . . I don't know. The environment, I guess. Just like you. Also, I hate cis men, and there are none here."

It's a half joke; I've been bitter about the way men treat me ever since my best friend from childhood sort of abandoned me when he got into his first relationship. He used to be my example of the one *good guy*, and then he turned out not to be. I mean, yeah, I still had cis male friends in high school, and they weren't awful, but that's beside the point.

"Yeah, that's what I thought." Jo leans back in their seat, looking far more satisfied. "How does your family feel about it?"

"About Wellesley?" Well, they hate it.

"Yeah. It's kind of far away, right?"

Oh, that's what Jo meant.

"Uh, yeah, it is kind of far, but I don't think we really mind the distance," I say. "To be honest, I think my parents are more concerned about how prestigious the school is. They're, like, kind of elitist when it comes to colleges."

When I got my college decisions last year, my parents were dismayed to find that I hadn't gotten into a single Ivy League or Ivy-adjacent college. That's far from a good hallmark for what school is best for you, or even what schools can be considered "good," but the mythical American Dream runs deep in my parents' minds. They wanted more.

It took me a while to understand it. When I spent sleepless nights my senior year crying about how I'd disappointed them, that I'd be headed to a small liberal arts college, I couldn't grasp why my mom and dad were so angry that I hadn't made it further. All I knew then was that I loved Wellesley and I wanted them to love it too.

It wasn't until last semester, when I had some time and space away from my family, and after I'd talked to Izzy and Priya about it in great depth, that I realized it all stemmed from their upbringings in China, in the decades following Mao Zedong's Great Leap Forward and Cultural Revolution, full of uncertainty and chaos. Higher education was one of the best ways out. Naturally, that mindset remained when they had kids.

The thing is, I had a good upbringing thanks to my parents' hardships. We were financially secure, and we lived in a place that was relatively safe for people who looked like us. So I don't need the Ivy League to get me further. Wellesley is already doing more for me than I need.

Jo grimaces. "Sorry about that. Where'd they go to school?"

It takes my mind a moment to shift to Jo's question. "Uh, for undergrad, my mom was at Tsinghua University in China, which is one of the most elite colleges there. My dad went to Georgia Tech. And they both went to the University of Illinois at Chicago for grad school." It's where they met. My dad was in nursing school; my mom was getting a degree in finance.

"Seriously?" Jo says. "What gives them the right to hate Wellesley? That's all, like, below Wellesley's level of prestige. At least in terms of how much rich white people care about them."

"Well, here's the thing," I say. It'll take a moment to explain my family's convoluted line of thinking, and it's probably oversharing, but I feel like I need to explain it so Jo doesn't get the wrong idea. "My parents care a *lot* about upward mobility and achieving as much financial stability as humanly possible. It's probably because of"—I gesture around—"twentieth-century Chinese historical events."

"Ah. Right."

"So they wanted me and most likely my little sister to go to as prestigious and elite of a university as possible, to keep the cycle going. And for them, Wellesley isn't enough. They want the *really* big ones."

"Like . . . Harvard?" Jo asks.

"Like Harvard," I solemnly confirm.

Of all the college rejections I got, Harvard hurt the most. Not because I even wanted to go there, but because I knew how disappointed—how mad—my parents would be. It has a reputation. It's "the best." Every parent wants their kid to go.

Jo shakes their head. "It's always Harvard."

I shrug. "I'm here now. It is what it is."

Just then, a group of students walks past us, and one of them says, "Oh my god, Sincerely, Wanda was so right. Like, yeah, sometimes I *do* need to calm down."

Sincerely, Wanda was "*so right?*"

Just like that, I am no longer thinking about my parents and Harvard and high school. I know what post they're talking about. This morning, Wanda replied to someone who was paranoid that their partner didn't love them. The response definitely wasn't what I would've said. Wanda told the person to consider whether the partner wasn't the problem, but rather that they were.

How could this happen? Wanda isn't right. Wanda is just somebody making fun of me, and really poorly at that. I refuse to believe that this person is actually taking Wanda's advice.

Jo looks at me, and I look at them, and I try my best not to look offended or alarmed.

I laugh nervously. "Did you hear that?"

"Yeah," Jo says, frowning. "Do you know about Wendy and Wanda?"

"Um . . . yeah, I know about them. But I don't follow them." It's true; I don't follow either account on my personal Instagram. I think it makes me seem less suspicious. If anyone asks how I know about them, I tell them Priya's really invested, which isn't technically a lie.

Jo shrugs. "That makes sense. Pretty much everyone knows about them."

"Do you follow them?"

"Of course."

"Who do you like better?" It had better be me.

And again, Jo shrugs. "I don't know. They're pretty different, you know? Like, I follow them for . . . different reasons."

It's a boring answer, but it's better than having an overt preference for my newfound archnemesis. It makes sense; most people must follow me for actual advice, and Wanda for when they want a laugh. Except that person who just walked past us and had the audacity to take Wanda seriously.

It's fine. I'm fine. I do *not* feel threatened.

It's my turn to shrug. "Let's get back to the reading."

Jo has a class in the afternoon, so we wrap up pretty soon, and I come back to my room with a to-go sandwich from El Table, a café on campus. Priya's sitting cross-legged on her mattress and holding her phone to her ear. She's speaking in Bangla, which means she's talking to her dad. I may not understand the words, but the frustrated look on her face and the harsh tone of her voice tell me quite clearly that this is not a fun conversation.

I make eye contact with her, and I point to the door, eyebrows raised. *Should I go?*

She shakes her head and holds up one finger, mouthing the words *one minute.*

For a couple minutes, I pad around the room, eating my sandwich, tidying some trash, checking on our plants. I'm a bit fond of our newest addition, a succulent that Priya insisted we name Adora, after Izzy, whose full name is Isadora. (I think she also named it after Adora from *She-Ra.* I never got around to watching it when it was popular.) I take a picture of Adora and text it to Izzy, who responds with a bunch of heart-eye emojis.

Priya is speaking quickly and urgently, and I recognize this tone. It's the same one I use when I'm talking to my own parents.

As I'm plucking out a shriveled, dry leaf from the bottom of Adora's stem, I hear Priya say, "Bye, Dad."

I look up. Her shoulders are slumped. She looks pissed.

"Is everything okay?" I ask.

She closes her eyes for a moment. "Yeah," she says, and then sighs. "It's just . . . every time I bring up Izzy, he tries to change the subject. What am I supposed to tell him when he asks what I did last weekend? No, I didn't hang out with the love of my life for twenty-four hours straight. I spent all that time alone, or with my roommate, or with my other friends. Fully clothed and not touching."

I clear my throat. "Okay, I know you don't talk to your dad about sex."

She glares at me. "Obviously not."

I get up and sit on the edge of her bed.

Being a queer child of closed-minded immigrants can be very frustrating. Your parents go through so much hardship to get where they are, and then they thrust a different kind of hardship on you without knowing the damage they're doing.

Priya's dad, a widowed Indian Bengali immigrant, is fine with Priya's lesbianism in theory—she's been out to him for a while—but he refuses to acknowledge that Izzy exists as anything besides a friend. My parents, Chinese immigrants, think my sexuality is a choice. I'm eighteen years old, nineteen this August. I will not be "growing out" of being aroace.

There's so much to love about both of our parents. Priya's dad has the best stories about shenanigans he got into when he was young; my dad sends me countless food pictures and tries way too hard to give me money for takeout when he thinks I'm getting sick of the dining hall; my mom gives oddly good advice just when you need it, and the fact that it comes off a little harsh actually makes it better because you know she's not toning it down. But nobody is perfect, and it just so happens that our parents' imperfections include their lack of understanding about queer identity.

Priya leans her head on my shoulder. It's not a good idea—we're both a bit too bony for it to be comfortable—but physical touch is a form of emotional support for her.

"It'll get easier," I say.

"When?" Priya asks. "In a year? Five years? When I get married?"

That strikes a nerve. I don't even have marriage to force my parents' acceptance. I wonder if, at some point, I'll simply go from a "straight" girl who's picky to a straight-up spinster in my parents' eyes. I don't share this thought with Priya; she knows well enough how I feel, and I'd do better by lightening the mood instead of dragging myself down with her.

"Are you telling me that you won't be married in five years?" I joke.

Priya chuckles. "Twenty-three's too early for Izzy."

"But not for you?" I know for a fact that her parents were married at twenty-two.

"Shut up."

Priya's phone buzzes. The vibration is a custom pattern: two short taps, a pause, and then three more short taps. Izzy's initials, in Morse code.

"Speaking of," I say.

"I never said I was marrying her," Priya retorts, but she's smiling as she reads her texts.

"We'll see about that." I pause for just a moment. "So what did she send you?"

"Um." She's smiling more now, shaking her head; I'm sure her cheeks would be flushed if her skin were paler. "She found a poetry night at a café in Boston this weekend. It's open mic."

I know how much Priya cares about her writing. Even Izzy usually isn't allowed to see it until it's close to being finished. I've only read her already-published pieces and a snippet of the novel she's working on, something all sapphic and literary and full of metaphors.

"So you guys *have* to go," I say.

Priya laughs. "I guess so. Do you want to come?"

I've been a third wheel on their dates before. It's not too awkward since I'm friends with both of them, but I don't particularly want to sit through open-mic poetry I won't understand.

"I think I might be busy. But send me pictures!"

Priya nods and looks back down at her phone, still grinning.

It's quiet moments like this, more than any grand and public display of affection, when I know how much the two of them mean to each other. A simple act of caring: *I found this thing that I think you'd like, so I'm sharing it with you.*

Priya is now texting at a rapid-fire pace, probably telling Izzy about the call she had with her dad, so I hop off her bed and sit at my desk. Their basically perfect relationship always reminds me to check up on my Dear Wendy submissions.

# CHAPTER 7

# Not This Train of Thought Again

## JO

I come back from my Wednesday-afternoon computer science lab to find Lianne sitting on the sofa in the Stone-Davis Hall living room, swiping on her phone. Katy is leaning against the sofa behind her.

"She looks cute," Katy says.

"Absolutely not, she's said some fucked-up things in our anthro class," Lianne replies, and she swipes.

"Ooh, what about her?" Katy says.

"No, I see her all the time when I study at Harambee, it'd be weird."

Harambee House is a space on campus for Black students. The college never had any intention of giving it almost the same name as a dead gorilla—that would be *so* racist—but it is pronounced the same way; it's a term in Swahili that, according to the college website, means "working together." We also have a house for Asian and Latinx/e students, and the top floor of the building WZLY is in has a space for LGBTQ+ students.

"Hey, guys," I say, and the two of them look up. "What are you doing?"

"Bumble," Lianne says.

The word itself incites anxiety in me. I hate it when my friends spend time on dating apps. The whole concept of dating apps is kind of weird to begin with—I don't get how you can look at a picture of someone, read a few facts about them, and decide if you're attracted to them.

It's pretty easy to come across other Wellesley students on dating apps because our school has a huge LGBTQ+ population. Like, I've heard estimates around 50 percent.

And still, it's hard to find people like me. The asexual community is small enough as it is; there are fewer aromantic people and even fewer people who are both.

Or maybe I just don't know anybody at all. I don't have that many friends.

The ramifications of my sexuality around my gender just make things worse. Does not being attracted to men make me less female, since so much of the female experience is tied to the male gaze? Or what if, because a lot of femme-presenting people at Wellesley also use they/them pronouns, I've come to associate those pronouns with femininity? But also, pronouns don't equal gender, right?

Ugh.

Not this train of thought again.

I deflect with a joke, hoping neither of them noticed my silence. "Not Hinge or Tinder? You're *really* desperate."

"Shut up," Lianne says. "There are some okay people here."

I peer over at Lianne's phone. On the screen now seems to be another Wellesley student, based on the college sweater she's wearing in her picture. Alicia, 19, is "a hopelessly romantic, bisexual girl looking for love." Her hair is dark and curly, the curls tighter and more sharply defined than mine, and she has light brown skin and a wide smile.

"She's cute," I say.

Lianne considers for a moment and then swipes right, and I flop down on a chair across from her.

"Tell me if you see anyone else we know," I say, pulling out my own phone.

"In the last three days," Lianne says, "I've seen Emma, Sydney, *and* Georgia." Three of our friends from our dorm.

"Jesus," I say. "How close did you set your location range?"

"Five miles," Katy says.

"Well, that explains it," I say. There are maybe two other colleges within five miles of us. "So did you swipe right on any friends?"

"God, no," Lianne says. "That'd be so awkward. Plus, none of them are my type."

I know for sure that Sydney is exactly Lianne's type: tall, thoughtful, stylish. Just like Katy. But I wouldn't dare say that.

"Better than that time you accidentally matched with Bea on Hinge," I reply instead.

She's our house president, the student in charge of our dorm.

"Don't talk to me about that," Lianne groans. "I couldn't look her in the eye for weeks."

"I can't look her in the eye normally, so you're doing okay," Katy says.

All right, we get it, the whole dorm has a crush on Beatrice Park.

I grimace. "Yikes. Well, have fun finding your soulmate. I'll be over here, wallowing."

"Wallow safely," Katy says.

I meant it as a joke, but as soon as I stop talking to them, my thoughts start to spiral.

I've seen this happen before. Katy was desperate to date people last semester, and she ended up with the worst man in the world. In high school, my friend group was always in flux, people going in and out as they dated and broke up.

Trying to find love never works.

I mean, obviously it does work out sometimes. My moms found each other. They're still in love about thirty years after they met. But most people are not my parents. Most of the time, it does not work out, and I'm left to deal with the consequences, so sue me if I would prefer that my friends remain single.

Lianne's voice snaps me out of my thoughts. "Okay, I'm done." She hands her phone to Katy. "Don't let me touch this for at least the next hour. I need to do a p-set."

"Should I take it with me to dinner?" Katy says.

Lianne frowns. "Give it to Jo."

"Cool," I say as Katy hands it to me. I tuck it into my pocket while Lianne takes out her homework.

Katy leaves for dinner, and when she exits, Lianne's eyes linger in that direction.

"You okay?" I say.

"Huh?" She looks dazed. "Yeah. All good."

"Let me know if you need anything."

"Thank you," Lianne says, and she turns to the packets of readings on the seat next to her.

Part of me is sure that Lianne has feelings for Katy. There've been a few signs; it started with a bit of jealousy when Katy got with Jason, then a lot of concern during that relationship. Now Lianne just stares at her a lot.

But maybe Lianne is merely worried. It's been a few weeks since the breakup, and Katy seems much happier, but I guess it's normal to still be a little concerned.

I don't know if Lianne plans on doing anything about her feelings, if they do exist. She didn't figure out she was gay until late in high school, so she has no dating experience from before college. And at Wellesley, she's maybe hooked up with, like, two people.

She and Katy wouldn't work, though. I would certainly hate it if they dated; it took us so long to curate our perfectly chaotic friendship dynamic.

The two of them together would ruin it.

Dear Wendy,

I can't help but feel like this entire campus is sexually active except me. I'm in a relationship right now, but I just don't feel ready yet, and neither does my partner. Maybe it's the Catholic guilt? I don't know. I don't think I'm asexual because I do want to have sex one day, but I'm not sure why I don't right now.

Sincerely,
Not Horny

Dear Not,

It is completely normal to not want sex.

It doesn't matter your age, gender, sexual orientation, relationship status, past sexual history—you're allowed to not want to have sex for any reason or for no reason at all.

I am not an expert on Catholic guilt, but our society does cause a lot of people to feel a sense of guilt around sexuality. That alone isn't always a reason for people to not want sex at all, but sometimes it is, and that's normal! And you don't need to be asexual to not want sex, nor do you need to not want sex in order to be asexual; asexuality is defined by a lack of sexual *attraction*, not sexual desire or libido. Maybe that describes you, or maybe it doesn't, and that's perfectly fine.

It's okay not to be ready. It's okay to never be ready. It doesn't make you broken, and it doesn't make you lesser than. As long as you and your partner are happy, that's all that matters.

Yours truly,
Wendy

**wandawellesley69** 1h
this is a familiar question . . . check my page
3 likes Reply

**_lianne** 27m
**@joanna.ephron @katymurphyart** not the catholic guilt
2 likes Reply

> **joanna.ephron** 20m
> **@_lianne** ??? why did you tag me
> Reply

> **_lianne** 14m
> **@joanna.ephron** wasn't your mom raised catholic??
> Reply

> **katy.e.m** 10m
> **@_lianne** WHY did you tag my art account
> Reply

---

**anon:** is it normal to not want to have sex? it feels like everyone else here does, but I don't?? I know this is a fun page most of the time but I really want answers

**answer:** yeah! lol perfectly normal. if anyone's making you feel like you should do it, then don't listen to them?? haters gonna hate. lots of ppl at w are, like, super horny, but they're also loud. (not in bed. just loud in general.) kinda fucked up how in our society, you're a prude if you don't have sex and a whore if you do! misogyny will do what misogyny does. bottom line: you do you!! xxx

**dearwendywellesley** 28m

Well. I see what you meant by "familiar question." And is that . . . a serious answer? I thought that was my territory! Who are you and what have you done with Wanda?

Reply

> **wandawellesley69** 16m
>
> wendy. honey. i've BEEN giving serious answers. you don't take me seriously
>
> Reply

> **dearwendywellesley** 10m
>
> @wandawellesley69 Maybe I would take you more seriously if you gave good advice
>
> Reply

> **floresalicia214** 8m
>
> uh oh the girls are fighting!!!
>
> 1 like Reply

# CHAPTER 8

## Officially Embroiled in Battle

### JO

The girls are, indeed, fighting.

Sort of.

I know the phrase is just a saying, but it still makes my stomach drop for a moment when I see it. I don't mind being called a girl by my friends and family, but when strangers do it, it's off-putting.

When I look at myself in a mirror, I think, *That's a woman.* I'm wide at the hips, my bra size is in the double Ds, and my face is too soft to be seen as anything but female. I like my body the way it looks. I like the way I dress. It's me.

But when I consider the role I want to play in society, I think, *That's not exactly a woman.*

I'm comfortable being grouped together with girls and women, but I feel very detached from it. And I think gender is just weird. That nuance is lost on people who don't know me.

@floresalicia214 has no way of knowing that; it's not like I put my pronouns in my Wanda account's bio, which would make it easier for people to narrow down who I am. And "the girls are fighting" is just an expression.

I should really be more worried about these comments. Dear Wendy is getting on my nerves.

"Jo?" Katy says, and I look up from my phone screen. She's lounging against our beanbag chair, drawing in a sketchbook.

"What?" I say.

"You look like you've seen a ghost," she says. "Everything okay?"

"Huh? Oh. Yeah. Uh . . . here, take a look at this."

I walk over to her corner and show her my phone. Instead of looking at it like any normal person, she grabs the phone from my hand and squints at it, just like my moms do.

"Ooh," she says. "So you guys are fighting."

"I mean . . . *fighting* is a strong word. This is pretty much what we've been doing."

Katy rolls her eyes. "And what would you call that?"

"Uh . . . I don't know. Um. Casual banter. Publicly. In Instagram comments."

She shakes her head and hands my phone back to me. "You might as well declare on your story that you and Wendy are officially embroiled in battle."

"I would never use the word *embroiled*."

Katy ignores me and says, "I can't believe this is happening. Didn't this come from you making fun of Jason?"

"I mean, yeah, kind of."

"Glad he was good for something," Katy says.

I laugh, but then I realize something. Katy doesn't voluntarily bring up shitty-ex-Jason very often, if at all. Maybe she's finally ready to joke about it. And then it'll be only a matter of time before she's ready to date again, and great, more things I'll need to worry about!

But not right now. At the moment, I have my Instagram. It's kind of fun getting Wendy to let their guard down. Not that they seem to be letting their guard down much, since all these comments still seem so prim and proper, but all the same.

My phone vibrates with a notification. It's another comment.

**veronica.verdier 1h**
hi i was anon lol . . . ngl this helped me more than dear wendy did so thank you
3 likes Reply

Oh. I know Veronica. She's in my Spanish class.

And I helped her. More than Dear Wendy.

The more I think about it, the more I think Katy is right. It's kind of self-righteous for Dear Wendy to have such a sense of superiority. I may not be an expert in relationships, and I may be writing my Instagram posts in a joking tone, but I'm also not entirely wrong.

It would be funny to knock Wendy down a peg, wouldn't it? I could just humble them a bit.

Of course, their advice is undeniably better than mine most of the time, given that most of the time, my answers are a joke. But maybe I should slip in my real opinion more often, and I'll see if that actually helps people, and if it does . . . then that would be really funny.

"Okay, wait," Katy says when I tell her and Lianne my plan later in the evening. "So you want to give real advice now?"

"Just a little," I say. "Just to step on Dear Wendy's toes a bit."

"And why do you want to do that?" Katy asks.

"Because it's fun."

"Can't argue with that," Lianne says.

And so begins Operation: Humble Dear Wendy. I take a screenshot of Veronica's comment and put it on my story.

lmao i just helped someone more than **@dearwendywellesley** did??? hey wendy, what are the odds that my advice IS actually better than yours?

And now I wait for Dear Wendy's response.

# CHAPTER 9

## Better

### SOPHIE

I cannot let myself be made fun of like this.

"This isn't funny anymore," I say.

Priya looks up, across from me at the table in the common room. She's working on her homework; I'm browsing my social media because I'm done with my assignments for the day.

"What?" she says.

"Look at this." I pass my phone to her, showing Wanda's Instagram story, where they've extremely rudely decided to tag me, as if I don't check their account religiously at this point.

"So?" Priya says, handing me my phone back.

"So . . . so this *joke account* is now giving better advice than me? This can't be happening. I'm better than this. *Wendy* is better than this." I can feel my face growing hot.

Priya drops her voice. "How about you say that a little bit louder so everyone in Claf can figure out"—she whispers this last part—"*you're Wendy?*"

"This isn't cool. I can't have someone who's mocking me be better than me."

"Sophie, have you considered that maybe you're overreacting a tiny bit? Just a little?" Priya looks completely exasperated.

Maybe I am overreacting. But also, I'm being attacked, and I can't have that.

I cross my arms and heave another sigh. "You sound like my mom."
"And you sound like my little brother. Calm down."
"Ugh. Fine. But this isn't over."
Priya rolls her eyes. "Okay. Just don't drag me into this."
There's no way Wanda can be better than me. I open my DMs and start furiously composing a message.

**@dearwendywellesley:**
This story is NOT FUNNY

**@wandawellesley69:**
lol??
don't tell me you're going to make me take it down

**@dearwendywellesley:**
No
I won't
Because you're obviously wrong

**@wandawellesley69:**
wow okay! uh. kinda harsh
is there something you want from me?

**@dearwendywellesley:**
Could you stop infringing on my territory? Perhaps?

**@wandawellesley69:**
lmao no

**@dearwendywellesley:**
Fine

**@wandawellesley69:**
"cute" ???????????

**@dearwendywellesley:**
Oh no, was that too demeaning?

**@wandawellesley69:**
my god you are so annoying

# CHAPTER 10

## *Sexiled*

## SOPHIE

I spend lots of time outside my dorm. I hang out at Acorns House, the Asian and Latinx/e space. I run outside when it's warm enough. And, of course, I go to the library to study, which is where I just came back from. I've been there all day, hours upon hours of productivity with a break in the middle for lunch, and I am tired beyond belief. I just want to lie down for a while and maybe pore over Wanda's latest posts to see if there's anything I can use against them.

But the one time I really need to be in my room, I find a Do Not Disturb sign, pilfered from a hotel, hanging on our doorknob. And I remember that Izzy is visiting this weekend. She and Priya are going to that poetry night they were talking about.

I've been sexiled.

I knew this would happen eventually, ever since last October when Priya blurted out over breakfast that she and Izzy had had sex for the first time when she visited Brown that weekend. Very awkward day for both of us. Since then, I haven't been locked out—I've voluntarily kicked myself out, which is different—but today, of all days? I was so busy working that I didn't even remember to turn my stuffed animals to face the wall this morning (it's a thing I do; it makes me feel better), and now they're probably all watching whatever Priya and Izzy are getting up to.

I sigh and turn around, then walk down until I get back to the first floor. Our main common room is two stories tall, with *Alice in Wonderland* carvings along a balcony (in memory of the architect's dead daughter, Alice, who according to Claflin legend is a ghost living on the fourth floor). I immediately sink into the worn leather seats of a couch.

It's nice to be here. Calming. Well, as calming as it can be to sit on a couch that countless people have puked on. I'm not sure how long I stare at the molding along the ceiling.

Eventually, my friend Alicia walks in. She's my hallmate next door. She wants to become a TV or radio journalist someday, has a lot of opinions about the season finale of *The Good Place*, and is kind of a third roommate to me and Priya because her roommate, Hadleigh (yes, it's really spelled with an -eigh), constantly claims the room for . . . things that Priya's probably doing right now.

"Hey," she says, waving at me.

She's wearing a gray sweater that has WELLESLEY COLLEGE embroidered across the front. Her curly black hair is nearly waist-length, and she has a thin gold septum ring. She's very tall, a half foot taller than me, and she always seems to carry herself with an air of confidence.

She gestures at the sofa across from me. "Anyone sitting here?"

I shake my head. "Feel free. What's up?"

She sits down, folds her hands in her lap, and says, "Hadleigh's boyfriend is here, and the two of them have closed off the room for unspeakable purposes, and I don't have my OneCard 'cause I was studying in the basement, so I can't go anywhere."

Ah. The usual.

"The same thing just happened to me," I say. "Except I've been outside all day, and I really want to take a nap."

She gestures around us. "You can nap in here if you're desperate."

I chuckle. "I'm not quite at that point yet."

Truly, Alicia is one of my favorite Claflin residents. She's extremely easy to talk to. I think she's the kind of person who'd be the subject of my Dear Wendy questions: *Dear Wendy, how do I ask out the coolest girl I've ever met?*

"How long do you think Hadleigh will be?" I ask.

Alicia shrugs. "Eh. I don't know. Maybe five more minutes? You know how it is. She doesn't usually take too long."

"How sad," I say. "Straight people deserve good sex too."

"Well, quality over quantity, right?"

I snort. "I guess that's fair."

"Although," she says, eyebrows raised, "they're probably not getting much quality either, from what it sounds like."

We laugh, and then Alicia jumps. "Oh! Sorry, it's my phone, one second." She pulls it out of her pocket and then scoffs. "Just Bumble."

"Can I try swiping through your potential matches?" I can't lie, it is fun to judge other people's profiles.

She shrugs. "Might as well. Maybe I can get back at Hadleigh tonight if I match with someone on campus."

She opens up the app. It's a sea of mediocre white boys that I immediately begin making fun of. Alicia and I swipe left on almost all of them.

"Honestly, I swipe left on pretty much all white people these days," Alicia says. "I don't have the time to teach my culture to someone who barely wants to learn, you know?"

"Makes a lot of sense," I say.

Finally, I recognize one person: "Lianne, 19," a girl with glowing brown skin, a round jawline, and a buzzcut.

"Oh, I know her!" I say. "She was in my astronomy lab last semester."

"That's cool. Is she a first year?"

"I don't know. We haven't talked."

Alicia scrolls through her page, considers for a moment, and swipes right on her. The screen lights up yellow, showing Alicia's and Lianne's faces side by side. It's a match.

"Oh, wow," I say. "I didn't know what that looked like."

"What, matching?" Alicia says, grinning.

"Well, neither Priya nor I have a need for dating apps, so I've never seen it happen."

"It's not that special after a while," Alicia says. "Okay, what do I say to her?"

"Uh . . ." I may be Dear Wendy, able to answer any question about love and sex, but I don't know how to flirt. "How about 'East or West Side?'"

Since she goes to Wellesley, she must know of the debate about which dorms are the best. We live on the west side of campus, which is closer to the academic quad and the campus center. East Side is near the science center and the Ville, our downtown area. The arguments over which is better are never-ending.

Alicia looks at me, bemused. "Are you sure that's a good pickup line?"

"Starting off with that could work well," I say. "It can get someone talking."

She rolls her eyes. "Okay, just for you."

She types and sends it, and we continue swiping through potential matches. Only a few minutes later, though, Alicia has an answer from Lianne.

*wow, i've never heard that one before*, it says, with an eye-roll emoji. Maybe I should've come up with a less common question.

"Shit, what do I say now?" Alicia says.

I shrug helplessly.

Alicia frowns as she types out an answer, then deletes it, then types something else. "Uh, I told her that I'm not used to matching with people from Wellesley. Does that sound all right?"

"Sure," I say. I don't really know if that sounds all right, but it's a reasonable explanation.

Alicia sighs. "Why do I date at all? Maybe finding love is a waste of time."

"Personally, I do think it's a waste of time. But maybe that's just me."

There are plenty of issues to struggle with when you discover that you're probably incapable of experiencing romantic love, but for me, there's also been relief. Joy, even, to know that there's a word for what you feel—or don't feel. I wish I had more people to share that with.

"Good for you, Sophie, but you might have ruined my chances with her."

I grimace. "I'm sorry. I hope she's forgiving."

"I hope so too." She looks through Lianne's photos again. "I mean, she looks really nice."

"Uh . . . yeah. Very cool. Super hot."

She snorts. "Okay, no need for any of that."

"Sorry," I say again. "I have no idea how this works."

I think I need to do some research on how to interact with people on dating apps. In case someone asks Dear Wendy.

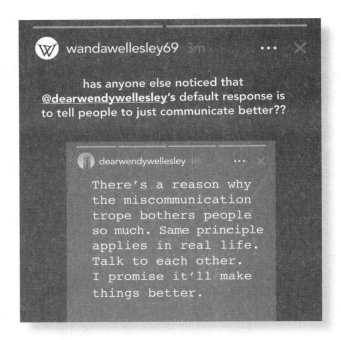

min yoongi's ACTUAL waking nightmare @not_sue_chen · 44m
has anyone else been following along with wendy
and wanda's rapidly escalating feud on
instagram lol??

roche bros hater @aaliyahjones · 39m
replying to @not_sue_chen
YES IT'S SO FUNNY LMAO

min yoongi's ACTUAL waking nightmare @not_sue_chen · 38m
replying to @aaliyahjones
omg glad it's not just me . . . they hate each other
so much for like no reason???

# CHAPTER 11

# First Date Tips For a Cottagecore Lesbian

## JO

Sophie and I give a pretty good presentation.

To be fair, we don't do *that* much presenting. We talk for five minutes, and then our classmates spend fifteen minutes going around and adding their own insights. Our class has a lot to say about trans exclusion.

When we go back to our seats, Sophie and I exchange a glance. She grins and gives me a quick thumbs-up.

"All right, thank you again, Jo and Sophie," Fineman says. "We're going to move on now to talking about your next assignment."

Our midterm (god, midterms already?) is a research paper based on course readings. There's a quick shuffle for everyone to take out their devices and open the course website, where Fineman has posted a more detailed explanation. I glance at Sophie, who looks like she's about to jump out of her seat with excitement.

She already has an idea? She's *excited* about this?

I've got a few thoughts in mind. Maybe something based on the readings we just presented? Or that period of time when some lesbian activists considered lesbians a gender entirely separate from women, and how that's sort of coming back now. Or maybe one about the internet's influence on sexual identity.

After class is over, Sophie immediately turns to me, a grin on her face.

"What are you so happy for?" I ask.

"I know what I'm going to write about," she says. She looks so giddy.

"Okay . . . ," I say as I gather my things. "Care to share?"

"The way gender affects relationship dynamics," she says.

"That sounds cool," I say. "What inspired you?"

"Oh, you know," she says, clearly trying (and failing) to sound chill. "Just the overall vibes at Wellesley."

I've only known her for a couple of weeks, but Sophie does not seem like the kind of person who uses the word "vibes" in face-to-face conversation. The way she's attempting to contain her excitement is kind of adorable.

"That's fun," I say.

She's right that our dating scene is extremely different from the average college. My Wanda submissions are proof of that. I got one this morning from someone asking for *first date tips for a cottagecore lesbian*. I told them that they should have a picnic on Green Beach, the lawn by Lake Waban, and added that I think "cottagecore" is an extremely cringe term.

Maybe I've brought this on myself by thinking about it, or maybe this is just a weird coincidence, but I hear a classmate, Kiara Woods, saying, "Wait, so you're actually having a picnic on Green Beach? It's February! You'll freeze!"

"Oh," another classmate, Clara Gonzales, says. "I didn't really think about that."

I turn around and look at them as subtly as I can. Sophie notices and whispers, "What are they talking about?"

I hold up a finger.

"They probably suggested Green Beach as a joke," Kiara says. "You know, since their whole page is satirical."

"I don't know," Clara says with a sigh. "They've started giving actually useful advice sometimes."

There's no doubt now that this is about me. But I can't let anyone know, so as much as I want to eavesdrop further, I think I need to let this go.

When I look back at Sophie, she looks a little amused.

"Was that something about Sincerely, Wanda?" Sophie asks.

"Sounds like it," I say. "Have you, uh, seen their latest post?"

Sophie shakes her head quickly. "I don't follow it, remember?"

Right. "It . . . wasn't that interesting," I lie. There's no way I'm letting her find out that it's me.

Sophie shrugs. "Oh well. I don't really care anyway."

We pack up our things and head out of the classroom—Sophie continues to yammer about her essay idea. She goes as far as to pull up JSTOR on her phone, already looking for sources she can use. I can't help but laugh at how intense she is.

"Stop laughing at me!" Sophie says, indignant. "Don't tell me you've never gotten excited about an assignment."

"I mean, I've gotten excited about an assignment before," I say. "But not so excited that I'm accessing PDFs of journal articles using the Safari mobile browser."

"Well, I have no time to waste."

"Uh, yeah, you do. This isn't due tomorrow or anything."

"You don't get it, Jo," Sophie says. She shakes her head, though I can tell she's not actually judging me. "I need to stay on top of everything so that I never fall behind so that I can always ensure my success if something *does* happen to slow me down."

"What is it like to have your life together?" I reply.

"It's stressful," Sophie admits, and we both laugh.

"So, the same as not having your life together, then," I say. "Except less fun."

I chide Sophie for her perfectionism all the way down the hall and out the door of our building. When we split off in different directions, going back to our separate dorms, I pull out my phone. There's a new comment on Sincerely, Wanda.

**@claragonzales14 11m**
lol any other suggestions that won't have me freezing my toes off?? maybe **@dearwendywellesley** has ideas?
Reply

Great. There's no doubt Dear Wendy will have more to make fun of me for now.

**anon:** any advice for people caught up in the middle of friend drama? i don't want to take sides . . .

**answer:** drop all of them, leave wellesley, and go live your best life in a remote cabin in the woods. alternatively, talk with your friends and tell them to make up unless they want you to never talk to them again. xoxo

**dearwendywellesley 3h**
The first option is not a good idea, please don't drop out of Wellesley :(
2 likes Reply

**wandawellesley69 2h**
um if they want to have fun don't ruin it for them
4 likes Reply

**dearwendywellesley** 4h     •••   ✕

You probably don't need me to tell you this, but please do not escape to a remote cabin in the woods just because of some friend drama.

 **wandawellesley69** 3m     •••   ✕

# LMAO PLS DW IS SO OFFENDED BY THIS???

**anon:** any advice for people caught up in the middle of friend drama? i don't want to take sides . . .

# CHAPTER 12

## Same

### SOPHIE

A few days after our presentation in WGST 110, Jo and I decide to have dinner together after class. We disagree initially about which dining hall to go to—each of us prefers the ones nearest our dorms—but we settle on Lulu.

The Lulu Chow Wang Campus Center is not at the center of campus, but the four-story building houses many important things. Mail Services is right at the main entrance. On the ground floor are a pub and a café run by student co-ops. The top floor is where you'll find the bookstore and the Bae Pao Lu Chow dining hall, which we weirdly also call "Lulu."

Lulu might actually be my favorite dining hall on campus. It's very open concept, with floor-to-ceiling windows. The view during sunset hours is to die for. The food itself isn't particularly special—it's just the same food you'll find in all the other dining halls.

After we get our meals, we sit at a small table in an alcove by the stairs. I have a cheeseburger and fries; Jo's eating mac and cheese and sautéed spinach. I send my dad a picture of the burger; he reacts with a thumbs-up. After a few bites, the small talk begins.

The little dance people do to socialize in college is entirely too pre-dictable. You cycle through a few topics: the dining hall food, your home-town, your classes. If you get lucky, you find a common interest and talk about that for the entire time. Otherwise, you might be stuck, like us, talking about life at school.

Jo tells me she was in the drama club's production of *Rosencrantz and Guildenstern Are Dead* last semester and that she DJs for WZLY; I show her some of the articles I've written or taken pictures for at the *Wellesley News*. She's thinking about majoring in sociology just because she really liked her sociology professor last semester; I'm fairly set on psychology but am considering adding on women's and gender studies. I tell her a little about Priya; she tells me her roommates are called Katy and Lianne.

"Wait, *Lianne*?" I say. "Is there any chance this Lianne matched with a girl named Alicia on Bumble recently?"

"Uh . . . yeah," Jo says. "How do you know?"

"Oh my god. Alicia lives next door to me! We're really good friends."

"That is so embarrassing," Jo says. And then she clarifies, "For them, not for us."

"Why? Because they know people who know each other?"

"Exactly!" Jo says. "What if we were super judgy?"

"Are we?" I say, a smile growing on my face.

"I don't know. I think we are. A little. You seem the type. And I guess by saying you seem the type, I *am* the type."

We both laugh. She's not wrong.

"I mean, I guess it's inevitable that they'd have mutual friends," I say. "I'm pretty sure everyone on this campus has, like, three degrees of separation at most."

She sighs. "I don't know, that's not really what I'm worried about."

"Oh. You're worried about something?"

"Yeah, it's just . . . this is totally oversharing"—she leans in, as if she's imparting a secret—"but I think Lianne has a crush on Katy and is trying to pretend it doesn't exist by meeting people on dating apps."

"Oh no," I say. "Does Katy know?"

I'm already thinking about how I might respond to this if it were a Dear Wendy question. Suppressing your feelings isn't usually a good thing; if you have confirmation that the other person isn't interested in you, then yes, you can do something to try to get over it, but otherwise, you could be wasting your time. Also, I'm worried about Alicia now.

"No, she doesn't," Jo says. "I swear, she's so weirdly oblivious. And now I'm in this super awkward place where I know, but Lianne doesn't know that I know, and Katy doesn't know anything, and I can't do anything about any of it, so I'm just sitting with this information. You know?"

It takes me a moment to put together what all of that means; I'm suddenly reminded of that scene in *Friends*: "They don't know that we know they know we know." I think if Jo sent all this to Wendy, I'd tell her to leave it alone and try not to overthink things. If Lianne came to Wendy asking about this, though . . . I've always had a hard time figuring out when I should and shouldn't tell someone to confess to their crush.

I bet Wanda would have a field day with this one. They'd probably tell Jo to blurt it out to everyone and let the situation get resolved ASAP. Or maybe they'd say the same thing as me, but super aggressively: *Uh, dude, mind your own fucking business, this isn't about you.*

Of course, I can't share that with Jo, so I raise my eyebrows and say, "That's fantastic."

"Absolutely amazing for me," Jo agrees.

"But no drama on your end, at least, right?"

"Yeah, no, I'm fine." Jo shrugs. "I don't get crushes, so."

*Don't get crushes?*

Every time someone tells me they experience some lack of attraction, I always think, *hang on, this person could be like me.* Ninety-five percent of the time, they aren't; they're just exaggerating their experience. But there could be a sliver of a chance.

"You know, I don't either," I say. "I'm aroace. Not sure if you're also . . ."

A smile creeps onto Jo's face. "Oh. I am too."

Oh my god.

Jo's aroace.

My heart is racing. I'm . . . astounded. Four years of knowing my sexual and romantic orientation, and I've never once met another aroace person. I'm almost convinced this is a dream.

This is amazing! Absolutely phenomenal! The best news I've heard since the day I got my Wellesley College acceptance letter. I've finally found another aroace person on campus, and it seems very much like we could easily be friends. We sort of are friends already.

At this moment, I cannot say any of that. All that comes out of my mouth is: "What?"

It's a terrible answer; a little rude, considering Jo technically just came out to me. But I came out to her first, so actually, I think this is completely, totally fine.

Jo chuckles nervously. "Yeah. Um . . . I haven't met anyone else at Wellesley who is."

"Me neither. That's why I was so surprised."

I don't know a lot of a-spec people at all. I met one online when I was fourteen, but we fell out of touch. I follow a few on TikTok. And Izzy is demisexual, though our experiences aren't really that similar.

"Does anyone else know?" Jo asks. "I would've never figured it out just from your social media."

"Yeah," I say. "Um, my family knows." Even if they're less-than-accepting about it. "And all my friends do. I just don't really talk about it online."

"Makes sense. I'm pretty much the same way."

"That's nice."

Jo looks really happy. Calm and cool about it, even. I think her experience with coming out and being out must not be nearly as fraught as mine. Or maybe she's freaking out on the inside. Who knows.

"So . . . wait," Jo says. "Can I ask a mildly invasive question?"

"Yeah, uh, go for it."

"Are you, like, totally, completely not attracted to people? Or is there any gray area? 'Cause I'm just not. At all."

"Oh. No, I'm not attracted to anyone, ever."

I have so many questions I could ask her. When did she figure it out? Does she also talk with a lot of people who say ignorant things like *You're so lucky you don't have to worry about love*? But at the moment, I can't voice any of these thoughts. I'm just happy to find someone who identifies the same way as me.

"I guess we have quite a bit in common," Jo says.

"I guess so."

Before I can say anything else, Jo's phone buzzes with an alarm, and she jumps, looking, well, alarmed. "Shoot, I have to go."

"Oh. Okay. Let's—let's keep talking later."

"Oh my god, yeah, I have . . . *so* much to say."

She starts gathering her things, and I stand up and do the same. We put away our dishes and start down the staircase.

"I'm so sorry," Jo says. "It's just—I always call my parents on Fridays."

"Right, yeah, of course." I've always envied people who call their parents on a regular basis. I wish I could do that, but at the same time, I probably wouldn't want to. My food texts with my dad are usually enough.

"But thank you so much for hanging out!" Jo says. "It was . . . *really* nice to talk."

"Yeah. Thank you, too."

She smiles. "All right. Are you going this way?" She points out the door.

"Oh, I was gonna get my mail and then head out the back."

"Cool. See you later?"

"I'll text you."

She gives me a thumbs-up and leaves through the front door. After I check my mailbox, where I find my weekly copy of the *New Yorker*, I go in the other direction, to the back door that leads to a hilly shortcut to my dorm.

And as I walk up, I can't help but wonder if Jo is about to become very, very important in my life.

# CHAPTER 13

# There Are No Take-Backsies

## JO

A real live asexual? Right here? Finally, after literal years of being out to my family and friends, someone I can truly relate to?

How can I talk to my moms when I have *this* to think about?

Is it too early to decide Sophie will be my new best friend? Will she even want to be my friend? She's so confident! So sure of herself! So put-together!

When I come back, it looks at first like my dorm is completely empty, but then I see Lianne on the top bunk, scrolling through her phone, the bluish light illuminating her face.

"How long have you been sitting there?" I ask, and I turn on the overhead light, which makes Lianne squeal and shut her eyes.

"Not that long! Turn it off!"

"Not even the string lights are on," I say, but I do as she says and flick off the switch. "You've been here fully in the dark?"

"In my defense, I was texting someone."

"For long enough not to notice the sun going down?" I say. "Who was it?"

"Literally nobody."

"The tone of your voice suggests that whoever it is, it's definitely *somebody*."

Lianne rolls over on her side. "It's the Wellesley student I met on Bumble. No big deal. We haven't even met in person."

Alicia. Sophie's friend.

I feel, for just a moment, like my insides are twisting upon themselves, but before I can let myself feel this further, I shake my head. No time to think about this; I need to call my parents.

Since the overhead light is still a no-go, I plug in our string lights and turn on a lamp at my desk so I can see my computer screen.

The FaceTime request comes two minutes late, which is pretty early for them. I hit the answer button, and their faces pop up on my screen: Mom, a thin, pale woman with salt-and-pepper hair styled in a pixie cut, and Mama, who's fat and wears thick glasses and has the same curly brown hair as me.

"Hi, Jonie!" Mom says, using a nickname only my family members ever call me. Mama waves.

"Hey," I say. "Sorry it's kind of dark. Lianne refuses to turn on the lights."

"It's good for the ambience!" Lianne says, and my moms laugh.

"Well, how was your week?" Mama asks, and I start to give them a recap on my classes and extracurriculars. I'm thinking about auditioning for the theater club's next play, but I hate the girl who's directing, and Mom tells me it's not worth my time if I'll be miserable.

Naturally, I can't focus at all during this call, nor do I really want to. We chat about who knows what, but my brain has gone back to focusing on Sophie.

Sophie, who's super smart and talks like Professor Fineman when she's excited. Whose hair is perpetually up in a neat ponytail or a simple braid. Who's aroace.

Like me.

I see a few text messages pop up on my phone, including one from Sophie saying she's really happy we talked today. I need to respond, but I can't ignore my parents like that.

After about twenty minutes, Katy comes back from wherever she's been—maybe a club meeting, since it's Friday—and immediately,

Lianne's out of her social-media-doomscroll hole, hopping out of bed to chat with her.

Not subtle, dude.

The two of them leave our room, probably to sit in the living room, and after my parents and I say good night to each other about six times, that's where I go to find them.

They're sitting on the long couch, this ugly green thing behind a scratched-up coffee table, and I join them on a purple armchair right next to it. Katy's laughing about something, and Lianne is awkwardly chuckling along. When I ask what's so funny, Katy dissolves into giggles.

"We're talking about my siblings," Lianne explains. "Katy thinks they're ridiculous."

"I can't believe your sister regularly calls you a whore," Katy says.

"It's affectionate!" Lianne insists.

Katy's an only child, so she has no clue how sibling dynamics work. Once, I told her about how my younger brother and I didn't speak for a whole week because we just forgot. She got so concerned that she almost made me go home and apologize to him.

"Anyway," Lianne says, "Jo, how was your call?"

"Same as usual," I reply. "My parents say it's lonely without me. My brother is doing fine. They might bring us some groceries this weekend."

"Fun," Katy says. "And how was dinner?"

I cover my mouth. "You guys. Sophie is *so* cool."

I tell them about my casual meal with Sophie and how it turns out she's basically the first aroace person I've ever met in real life, and Katy is immediately ecstatic.

"Oh, this is incredible. You guys are gonna bond, and you're gonna become best friends, and you'll be able to complain to each other about allos"—*allosexual*, or non-asexual people—"together for the rest of your lives, and it's gonna be amazing and exciting and majestic."

I frown. "Majestic?"

"Yes. Majestic."

"Thank you for your encouragement," I say, "but Sophie and I have only talked, like, three times including over text, so I think it's a *little* early to be making any assumptions. Besides, I don't even know if she actually likes me. We barely know each other."

"What?" Lianne says. "You said she texted you afterward saying she had a 'fun time.'"

I hum and grimace. "I don't know, it's just . . . she seems really cool, and put-together, and like she knows everything, and I feel like I know nothing, and I'm still trying to figure so much of myself out, and I don't know if she wants the burden of being friends with me."

As soon as I say it, I know I'm being ridiculous, but there are no take-backsies, so . . .

"You're not a burden," Lianne says.

"And there's nothing wrong with being unsure about yourself," Katy adds. "You're literally eighteen."

"It's not that I'm unsure," I say. "Like, I know that I'm aroace. But I haven't figured out what that means for me, you know? Like, what's my life gonna look like when I grow up?"

"Super valid concern," Katy says. "For a little while, I didn't realize being bi meant I could very well *not* spend my life with a man."

I snort. "So far, the men you've been with haven't been worth your time at all."

"And I've learned my lesson," Katy says. "Have I dated anyone since Jason?"

"Fair enough," I say.

I glance at Lianne, who's looking away furtively. I need to talk to her about this soon. She can't have a crush on Katy while also talking to people she's met on dating apps. That's, like, not allowed.

"Anyway," Lianne quickly says, "don't get all caught up in your assumptions about Sophie. She seems cool."

"She is," I say.

"Then that's great," Lianne says. "Go be friends with her."

"Okay. But what if—"

"Jo, come on," Lianne says. "Chill out!"

I shrink in my seat. "All right. But—"

"*Joanna, please,*" Katy says, and I hold my hands up in surrender, the three of us all laughing. "At this point, you're going to have to ask Dear Wendy for advice on how to make a new friend."

I fake a gasp in horror. "I would never." Especially not now, when our accounts have progressed to the shaming-each-other-in-our-stories phase. "Seriously, I'm just freaking out for no reason. I'll be fine."

"But is it really that bad if you ask for help?" Katy asks. "It's not like Wendy would know who you are."

"Katy, it's a matter of principle," I say. "If I ask them for help on something that I honestly do not need help with, that would be so deeply embarrassing for me and everyone involved."

I assure the two of them that I'll be fine, that it's just been a little too long since I've made a friend here. I'm pretty sure they believe me.

Later, though, when we go to bed and I'm alone with my thoughts, I wonder if Sophie really does want to be my friend.

I've never been great at making friends. I had people at school I hung around with, but with people constantly going in and out of the group, I never really hung on to any of these friendships. We graduated, school let out, and I pretty much never regularly talked to any of them again.

The worst part is that I don't really care. They moved on. I was just hovering in the background, an extra bit of filler for their conversations. I don't expect to speak much to anyone from high school until I start getting wedding invitations in the mail in five or ten years.

If even that. I don't really know how weddings work. Are they big enough to invite that person who happened to be in at least one class with you every semester that you shared homework answers with? Or how about your castmate from *Mamma Mia!* who played your daughter and sang "Slipping Through My Fingers" with you while crying on closing night?

I mean, it doesn't really matter. I hate weddings. I haven't been to one since my parents renewed their vows in our backyard a few summers ago, which I don't think even really counts.

Why am I thinking about weddings again?

When WGST 110 is over, will Sophie still care to talk to me? Or will we bump into each other one day, talk about how we *have* to get lunch soon, and then never get around to doing that?

I think maybe I need to go to sleep.

# CHAPTER 14

## Drained

### SOPHIE

My mom has an Android phone, so her video calls always come in from WeChat. It's the Chinese equivalent of Facebook and WhatsApp. The video quality is so poor that I might as well be on an audio call with her.

"Lèle!" she says when I answer the phone on the way back from studying at the library, fumbling to plug my earbuds in. "Are you busy right now? Where are you?"

"Hey, Mom," I say. "I'm walking back to my dorm. What's up?"

"I wanted to see you. How was your week?"

My mother looks a bit like if my sister or I were forty-eight years old: sharp and narrow jawline, high cheekbones, stick-straight hair that's graying but gets dyed black every few months. She still calls me "Lèle," my little name in Chinese that means "happy," which I got as a baby because I fussed a lot and my parents wanted to counterbalance that temperament. I don't talk to her and my dad as much as most people seem to talk to their parents; mostly, it's just the food pictures. But sometimes, Mom calls anyway.

"Uh, nothing has really happened this week," I say. "What about you? Anything going on at home?"

"Mm," she says. "Nǐ mèimei zuótiān bù kěn shàngxué."

My sister, Abby (Yuányuan, in Mandarin), is a freshman in high school. And according to my mother, she wouldn't go to school yesterday.

She actually talks to me more often than my parents do, texting or calling me to ask extremely basic questions or rant about her friend drama.

"What?" I ask. "Why would Abby skip school?"

"Tā shuō tā shēngbìng le, dàn wǒ juéde tā jiùshi búyào qù."

"Uh, that's not like her," I say. Abby wouldn't fake being sick just to skip class. "But, so, you just let her?"

"Yeah," Mom says, and she looks almost dumbfounded. "Wǒ hái néng gàn shénme?" *What else could I do?*

"Mom, you never would've let me skip school like that."

"You never want to skip school like that."

"Because I thought you'd get mad at me!" I say. "You lectured me for getting a B+ in fourth-grade math." I know what she's going to say next.

"Because I *know* you can get an A if you don't spend all your time reading your Percy Jackson books," she says.

Exactly as I suspected. "Mom, not this again."

We always get into the same few disagreements every time we talk. Next thing I know, she's going to bring up how I could've gotten into Harvard if I'd done one more piano competition, or how I'd have a summer internship lined up by now if I wasn't at my "tiny liberal arts school," or how I shouldn't have made yearbook my main high school activity because now it's the only thing Abby wants to do.

Thankfully, my dad has wandered into the living room; I hear his booming voice through my tinny phone speakers. "Zhū Yǐng, nǐ zài gēn shéi liáotiān?"

"Shì lǎodà," Mom says. *The oldest kid.*

My mom turns the phone to my dad, and I can see him standing behind the living room couch. He's wearing rectangular wire-rimmed glasses and has a clean-shaven face, though he always seems to miss a spot on his cheek. He's still wearing his coat from work—he's a nurse practitioner.

"Hi, Lèle," Dad says. He smiles blankly. My dad is so awkward.

"Hi, Dad."

"Are you walking home right now?" he asks. "Why can't I see you?"

"Yeah, I'm almost there."

"How was your week? Did you learn anything interesting during any of your classes?"

The back-and-forth Q&A lasts until I get in the elevator, and during my thirty seconds of no reception, I feel utterly drained. There was plenty of big stuff that happened this week. I did my WGST presentation, I got into that whole argument with Sincerely, Wanda on Instagram, and I had a big conversation with Jo about our sexualities.

But I can't possibly bring up any of those things. My mom thinks women's and gender studies is a pointless field of study, my parents don't know about Dear Wendy, and they certainly wouldn't take well to hearing I've found an aroace friend, given how they feel about my sexuality.

It isn't *that* bad. They accept my "choice" not to date, and they've stopped constantly asking if I've met somebody yet. But they refuse to acknowledge that I don't feel that way about anyone. That I'm *not* just picky, I'm *not* just focused on school, and I'm *not* attracted to anyone.

It's okay, though. I don't need to talk to them about this part of my life. I'm very used to keeping things to myself at this point; really, who needs to hear about my latest petty problems when they'll fade away in a few days? As Dear Wendy, I have other people's problems to fix, situations that are much more dire.

The elevator doors open, and a few moments later, my connection returns. Once I'm back inside my room, I see that Priya's taking a nap, so I tell my parents I need to go, asking them to make Abby text me back because she hasn't replied to my question about what kind of pens she wants from Muji. I tug my earbuds out of my ears, throw my phone onto my mattress, and thank the universe that I made it through this conversation.

I'm just irritated enough that I think I can put this energy into productivity; I vacillate between a few different options (finish a p-set, write my assigned *Wellesley News* article, check my Dear Wendy submission form) before settling on the thing I know best. Good thing I do, because the most recent submission says:

dear wendy,
this isn't an actual question. just wanted to say . . . your posts
are boring. and you're boring. and i don't like you.
sincerely,
wanda <3
p.s. you suck!

Oh my god.

Dear Wendy,

I'm graduating soon and moving in with my partner. Any advice
on how to deal with money together? When is a good time to
create a joint bank account?

Best wishes,
Someone Who Should've Taken an Econ Class

Dear Someone,

I don't think an econ class would've helped much with this! Money
is a very personal decision in a relationship. If I had a little more
context about your relationship, I might be able to answer this
better, but here's my general advice for people who are ready to
move in together.

Some people see merging your finances as a sign of commitment, but I don't really buy that (pun absolutely intended).
You're in your early twenties and probably don't have many

shared expenses besides rent, utilities, and groceries. Most likely, you aren't married, so you'll still be paying your taxes separately. I don't think you really need to worry about pooling your money together for a few years at least.

Also, there are married people who keep separate bank accounts! Especially if one has very different spending habits from the other, it reduces the chance for arguments about how much money you're spending.

Best wishes,
Wendy

**wandawellesley69 25m**
congrats, wendy, you just won the award for the least interesting answer you've ever given
Reply

> **dearwendywellesley 20m**
> What would YOU have said??
> Reply

> **wandawellesley69 12m**
> i simply wouldn't get this question in the first place. you're boring!
> Reply

# CHAPTER 15

## Meeting

## SOPHIE

I've gone to all of my professors' office hours at least once. I'm not trying to suck up to them—I think I might have gotten a worse grade in PSYC 101 last semester because of how much I rambled in office hours—but talking with professors is comforting, a reminder that they're real people.

But I've been putting off meeting with Professor Fineman since the semester started. Which was less than a month ago, but that's a long time for me. She may not intimidate me as much as she does Jo, but she's such a powerful presence that I'm a little scared to talk to her. I'm finally meeting with her today to talk about the midterm essay for this class.

"I haven't even looked up any of her research," I say to Priya as I neatly braid my hair.

"Sophie, do you really think most students actually look up their professors' research?" she replies, eyes trained down on a problem set she's doing. It's probably linguistics; she's taking the intro-level class so she can better understand word-nerd Izzy Sun's ramblings about dialects and syntax.

"I don't see why you wouldn't!" I say. "What if they're doing something super cool that you want to hear more about?"

"You are *such* a Wendy," Priya says.

"That's a compliment to me," I say, and I walk out the door.

When I get to her office in Founders Hall, Professor Fineman is sitting at her desk, typing something. Outside of class, she looks a lot more relaxed: Her posture isn't so perfect, and her blond hair is tied in a messy ponytail instead of a neat bun. The door is already open, but I still knock as I enter.

"Hi, Professor," I say.

When she looks up from her computer, she smiles warmly. "Sophie! Sorry, I got a bit caught up replying to emails. Come in, have a seat."

There's a wooden chair in front of her desk. I put down my bag and sit down, legs crossed. I want her to think I'm completely nonchalant, but I can't lie to myself—I'm nervous.

She unceremoniously pushes her computer to the side. "So!" she says. "What brings you here today?"

Why *am* I here? "Well, I, uh, I try to talk to all my professors a couple times in the semester, you know, because I feel like it helps me know you outside of a classroom. And I thought it'd be helpful to brainstorm essay ideas with you."

She nods, a small smile on her face. She's probably used to students like me.

"Got it," Professor Fineman says. "It's great to hear that you're interested in talking with your professors. I really wish more students would come to office hours, even if they don't have anything class-related to talk about. One-on-one conversations are my favorite part of teaching."

"Yeah! It's more . . . reciprocal."

"Exactly," she says, and now she's grinning. "So you want to talk about your midterm essay. Do you have ideas already?"

"Yeah, I do." I explain my initial idea: gender dynamics in romantic relationships. And then I list off a few more that I've come up with, in case she hates the first one, but as she nods and says "Uh-huh" to everything I tell her, I have no clue what she thinks.

"And which one do you think you'd like to write the most?" she asks when I'm done.

"Probably the first one," I admit.

"Then go for it!" she says. "Simple as that. You don't need my permission to write what you want."

Really? That's it? "So you don't think one of the others would be a stronger topic?"

"I think the strongest topic is whichever one you're most excited about," Professor Fineman says. "Are you interested in talking about relationships?"

"Um . . . yeah, I am." Time to tell her about how cool I think relationships are without having to delve into my own sexuality or Dear Wendy. "I've always been so fascinated by society's ideals about romance. Especially how Western culture has influenced the rest of the world. Like that study you had us read about heteronormativity in Chinese boy's love stories? I hadn't realized there were actual studies on something I've only seen criticized on social media."

She chuckles. "I hear that a lot from my intro classes. It's disappointing that kids aren't being formally taught about gender and sexuality studies during school. But it sounds like this is a topic you're passionate about, so if you want to write about it, then I think it'd be a great idea."

"Cool!"

"Actually, I think I have a few more articles I could send to you, if you're looking for more resources. Have you learned how to use the library's database search yet?"

Just like that, we spend way too much time looking through articles I might be able to use. It's like Professor Fineman has an internal repository of readings that she can provide. That must be what happens when you've been teaching for . . . I don't even know how long. She has one of those timeless faces that could easily be twenty-eight or fifty-five.

We compile a list of articles for me to look at, and Professor Fineman emails me a list of links and prints out a couple of the more relevant ones. It's on a desperately slow inkjet that clearly isn't school-provided, but she's being too nice for me to say no. I stare at the printer for approximately ten seconds of it slowly spitting out paper before looking back at Fineman.

"Uh . . . so, Professor, I was wondering—" I start. I have no idea where

I'm going with this sentence. What's something I can ask? "Um . . . could you tell me a little about your research? I realized I don't really know what you do outside of class."

Instantly, she lights up. "I am *so* glad you asked. You'll see in a few weeks during class, but I am particularly passionate about our unit on queer studies because it's what I focus my research on."

Oh, of course her focus is on queer studies. No wonder we've had so many readings on queer issues already, especially the intersections of queer and BIPOC issues. I was surprised at first; I'd expected women's and gender studies to mostly focus on straight white women.

"So for example," Fineman continues, "my most recently published article was on how the queer studies field represents trans voices, and of course, they're vastly underrepresented, as they are in pretty much any queer spaces. But most of the research I do is more focused on sapphics, which would make sense, considering I am one."

Wow. I don't think I've ever had an openly queer teacher before.

"That's so cool," I say, and I hope I don't sound like I'm choking or something even though I could probably explode into a hundred thousand smithereens right now. "Do a lot of professors end up researching things that, uh, also apply to them?"

"It depends," Fineman says. "In some fields, yes; a lot of my colleagues have a personal connection to their work. But not always. In any case, we're very passionate about what we do."

"That's good to hear," I say weakly.

I'm still processing the last couple of minutes of this conversation. I have so many questions now, and I also have no idea what those questions are. Is this what people mean when they say they have a crush on their teacher? No, it obviously isn't, but I think being starstruck by my extremely cool professor is probably the closest I'll get to that.

We chat for a while about one of her favorite articles she's ever put out, where she got to interview some sapphic Wellesley students about their experiences. It sounds like a study that's perfect for our campus.

I wonder if she's ever done anything on asexuality or aromanticism, or knows someone who has.

"Oh my gosh!" Fineman suddenly exclaims. "It's 4:15. I've kept you for so long."

"Really?" I look at my wrist, where a battered-up analog watch definitely reads 4:15, over an hour since I came into her office. "Oh, wow, yeah. It did not seem like that much time."

"I hope I didn't make you late for anything," Fineman says, laughing. "I tend to ramble a bit about my research."

I tell her not to worry about it, and she hands me the articles she recommended, which have been sitting in her printer.

I'll definitely be coming back to this office soon.

**@saguarolasagna:** okay buckle up for this one. i've liked this one person since last year, and we were about to go on a date, but we kept canceling because of various other commitments, and then we had to go home for the summer, so i ended up not going on a date with them, and now we're friends. fast-forward to now. i just got set up with the first person's roommate, and lowkey they're kind of cute too. but then also the first person just texted me asking if we want to do a do-over??? so like. what do i do. who do i go with. wtf.

**answer:** lmao???? take both of them on a date. at the same time. figure out who you like more then.

---

**dearwendywellesley 15m**
OMG do NOT do that!!!!!!
Reply

> **wandawellesley69 7m**
> why not? it's efficient
> Reply

**e.vie.dawson 39m**
omg **@saguarolasagna** bold of you to send this in non-anonymously
Reply

> **saguarolasagna 28m**
> I THOUGHT I'D HAVE IT FIGURED OUT BY NOW
> Reply

**e.vie.dawson** 20m
YOU DON'T????
Reply

 **dearwendywellesley** 4h ··· ✕

Some unsolicited advice from me: since
they are roommates, you're in a sticky
situation. I would postpone everything,
give it time, and see who you truly want
to pursue a relationship with. That said,
since this was posted non-anonymously by
@wandawellesley69—bad move, Wanda—they may
have seen this post already; you may want
to talk to them about that.

@saguarolasagna: okay buckle up for this one. i've liked this one
person since last year, and we were about to go on a date, but we
kept canceling because of various other commitments, and then
we had to go home for the summer, so i ended up not going on a

 wandawellesley69 3m ··· ✕

hey @dearwendywellesley maybe don't just inject
your advice into my posts, they could've submitted
to you if they wanted to hear your thoughts??
just saying??

 dearwendywellesley 4h ··· ✕

Some unsolicited advice from me: since

# CHAPTER 16

## A Dear Wendy Sympathizer

### JO

Wellesley doesn't have a midterms week, instead leaving the semester's timeline up to each professor's discretion. As a result, from about late February to early April, it's just always midterms season. You can tell that the mood has shifted from the beginning of the year if you set foot in any classroom. Most people's eyes are trained on their laptops as they pretend to take notes while working on p-sets, readings, and papers for other classes, or alternatively, browsing social media out of boredom.

The other thing about midterms season is that some of us lack the energy to properly participate in class activities. In today's WGST 110 lesson, we're supposed to be talking about gender as understood by young children—a very important thing to talk about, of course—but Sophie and I are really just telling each other about our childhoods in general.

"I remember when I was about six and Abby was two," Sophie says, telling me a story about her sister, "she got really mad that we had to wear these matching dresses for a photo shoot we were doing at some photo studio."

I laugh. "You were one of those families?" My family's photo collection consists entirely of pictures we took ourselves and portraits from school picture day.

"We sure were. And she just refused to look the same as me. She was, like, crying and screaming whenever we put her in the dress. And the only other outfit my mom had brought for her was this traditional Chinese outfit. You know what I'm talking about?"

"I think so."

Sophie shows me anyway after a quick Google search. "This one looks kind of like Abby's," she says, pointing to a baby wearing a red buttoned shirt and pants. "But yeah, so all the photos we have from that day with Western clothes are of her either crying or wearing a Chinese outfit that totally clashes with everyone else's clothes."

I'm pretty sure we got to this topic from talking about gendered clothing for kids, but I'm not totally sure.

"I mean, at least you have pictures in Chinese clothes, right?" I say.

"Only pictures of me and Abby," Sophie says. "My parents didn't do an outfit change."

"Tragic."

There's an awkward pause. I don't really have anything else to add, and Sophie's clearly done with her story. But in the five seconds we're silent, I hear the name "Wendy" behind me, and I tune into the conversation our classmates are having.

"It's honestly embarrassing," Meha Ahmad says. "Like, just let them be, you know? Not everything is about you."

"Right!" Lulu Hernandez replies. "If I were Dear Wendy, I would just go back to what I was doing before. The advice was easier to take when it was just one person speaking objectively."

As I suspected, they're talking about Wendy and Wanda.

"Oh, you're so right," Meha says. "But you have to admit, the fighting *is* pretty entertaining."

"Well, duh," Lulu says.

Their voices fade out as they keep talking, my attention returning to Sophie, who seems like she was also listening to them.

It kind of sounded like they were on my side. Or, at least, against Dear Wendy's antics. They're so right! Wendy needs to leave me alone!

"Did you catch that?" I ask.

I don't want to get too much into a discussion about the accounts with Sophie; she might start figuring out that I'm one of them, and I am not ready for anyone to know my identity. But I can't help but wonder about her thoughts.

Sophie coughs. "Yeah. Weird, right?"

"I think the whole campus takes this kind of drama way too seriously," I say. It's true—every minor incident gets blown way out of proportion here.

"I guess I understand where they're coming from, though," Sophie says. "Wendy and Wanda, I mean."

"Yeah? How so?"

"Well," Sophie says, frowning a little, "if I were Wendy . . . I think I'd also feel a little threatened by Wanda."

Okay, so Sophie's decidedly not on my side. But she doesn't even know the full story. Now I feel like I need to explain myself.

"I mean, you don't follow them, right?" I say. "If you actually look through, I don't really think Wanda is actually trying to usurp Wendy or whatever." I shrug. "I feel like if Wanda was really attempting to give better advice, they'd . . . you know. Clean up the page a bit."

I am having doubts about using Comic Sans for everything.

Sophie seems to consider this. "Maybe. I think Wendy is just trying to make sure people don't end up taking bad, fake advice."

"People can tell the difference between real and fake advice." At least, they should.

"You never know," Sophie says. "Before we got on campus, one person in my orientation group asked our mentor if we have to bring our own mattresses."

"You're kidding."

"Someone else replied 'Yes' as a joke, but we all started freaking out until our Orientation Mentor debunked that claim."

I laugh. "Okay, well, like that person in your OM group, Wanda is likely trying to provoke a reaction. It's probably good-natured."

"If it was so good-natured," Sophie says, "I don't know that it would've gone for this long."

I wonder if she's actually making a good point. At what point does my teasing of Dear Wendy become outright bullying?

Oh, who am I kidding? I'm not *bullying* Wendy. If anything, they're bullying me. Sophie doesn't really have context for the situation since she doesn't follow the accounts, and she also has no idea that I run my account. I can't blame her for being a Dear Wendy sympathizer.

Before I can come up with a proper rebuttal, Fineman calls for our attention back to the front of the class, moving on with our lesson, and I sit and wait for the next twenty minutes to pass so that I can start my weekend by finding more Dear Wendy posts to comment on.

# CHAPTER 17

## Break

### SOPHIE

Jo really seems to have no idea that I'm Wendy, but somehow, the conversation we had has actually helped me. If she's right that Wanda has no malicious intent, then that means I can wear them down.

"Wear them down?" Priya asks when I tell her about my thoughts over dinner. "Did you never get taught about how to, like, be assertive in elementary school?"

"What? No. What does that have to do with this?"

"I feel like you've gone from assertive to just plain aggressive," Priya says. She takes a bite of her dry-looking pasta, pretends to gag, and swallows it painfully. "God, this is gross."

"I am not being aggressive," I say.

"Sophie, you posted an in-depth analysis of Sincerely, Wanda's most recent post on your story for thousands of followers to see. That post was, like, two sentences long. All they said was basically 'LOL, break up, then.'"

I consider it. "Okay, maybe that was a little aggressive."

"How about this?" Priya says. "Until you're done with your midterms, you should take a break from the Wendy/Wanda drama."

"What? No. I need to keep up my posting schedule." But the idea does appeal to me. Specifically, the part of me that's getting stressed about the fact that I have an essay for WGST, another essay for my writing class, and a calculus test all due or happening in the next two weeks. And that's not even mentioning all the work I'll have to do for Abnormal Psychology soon.

Why did all my professors decide to make midterms happen at the same time?

"Just go on hiatus from being mean to Wanda, not from your whole account. You can come back to it with a fresh mindset."

I sit back in my chair. "I could do that."

She takes another bite of her pasta. "God, I can't eat this." She gets up, preparing to take it to the compost bin, but I stop her and take a picture for my dad.

> Me (5:54 PM)
> [attachment: IMG_1130] Priya's pasta

Bowen (5:54 PM)
They need to hire better cooks! 🙄 💀

My dad needs to have better appreciation for unionized workers.

> Me (5:55 PM)
> The cooks aren't the problem, we all love them and they're very underpaid and overworked
>
> I think the supplier is the real issue

Bowen (5:55 PM)
I see

As Priya dumps out the rest of her food, I sit back and pick at my salad (which is probably also doomed for the compost). My phone lights up with a Dear Wendy notification, and I have to fight the urge to check and see if it's Wanda, laughing at another one of my posts.

Priya's probably right. I don't need to feel so attacked by everything Wanda says. But I can't deny that I experience a twinge of glee every time I find something about them that I can point out. No matter how many people tell me that I shouldn't take this so seriously, I'm still going to. This is my account, one that I've built up for months now, and I work really hard to make sure my advice is of the highest quality. Wanda is trying to undermine me, whether for fun or for more nefarious purposes. I can't let them win.

When Priya sits back down at our table with a glass of lemonade in hand, I say, "Okay. You're right. I've gotten a little in over my head. I'll take a break."

"Good," she says.

"But after my midterms are done, I will not stop until Wanda gives up on their attacks."

Priya rolls her eyes. "You do you, Sophie."

Taking a break is easier said than done. When Priya and I go back to our room for the night, I see that I do, in fact, have yet another new comment from @wandawellesley69. It's under my most recent post.

Dear Wendy,

Last weekend, I went somewhere with somebody (I won't say what because that would very obviously reveal my identity if they follow you). I assumed we were just hanging out, but at the end, they tried to kiss me??? It was at this point that I realized that I had gone on a date with someone without knowing that it was a date. I feel so awkward and so naive for not figuring it out sooner. What do I do?

Sincerely,
Single Not Ready to Mingle

Dear Single,

You wouldn't believe how common it is for people to accidentally go on dates. Personally, I have multiple friends who have done so, usually with disastrous results. That being said, you can and will recover from this. Life is embarrassing, after all, and dating especially so. In your case, if you haven't already, I would definitely apologize to the person you went on a sort-of-date with; just be honest in saying that you had no idea what the purpose of your outing was. Then, if you find that you do feel the same way, tell them that as well and talk about what comes next. If you don't feel the same, emphasize that you'd just like to stay friends, and assert boundaries if necessary. In any case, as usual, my advice is for clear, healthy communication.

Best wishes,
Wendy Wellesley

**wandawellesley69  16m**
hey wendy have you ever gone on an accidental date? just wondering
Reply

Do I even respond to this?

The answer to this question is no. I'm fairly certain that nobody has seen me as desirable enough to ask out. I wasn't friends with a lot of people growing up, and I didn't want to be, but those I was friends with had all been on at least one awkward teenage date—many accidental—by the time we graduated from high school. Two of my friends even dated each other (and then proceeded to drop me as a friend; it was a whole thing). I was the only one who had never been asked out.

Well, okay. There was one time my senior year. Miles Johnson, a white boy in my grade whose main personality trait was being a gym bro, walked up to me one day during lunch while I was editing yearbook spreads. His friends a few tables over snickered as he asked me if I wanted to go to homecoming with him. I rolled my eyes and said no; he returned to his table, friends laughing even harder.

I still don't really know what the point of that was. Izzy thinks that he wanted me to say yes; Miles probably thought I was an unlikable bitch who would fall to my knees if someone finally showed interest in me.

Needless to say, I wasn't out as aroace in high school. Nobody knew about my identity except a close circle of friends. I didn't even really come out to my parents. I just kept on talking about asexuality and aromanticism, and they figured out that was how I identified. Of course, because I was a tween when I first talked about it, they thought I'd grow out of it.

I didn't.

I feel my phone buzz with a notification and look up from where I've been staring into space. What am I doing? This is a few too many feelings about high school, which is all in my past. All this after what was probably an offhand comment from Sincerely, Wanda. I really should listen to Priya and take a break.

I decide I'm not going to reply to that comment after all. Nothing good will come of it. I am going to succeed at all my midterms, and that means I'm not going to let Wanda's remarks get to me.

I check my phone for a notification. It's a text from Jo.

Jo (7:17 PM)

> hey!! this is kind of random but do you want to hang out this weekend? maybe go to boston or something?

I reply immediately that I'd love to hang out tomorrow or the day after, and then I put my phone aside and pull a book out of Priya's extensive collection on her shelf. When in doubt, I can always escape the worst thoughts in my mind by immersing myself in a story. Soon, my mind wanders away from my memories and into a witty small-town romance. I may be aroace, but I love a good love story.

# CHAPTER 18

# The Meaning of Life and the Inevitability that You'll Die Alone

## JO

I hate the Wellesley/Boston shuttle bus.

I've had motion sickness since I was little, and it's never been too bad, but something about the coach buses from the company contracted by our school just doesn't agree with my stomach. I know I should probably just go to my doctor and get a nondrowsy motion sickness medication, but that would require me to have my life together far more than I currently do.

I warned Sophie already that I would be entirely out of commission during our forty-minute ride into the city. She seemed sympathetic but clearly doesn't relate. While I stare out the window, she's reading, an absolute no-no when you have carsickness. I sneak a look at the book in her hands, a paperback with a blue cover depicting two people sitting on . . . are those giant sandwiches? No, those are suitcases. Is my nausea affecting my eyesight too?

She doesn't even give me a glance. I shouldn't have asked her to hang out with me. I bet she's so annoyed right now that I invited her out but won't even talk to her. Or maybe she actually doesn't want to talk to me at all, and she's dreading the coming hours.

*Or maybe,* says a voice in my head, *she's just having a good time and enjoying her book and will be happy to talk to you when you're not dizzy and nauseated.*

I don't know. I'll have to see.

We get off at the first stop, Harvard, because I can't stand to be on the bus any longer than I have to. There's a T stop right here, so we can take the subway the rest of the way to the Friendly Toast, where we're getting brunch. We walk down to the platform, pausing so Sophie can refill her CharlieCard.

"Are you feeling better?" Sophie asks as we wait for the train.

I cough. "Yeah. It usually clears up pretty quickly."

"So you'll be fine to eat, then?"

I laugh and tell her it'll take a while just to get to the restaurant and probably even longer to be seated; the Friendly Toast is known for having absurdly long lines because of its popularity among tourists and college students.

Once we get on the train, it doesn't take long for us to start talking in earnest. I ask Sophie if she's been doing anything interesting lately. She immediately proceeds to give me a rundown of her first-year writing course.

"Yeah, so my class isn't super English-y?" she says, gesturing as she talks. "It's about how we assign names to things and how that changes our perception of those things. My first-choice writing class was very literature-based, but I didn't get in. So far, it's pretty fun, though."

I say this in the nicest way: Sophie sounds like such a Wendy right now. Imagine liking a required class that you didn't choose to take.

I shouldn't have asked this question. This isn't relevant. We could talk about literally anything else. I hate that social conventions force me to perform a bunch of requisite small talk before getting to anything of interest.

"You're bored, aren't you?" Sophie asks.

"Sorry," I blurt. "It's just . . ."

"No, you're fine." Sophie waves a hand in the air. "I was kind of hoping you'd tell me to stop by now."

I smile sheepishly. "I was hoping we'd talk about . . . ace . . . stuff? I didn't know how to bring it up."

"You should've said!" Sophie laughs. "I thought maybe you didn't want to talk about it since you hadn't brought it up."

"I didn't want to make things awkward."

She shakes her head. "Not awkward at all. I've actually been thinking about things to talk about with you. Like . . . do you ever get people who are like"—she pitches her voice down—"'Oh, wow, I'm so jealous of you, it must be so nice to not think about your crush all the time.'"

"Yeah. It's exhausting."

"Right? Yeah!" Sophie throws her hands in the air. "Because I never know what to say to that! Like, yeah, my mind has other things to fixate on. They're not *better* things."

"More time to contemplate the meaning of life and the inevitability that you'll die alone."

Too much? Maybe that was too much.

Sophie has a shocked look on her face, but then she nods. "Yeah. Basically that."

"Glad to know we're on the same page."

"I can't help but think that I would have saved a lot of stress if I'd seen more examples of a-spec people growing up," Sophie says.

"Right! Does it ever annoy you how little representation we get in the media?" I ask.

"All the time," Sophie says. "It's like nobody knows ace people exist, let alone aromantics."

"And when they do know, their idea of it is so black and white!"

Things I hear a lot: that all ace people don't want to have sex, that all ace people are also aromantic, that *no* ace people are aromantic, that ace people can't be in a relationship.

The worst is ace discourse. People are *still* debating whether asexual people are queer. I mean, hello, what do they think the *A* in LGBTQIA stands for?

"Are your parents supportive?" Sophie asks. "If you don't mind me asking."

"Oh, yeah," I say. "I mean, they're lesbians, so. Makes sense they'd be accepting."

Her eyebrows shoot up in pleasant surprise. "That's so nice!"

"Yeah, they're really great. How about your parents?"

I know her parents look down on Wellesley as an institution, but that doesn't necessarily translate to bigotry in all forms.

Sophie sighs. "Well, it's—it's a little complicated."

Never mind, then. "Oh. Uh, you don't need to share if you don't—"

"No, they know. They just think I could change my mind someday."

I raise my eyebrows. "So they think it's a phase."

"Yeah."

"But you don't think so."

She grimaces and nods. "I mean, I know myself. I know that I never will. I tried to tell my mom, like, hey, how do you know *you'll* never be attracted to a woman, and she was like, 'Oh, that's different, because I already know I like men.'"

*I know myself.* Damn. I wish I knew myself.

"Mm, casual biphobia," I say.

Sophie sighs again. "Yeah, I'm fairly sure my parents don't think bi people exist."

"What the fuck? What do they think the *B* in LGBTQ stands for?"

She rolls her eyes. "I don't know, *bullshit*, I guess."

The word surprises me enough to choke out a laugh. It's so blunt. I haven't heard Sophie swear before, and in her voice, it rings with emphasis.

"Anyway," Sophie says. "At least my sister is cool with it. And most of my friends."

"Ah, that's nice! Yeah, my friends from high school were all right too. Although a few too many of them have dated each other."

Sophie hisses. "That's got to be a little weird for you."

"A bit. I don't know. I think it was annoying seeing them make each other so happy. Like, do I not have this effect on you? Or on anyone?"

"I know what you mean," Sophie says. "It's really frustrating."

We keep talking all the way to the Friendly Toast, through a transfer from the Red Line to the Orange Line, and as we exit out of the Back Bay MBTA stop. When we go up to the front of the restaurant, which is totally packed with people, the host tells us that we have a forty-five-minute wait for a table for two. Absolutely ridiculous as usual, but luckily, we planned for this. Sophie gives them her phone number to contact her when our table is ready.

With that, we set off toward the Boston Public Library's central location to browse their books, chatting a bit about a workplace sitcom we've both seen. It's a windy day—not unusual, since we're so close to the ocean—and my hair blows around wildly. Dammit, it's going to get so messy. I should've put it up.

While we're waiting at a traffic light, Sophie says, "Oh my god, wait," and waves to a couple in the distance, one of whom waves back.

"That's my big," Sophie explains. "On a date, I think. It's so funny we'd run into each other."

Right. Every first year gets assigned a "big sibling" on Flower Sunday, a pseudo-religious event in September organized by the Office of Religious and Spiritual Life. Bigs and littles can have a wide range of relationships; some of them never speak after Flower Sunday (like me and my big), some are casual acquaintances, and some are good friends.

"Oh, cool," I say. "What's their name?"

"Darcy."

"Like from *Pride and Prejudice*?" I have many thoughts about Fitzwilliam Darcy. Namely that if he proposed marriage to me, I would say yes, aromanticism be damned.

"Yes, exactly that. I'm pretty sure their parents named them after him. It's the total opposite of a fitting name, though."

"Wait, how is that name not fitting?"

"Oh!" Sophie laughs. "Fictional Darcy sucks at romance. But Darcy, my big, managed to find what will probably be their life partner within the first two weeks of freshman year. They've been dating the same person for three and a half years now."

"Damn. Good for them."

"Yeah. They're a good person to go to for love advice."

Love advice. Huh.

*What if Darcy is Dear Wendy?*

There's no way for me to find out. I don't know them, and I can't get Sophie to investigate without telling her my internet persona. And tons of people are good at love advice. That's not a rare trait to have. And, like, it would be a little weird if they were Dear Wendy. It sounds like they're a senior. Oh god, what if I've been arguing with a senior this entire time? That's so embarrassing. For me and for them.

"Anyway," Sophie says. "Do you like *Pride and Prejudice*?"

A good change of subject. "I feel like such a basic bitch for saying it, but yes, I love it."

Of course I love it. I don't know anyone who doesn't want to date or be Lizzy Bennet.

"For a while in high school, all I could think about was the 2005 adaptation with Keira Knightley," Sophie says.

"You mean, you don't *still* think about it every day?"

"Ah. You've got a point." Sophie raises her eyebrows, looking off toward the library, which is in view now, a large stone building with arched windows. "Hmm. I really do like romances."

"Do you think it's weird as an aroace person to like romcoms?" I ask.

Sophie shrugs. "I mean, we don't have to dislike romance just because we don't want it for ourselves. Of course there are some of us who are really averse to romance, right? And that's totally normal. But that's not all of us."

"Well said." I've definitely got a limit to how much romance there can be for me to enjoy it. But a little bit of it is fine.

"Thank you! But yeah, it's like, do people who listen to true crime podcasts genuinely want to commit murder? Do dystopia readers want to live in an even more oppressive society? Do people who watch Food Network actually know how to cook?"

"Damn, that last one hurts," I say, and Sophie giggles.

We've only known each other's identities for a couple of weeks or so, but it feels like Sophie has so much wisdom about it. I can't begin to voice all my thoughts about aroace-ness and how it affects me, and here she is, waxing poetic about media consumption.

"Wait, that reminds me," I say. "Do you know if people who, like, enjoy . . . horny media?" Sophie snorts. "Do they *actually* go around thinking about how they want to have sex with other people?"

I know the answer to this is a resounding yes. Lianne and Katy have proved that to me time and time again. But I think I need to hear it from her.

"Unfortunately, the answer is yes," Sophie predictably replies. "I asked Priya that a while back, and, yep, allos can really be that horny."

"Oh god." Meanwhile, when *I* try to picture having sex with people, it straight-up triggers my fight-or-flight response.

Pretty soon, we're listing things we don't understand, back and forth, as we enter the library.

"Why do people think muscles are hot?" I ask while we ascend the stairs.

"Why do elementary schoolers pretend to date?" Sophie asks when we walk through the courtyard, a fountain spewing out water in the middle.

"How hard is it to *not* cheat on someone?" I say when we're browsing the new book displays on the main floor.

"Why are there so many movies where losing your virginity is a plot point?" Sophie asks as we pass by a display with a DVD copy of *The 40-Year-Old Virgin* on our way up to the teen section.

"Where is the line between platonic and romantic attraction?" I say as I read the jacket copy on a friends-to-lovers romance with two South Asian kids on the cover, a starry night in the background of the illustration.

"Why the *hell* is there still ace discourse?" Sophie asks when she and I find a book published several years ago that heavily involves Tumblr.

"How are there not more stories for teens that focus on friendship?" I ask, which a librarian overhears. They recommend we look out for a book about music and Deaf identity coming out this summer.

By the time Sophie gets a text saying our table is ready, I've fully ranted to her about the terrible ace representation in a show that she hasn't even seen. She's listened intently the entire time. She seems personally offended by some of the things I'm describing.

Yeah, I think Sophie does actually want to be my friend.

# CHAPTER 19

## Debrief

### SOPHIE

Joanna Ephron. What a wonderful human being.

While they get up to use the restroom, I poke at my eggs Benedict and look around at the restaurant. It's packed with people: an elderly couple at one table, a group of guys at the bar cackling at something one of them must have said, and two girls about my age sitting in a booth nearby. One of the girls, with curly hair and light brown skin and a surprisingly stern gaze, looks oddly familiar to me; maybe a Wellesley student? But no, they're both wearing sweaters with the logo for another Boston-area college.

I can't people-watch for very long; quickly, I find myself musing on my conversation with Jo. This is probably the most I've talked to another a-spec person about a-spec things. Sure, I've had plenty of long discussions about sexuality with friends from home, with Priya or other people I've met here, but none with a similar experience to me.

I feel so *seen*.

But what if I've come off as too full of it, too judgmental? I get a sense that Jo is less secure in their sexuality than I am. But I haven't *had* many meaningful interactions with other a-spec people in my life, so I've never had to contemplate the minutiae of different experiences before.

A few seconds keep replaying in my head. While we were waiting for our food, Jo asked me about the line between platonic and romantic attraction, and I was a little lost.

"I guess it differs from person to person," I said. "I don't know. I feel like . . . I kind of *know* that that's not me. You know?"

They looked back at me, eyes wide. "No. I don't."

I mean, what do you say to that?

I wince at the memory of my response: "Oh, um, I mean, that's normal. Don't worry about it. It's all right to be unsure."

Dear Wendy would be way more coherent than this. But Jo seemed to be okay with my response. They seemed to be okay with this whole conversation.

I really hope they liked it as much as I did.

When Jo reappears, they raise their eyebrows at me as they walk back. I'm not really sure what that means until they sit down and say, "I think I might have just walked past a vaguely famous person?" and for the rest of our meal until we get our check, Jo and I try our best to subtly google a US champion figure skater who we're pretty sure is sitting right by us, shushing each other whenever we get loud enough to be overheard.

This day might be the most fun I've had all semester.

When I return to campus, expecting to debrief with Priya, she's not in our room. Instead, I find her girlfriend. Izzy Sun, a petite Chinese American with chin-length hair dyed pastel pink at the ends, sits cross-legged on Priya's bed, wearing one of Priya's T-shirts from high school, reading something on her phone. While I was gone, the two of them have been spending the day together.

"Sophie, you're back!" Izzy says, looking up at the sound of me entering the room. She locks her phone and turns it face down.

"Hey!" I say. "I thought you'd be back at Brown by now."

"Did Priya not tell you I'd be staying the night?" Izzy says, eyebrows wrinkled in concern. "I hope that's fine."

"Yeah, it's totally fine!" Izzy doesn't snore, and when I'm around, the two of them don't do anything more than cuddle. "I think she forgot to mention."

"Cool. I'm sorry." She looks deeply apologetic. She really shouldn't be; I've been friends with her longer than with Priya, so it's always nice when she's around.

"It's really not a big deal," I say. "Hey, where is she right now?"

"Doing her laundry," Izzy says. "She's been gone, like, ten minutes."

"Oh. Well, laundry's kind of hard in Claf." Our laundry room is in the basement, only accessible by staircase. There are four washing machines for the whole hall, and they have an offensively small capacity.

"I've heard." Her phone buzzes, a series of vibrations that I know spell out the letter *P* in Morse code. "Oh, that's her. *'I fucking hate laundry.'* Uh . . . I hope everything's okay." She taps out a quick response and then shuts her phone off again. "And how are you?"

"I'm great! I just hung out with a friend I met in class."

She nods. "Cute. What'd you guys do?"

"We got brunch and talked about being aroace."

Izzy gasps. "You found one?"

I've told her a few times about my struggle in finding a-spec friends. Izzy is demisexual, which is part of the asexual spectrum, so she's been really helpful to me. That being said, we very much are not the same, given that she is in a committed romantic relationship, whereas I am repulsed by the mere idea of being in one.

"Yeah," I say. I can't help but smile a little. "She's really cool."

Izzy nods. "That's great."

I really want to spill everything right now, but unlike Priya, Izzy won't pry for more details, and in any case, I'd prefer to wait until Priya comes back so I only have to tell this once.

"And how are you doing?" I ask Izzy.

"I'm good," Izzy says, smiling. "I like hanging out here."

"Have you and Priya done anything fun?"

"Well . . ." She looks up for a moment. "We watched a couple episodes of *Abbott Elementary*. Uh, mostly we just cuddled and talked."

"Gross."

She smirks. "That's not the grossest thing we did."

"Let's not go there today," I say. "Priya tells me enough."

"What?" Izzy's smile drops off of her face entirely.

Maybe I should not have said that.

Yes, every now and then, Priya reminds me (with absolutely no specific details) that she and Izzy have really awesome sex, and I am perfectly okay with that. I thought Izzy was too. She knows I know what they get up to. She's seen how I arrange my stuffed animals when she's over.

"It's nothing graphic," I blurt. "At all."

Izzy blushes and squeezes her eyes shut. "Oh god. I'm sorry."

"If it makes you feel any better, it's all good things," I say, trying not to laugh.

This only makes Izzy blush harder. She keels over and hides her face behind one of Priya's stuffed animals, a cat named Señorita Gatita. Of course, Priya chooses this moment to enter, holding a hamper full of laundry and panting dramatically.

"I hate those stairs," she says, letting out one final breath. "Hey, Sophie."

"Your girlfriend just passed away from embarrassment," I say. I tilt my head toward Izzy, who's still hidden behind the cat.

"Oh no," Priya says as she sets down her laundry basket by our closet. "Iz, what happened?"

"Apparently, you told Sophie I'm good in bed," Izzy says, sounding a little whiny. "So now I can never show my face in public again."

"Oh, please," Priya says. "Your face has been in worse places than in public."

I snort, and Izzy groans and says, "Priya, no, that's the whole point!"

This makes Priya burst into laughter. She sits on the edge of her bed and rubs Izzy's back, which is intimate enough of a gesture to make me look away for a moment.

"All right, we'll stop torturing you," Priya says. "Let go of Señorita."

Izzy sighs and sits back up. "Okay."

Priya smiles and kisses Izzy on the forehead, which makes Izzy giggle and lean into Priya's touch. I don't know if it's just me, but forehead kisses seem a million times more private and personal than regular kissing. The only way I could feel more awkward right now is if they started making out in front of me.

"So!" Priya says, looking back at me as she throws an arm around Izzy's shoulder. "Sophie! Tell us about your day."

"Oh. Sure. Uh . . . Jo is really cool."

"She sounds cool," Priya says.

"I guess I'm a bit overwhelmed because I never realized how . . . how *easy* it'd be to have an aroace friend," I say. "Like, no offense to you guys, but she really understands it."

Izzy and Priya look at each other with knowing smiles.

"Yeah," Izzy says. "I mean, Priya was my first lesbian friend, and it was so nice knowing someone with such a similar experience. With the compulsory heterosexuality, and the general disgust at the idea of being seen by a man."

"Of *course* you ended up falling in love with your first lesbian friend," Priya says. "That's, like, so gay, dude."

"Hey!" Izzy slaps Priya's arm gently. "I knew plenty of queer people before you! Just . . . not lesbians."

I laugh. "Yeah, it was pretty nice to talk to her."

"Might be nice to know someone who'll never need your Dear Wendy advice, huh?" Priya says.

I flinch automatically upon hearing Priya talk about Dear Wendy in another person's presence, but I have to remind myself that Izzy knows already. Priya's great at keeping secrets from everyone . . . except her girlfriend.

"Wh-what—well, I—I give platonic advice!" I stammer. "Maybe not as frequently, but . . . but when people ask, I'll answer!"

I expect Priya to play it off as a joke, but she raises her eyebrows and says, "Right, sorry. My bad."

I relax a little. "Anyway, it's cool talking to Jo. I wish I'd met her earlier.

But it's so hard to meet other aro and ace people here. The queer orgs don't really carve out a space for us."

Izzy frowns. "Is there not a club for a-spec students? Someone started one at Brown recently. I've been meaning to go to one of their meetings."

I shake my head. "We used to have one, a few years ago, but apparently everyone in it graduated."

There's a 2018 *Wellesley News* article that mentions Wildcards, a discussion group for asexual and aromantic students, but when I emailed our director of LGBTQ+ services back in August, she told me it hasn't been running for a few years now.

"It sounds like there's still a demand for it," Priya says.

"So, what, are you saying I should start it back up?" I snort. The prospect of starting a whole club is almost too ridiculous to imagine.

"Why not?" Izzy says. "It might help some people."

Oh, they're serious.

"I . . . I guess I could," I say.

But how would one go about starting a club? I wouldn't even know who to contact. Is it even possible to get a club up and running during second semester? How many people here would even be interested in joining?

"Oh!" Priya says. "And you could get Jo to help. And you can advertise on Dear Wendy! And maybe you could ask Darcy to help since they started the geese-watching club."

"Sorry, you have a *geese*-watching club?" Izzy says.

"Yeah, my big started it," I say. "It has, like, a hundred members signed up for email list. But that's beside the point. I didn't even say I'd start anything."

"But you implied it," Priya says defiantly, crossing her arms.

She's got a point. I can ask Jo if they're interested in working together. Working on our WGST project was fun, and if we both want to do this passion project, it could be super worthwhile. And I could definitely ask

Darcy how to start a club and who in admin to contact (although I'm not sure starting an org for observing our campus's many flocks of geese is quite the same process as starting a discussion org). But advertising on Dear Wendy? No way. People would definitely figure out I run the account.

As Priya and Izzy start chatting about other things, I think about whether this can happen.

It would be nice, wouldn't it, to have a space for people like me.

Me (5:28 PM)

Hi! So I have a question for you

How would you feel about starting an org for a-spec people?

Jo (5:35 PM)

omg

i think that is a terrific idea

Me (5:36 PM)

Ah okay!!!

Yeah so there used to be one a long time ago but now it's gone??

Jo (5:36 PM)

rip

Me (5:36 PM)

Yeah lol

I was thinking that we could ask Darcy how to do it since they started the geese-watching club

Jo (5:37 PM)

uh

who's darcy

Me (5:37 PM)

My big??? the one we saw in Copley Square today

Jo (5:37 PM)

RIGHT yes duh

wait THEY started the geese-watching club???

i've been on the mailing list forever

Me (5:38 PM)

Yes HAHA it's their proudest achievement

Jo (5:38 PM)

that's actually incredible

but yeah that sounds great!! i'd love to make this happen

this is so exciting

Me (5:38 PM)

I'm glad you're excited!

Got to go now but let's talk more about this later!!

**@hadleigh.912:** this isn't relationship-related but just wondering what pronouns i should call you by?? you've come up in conversation a few times

**answer:** omg i'm famous enough to come up in conversation . . . you can use any pronouns lol, if i reveal my personal pronouns it'll make it easier to figure out who i am lmaooooo

> **dearwendywellesley 47m**
> For what it's worth, I've been using they/them to refer to you
> Reply

> **wandawellesley69 31m**
> oh. uh. thanks?
> Reply

# CHAPTER 20

# No, That's a Fender Bender

## JO

"What even *is* gender?" Katy asks.

I know it seems like all my roommates and I do is help each other through various identity crises, but that's all Wellesley students *ever* do with their friends.

But I am *not* the person to be answering Katy's question.

I remove my earbuds and look up from my computer, where I'm putting together a playlist for WZLY. "Gender is . . . the baby food brand that does, like, mashed vegetables."

"No, that's Gerber," Lianne says from her spot on the top bunk. "Gender is those little fruit snacks with the juice inside."

"No, those are Gushers," I say. "Gender is the description of someone who's really kind and loving."

"No, that's gentle," Lianne says. "Gender is a minor car accident."

"No, that's a fender bender. Gender is the thing where rich people move into poorer areas and slowly displace all the existing residents."

"No, that's gentrification," Lianne says. "Gender is—"

"All right, stop, I get it!" Katy says, before I can get a chance to make a joke about chicken tenders. "None of us fucking know what gender is!"

"Oh my god, Kaitlyn Murphy, saying a swear word?" I say. "How blasphemous."

Katy sighs. "Sorry, guys. It's just . . . I watched one of those oddly specific videos that ends up saying, like, 'If you relate to this, you might be nonbinary!'"

I hum. "I relate to some ADHD TikToks, but I don't have ADHD."

"That's great, Jo," Lianne says, "but unfortunately, gender cannot be diagnosed."

Ouch. She's right.

"Well, Katy," I say, "we will support you regardless of how you identify."

"I think that for now, I'll keep on scrolling through social media to try and forget about all this," Katy says.

"Good plan," Lianne says. Her gaze remains on Katy for a second longer than it should.

I don't like it.

I shake my head and return to my playlist. WZLY has a strict one-song-per-artist-per-hour policy, and I need a few more songs to fill the hour I have for my show. My show is tomorrow evening—I dropped my morning one and picked this up instead so I can get some rest after being out in Boston with Sophie today—and I need to fill this up soon.

I ask Katy and Lianne if they have any requests, and they do, so I add a song by girl in red for Katy and a song by SZA for Lianne.

The playlist is five minutes short of an hour, so I still need one more song. I could throw in something classic, maybe Mitski or Troye Sivan, but I kind of want something new.

Maybe I should ask Sophie. She texted me earlier today with more plans for the a-spec club we're apparently starting.

Me (8:42 PM)

hey! so idk if you remember but i dj for wzly

and i'm making my playlist for my show this week

do you have any song recs?

Sophie seems the type to either have fucking phenomenal music taste or the trashiest taste imaginable. I sincerely hope it's the first.

Half an hour later, I find out it's not the first.

Sophie (9:14 PM)

Omg that's so cool!

Wait when is your show??

This is super basic but

Could you do All Too Well by Taylor Swift?

The ten minute version if time allows??

Of course she's a goddamn Taylor Swift fan. Wouldn't expect any less.

I mean, I like Taylor Swift too. It's practically a requirement for my generation. So I won't judge. But I am not playing a ten-minute song during my sixty-minute show.

I tell her my show time for tomorrow, and then I try to soften the blow of saying no to "All Too Well."

Me (9:17 PM)

unfortunately i'm already playing nothing new feat. phoebe bridgers this week bc i'm a sad bitch

so i need a different artist

Sophie (9:18 PM)

Oh no!

Okay lol how about Never Been in Love by Will Jay?

116

> Big aroace vibes

> Although he has another song where he says he was already in love when he released this song lol

I have not heard of this one before, but I'm always looking for aroace vibes, so I plug in my earbuds and give it a listen.

Sophie is right. Big aroace vibes. It's . . . so *happy*. He sounds so *proud* to be single.

Yeah, this is giving me lots of serotonin. I feel very validated. This is good. Very good.

I put the finishing touches on my playlist, but before I can close my computer, my phone rings. It's my moms.

Melissa (Mom) and Becky (Mama) Ephron are absolutely wonderful people, but they do this mom thing where despite our regular weekly phone calls, they'll also call me randomly without any warning, usually at incredibly inopportune times, to discuss something entirely pointless.

I answer, and their faces pop up, the two of them sitting side by side in our living room.

"Hey, sweetie!" Mom says, waving at me. Despite having lived in Massachusetts for over twenty years of her life, she still sounds super Midwestern. "Are you free to chat?"

"Uh, depends," I say. "Is it urgent?"

"If 'your moms miss you' is considered 'urgent,'" Mom says, "then yes, it is *very* urgent."

Mama laughs. "Theo says hi too."

They flip the camera and show my twelve-year-old brother sitting on our sofa playing on the Xbox.

"Go away," Theo says, despite the fact that I'm already away. "Home is better without you."

My parents laugh and turn the phone back around.

"You know, I got to hang out with a new friend today," I say.

"You actually made a friend?" Theo shouts, which makes my parents laugh.

"She's *actually* really great," I retort. "Her name is Sophie. We're in the same class."

"Well, good for you," Mom says. "You'll have to bring her over sometime."

"I probably will at some point," I say. "So anyway, why did you call?"

"Oh, we wanted to know if you'd like to come home for breakfast tomorrow," Mom says. "We're making biscuits and gravy."

"From scratch?"

"Jonie, what do you think?" Mama asks, looking incredibly taken aback. "I would never make you store-bought biscuits."

I roll my eyes. "Fine, come pick me up whenever."

"I'll swing by at 8:30," Mom says. "Do Katy and Lianne want to come?"

"Uh . . ." I look at my roommates, who've clearly been listening in, and both of them shake their heads. Katy mouths something that might be *sleeping in.*

Mom rolls her eyes. "You girls are so busy."

I shrug. "Maybe they just hate biscuits."

"Hey, you're still fine with being called a girl, right?" Mama asks.

Every day, I thank the universe that I have lesbian parents. Most people wouldn't bother to check.

"Yeah, that's cool," I say. "I don't really care when you guys do it." It does bother me when people assume I'm a girl without asking, but that's obviously not the case here. "Okay, if that's it, then I think I need to go now."

"No, wait!" Mama says. "We need to tell you about the dishwasher!"

I sigh. "What happened to the dishwasher?"

"Your mother decided to put dish soap in it," Mama says. "Even though she's been capable of loading a dishwasher for at least thirty-five years."

"But *you're* the one who bought the Trader Joe's wine that got me tipsy enough to mix the dish soaps, so who's really to blame?"

"Can you not wait to tell me about this during dinner?!"

"No, wait, I want to hear it!" Lianne says.

I bury my face in my hands as my parents and roommates laugh.

Dear Wendy,

I just started dating someone, and I feel like our communication isn't as strong as I expected it to be. Like, I tell them all the time how much they mean to me, but they never really say it back. Is our relationship doomed?

Sincerely,
I Just Want to Be Loved

Dear Loved,

Your relationship isn't doomed! Think about other reasons why you might be feeling this way. It can seem like you're giving more than you take even if that's not the case. I often think I'm the one who texts people first or who makes all the plans, when the real distribution is close to 50/50.

Also, maybe your partner expresses their love differently from you. Have a discussion with them about how you like to show your love. Do you express it in words, actions, or some combination of the two? (Personally, I think you can't go wrong with making someone a playlist.)

In other words: Talk to each other. See what works for each of you!

Best wishes,
Wendy Wellesley


**wandawellesley69 21h**
holy mother of god why did you post this at 5 in the morning
Reply


**wandawellesley69 3m**
omg no response, wendy?
Reply

# CHAPTER 21

## Dignity

### SOPHIE

It really is nice to not always be the one who texts first.

I am extremely chatty. Even with my closest friends, I tend to be the one who initiates a conversation. Maybe it's just because I'm on my phone a lot—I have to stay in the loop as Wendy—but when somebody texts me first, even once or twice, that's basically become a sign to me that we are, in fact, friends, and I'm not reaching out in a one-sided way.

Jo (10:11 AM)

omg

have you read this before

[attachment: IMG_1221]

Me (10:11 AM)

I have!! OMG Loveless was a turning point for the aroace community

I got it as soon as it came out

The book in question is a YA aroace coming-out story. It's one of my favorites.

Jo (10:12 AM)

i've been meaning to read it for so long and was just reminded that it exists

there are a bunch of holds on it at the library

Me (10:12 AM)

If you want, you can borrow it from me! I have a copy in my dorm

Jo (10:12 AM)

wait please that would be so nice

At the sound of my phone buzzing on the common room coffee table yet again, Priya puts down the book she's reading—a sapphic thriller/mystery with a spilled milkshake on the cover—and the motion causes Alicia to look up from her homework problems.

"Why is your phone blowing up so much?" Priya asks.

"It's Jo," I say.

"Ooh." Alicia smirks. "Are you guys going on another date already?"

The two of them have been trying to get me to reclaim the word "date." I appreciate the thought—*Why can't any special outing be considered a date?*—but it just sounds wrong. I don't need to apply romantic terminology to fit my life.

I try my best not to make Alicia feel bad. "Mm, I don't think 'date' is working for me."

"Are you going on another outing?" she suggests.

"That sounds weird too."

Priya clears her throat daintily. "Are you furthering your bosom friendship by spending your *leh-zure* time with one another?"

"If I say yes, will you stop coming up with innuendos for hanging out?"

Priya props up her legs on the coffee table. "Maybe we will, and maybe we won't."

"Cool. Great."

Alicia and Priya smirk at each other, and I look back at my computer, where my WGST essay sits in a Google Doc. It's due in a little over a week, and I don't want to keep looking at this draft.

I am incredibly tempted to open up my Instagram and take a look at Wanda's account. Just a peek. Against Priya's hopes, my break hasn't made me calm down or take things any less seriously. I won't say anything mean, though, so I'll technically still be on my break from drama.

I glance at Priya now, engrossed in her work. She won't know if I just sneak a glance.

I pull out my phone and open the Instagram app. Right up at the top, I spot it: Sincerely, Wanda's signature Comic Sans on a white background. But my eyes barely manage to scan half of the first sentence—*so i've got some petty friend drama you're gonna love*—when Priya smacks my phone out of my hand. It lands face down on the floor.

"Hey!" I yell. "What was that for?"

"Oops," Priya says, smiling innocently. "How clumsy of me! Sorry!"

Alicia narrows her eyes at Priya but then shakes her head and looks back down. Yikes, that was close.

Just another week. One week, and then I'll be able to tell Wanda every one of my thoughts about their annoying, unprofessional, chaos-inducing posts.

# CHAPTER 22

## Never Say Those Words Again

### JO

Sophie and I get lunch at Lulu to talk about how to start a club. (Our food is almost certainly going to taste worse than what we got at the Friendly Toast yesterday.) I kind of have no idea what to expect, but leave it to Sophie to have way too much to say already.

"I would've invited Darcy to this," Sophie says, her voice echoing in the dining room, "but they're super busy with classes."

"Aren't we all."

She nods solemnly. "I did manage to ask them a few questions about how they started the geese-watching club, though, so it's gotten a little clearer."

She launches into an explanation of how clubs work at Wellesley and what it takes to get official approval. I get lost several times in the number of acronyms of different groups on campus we need to talk to so we can get through different stages of the org's creation—one committee for org approval, one committee for funding, one office for administrative support, and on and on—but eventually, I think I get a good idea.

"Okay, great," Sophie says. "Those are all the steps to make a constituted org. But there are actually a lot of campus orgs that don't get funding or admin support at all—they basically just run underground—and I actually think that's the way to go for us."

I nearly spit out my omelet. "Are you kidding me? Why did you explain all that, then?"

"Just in case you wanted to know," Sophie says, twirling a strand of pasta around her fork. "Isn't it fascinating? Bureaucracy is so interesting."

"Never say those words again," I say. "Anyway, why shouldn't our Wildcards revival be constituted?"

"Well, I was talking to Darcy, and they mentioned that a lot of queer orgs aren't constituted because then they have to submit an official member list to admin, and that has the potential for outing people who are in the closet."

"That makes sense," I say slowly. "But then how do we get people to join?"

"That doesn't really depend on administrative approval," Sophie says. "Anyone can advertise with flyers around campus or in College Government's email blasts as long as you follow spamming guidelines."

"Oh, okay." I don't know why I didn't think of that. I see flyers for so many things around campus.

"From here," Sophie says, "I think the first thing we should do is check with the director of LGBTQ services and see if we can use their space to hold meetings, and then we should see if there's even any interest in having an a-spec org at all."

"So . . . do *I* actually need to do anything?" I ask. "Because I hate emailing people, and I don't have any friends."

Immediately after I say it, I want to kick myself; it sounds very much like I don't want to do any work and just want credit for being involved. Which is not the case. I just don't want to do those two things specifically.

Sophie laughs. "Uh, I guess not for now. But once we have that figured out, there'll definitely be things for you to do."

She doesn't *look* like she's mad at me or judging me. But who knows.

"Should it still be named Wildcards?" I ask. "I always thought that name was a little weird."

"I think it's a bit of a play on words," Sophie says. "Like, because of 'ace'?"

"I feel like we can do one better," I say. "Are there, like, any famous single people or something we should name ourselves after?"

Sophie laughs. "Real or fictional?"

"Either could be fine."

Sophie considers it. "Okay, maybe this is just my childhood Greek mythology obsession coming into play, but maybe we could name the org after one of the virgin Greek goddesses? Like Athena or Artemis?"

"Then people will think this is a Greek myths club," I say. "I mean, I would."

She sighs. "That's probably right. Hm . . . what about their Roman names? Minerva probably doesn't fit right, but Diana is, like, a normal name."

"That could work. The *Dianas*. I like the sound of that."

By the time we finish lunch, we have a plan for Sophie to put out some feelers this week. We'll see in a week or two where we are and then go from there.

"Oh, you know what?" I say as we walk down the stairs from the dining hall. "Artemis-slash-Diana is an archer, right? Like, she's got her band of hunters and everything."

"Yes?" Sophie says, clearly not getting where I'm going with this.

"So does that make her . . . an arrow ace?"

Sophie stops dead in her tracks. "Jo, please."

I slowly break into a smile. "So we are still employing wordplay in this org's name after all."

"You know, that isn't an original joke. I bet someone on the internet came up with it over a decade ago."

"It's funny and you know it."

She looks at me, eyes narrowed, but isn't able to keep a straight face for long. We both burst into laughter, the sounds ringing through the high ceilings.

"You're ridiculous," Sophie says, shaking her head, a smile lingering on her face.

# CHAPTER 23

## Hearts

### SOPHIE

Somehow, I've been spending a *lot* of time with Jo this weekend. Priya and I were planning to order Chipotle after Izzy went back to Brown, but then we didn't want to pay the super high delivery fee for just two people's food; we asked a bunch of friends if they also wanted Chipotle, and Jo was the only one who said yes.

This evening, Jo walks over to West Side so we can eat our dinner in Claflin, which she has somehow never been to before. We sit at the table in the middle of the main common room, and I have a full text exchange with my dad about how I got mild salsa because he didn't feed me enough spicy food growing up before Jo notices the Claflin carvings.

"Oh my *fucking* god, what are those?" she asks, pointing up at the wooden figureheads above the entryway. They're about a foot tall and painted in gold and red, seeming to stare angrily down at the room.

"Oh, that's the King of Hearts," Priya says. "And, uh, I think that one's the Queen."

Jo seems like she's nearly vibrating out of her seat. "Why the *fuck* are they there?"

"The Claflin architect's daughter Alice died, and he put these *Alice in Wonderland* carvings here in her honor," I say. "At least, according to what I've heard. Also, Alice is a ghost, and she haunts the fourth floor."

Jo gapes at the nonchalant way we're speaking. "He's . . . *watching* us."

"Uh . . . yeah?" Priya shrugs. "You saw Kulima in the lobby." Our unofficial mascot, a near-life-size plastic skeleton.

"*Kulima* is a plastic skeleton wearing a firefighter helmet," Jo says. "Nothing scary about her. But *this*? How do you guys sleep at night?"

"It's not like we sleep in *here*," I say.

"But . . . you sleep on the fourth floor. Which apparently is . . . haunted?"

"Eh." I shrug. "I don't believe in ghosts."

"I do," Priya says. "But Alice means no harm. She's just a little noisy sometimes."

"*NOISY?!*"

Eventually, Jo calms down enough that she's able to fill us in with some Stone-D lore, which is significantly less spooky than Claflin's.

"So a lot of decades ago, there was a dorm called Stone Hall that burned down, and Olive Davis, who was in charge of the dorm, had given such frequent fire drills that everybody was able to get out safely, and then they named the new one after her."

"Why was Wellesley so fucking flammable in the twentieth century?" Priya asks. "There was the College Hall fire too."

"Uh, do you see this room?" I say, pointing up at the carvings. "That's all wood. Still flammable."

"We've got a sprinkler system now," Priya says.

"But if it malfunctions," Jo says, "this whole room is burning down."

"Damn," Priya says. "This'd be a good place to commit arson."

"Um, please don't commit arson," I say.

As we explain to Priya why gratuitous burning is a bad idea, a few other Claflin residents walk into the room: Alicia, her roommate, Hadleigh, and a friend who lives down the hall, Sue Chen.

"Oh my god, hi, guys!" Priya says.

Alicia waves. "Mind if we join you?"

I look at Jo, who shrugs and nods. As Alicia, Hadleigh, and Sue sit down, Jo leans in and whispers to me.

"Who are they?" she asks.

"Other Claf residents," I whisper back. Then I turn to the others. "So everybody, this is Jo."

"Hi, Jo," Hadleigh says. She wiggles her eyebrows expectantly and tucks a strand of her blond hair behind her ear. "Ooh, should we all go around and do the Wellesley intro thing?"

Sue smirks and pushes up her glasses. "Ah, yes. Name, pronouns, dorm, prospective major, hometown, and . . . what am I missing?"

"Fun thing you've done this weekend," Alicia replies.

The rest of us laugh.

"Please don't make me do that," Jo says.

We still go around with our names and pronouns, even me and Priya just for laughs. Jo makes brief but piercing eye contact with me when Alicia introduces herself, and I try to convey to Jo that yes, she's *that* Alicia.

Jo is last to introduce herself.

"Jo, she/they, and, uh, I know we're not doing fun facts, but my fun fact for you is that I picked up a WZLY show tonight, so I actually need to leave in about half an hour."

"You're a DJ?" Hadleigh says. "I'm interning right now!"

"Yeah!" Jo says. "How's it going for you?"

"I'm still recovering from the fact that we're not allowed to just play Lorde on repeat," Hadleigh says.

"*Right?*" Jo says. "I have 'Royals' on my playlist for tonight."

It turns out all six of us have strong feelings for Lorde's music, but doesn't every liberal arts college student? My favorite of her albums is *Solar Power*, but Jo insists the best one is *Melodrama*, and Priya betrays me by agreeing with her. The Lorde discussion continues for so long that we even go into the fan conspiracy PowerPoint, and all too soon, Jo has to leave.

"Please listen to my show!" Jo says as she stands up to go.

"We will!" I reply.

Some of the others also leave, but Priya, Alicia, and I stay, looking up the website where we can tune in.

# CHAPTER 24

# The Man, the Legend, Harry Edward Styles

## JO

Once people know your music taste, they start to think differently about you. So yes, I am nervous for Sophie's friends to hear me on the radio after they've only just met me.

As usual, I walk into Studio A and begin my show by announcing, "You're listening to WZLY Wellesley, 91.5 FM. My name is Jo."

I look over at Spotify on the computer screen. "Our first song for tonight is 'Adore You' by the man, the legend, Harry Edward Styles, off his critically acclaimed album *Fine Line*. In the words of Harry himself, it is a song about a fish."

The broadcast runs on a few seconds' delay, so it takes a few beats for me to get any texts from my friends. The first to come in is from Sophie.

Sophie (7:01 PM)

Of course you're a Harry Styles stan

Me (7:01 PM)

when did i EVER say i was a stan

Sophie (7:01 PM)

You said his middle name

Me (7:01 PM)

how do YOU know his middle name??

Sophie (7:02 PM)

I googled it to see if you were right

Me (7:02 PM)

what's wrong with being a harry styles stan?

Sophie (7:02 PM)

Absolutely nothing

Me (7:02 PM)

good

Is it a little basic for Harry Styles to be your favorite member of One Direction? Yes. But is he objectively the most correct option? Also yes.

My roommates are the next to text me.

## the unfortunate residents of STO-202

lianne not-a-butler (7:03 PM)

this is like the third time you've done adore you

Me (7:03 PM)

okay and?

katy kissed a girl and she liked it (7:03 PM)

Harry has a much bigger discography than this one song

> You only have so many chances to play his music, you should be switching it up

> I mean this is one of his most popular singles

Me (7:04 PM)
> shut up

I switch over to my messages with Lianne now. There's something to tell her that Katy doesn't need to know.

Me (7:04 PM)
> you know

> alicia flores is listening to wzly today

lianne not-a-butler (7:04 PM)
> jo please don't remind me HAHA

> at this point she's just a failed bumble match

Me (7:04 PM)
> failed?

lianne not-a-butler (7:04 PM)
> i lowkey ghosted her bc i forgot to respond one day and then kept putting it off

Hmm. Maybe it's a good thing that the Bumble match hasn't worked out.

After answering the usual texts from all my other friends, I open up Instagram and begin my usual doomscroll.

The third post on my feed is a Dear Wendy post, someone asking about what to do if you're caught between two friends' petty drama. (Apparently, one of them went as far as to tell the person asking the question that they can't hang out with the other friend.) It's the first thing I've seen from Wendy in days—they've been awfully quiet this week.

Oh well. Better for me. I type a comment under the post.

**wandawellesley69 1m**
idk i feel like maybe you should just drop both friends?? just a thought
Reply

All things considered, a pretty tame comment, but we'll see if Wendy even responds.

# CHAPTER 25

## Confrontation

### SOPHIE

can't take it anymore. I need to see what Wanda's been posting.

I still have the rest of this week before the peak of my midterms is over, but it's been gnawing at me. They've been making comments on my posts this whole time. So I open Instagram and start reading.

Except as I scroll through their posts from this past week, I can't find much to talk about. Wanda's advice is shockingly sound.

There's this one from yesterday:

**anon:** my professor refuses to provide me my accommodations (which i won't say for privacy reasons). i've tried talking to them and they said my accommodations are unfair to other students. wtf do i do?

**answer:** okay so that is very much illegal discrimination and you should talk to the title ix office, your dean, ADR, and maybe the ombudsperson. best of luck, and whoever that professor is, i hope they get what's coming for them.

Yeah, they're right. That's illegal. And I would've given the same answer. Maybe not threatening the professor—I don't want my account taken down for harassment—but the rest I agree with. I wouldn't really call this relationship advice, but I would have answered this.

And then there's this from a few days ago:

**anon:** okay i have nowhere else to put this but i just want to say i'm pretty sure my partner is going to propose after we graduate this may and i'm really fucking excited, we've been together since high school and i just want to be married already

**answer:** oh good for you i respect a long term couple! i expect an invitation to the wedding. also wtf wait people my age are already thinking of marriage?? am i . . . growing up??

It's cute. I probably wouldn't have answered that question if it were in my inbox—it's not seeking any advice—but this is a fairly appropriate answer. It's pretty weird to imagine people not much older than me getting married (where I'm from, it's much more common to marry in your late twenties or later), but it is normal for a lot of people.

The next one just makes me feel bad for the person who asked the question:

**lolquirkyusername:** my parents don't approve of my relationship (they won't let me date until after i graduate college) even though my bf is literally the ideal bf for me (harvard student, perfect gpa, premed, amazing at playing the cello, family is from the same culture as mine). what should i do about it? pretend we broke up? ACTUALLY break up?

**answer:** not until you graduate college??? god! i literally just answered a submission about marriage! i think a lot of parents try to exert a little too much control over their kids who are

actual adults, and that's really not fun, and i'm sorry. if you
haven't already, talk to your bf about your options; the two
of you probably know better than me what your parents will
react best to because i don't know your culture or the particular details of it. but please don't actually break up over this,
he sounds nice lmao

The response is impressively culturally sensitive. (Although I guess
cultural sensitivity hasn't ever been an issue with Wanda.) I definitely
knew some people whose parents didn't want them dating in high school,
leading them to sneak around and lie, because that would usually end up
with a better outcome than being honest and trying to talk about it.

When I get to the last post from this week, though, I feel like I've
struck gold.

**anon:** this is literally such a tiny issue but this friend of a
friend like totally has a crush on me and they keep trying to
hang out with me one-on-one and i am TIRED. how do i get
them to stop. i don't feel the same way!!

**answer:** i know you want me to say that you should tell
them no or ask your friend to talk to them, but i actually
think you should just keep hanging out with them until they
get tired too because confrontation is hard!!! i mean unless
you're like super annoyed with their mere existence or
whatever.

Confrontation is hard, yes, but it's necessary. Wanda is just advocat-
ing that this person waste their time and energy on a person they don't
particularly care for.

I think about how I can respond as I hop out of bed and get dressed in
my workout clothes. The post is definitely in a more joking tone than the

others, but I still don't want the person who asked this question to take the answer seriously, and it's a lazy move for Wanda to answer like this, especially when their other answers were all so . . . decent.

That one bit keeps nagging at me. *Confrontation is hard.* And then I realize why it's bothering me so much.

I repost the post to my story, adding just a bit of text: *Oh, really? Confrontation is hard? Wanda doesn't seem to have much of an issue confronting ME, given the number of comments they've made on my page while I was too busy with midterms to do more than queue my usual posts. Take a look for yourself if you don't believe me!*

Satisfied, I put away my phone and start on my run around Lake Waban.

**@wandawellesley69:**
okay wow, low blow
so maybe i do enjoy confrontation. anything wrong with that?

**@dearwendywellesley:**
Of course there's something wrong with that
My page is littered with your comments

**@wandawellesley69:**
you're one to talk LMAO
wendy. bestie. i am just trying to have some fun!!

**@dearwendywellesley:**
I understand that!
I just think that maybe you can have fun without putting
others down in the process

**@wandawellesley69:**
okay lol i'll back off
but only if you'll do the same

**@dearwendywellesley:**
I can't promise that

**@wandawellesley69:**
then i can't promise anything either!

**@dearwendywellesley:**
Fine
May the best W. Wellesley win

**@wandawellesley69:**
WHAT IS THERE TO WIN????????

# CHAPTER 26

## SOPHIE

I don't know when Wanda and I started acting like this with each other, but in just over a month of their existence, we've gone from amicable to downright hostile. The weird part is that I kind of like it. I like poking holes in their arguments. I like stirring up a little drama. I even like that they fire back; it's a mutual thing, so it's not like anyone is really being bullied.

I do deserve to win, though.

It's been a day since we had a conversation on Instagram about not backing down. That isn't a problem for me; I'm going to keep on making my posts and commenting on theirs, and we'll just have to see what happens. If anything even happens from this.

I'm in the middle of writing another comment to Wanda when I get a text from my mom, breaking me out of my Wanda-induced reverie.

Ying (7:58 PM)

We went to party at Zhou Ayi's house last weekend.

I just remember, Zhou Ayi said she has a coworker with a son at MIT.

Sean Ma, you know him?

I have to laugh. It's the only reaction I can have besides pure irritation. MIT has thousands of students; why would I know this one MIT boy?

Ever since my mom found out that Wellesley has a cross-registration program with the Massachusetts Institute of Technology—one of the only reasons she's okay with me going here—she's assumed that means I know everyone who goes there, despite the fact that I have yet to cross-register in a single MIT class.

> Me (7:58 PM)
> No, Mama, I don't know him
>
> There are many people at MIT
>
> And I haven't been there yet

> Ying (7:59 PM)
> Zhou Ayi said he has girlfriend at Wellesley.

> Me (7:59 PM)
> That's great, mom

> Ying (7:59 PM)
> Maybe you can find MIT boyfriend too.
>
> If you want someday.

I knew this was where she was going.

> Ying (8:00 PM)
> Are you in MIT class?

Me (8:00 PM)

No, not this semester

Ying (8:00 PM)

Remember to take one next year.

Good for resume.

And important to meet people with different opinion.

Wellesley girls all very similar to you.

And with four text messages, my mother has delivered *several* micro-aggressions. *Meet people with different opinion than you*? That just means she thinks my politics are too far left. And, of course, "Wellesley girls" is a misnomer, given that so many of our students are trans or nonbinary. All things I can't discuss with my mom without getting into a fight.

My mom and I have very different viewpoints about the purpose of college. For her, it's simply a necessary step into the adult world, the place where you get a degree so you can get more degrees or get a job, maybe where you meet your eventual spouse. The better the college, the better opportunities you'll get later. Which, sadly, is true to some degree—saying you went to Harvard on your résumé can get you further in the job application process, after all.

But for me, college is more than another thing you do to get elsewhere in life. It's a pivotal point, the place where you learn your values and find your people, where you can walk around and exist in a place with a rich, important history and set foot in places that thousands of students did before you. It's my home, more so than my suburban hometown has ever been. For the first time in my life, I'm in an environment where people care about me—the *whole* me. I wouldn't get that at MIT or Harvard, where so many legacy students with trust funds are roaming around, where there are so many people with egos about the fact that they go to one of the most prestigious schools in the country.

I groan loudly, which makes Priya turn from her spot at her desk and ask me what's wrong. She probably suspects that it's Wanda, but she won't say anything with Alicia here. Alicia looks up too; she's been sprawled out on our floor doing a reading.

"It's my mom," I say. "Pressuring me to take classes at MIT."

"You're not the only one," Priya says. "A couple days ago, my dad texted me a picture of the MIT literature department's course browser. I don't even know how he found it."

"Sometimes," I say, "it feels like the only reason my parents are paying my tuition is because they expect some of it to go toward MIT classes."

I know they wouldn't actually stop paying my tuition, but it still feels like it.

Alicia shrugs. "What can they do? It's not like they can force you to go there."

"I mean, I might. If I find a class I want to take." So far, I haven't.

"We can all take one together so we're not suffering alone," Priya says.

I reply to my mom's texts with a thumbs-up emoji, which is always a great way of ending a conversation. I sincerely hope she doesn't actually want me to date an MIT guy.

"If it makes you feel better," Alicia says, "my parents will *not* stop bothering me about getting an MIT boyfriend, and that's, like, a million times worse than making you take classes."

"Damn," Priya says. "They still don't know you're mostly seeing people at Wellesley?"

Alicia shakes her head. "They don't need to know right now. I'm not worrying about coming out unless my hypothetical long-term partner turns out not to be a man."

Alicia's parents aren't immigrants like my parents and Priya's dad, but her grandparents came to the US from Puerto Rico, so she's only one more generation removed from the baggage that comes with being a child of immigrants.

"You know what I don't get?" Priya says. "I'm literally out to my dad, and he knows I have a girlfriend, but he refuses to talk about her. Ever."

"Not to make excuses for him, but do you think he'd be the type to talk about your boyfriend if you had one?" Alicia asks. "Some parents just don't want to talk about relationships."

"Hmm," Priya replies. "Maybe not. I don't know."

"Do you think your grandparents talked to him about relationships?" I ask. "If not, that might have influenced him."

She sighs. "I know they weren't super happy when he told them he wanted to marry my mom."

As I've learned from another deep conversation about BIPOC struggles like this one, Priya's mom, who died when Priya was about five years old, was Punjabi, and her dad is Bengali, and in India, it's generally more acceptable to marry within your ethnic group than outside of it.

"Maybe relationships are a sore spot for him because of your mom," Alicia says.

"It's so weird," I say. "My parents *wouldn't* be the type to talk about relationship stuff, but I think after she realized I identified myself as aro-ace, my mom started talking about my dating life *more*."

"Weird," Priya says.

"I wish my family would get that Wellesley isn't just a place where women find their husbands," Alicia says. "I'm getting a whole degree here."

That always strikes me every time I talk about Wellesley as an institution or about the older generations' opinions on it. It seems like wherever you go, you'll find people who still think so-called women's colleges don't serve a purpose other than eventual marriage. We're here because it's a phenomenal school and a safe space for us. Maybe some people—or a lot of people—do want to date, but that's true anywhere you go.

"I think we generally need to let go of the concept that college is where you find The One," Priya says.

"Easy for you to say," Alicia fires back. "You found The One in high school."

"And you *never* shut up about it," I add.

It's at this point that the conversation derails from our family struggles to us making fun of Priya for being obsessed with her girlfriend, but this part of the conversation sticks with me even as our mocking of Priya grows increasingly silly.

When I look back at my phone, my half-finished comment to Wanda still sitting there, I sigh and delete what I've written. I'm too tired for this today.

It's *hard* to be queer and part of any diaspora. Even if your parents are trying their best.

I want things to be better. I know they can be. I just don't know how, and neither does Priya, and neither does Alicia, and we're doing what we can to have a good relationship with our parents, but it sucks what we have to sacrifice to make that happen.

# CHAPTER 27

## Movie Night

### JO

Sophie (6:34 AM)

[link: TikTok.com]

 You

It's cool that Sophie and I text now. It's *not* cool that she regularly wakes up before 8:00 A.M.

The link is to a TikTok of a person saying, "Look, I *love* the fact that I don't have to be confined to society's heteronormative ideals. I love the idea of being single. But when Mr. Fitzwilliam Darcy shows up in the middle of that field at the asscrack of dawn? Suddenly, I have a *visceral, physical need* to be in love *right the fuck now*."

I stifle a giggle, trying not to wake Katy, who's still asleep after we stayed up until 3:30 A.M. binge-watching *Top Chef*. (Okay, maybe this is why I'm tired, but I had a good reason for doing this. It was the season where the winner was a Korean American lesbian. She's amazing.)

Me (9:12 AM)

oh what a great way to start my day

being called out by a stranger on tiktok

also why tf were you awake at 6:34 AM

Sophie (9:15 AM)
I go on a run at 7 every day

Of course Sophie's a runner.

Me (9:15 AM)
what the hell

there have been days when i go to sleep at 6:34 AM

also since when do you run??

Sophie (9:16 AM)
Since my parents made me join cross-country when I was in seventh grade

It was shockingly enjoyable

It's very popular! In high school our team had 150 people

Me (9:18 AM)
holy shit how big is your high school

Sophie (9:18 AM)
2,550 students

Me (9:18 AM)
that was an oddly specific number

Sophie (9:18 AM)

Lol

I was editor-in-chief of my yearbook

We had to put that number in the opening pages

And I double-checked it many times before we submitted it

So now I remember it

Me (9:19 AM)

omg cool

i was a theater kid 🎧

Sophie (9:19 AM)

I knew so many of those

One of my friends in high school was a theater kid

Another did show choir

Priya's girlfriend went to my high school and she did improv

Me (9:20 AM)

oh cool i didn't know she had a gf

Sophie (9:20 AM)

Yeah lol! Her name is Izzy

> Priya's off visiting her today

> And probably for the rest of this weekend

If Priya's gone, that means Sophie is spending the weekend alone. I hope she won't feel too lonely. I don't know if I've ever spent a night here without Lianne or Katy, and honestly, I like it best when they're both here. It's comfortable.

> Me (9:20 AM)
>
> oh cool

> Sophie (9:21 AM)
>
> Yeah they're kind of a perfect couple

Yep. Yeah. Cool. Good stuff.

How do I reply to this? Gotta love it when you run out of things to say in a text conversation, but you have read receipts on, so you need to say something else now or else it'll be awkward.

> Me (9:22 AM)
>
> well if priya's gone for the weekend
>
> is there any chance i could pop by?? and hang out??
>
> and not do any work on the dianas whatsoever??

Fingers crossed that Sophie won't think I'm being annoying. I really don't want to impose on her, but also, I want to spend time with her without needing to do work. I'm excited about our club, I really am, but I need a break from productivity.

Sophie (9:22 AM)

You are more than welcome to do so :)

Lol I need a break from club planning too

Sophie ends up inviting me to watch *Inside Out* in her dorm room in the evening. I arrive wearing my pajama pants, which are yellow and patterned with pictures of cats, and I bring with me two bags of microwave popcorn and my favorite stuffed animal. Because when I have a movie night, I *have a movie night*. This is *Inside Out*. I will need Sammy the Frog to get me through this.

When Sophie opens the door, she says, "Oh my god, you look so much cuter than I do right now."

She's still wearing her daytime clothes: a purple pullover with Taylor Swift lyrics and a pair of Adidas joggers.

"I can guarantee you I will *not* look this cute by the time this movie is over," I say. I hold up the two packages of Orville Redenbacher's Movie Theater Butter popcorn. "You want some?"

Sophie raises her eyebrows. "Yes, please."

She shows me to the kitchenette on her floor, where there's a communal microwave. After we pop the popcorn, we go back to her room.

It's a little smaller than mine, which makes sense since only two of them live here. The ceilings are a bit sloped. Her bed has a cute bedspread and a matching pillow, and it's made perfectly neatly. There's a row of stuffed animals on it . . . all turned to face the wall?

"Why are your stuffed animals all looking away?" I ask.

Sophie blushes. "I do that whenever Priya's girlfriend comes over. I forgot to turn them back around."

"Uh . . . why do you do that?"

"Just so they don't have to, you know . . . witness . . . whatever goes on."

I burst into laughter.

"Stop!" she says. "It's not funny!"

"This is the funniest thing that you've ever done," I say, trying to catch my breath.

"It makes me feel better!"

"They can't see! They're not alive!"

"You take that back!"

Once I finally stop laughing, we sit on the fuzzy rug on Sophie's floor, and before long, we're sobbing about the death of an eleven-year-old's imaginary friend. As Riley returns home and tells her parents how much she misses Minnesota, I start crying along with them, which is *so ridiculous* because I can visit home at any time, but you know how it is.

As the credits roll, Sophie looks at me and frowns. "Are you all right there?"

I give her an uncomfortable smile and two thumbs up. "Great. Spectacular."

Sophie tilts her head. "Do you need a hug?"

I sniffle and nod, and that's enough for Sophie to pull me close as I whimper about Bing Bong and all of Riley's lost memories.

"There, there," Sophie says, awkwardly patting my shoulder. "It's just a Pixar movie."

"*Fuck* Pixar," I say.

I sniffle again. Sophie gives me yet another tissue (I hope she doesn't run out because of me). I blow my nose in a loud honk, and Sophie giggles.

Eventually, I regain my composure enough to speak in full sentences, and I say, while staring at the crack underneath Sophie's door, "Sorry I'm such a mess."

"Don't be," Sophie says. "We all have a lot of feelings. That's kind of the whole point of the movie."

I sigh. "You know the part with the boy at the end where all his emotions are running around when he sees Riley?"

"Yeah? It's hilarious."

"Is it bad that I wish that were me?"

Sophie looks at me in a way that I can't read, her lips pressed together and her eyebrows wrinkled.

"No," Sophie says. "It's just amatonormativity."

Right. Amatonormativity, a cousin of compulsory heterosexuality. Feeling like you *need* to be in a relationship because that's what everyone feels. Wanting, but also not.

"Do you ever feel like that?" I ask.

"Sometimes," Sophie says, which surprises me. The way she carries herself, it's like . . . she knows she's never going to be in love, and she's proud of it.

"I think I'm used to it now," Sophie continues. "You know, I'll see a happy couple, and I'll be like, 'Oh, gosh, I'll never achieve that kind of happiness in my life,' and then I remember that that's just my immigrant mother's insistence that marriage and children are the only way to be happy."

"I don't know if it's just an immigrant parent thing," I say. "It's kind of all around us." The fictional narratives we consume. The real ones too. The entire celebrity gossip industry. Your friend in a committed relationship who constantly waxes poetic about their lover. All of it.

"Oh, yeah, for sure," Sophie says. "And it varies between people. I think for me, it's more obvious with my mom. 'Cause my dad kind of goes with whatever my mom says."

"Did your parents have some sort of big grand love story?"

Sophie chuckles. "Not exactly. They met in grad school. I think they had a mutual friend."

"Still pretty fun."

"What about your parents?"

Oh, this is a good one. "Do you want the long version or the short version?"

"Long, absolutely."

I smile. My moms have told this story so many times.

"Okay, so picture this: It's 1993, and hate crimes against queer people are increasing, and Don't Ask, Don't Tell is being implemented, and HIV drugs are only barely starting to come out. So in April, there's a protest in Washington, DC."

"And your parents were there," Sophie correctly guesses.

"That's right," I say. "They were both college students. They'd traveled hundreds of miles to be there, Mom from Illinois and Mama from New York. And they just bumped into each other while they were protesting in front of the White House. Mom likes to say it was like magic. Mama insists that they didn't *really* hit it off until they went for drinks that evening."

"Wild," Sophie says. "Then what?"

"Then they started dating. And then a decade after they met, Massachusetts legalized gay marriage, so they moved here and got married. And then they had me using my uncle—Mom's brother—as a sperm donor, and then they had my brother six years later."

"That's . . . really cute, actually," Sophie says.

"I've spent my whole life hoping I'd get a love story as good as that," I say.

"But you won't."

I thought it sounded like a joke, but Sophie has clearly figured out the real pain behind it. I see my parents, and they're incredible, pretty much exemplary of the ideal relationship, and that's all that's been modeled to me my whole life.

And I don't know how else to be happy.

I look up at Sophie. How can she so easily, so effortlessly, say those words, words that I can barely admit to myself?

I sigh. "Yeah."

I take this lull in conversation as an opportunity to clean up. I pick up some tissues scattered across the floor, stuff them in an empty popcorn bag. Sophie does the same.

"Is there anything else you want to do?" she asks once the rug is free of all evidence of our movie-watching.

I think this might be an invitation for me to go back to my dorm.

We've seen a movie; the objective of our night is over. So I should go now, right?

Or maybe I'm overthinking. Maybe she simply wants something to do.

"I don't know, what do people usually do when they hang out with friends?" I say.

"We could do some work?" Sophie suggests.

"Absolutely not."

"That's fine," Sophie says. "Yeah, I didn't really think that through. How about . . . oh, we could do some slumber party activities!"

"Like what?"

"Paint each other's nails. Watch a murder show. Dissect your deepest emotional wounds. Eat a bunch of junk food. Talk about how scary it is to be a living human being. Play Mafia, if you're with multiple people."

"Whoa, whoa, whoa, some of those things are *not* like the others," I say. "Emotional wounds?"

"Have you never been to a sleepover where you accidentally open up to each other *way* more than necessary?" Sophie says. "That was the best part of middle school."

"Oh. I mean, that's kind of what it's like having two roommates."

"Exactly, so you do know what I'm talking about. Do you want to do that?"

I feel my face flush. "Um . . . maybe we can do one of the other things first."

I'm not ready to unload all my innermost thoughts and feelings on Sophie. We've only really known each other since the semester started. Barely over a month.

"Fair enough," Sophie says, shrugging. "Usually, that sort of thing happens naturally, and asking if you want to is anything but natural."

Sophie ends up pulling some coloring books from her bookshelf, and we sit on her floor coloring with a set of Crayola washable markers. For some background noise, Sophie puts on a Crash Course video, which is so unbelievably nerdy that I have to laugh.

Soon enough, we're giggling at our horrible coloring technique and chatting about our families, high school activities, cringey middle school phases, and the numerous houseplants on Sophie's windowsill.

We only realize an hour has passed when Sophie's phone alarm goes off, reminding her to take her birth control, which she tells me she uses to manage her period cramps.

"Setting a birth control alarm is peak Wendy Wellesley behavior," I say. In fact, I bet Dear Wendy would do the same thing.

Sophie raises her eyebrows, like she's surprised I'd say that about her, and then turns around to pop a pill out of her packet.

"A real Wendy would remember all on her own to take her medications," she says. "But anyway, it's getting a little late." It's not, but good for her for thinking it is. "Do you want to just sleep over for the night?"

"Honestly? Yeah, that'd be great."

While I'm silently freaking out because I've never slept in someone else's room at Wellesley before, Sophie gives Priya a quick call to make sure it's okay for me to be sleeping in her bed, upon which Priya says, "As long as she's fine with the things that have happened in that bed."

"Gross," Sophie says, and then she says her goodbyes and hangs up. "Uh, Jo, there are some clean sheets in the closet—"

"Yep," I say, already opening the door.

"The closet outside," Sophie clarifies.

"What?"

This is how I learn that the fourth-floor dorms in Claflin were all built with one closet, and every group of first-year doubles has an extra one in the hallway.

"That's so weird," I complain while we're changing the sheets. "Why couldn't they build two closets? I mean, at least you get an extra one in the hall and aren't stuck with one tiny one like in a bunch of the other dorms, but still."

"Beats me," Sophie says. "I'm getting a feeling that you kind of hate Claflin."

"So much of it doesn't make any sense."

Sophie insists that I brush my teeth even though I tell her I'll be fine for one night. She gives me an unused toothbrush that's clearly a freebie from the dentist. Her toothpaste is so aggressively minty I nearly choke on it.

Right when we settle into bed, Sophie lets her hair out of its ponytail. There's a dent in her hair from being held up all day. From the way it frames her face, I can barely recognize her.

I've seen her hair in a braid, in a bun, in ponytails of various heights, but never unstyled.

She looks so vulnerable like this.

"Hey, why do you never wear your hair down?" I ask her.

She raises her eyebrows. "Oh. It's lower maintenance. And . . . I don't know, I think people look at me differently when my hair is down." She must notice the quizzical look on my face because she adds, "Like, they take me less seriously."

"Huh. That's interesting." Frankly, I do not care if her hair is down or up, but I'm not going to just say that because it'll sound like I do care.

"I know it's supposed to be bad for your hair, but I don't notice a difference."

"If you ever decide your hair needs a break," I say, "Lianne gives haircuts. I think a shorter style could make you seem more serious."

She frowns. "I've tried that before, and it makes my hair curl up at the ends like I'm stuck in the 1960s."

"Ah. Yikes."

My hair is its own thing. I've learned what products work with it, what I need to do to make it look nice. Curly hair is difficult, but I like it.

"Does it ever get tiring for you?" Sophie asks, like she can sense what I'm thinking. "Managing your appearance? Like, who are we doing it for? It's not to look attractive."

Whoa. We're getting a little deep. "I mean . . . yeah. I think about that a lot. Especially since, like, the world perceives me as a girl, and the way I choose to make myself look is the reason why, but also, I don't want to be?"

"Be a girl? Or be seen as one?"

I pause for a moment. "The second one."

"But do you like the way you look?"

"Yeah," I say. "I'm very happy with it."

"Then . . . it's not your job to make people aware that your gender doesn't have to match your appearance. So do whatever makes you feel good about yourself."

She says it as if the solution is so simple. And I guess it is. Stop caring what other people think. But she obviously cares about what other people think, too, if her hair is any indication.

"Okay, well," Sophie says, reaching toward the light. "Good night!"

"Oh my god, you can't just turn off the light and expect me to fall asleep!"

"Really?" Sophie says, frowning. "That's what Priya and I do."

"You're so weird."

"*I'm* weird? How do you and your roommates go to bed?"

I shrug. "We go to sleep when we want to. And if the light is still on, I'll put on a blindfold, but I'm, like, always the last to go to bed."

"I'm sure Lianne and Katy will be glad you're not keeping them up tonight, then."

"Stop, I'm actually so worried about them."

"Really?" Sophie says. "Why?"

"Uh . . ." Oh no, I've fallen into the deep end. "So, you know how Lianne probably has a crush on Katy?"

"Yes, we've been over that."

"I guess I'm just worried that if I'm not around, she'll do something impulsively that will not go well."

"What if Katy likes her back?" Sophie says.

"She doesn't," I say.

I don't know if Katy likes Lianne. But there's no way. The whole idea of Lianne being in a relationship is ridiculous to me—doesn't matter who it's with.

"I'll take your word for it," Sophie says. "I mean, I could definitely tell when my high school friends liked each other."

"Did they date?" I wonder if her high school friend group was also chronically in conflict because of relationship drama.

"They sure did." She rolls her eyes, and a bitter sort of expression clouds her face, a sure sign that something complicated happened.

I clear my throat. "Do you want to elaborate?"

"It's a long story."

"I have time."

She looks like she's thinking a lot about what to say, and I'm about to tell her it's fine if she doesn't want to explain when she starts speaking again.

"Okay. Well . . . so, the first thing you should know is that I have moved on from this. It's something I processed, like, two years ago. I wrote an essay about it in a creative nonfiction class last fall."

"Oh my god, you're about to tell me something horrible." Someone got hurt. Or maybe hurt Sophie. Or—

"No! I mean, nobody died or anything. It's just . . ." Sophie frowns. "Basically what happened was my best friend of sixteen years slowly ended our friendship as he grew closer and closer with our other friend, aka his crush and eventual boyfriend, and I saw all the signs but didn't realize it was happening until it happened, and now I only speak to him when I wish him a happy birthday and then he tells me happy birthday back a week later. And that really made me think for the first time about how this could happen with any friend who's not also aroace. Like, my person, my closest confidant, will probably always have someone else—a romantic partner—that they're closer to."

*Oh.*

I don't know why I assumed that Sophie's life before Wellesley was perfectly peachy, no drama, no identity struggles. We all have stuff to deal with, don't we?

I have about a million questions now, but I ask a simple one. "How did you become friends?"

"Oliver's my next-door neighbor at home. I guess technically our parents introduced us when we were babies."

"Damn."

"So you can imagine that growing up with him basically being like a brother, or at least a really close cousin, and then suddenly getting cut off, was a very difficult experience for me."

"No kidding."

"But because of this, I became closer with a few of my other friends, including my friend Izzy, who did *not* totally abandon me when she started dating Priya." I remember Sophie mentioning having gone to high school with her roommate's girlfriend.

This sounds very simple. Too simple. "You've definitely glossed over a lot of stuff in between, haven't you?"

Sophie rolls her eyes. "I mean, yeah, it was a very emotionally taxing experience. If that's what you're talking about."

"Sort of. I mean . . . nothing nearly that bad happened to me in high school, but I feel like I still constantly dwell on my old high school drama even though I'm not friends with any of those people anymore."

"Really?" Sophie smirks. "What happened to *you* that was so bad?"

And just like that, I'm explaining all the different configurations of my high school friend group since freshman year, from the first awkward relationship formed from two queer people very clearly experiencing compulsory heterosexuality to the rifts that ensued when particularly problematic people were brought in.

Theater kids are the worst.

". . . and probably the worst thing that happened," I say, "is when my friend Brooke dated my friend Brynlee—"

"There are actual people named *Brynlee*?" Sophie interrupts.

"Yeah, her mom was, like, an early mommy blogger. Their kids always have weird names. Anyway, my friends dated, and then they had this big dramatic breakup, and the thing was, some people in our group were super good friends with Brooke, and some were way closer to Brynlee, and so when the breakup happened, different people heard way different sides of the story and, as you'd expect, took sides themselves. But I wasn't really great friends with either of them because I suck at making friends, so I was kind of stuck in the middle hearing everyone's drama and not really knowing what to do with it. But then Brooke stopped auditioning for plays, so things finally calmed down. And Brynlee is lowkey a Republican even though she's literally bi, so I don't talk to her anymore."

Sophie stares at me. "Whoa."

"Yeah."

"This explains so much about you."

"What the hell is *that* supposed to mean?"

She starts tripping over her words trying to explain how my personality is "just, like, a lot sometimes," and I have to quickly tell her I'm not offended. And we can't stop laughing.

Sophie and I talk like this for probably another hour. It's effortless how we can keep a conversation going. But eventually, Sophie falls asleep in the middle of a sentence, and that's my cue to turn off the light and go to sleep.

I lie awake in bed for a while longer. I'm not bothered by, as Priya said, "the things that have happened" in this bed. But it's weird to be in here.

I've never slept over in another person's dorm. Is that a thing that people do? Probably. But I barely have any friends besides Lianne and Katy. Maybe people just don't like me. Maybe I don't make enough effort to have any friends. I don't know.

Having friends in high school was so hard. Keeping them, anyway. I floated through groups of people: whoever was doing the school play every season, or the people I shared a lot of classes with. And now that I'm in college, I kind of just go along with whoever decides they want to be my friend. Which is only my roommates, to be honest. And now, Sophie.

I fall asleep hoping Sophie actually wants to be my friend and doesn't secretly hate me.

Dear Wendy,

One of my friends got into a relationship recently, and it feels like they've stopped talking to me. Maybe not completely stopped, but I've been talking to my major advisor more than this friend lately. I want to approach them about it, but am I being too selfish? Where do I draw the line?

Best,
Third Wheel

Dear Third,

The easy answer is to tell you to wait it out, that things will calm down, but in my experience, I think that approach tends to be pretty terrible for friendships in the long run. So . . . try this.

(Before I begin, it's natural for someone to fall off the radar if this relationship is *very* new. If it's been under two or three weeks, you could give it a minute, but otherwise, keep on reading.)

First, text and ask if everything's okay. There could be something else going on in their life! If they've just been "busy," I'd suggest arranging a time where you can hang out. If you're not in the same place, schedule a call! As gently and politely as you can, *make* them make time for you. If in a few weeks, you haven't seen any improvement, then you can sit down and have an honest conversation.

I'm running out of space on this answer slide, so DM me if you have any other questions! This is something I have . . . a lot of experience with.

Best wishes,
Wendy Wellesley

**wandawellesley69** 41m

dude it should not take this long to say "communicate with each other"

Reply

> **dearwendywellesley** 22m
>
> If I just said that for every answer I give, I might as well shut down this account
>
> Reply

> **wandawellesley69** 10m
>
> that would be a great idea actually! shut it down!
>
> Reply

> **dearwendywellesley** 4m
>
> I will not be doing that.
>
> Reply

**wandawellesley69** 40m

also what do you mean "a lot of experience"??

3 likes Reply

> **dearwendywellesley** 21m
>
> Don't worry about it!
>
> Reply

> **wandawellesley69** 5m
>
> you're literally so cryptic and for what
>
> Reply

**anon:** alright i'm taking this to you too in case you and dear wendy have different thoughts. what do i do if my friend is dating someone and clearly prioritizes their partner over me? i'm getting tired of them falling off the radar every time their SO is around.

**answer:** the only time that's ever happened to me, my friend's SO was also a total asshole, and she hated him and dumped him, but that's probably not a great solution LMAO. i mean personally i would just deal with it. like accept that that'll happen? but you're right that's not fair to you so. idk do what dear wendy says i guess?

> **dearwendywellesley** 3h
> So you admit I'm right!
> 2 likes Reply

>> **wandawellesley69** 2h
>> no stop shut up that's not what this is
>> Reply

# CHAPTER 28

## Aggravating

### SOPHIE

It was nice hanging out with Jo last night. I learned a lot about her. She's a sperm donor baby; she's incidentally vegetarian most days of the week because the Stone-Davis dining hall doesn't serve meat; one of the ways she figured out she was aroace was doing stage kisses during her high school production of *Almost, Maine*. She cares a lot about her roommates, but I think she's scared of how her relationship with them might change in the future.

I like her. A lot.

Our conversation last night reminds me a little of my sister, Abby, who's four years younger than me but often acts like we're the same age. We mostly joke around with each other, but every so often, we end up in a pretty deep conversation.

As if my thoughts have summoned her, I get a FaceTime request from Abby, which I answer immediately. She shows up on my screen at an awkward angle, her phone held below her chin, the bottom half of her face out of frame. According to everyone we know, we look identical—same sparse eyebrows, same angular jaw, same high cheekbones.

"Yes, Abby?" I say.

I'm one paragraph away from finishing my final draft of my WGST paper, and then I have to pack up and head back to my dorm from Lulu, where I'm studying. She couldn't have called me ten minutes later?

"Sophieeeeeeeeeee," Abby whines. "I was trying to wrap a gift for

Madeleine's birthday 'cause I got her a mug that looks really cute, but then I DROPPED IT! And now it's BROKEN."

Madeleine is her best friend—and the younger sister of my ex-friend Oliver. (Madeleine dislikes Oliver as much as I do, so I welcome her presence in my life.) Now that I've told Jo about it, Oliver's been on my mind a bit.

Nobody talks about breaking up with your friends. It sucks. Especially when that friend ditches you to be with whoever they think is The One. In high school, I always wondered if I didn't do enough for him, but I know better now. He wasn't enough for me.

Abby looks like she's still waiting for a response from me, and I blink and clear my thoughts.

"How did you drop it?" I ask.

"One minute, it was in my hands, and the next minute, it was on the floor, shattered into a million pieces, along with my heart."

"Buy her a new one!" my dad's voice calls in the background.

"I don't have an income!" Abby shouts back. "Anyway, help."

"Abby, do you really expect me to be able to help from hundreds of miles away?"

"Tell me it's going to be okay and Madeleine won't hate me forever."

I roll my eyes. "You've been friends with Madeleine since before you lost the stump of your umbilical cord. I think you'll be fine."

"Ugh." Abby sits back. "I just want her to have a good birthday."

"And you think that mug is the make-or-break item for her birthday?" I ask.

"I—well—"

"Anyway," I say, "get her a new present."

"But—"

"I need to go, bye!"

I hang up, and not two seconds later, my phone is buzzing again with Abby's name.

"That was *so mean*," Abby says, pouting. "Go away."

"Okay." And I hang up again.

It's a fun little dance that we do. I love aggravating Abby, and she loves to irritate me too. It takes her three minutes to call me back again, during which time I manage to finish my paper.

When her face pops up on my screen again, I form a plan.

"Well, now that you refuse to let me go," I say, "I can tell you about the new friend I made."

"Oh my god, you have friends?" Abby says. "What a concept."

I ignore that comment. "Their name is Jo. We're trying to start a club together for asexual and aromantic people."

"That's boring," Abby says, and then she hangs up.

Oh. Wow. That was faster than I thought it'd be.

A few seconds later, though, she calls back. Her phone camera is aimed at her school-issued laptop, with the Instagram website pulled up to Jo's account.

"Is it this Jo?" Abby says. "She's a lot prettier than you."

"Oh my god. Yeah, that's Jo. Wait, hey, what do you mean she's prettier than me?"

Thankfully, before she can find another way to make fun of me, Abby gets called downstairs for dinner. And I end up eating in the Lulu dining hall with my family on FaceTime. It happens every now and then. I don't mind, except I miss my dad's cooking, especially when the dining hall food is so subpar. There are some days I would do anything for a simple bowl of rice and tomato eggs; unfortunately, since I don't have a wok or even a frying pan, I can't make it myself.

"And what are you guys eating?" I ask.

Abby flips her camera and shows me a bowl of fried rice. It's pretty standard, just rice, eggs, Chinese sausage, and a frozen vegetable medley from Costco. My dad makes it whenever he's home late from work since it takes so little time to whip up. As I look down at my overcooked spaghetti and barely seasoned meatballs, I feel extremely jealous.

"Are you sitting there by yourself?" Abby asks.

"Yeah."

"Oh my god. You really don't have any friends."

"Well—" I mean, I don't really have a good excuse. "Priya's probably doing a FaceTime dinner with her girlfriend. And—and it's late, so I bet all my other friends are done eating." I probably could've asked Jo, but we only just hung out yesterday, and I don't want to bother her.

"Lèle, you should get a girlfriend, too, so you can eat dinner together," Dad says, snickering, and I am instantly in a bad mood.

"How many times do I have to tell you?" I say. "I'm not gay."

"Maybe you should try to date someone so you know for sure," Mom says.

"Mom, stop," Abby says. It's a small gesture, but I love my sister for it.

"I told you guys," I say. "I don't like boys or girls." Or people who are neither, but they're absolutely not ready for a discussion about the gender spectrum if they can't even accept asexuality. "I am perfectly happy just having friends."

"For now," Dad says.

I can see Abby rolling her eyes. At least I have one ally in the family, but I do wish that I could stop having this conversation every couple of weeks.

"Anyway," I say. "I'm fine eating dinner alone sometimes. It's not that big of a deal."

But just like that, I've lost my appetite.

# CHAPTER 29

# To Be Attractive

## JO

Amid her usual ridiculously academic terminology, I think Professor Fineman is making a little sense.

We're talking about attractiveness in class today. We've just handed in our big essays—I'm very proud of my essay tearing apart J. K. Rowling's transphobic rhetoric using our readings on TERF ideology—so I guess now's the time to talk about something less deep. But as it goes in academia, this has become deep anyway.

Fineman puts a slideshow on the board with a ton of questions. *What does it mean to be attractive? How do our intersectional identities play a role in what we perceive as attractive and what others perceive in us? In a time of a renewed demand for racial justice, what does dating look like for BIPOC individuals?*

What's not there, though, is a question I thought about during all our readings for today. *What does it mean for me to be attractive, considering I don't ever want anyone to be attracted to me?*

"And with those ideas in mind," Fineman is saying, "I'd like you all to get into groups of two or three, maybe four, and discuss some of these questions in relation to your readings. And let's say we'll come back as a large group in twenty minutes, okay?" A few people nod. "All right, get yourselves into groups, and feel free to sit outside the classroom if it gets too noisy!"

I turn to Sophie. She turns to me. With a single nod, we make a silent agreement to work together.

The two of us find a small alcove in the hallway, away from the heavy chatter of the class. Sophie sits cross-legged and shuffles through her papers—our readings, all printed and stapled together. Pretty much nobody in this class stays on track during small group discussions, but Sophie likes to at least pretend to give our readings a glance.

She puts down the papers and sighs. "I do think that last question that Fineman had up was really interesting."

"Remind me what it was about again." I did not write down any of those questions.

"It was about dating as a person of color," Sophie says. "Which is totally irrelevant to us, but still interesting to think about, right? I think it's important to consider attractiveness through an a-spec lens. Like, none of these papers really talked about it, but it's so interesting what makes someone attractive to an a-spec person."

"What do *you* think makes someone attractive?" I ask, because I'm curious.

"I have absolutely no clue," Sophie says. "Doesn't matter your gender or sexuality. I mean, I guess I know when someone is pretty to look at."

I never really understood it when one of my friends said someone was hot. What makes someone "hot" or not? What does that even mean? Sexual attraction?

"It's kind of gross," I say out loud.

"What?" Sophie says, eyes wide.

"Attraction," I say.

She laughs. "Yeah. It kind of is."

"Do you like *being* attractive?" I ask.

I mean, I won't wear clothes I don't think look good on me. But I don't know if that's really about looking attractive. It's more about what makes me comfortable. I don't ever look at myself and think, *Wow, I feel attractive.*

Sophie frowns. "I guess to some very basic degree. I try to look presentable, I guess. But that's not as much about being attractive as it is just being taken seriously."

"But don't people take you more seriously when you're the right amount of attractive?" I counter.

"Ooh, that's a good point. If you look 'too attractive,' you're a whore, and if you're 'unattractive,' you're ugly or lazy or unprofessional no matter how hard you try." She uses air quotes while saying that.

"I think it's so weird to exist in this society where you *have* to be some baseline level of 'attractive' to be treated like a normal human being." I scratch my arm absently. "Like, it all comes back to the patriarchy."

It's so—I don't know. It's gross.

"Yep," Sophie says. "And in tandem with that, white supremacy, since many non-European societies weren't so heterosexist and patriarchal before European colonization, though, of course, that can't be applied to all precolonial civilizations."

God, she sounds like Fineman. But she's right.

I hate this. We really have to exist amid this. Because of fucking white men. The more I consider it, the more my skin grows hot with frustration.

"But what can we do about it now?" I ask.

Sophie shakes her head and shrugs. "I don't have a clue. I mean, even on the Wellesley campus, where there are almost no men to speak of, the male gaze still persists."

I decided to go here, as opposed to one of the coed universities I got into, because I was scared that, in an environment with so many cishet men, I'd be seen as an object.

Come to think of it, I don't know how many people have looked at me and seen something they liked. Or the things that they've imagined.

Thinking about it makes me feel trapped in my skin. This organ that has so much weight in my beauty, my attractiveness. Protecting me from the world, while also being the thing strangers scrutinize me for. At the end of the day, I'm just a body, and—

"Hey, are you all right?" Sophie asks. "Bug bite or something?"

I look down at my arm. There are streaks of pink from where my nails have been scratching away.

"Uh . . . yeah, I'm fine," I say. "I don't know. A little uncomfortable thinking about all this."

It's an anxious response. I do this sometimes, picking or scratching at my skin, needing it to feel right. It's better, I guess, than the panic attacks I'd get so often in middle school, that I still get every now and then.

"Okay," Sophie says, digging through her tote bag. "Even if that itch is psychological, I do have a tube of cortisone cream that might help it feel better."

"Why the fuck do you carry cortisone with you?"

"I had a bug bite in, like, September that was bothering me, so I put a tube in my bag and never remembered to take it out." She's still rummaging through her things.

"Um, I don't need any, but thanks. I think it's just me feeling anxious."

"Makes sense." Sophie finally abandons the bag. "Do you want to talk about the readings, but not in relation to us?"

"Yeah, that sounds like a good idea."

We spend the rest of our allotted time talking more broadly. It's still uncomfortable, thinking about how people look at me and judge me for how I look, but what can I do about it?

Nothing. That's what.

Once we get out of class, Sophie asks me if it's about time for us to advertise our interest meeting for the Dianas, and begrudgingly, I agree. We tried sending an email interest form, but nothing really came of it because nobody checks their emails enough at this school.

"Should we just do Facebook for now?" The college Facebook groups tend to be a bit less active but also a little more closed-off, reserved for the college community. And I don't want the stress of having another Instagram account to run just yet; we'll make an Instagram for the org at some point, but not now.

"Yeah, that's fine," Sophie says. "I'll make a graphic we can post!"

And just like that, we're about to start the club for real.

## Sophie Chi > Wellesley College Class of 2027

Hey sibs! Are you asexual or aromantic? Curious to learn more about a-spec identities? Come to the first meeting of the Wellesley Dianas, a discussion group for a-spec students and allies, on Saturday at 1:00 P.M. in the Penthouse of Billings Hall. Hope to see you there! (Questions: sophia.chi@wellesley.edu or joanna.ephron@wellesley.edu. Accommodations: accommodations@wellesley.edu)

## Joanna Ephron > Wellesley College Memes for Queer Leftist Teens

hello this goes out to all current students on the asexual or aromantic spectrum: come to the wellesley dianas!! see attached spam for more.

# Wellesley Dianas

first meeting, *Saturday at 1:00 P.M.*

**??: sophia.chi** or **joanna.ephron**
Accommodations: accommodations@wellesley.edu

# CHAPTER 30

## *First*

### SOPHIE

On our Facebook posts about the Wellesley Dianas, Jo and I put a form asking people to give us their contact information if they wanted to be added to a mailing list. It sort of doubles as an interest form for the first meeting. According to the form, there were at least ten people interested in going to our first meeting.

So why, then, are there only two other people here?

We're holding our first meeting in the Penthouse, on the fourth floor of Billings Hall, which is mostly an administrative building. The sloped ceilings are decorated with pride flags; there are mismatched chairs arranged around a coffee table, right by two bookshelves that hold lots of queer books.

At least the two people seem nice. Evelyn Dawson, a sophomore, is a waifish white girl wearing a pair of denim overalls over a green T-shirt, her long bleached-blond hair held back in a messy ponytail. Charlie Santos is a fellow first year; they're wearing a white graphic tee and ripped mom jeans, loose black curls poking out of their beanie and freckles dotting their light brown cheeks.

Sometimes I wish I looked more blatantly queer. I'm wearing a quarter-zip pullover and black leggings, and my hair is neatly woven in a French braid. All very nondescript. Even Jo looks more appropriately queer than I do, in her chunky cardigan and cuffed jeans, her curls just messy enough to show that she doesn't care too much about how she looks, even though I know she cares a lot.

The fact that I can look so out of place in such a small group is a big testament to my unrefined fashion sense. I really don't have time to dwell on my clothes, though, nor do I care *that* much about what I wear. Right now, I have a meeting to co-run.

"Okay," I say after we all introduce ourselves. "So, um, I was thinking for our first meeting we would keep things light and get to know each other. Like, I think that having queer friends is much more than all of you sharing an identity, you know?"

Evelyn perks up. "Yeah, for sure! Like, most of my friends growing up ended up being queer. We just gravitated toward each other."

I'm reminded of my friends from home. Nearly my whole friend group was queer, but a lot of us had known each other long before we knew what being queer even was. I don't talk to most of them anymore—especially not Oliver—but they were a lifeline to me for years.

"Yeah, with my friend group back home, not only were we all queer, we also all turned out to be neurodivergent," Charlie says. "There was a period of time where three of us were all waiting for neuropsych results. I feel like the fact that we all knew each other should've automatically qualified us for our diagnoses."

The rest of us laugh. Jo says, "Yeah, definitely agree that we all kind of flocked together. Like, no wonder I did theater."

Charlie looks up at the mention. "Wait, I did tech crew."

"Oh, man," Jo says. "Tech crew is even gayer than acting."

Charlie nods. "I wasn't out to a lot of people in high school, but the techies knew. They were, like, the only people who I could say 'Hey, I'm non-binary, demi, and pan' to, and they'd understand all those words right away."

"It was definitely a bit of a culture shock when I came here," Evelyn says. "Like, yeah, I still have to explain my identity every now and then, but people catch on so much faster."

Jo laughs. "That reminds me. This one summer, I went to camp, and I offhandedly mentioned to a girl that I was asexual, and she said 'Me too,' but she thought I meant I was celibate."

"Wellesley's not free from that either," I say. "I met this girl in class last semester who'd never heard of asexuality, and I ended up explaining my entire life story to her. Luckily, she was eager to learn."

Charlie clicks their tongue. "I forget how sheltered some people are before coming here."

"Some people are still sheltered after four years here," Evelyn says. "In fact, a lot of people are. Our experiences really aren't a good indicator of the average Wellesley College experience."

We start talking about other awkward encounters we've had here, and I'm honestly stunned by how easily the conversation flows from one topic to another. It's considerably easier to talk to people in college than in high school, but I've still never felt like I understood a group of people so quickly.

After our meeting is over, Jo and I debrief and decide to work on improving attendance. I already have a plan.

"I'll make an Instagram account," I say. "And I'll have Gretchen send out our flyer in her queer students mailing list." Gretchen, the director of LGBTQ+ services, has offered to help us advertise, but until this poor turnout, I didn't think we'd need her help.

Jo frowns. "Are you a Virgo?"

"Actually, yes," I say, very confused at how we arrived at this. "How did you—why—never mind. Wait, what are you?"

With no hesitation, Jo replies, "Gemini sun, Sagittarius moon and rising."

Of course Jo knows astrology. Wellesley has a weirdly large number of students who are into astrology.

"I have no idea what that means," I admit.

"You've been a Wellesley student for a semester and a half and still don't know what that means?" Jo says.

"What does this even have to do with what I was talking about?" I ask, laughing.

"You just sounded like such a Virgo," Jo says.

"Well, one of us has to be on top of all our stuff."

"And it's going to be you."

I'm okay with that.

Dear Wendy,

I recently found out that my boyfriend snores. We've been together for a few months now, and we hadn't found the time to spend a night together until recently because both of us have roommates we didn't want to disturb.

His snoring is SO LOUD. I barely slept a wink when he stayed over last weekend. My roommate, thankfully, was out of town, but I doubt she would have been able to sleep either. Seriously, it sounded like he was being exorcised or something. And it never stopped! It kept going on all night!

So what do I do? Do I confront him about it? I really like him, and I don't want to ruin things over something he can't control.

Best,
Tired Girlfriend


Dear Tired,

I'm not a medical expert, and this is not medical advice, but snoring that loudly for that much time, especially at such a young age, is quite possibly a medical condition. Could you ask him if he's ever been tested for sleep apnea? Is there anything wrong with his nose, like a deviated septum?

In any case, if you're planning to have him sleep over again, you should talk to him about the snoring. See if there are things you can do to muffle the sound, like turning on a white noise machine. Be kind and gentle about it! Don't just ignore it; your sleep is important, as is his health.

Sincerely,
Wendy Wellesley

**wandawellesley69 3m**
the not-a-doctor disclaimer is SO FUNNY omg nobody here thinks you're a doctor, wendy
Reply

**dearwendywellesley 2m**
I'm just trying to cover all my bases
Reply

# CHAPTER 31

## Connection

### SOPHIE

I go to Professor Fineman's office hours a few days after handing in my essay. After class last Friday, I booked the appointment on a whim. She said that she'd have our papers graded by the end of this week and to "See me if you have any questions," and I'm not quite sure what I want to ask, but I feel the need to talk to her again. Jo thinks I'm being ridiculous, but too bad.

"Sophie!" Professor Fineman says as soon as I knock on the door. "Good to see you!"

"Hi!" I say, a little bit too chipper. "How are you?"

"Good, good! Have a seat, I was just finishing your essay."

"Oh no, already?" I say, half joking, as I sit across from her.

I put so much effort into this paper. Ten pages of me talking about how your gender and sexuality can affect how you behave in relationships and how you see other people's relationships. How queer relationships are often so much more egalitarian, yet how oddly heterosexual and gendered the media tends to make them out to be. I wish I'd had another ten pages so I could talk even more.

Fineman smiles. "I can tell from that quick skim that you care very much about your topic of research."

"Ah. Thank you." She's so observant.

A little nod, and then: "Is there anything in particular you wanted to talk about today?"

"Oh! Yeah. Uh . . . I wanted to talk to somebody about what I wrote.

It's just, there's so much that's in my head now, and I don't want this paper to be the end of it all."

I expect her to think I'm being silly, but she chuckles and says, "I know the feeling."

Right. She's an academic. That's her main thing besides teaching: doing research and then telling people about it.

I feel myself flush. "Yeah, I don't know, it's really exciting. I spend a lot of time thinking about other people's relationship dynamics. I think a lot about my place in all of it too."

"Oh, really?" Professor Fineman says. "Tell me more."

There's so much more. The way I interact with my friends who are in relationships. My participation in fandom shipping culture in middle school and early in high school, before I got too busy to go on Tumblr. And that's not to mention everything that has to do with Dear Wendy. But I think I should settle on the obvious one. I trust her.

"Well, I'm aromantic and asexual," I say. "I don't know if you've seen the spam for it, but Jo and I are trying to start an a-spec discussion club, and we just had our first meeting."

"Oh, yes, I did see that," Professor Fineman says. "Congratulations on holding your meeting!"

"Thank you!"

"And how does that play into the way you experience relationships?" she asks.

"So . . . I have no desire to participate in a romantic relationship, but I find them really interesting."

I brace myself for Fineman's reaction, but she isn't fazed at all. "Funny how that happens sometimes, huh? I have a lesbian colleague who spends all her time studying men and masculinity."

"Oh, that's . . . cool."

My unease makes her laugh. "Yeah, I wouldn't make that my life's work either. But you seem to be comfortable thinking and talking about romance, even though, as you said, you have no desire to participate."

"Yeah. Um . . . I don't know, I think that because I don't want it for myself, I look at relationships from a really different angle than most people."

"How so?"

I look aside and breathe out a puff of air, trying to come up with the right words. "I'm a lot more objective, I think. Like, if my friend has a relationship problem, and they keep fluctuating on what they should do, I pull out a pros and cons list."

"Uh-huh."

"And I've known I'm aroace for a few years now, so I've gotten used to the idea of not needing a romantic partner to be happy and fulfilled."

"That's good."

"And I guess when I consume romantic stories, it's just another story for me. Like, a good Nora Ephron film will make me happy, but I don't want any of that to happen to me."

I tuck a few loose hairs behind my ear. This is probably the first time I've told all this to an adult, and . . . it kind of feels nice. And Professor Fineman does not follow up more with my feelings about romance.

"You know Nora was a Wellesley alum?" she asks.

I nod.

"Do you know if Jo is related to her? I noticed they have the same last name as her."

I didn't even make the connection. "I don't know. I don't think so? I feel like they would have told me."

It only occurs to me after I say that that Fineman used "they" to refer to Jo. A lot of professors tend to exclusively use *she/her* to refer to anyone whose pronouns are both *she* and *they*, so this is a pleasant surprise. I should tell Jo about this.

Fineman shrugs. "Anyway, it's great to be self-aware. And . . . oh, I just remembered something you mentioned in your essay. What's your experience with fandom culture?"

And just like that, I know I'm going to be in this office for at least another half an hour.

# CHAPTER 32

## Joe with an E

### JO

"Jo? Jo. Joanna? Joanna Middle Name Ephron!"

"It's Olivia," I say, not looking up from my phone, where I'm busy making Wanda posts. When Wendy answered a very oddly specific question about snoring a couple of days ago, I realized that I have a lot of oddly specific questions that I have yet to answer, and I need to catch up.

"What?" Lianne says.

"My middle name."

"Oh," Lianne says. "Jo, can you please pay an ounce of attention to me?"

I finally look up. "Yeah, what's up?"

Lianne is standing in front of me, holding up her phone, open to its lock screen. She points to the time: 8:26 P.M.

"You've been on your phone for two hours," Lianne says. "Don't you have work to do?"

"I *am* doing work," I say. "It's just Wanda work."

"I mean real work," Lianne says, not looking impressed.

I know what she means. And, yeah, maybe I do have a reading to do for WGST 110, and an essay to write for my sociology class, and coding to do for my CS class, and some vocab to study for Spanish, but right now, I do not want to do any of those things.

"Since when are you trying to make sure I get all my work done?" I ask. "Isn't that usually Katy's job?"

I don't usually rely on my roommates to keep me from procrastinating, but sometimes, Katy does take it upon herself to do just that. Her interventions are rude but necessary.

Lianne sighs. "Okay, fine, Katy texted me to make sure you were being productive."

"And you didn't want to disappoint her?" I say. "How very interesting."

She shakes her head. "Jo, you really do love jumping to conclusions, don't you?"

"It's my favorite pastime."

She sighs. "Take a break from the Wanda stuff. You can make fun of Wendy later."

I pretend to be offended. "Excuse me. I wasn't making fun of Wendy at all. I was writing up my own posts."

I'm not lying. I haven't been posting often enough for the quantity of messages I'm now getting. I have tons of unread DMs and submissions in my anonymous form that I have yet to post about. And okay, maybe I did get a little carried away with how much detail I'm putting in some of these responses, but it's all for the overall effect.

"Even so," Lianne says, "you do have to admit that you've gotten a little consumed by this account."

"That is not true," I say. "I am consumed by many other things. Like classes—"

"You know that's a lie."

"—and the Dianas—"

"You've literally had one meeting."

"—and watching reality television—"

"Jesus Christ, Jo."

"—and I'm just saying, you waste just as much time on dating apps as I do on my Wanda account."

"That's just plainly untrue. I haven't even touched Bumble or Hinge since that disastrous attempt with Alicia."

Okay. I think she wins. "Fine, I'll do homework now."

"Good."

"After I finish this post."

"You're fucking kidding me."

But Lianne is not Katy, so she lets me do it anyway, and it's only after I save the file that she says, "Wait, your initials spell JOE with an *E*?"

Oh. I had completely moved past that.

"Uh, yeah, my parents thought it was funny," I say. "And my aunt's name is Olivia, so it worked."

Lianne cackles and pulls out her phone. "Wait, are your brother's initials TOE?"

"Oh my god, ew, no! His initials are THE." His middle name is Henry. It does, in fact, spell the first three letters of his name. And, you know, the most common word in the English language.

She only laughs more. "That is so much worse."

"Please don't tell anyone. Not even Katy."

"Oh, that text has already been sent."

Right on cue, my phone buzzes. *OMG should I start calling you Joe?* says Katy in our group chat.

*absolutely not,* I type back.

# CHAPTER 33

## Phone

### SOPHIE

For some reason, Wanda has posted six times in the last twenty-four hours. There are multiple posts about confessing to your crush, one about someone's boyfriend crying during sex, and one about friend drama.

Six posts means six opportunities to call out Wanda's bad advice.

I pore over the first post—someone has a crush on their RA—when, across from me, Izzy says, "Sophie?"

I look up. We're sitting at a booth at a Korean restaurant in Allston, a neighborhood in Boston; Priya has just gone to the bathroom, and Izzy is finishing the tteokbokki we ordered. I, admittedly, went on my phone for a little bit when the two of them started talking in hushed voices about a high school situation I wasn't involved in.

"Yeah?" I say.

"Is everything okay?" Izzy asks. "You've been typing very intensely on your phone."

"Oh," I say. "Yeah. It's just a Dear Wendy thing."

She presses her lips together but doesn't say anything, but just that little expression tells me everything I need to know. Izzy never tells you when something is bothering her, but her face always shows it.

"Sorry," I say sheepishly. "I'll save it for later."

"Thank you," Izzy says. "Fish cake?" She holds up the last fish cake from our tteokbokki with her chopsticks, but I shake my head, already full.

I forget about the phone thing until Priya confronts me later, back at our dorm, while Izzy is in the shower.

"Izzy says you've been on your phone a lot when we're hanging out," Priya says. "She said it wasn't a big deal, but she also never says anything is a big deal, so."

"Oh." I don't really have anything to say to this. "I'm sorry."

I don't mean to be on my phone a lot. But I've been posting more, which makes Wanda post more, which means I have to post more about them, and—

"Alicia and I have been noticing this too," Priya says. "I just wanted to talk to you about it. Because this isn't like you, you know? You're usually on top of your shit and present in our lives, but ever since you started this whole drama with Wanda . . . I don't know, it's like you've gotten more careless."

My heart sinks to my stomach. Now that Priya says it, I realize she's right. Running my Wendy Instagram has taken a toll. But it's not the only thing consuming my time, and it hasn't disrupted my academics at all.

"Well—this isn't much of an explanation, but I have been busy with other stuff," I say. "Jo and I have been working really hard on the Dianas."

We've been sending out our interest form in any way we can—on our personal Instagram, through Gretchen's newsletter, and more—and we've also been talking more about whether to get administrative approval. We're holding another meeting tomorrow, and hopefully, attendance will be up a bit.

"I'm sure you have," Priya says. "I hope you aren't being so shifty with Jo."

"No, I—I would never."

"So maybe don't be like this with us either," Priya says. "Just because we've been friends with you for longer doesn't mean we deserve less respect."

"You're right," I say. "I'm sorry I haven't been giving you my full attention lately. That's not what a good friend does. And I'll apologize to Izzy too. And Alicia."

"Thank you," Priya says. "For the record, though, I do want you to win your fight against Wanda. They're kind of annoying."

I smile. "Thanks."

When I look back down at my phone, I close out of Instagram. Just for tonight. Priya is right; thinking about Dear Wendy and writing for Dear Wendy and making Dear Wendy posts has been minorly consuming my life.

# CHAPTER 34

## Frosted Sugar Cookies

### JO

I have to admit, I'm a little nervous for our second meeting of the Dianas. It's probably going to be awkward, regardless of whether we have impressive turnout or nobody shows up again. When I arrive at the Penthouse, only Sophie is there so far. We agreed to arrive fifteen minutes early, which for her probably meant twenty minutes and for me, ten.

"Hello," I say. "I brought food."

Inside an Office of Sustainability recycled-plastic tote, I have a bag of Cheetos and a container of green-and-purple frosted sugar cookies, which I saw at the grocery store and thought were fitting.

"Oh my god, I hate those cookies," Sophie says. "Why did you get them?"

"Do you not see the colors? This is the aro and ace flags representation we need at this meeting."

Sophie sighs. "Yeah, I guess that's cool."

I look at her expression and chuckle. "You still hate those cookies, don't you?"

"It's painful to even look at them."

In time, people arrive. Charlie and Evelyn are back, and right before we're about to start, someone new shows up, a curly-haired white person wearing a maroon cardigan over a black scoop-neck top tucked into dark-wash skinny jeans.

"Oh my goodness, hi!" Sophie says. "Are you here for Dianas?"

"Yeah!" they say. "I'm Hannah Rizzo, she/her, first-year."

That self-introduction script is ingrained in us all.

We all scoot over and make room for her, and once we all get settled, the rest of us introduce ourselves as well.

"So we have a range of options for what we can do today," Sophie says. "If anyone has something specific they want to talk about, we can go on a tangent about that, or we can choose from this list that I made."

What she doesn't tell the group is she has an entire spreadsheet filled with activities, organized by type (discussion topic, game, icebreaker). It's color-coded.

Nobody says a word, though, so I say, "Uh, how about we pick something from Sophie's list, then?"

"Actually," Evelyn starts, "I was wondering if we could maybe talk about navigating the LGBTQ+ community as an a-spec person? I know we touched on it last time, so I thought, you know. Maybe that would be something. It's been on my mind."

"I have so much to say about that," Hannah says, and Charlie nods too.

Sophie claps her hands together and smiles. "Great! Yeah, that sounds like a really good idea."

"Could I start, then?" Evelyn asks.

"You have the floor," I say.

"Great. Yeah, so, I think that both being aromantic or asexual can easily alienate you from a lot of queer spaces. Like, for me, since I'm an aromantic lesbian, whenever people talk about how desperate they are to find their other half or whatever, it feels so . . . suffocating. Like, I don't know how to tell people that I may never feel the same kind of emotional connection that they do toward me, you know?"

Lots of nods. I snap my fingers.

"And on the opposite end of that," Hannah says, "I think that being ace makes conversations about sex *so* much more difficult. Which is so hard when so much of the queer community revolves around a culture of hookups. Allocishet people too."

"I definitely feel super alienated sometimes," I say. "Like, when I found out that both of my roommates had already dated and had sex by the end of first semester, I was so shocked. I feel so weird knowing that they've opened themselves up in such a vulnerable way, physically and emotionally."

Sophie laughs. "I don't know, I think I try to sit out of dating and sex conversations if I'm not emotionally prepared to talk about it, and there's been a couple of times where I felt like that made me a burden to the conversation."

Charlie raises their hand. "I think that there are definitely a lot of people that like to shit on asexuality as being, like, inherently less queer. Like, I still identify in other ways that also make me queer, but I'd be curious to know what it's like for a cishet ace."

Hannah blows a stream of air through her nose. "You're in luck. You're speaking to one."

"Oh god," I say. "I am already sorry about all the exclusionists."

Ace exclusionists think that being asexual doesn't inherently make you LGBTQ+. I've seen the argument applied to aromantic heterosexual people, too, some bullshit about how *then horny teenage boys can call themselves aromantic and consider themselves queer*, as if that's how aromanticism works. It's the same kind of gatekeeping that left bi and trans people out of the conversation during the early gay rights movements, and sometimes even today.

Hannah rolls her eyes. "Yeah, it really sucks. I mean, even at Wellesley, I've met some people who don't think I should be joining queer orgs."

"Who?" I ask. "Drop their names."

She blushes. "I don't want to start anything."

Evelyn raises her eyebrows. "If they would start anything against you, you're allowed to expose them to us."

Hannah shrugs. "Fair enough."

Names are dropped, Instagrams are unfollowed, and then we move on. Thankfully, I don't follow any of them on my personal account, but I don't check my Wanda account. I follow back everyone on there, no matter their moral standing. I even follow this junior who likes to spend her time emailing the whole school all the conspiracy theories she legitimately believes in, primarily that the earth is flat.

Okay, maybe I should unfollow Flat Earth Girl. I'll figure that out later. For now, I should be paying attention to our discussion.

"Hey, I just remembered something," Charlie says. "I keep seeing these TikToks of people talking about, like, their 'cringey asexual Tumblr phase.' And I mean, there's something to say about the way the internet likes to excessively push microlabels onto people, especially ace people, but the way some folks talk about asexuality as a phase feels . . . very wrong."

"You know, I've noticed that," Sophie says. "Like . . . when someone figures out they're gay and not bi, or the other way around, it's not as frequently labeled as being 'cringey.' Of course, online queer discourse often involves biphobia or lesbophobia or some other combination of phobias, but asexuality is often dismissed in a very specific tone."

"I wonder if it has something to do with sex," Hannah says. "Like, we associate sexlessness with youth and immaturity."

Our conversation continues for nearly an hour, meandering between different topics that aren't even always related to queer identity. At one point, while we're talking about how we manage our schoolwork, Charlie persuades Hannah to consider seeking an ADHD diagnosis. In the end, Evelyn has the last word: "So, yeah, that's how my mom and stepdad unknowingly contribute to my ongoing existential crisis on a daily basis!"

As it turns out, none of us have perfect straight ally parents, unless my parents count, but they don't since they're not straight.

Charlie, Evelyn, and Hannah trickle away, taking the last of the cookies.

"See, I told you they would eat them," I say to Sophie.

"They're gross," she insists.

"You're outnumbered here."

"Whatever."

# CHAPTER 35

## Friend

### SOPHIE

"I think it's really interesting what Charlie said about microlabels," Jo says as we walk out of Billings. We decided to get dinner in Stone-D since it's nearby, so we're heading in that direction.

"Yeah?" I say, adjusting the tote bag on my shoulder. "How so?"

"Well, I don't know if it's just the side of the internet I was on in middle school, but a lot of people I followed liked to get really specific about the ways they labeled themselves. Like, three words for sexuality and two for gender that I had to google to understand."

I wasn't really on the side of the internet that Jo was on as a young teen, but I do know what they're talking about. I've seen a few video essays on the topic: young queer teens on Tumblr a decade ago and now on TikTok often identify themselves with very specific terminology for their gender and sexuality, sometimes with self-coined words that the general public isn't at all familiar with. It's often a way for people to grow more comfortable in their identities—but frequently, people drop these labels as they get older.

"Fascinating," I say. "I mean, I do think there's value in having labels, right? Like, being able to put a word to the way you feel helps validate that feeling. I definitely take comfort in my identity."

"No, me too!" Jo says. "That's not really what I mean, though."

"So what do you mean?"

Jo sighs. "I don't know. I think it's just—for me, having too many labels for myself feels like I'm, I don't know, closing myself off. Like I'm putting myself in these little boxes that only a few other people can fit in, or that I owe it to people to tell them all the different little ways I feel."

"When really, you're just . . . you."

I definitely understand this feeling. I'm aroace, sure, but even people who identify with that label have different experiences. Some are okay with having sex or totally enjoy it; I'm never going to, but I'm not totally disgusted by it when it doesn't involve me—I don't skip past sex scenes in movies and TV shows. There are words I could use to describe this: sex-positivity versus sex-negativity. But I'm not going to add that to my bio or tell that to people when I meet them, simply because I don't want to.

Jo looks at me, head tilted, curls blowing around a little in the breeze. "Yeah. Exactly." Then they sigh. "I don't know. It's all so complicated. Like, when *can* you claim a label for yourself?"

"What do you mean?"

"I mean . . . I use she/they pronouns, but I'm not sure that I can call myself nonbinary *or* a woman somehow. I have Jewish ancestry from my grandpa, but my parents didn't actually raise me with any religion, so I don't really call myself Jewish. I don't know. This is kind of getting off-topic."

"No, you're fine," I say. "I think that's something a lot of people struggle with. It's a classic dilemma for children of immigrants. I often hear things like 'I'm too American for China but too Chinese for America.'"

"Right."

We reach Stone-D, and as we get our food and sit down to eat, we keep on talking. After Jo asks, I tell them a bit about what it was like growing up in the Chicago suburbs, where there was a decently big Chinese community but still enough white people for me to have some tense experiences growing up.

"And I don't know if that ever really improved here at Wellesley," I say. "Because now all the Chinese people here come from way different places than I do and have really different life experiences. Like, I'm not going to have as much in common with someone from the Bay Area who went to a seventy percent Asian school, let alone a Chinese international student."

Jo nods intently. "That's got to feel a little weird."

"It's not too bad most of the time," I say. "I have a nice group of friends I can relate to, even if most of them aren't Chinese."

"That's good to hear," Jo says. "Do you wish you had gone somewhere with more people like you?"

I shrug and twirl some noodles around my fork. "Not really. There are enough people here who are like me."

It hits me all of a sudden: I am opening up a lot to Jo. And they're not making it all about them, which is a common problem in conversations at any PWI—or really, anywhere with a lot of white people. Usually, I just hold back on sharing much about culture and identity with my white classmates and friends, both here and back home. But I actually feel comfortable telling all of these things to Jo.

I feel comfortable telling a lot of things to Jo.

Wait, has Jo become one of my best friends?

Huh. Weird.

"So," I say, trying to shake off this revelation. "How do you feel like you fit in here?"

I've found my ways to fit in with the clubs I'm in and the people I spend my time with. I feel like Dear Wendy makes me fit in better, even if nobody knows that's me, simply because I get to interact with so many members of the community.

"That is a great question," Jo says. "Sometimes I feel like I don't really."

"Why not?" I ask.

From my perspective, it feels like there are a lot of people here like Jo: smart, witty, and active in campus organizations like WZLY and theater.

Jo chews on a forkful of salad before saying, "I think I spend a lot of time wondering if everyone I know actually hates me."

And then they shrug it off.

I've had my fair share of this feeling. For me, it was grounded in truth: There were people who hated me back at home—classmates who thought I took my work too seriously, yearbook staff members who found me too strict or too much of a perfectionist. But I didn't care after a while. Wherever you go, I reasoned, there'll be some people who don't like you. You can't please everyone. That's why Dear Wendy is anonymous—people can only judge me based on what I post there, not anything else about me.

"That's not true," I say, instead of dumping out all of those thoughts. "You're one of the most likable people I've met."

Jo chuckles awkwardly. "I'm glad you think so."

I meant it as a reassurance, but I realize I mean what I said.

Jo is definitely one of my best friends now.

How did this happen?

# CHAPTER 36

# *AHHHHHH THIS IS HORRIBLE*

## JO

My WZLY show this week is one of my favorite things I've ever created.

Seeing as we are not allowed to play more than one song per artist, I have found a loophole. One song from One Direction, one song from each of the members of One Direction, and a lot of covers of their songs.

I asked Sophie to listen to my show after we got dinner yesterday, not remembering that it was planned to be this playlist, but too late to turn back now.

Sophie says it's terrible, but then she says she'd do the same with Taylor Swift if she were a DJ. She live-texts me her reactions as she listens.

Sophie (11:02 AM)

Starting off strong!

Me (11:02 AM)

yeah, night changes isn't my ABSOLUTE favorite but it's up there

Sophie (11:02 AM)

Lol it's pretty fun! Thanks for reminding me to listen

Me (11:02 AM)

ofc lol

After a few more songs, I turn on the microphone. "That was 'Fireproof' by One Direction. Good morning to everyone listening, and by that, I mean good morning to the one person who's listening. This is WZLY Wellesley, 91.5 FM, and my name is Jo. Today, we're listening to as many One Direction songs as we can without violating the one-song-per-artist-per-show rule, so up next, here's something you're probably going to hate: the Glee Cast version of 'What Makes You Beautiful,' from *Glee: The Music, The Complete Season Three*."

As expected, Sophie is very upset.

Sophie (11:04 AM)

AHHHHHH THIS IS HORRIBLE

Am I allowed to turn it off??

I can't listen to this Jo

Am I the only one listening????

Can I call in to make a request that you STOP????????

Me (11:04 AM)

no <3

"What Makes You Beautiful" fades out, and Mike Tompkins's a cappella cover of "Steal My Girl" starts playing. I think I'm a genius for making this playlist. It goes in a pattern after the first song: two covers, then one solo song from a former One Direction member.

Sophie (11:07 AM)

Wait can I tell you a secret

Me (11:07 AM)

yeah?

Sophie (11:07 AM)

I HATE a cappella

Me (11:08 AM)

well that makes two of us lol

Sophie (11:08 AM)

Then why did you put this in the playlist???

Me (11:08 AM)

look i was trying to find 1d covers and there isn't as much variety as i'd like

Sophie (11:08 AM)

As long as you don't have any Kidz Bop versions on here

Me (11:08 AM)

oh hell no

Sophie (11:09 AM)

Good

You know you should tell Charlie/Evelyn/Hannah to listen to this

Me (11:09 AM)

slkdjfdlskjflksd WHAT

it is WAY too early for that

It would make them quit the club

Sophie (11:09 AM)

Fine, I'll do it myself

Before I know it, I get another text.

Unknown Number (11:10 AM)

hey, this is charlie!

sophie gave me your number and told me to listen to your show

i didn't know you were a dj??

(also do you know how she got my number lmao this is creepy)

Me (11:10 AM)

omg hi

i think we collected phone numbers in the dianas interest form????

sorry you were stalked but uhhhhhh thank you for listening lol of all days sophie HAD to pick the day i played my one direction playlist to tell you guys about it

This is so embarrassing for me.

Charlie (11:10 AM)

lmao no worries

i had a big 1d phase

harry is big gender envy

Me (11:10 AM)

OMG HE IS THANK YOU

All right, maybe this won't be so embarrassing after all.

**anon:** my sister uninvited me from her wedding because i refuse to wear a dress because of ~gender things~, what do i do?

**answer:** who gives a shit what you wear! that's awful of her! do you really still want to go to this wedding?

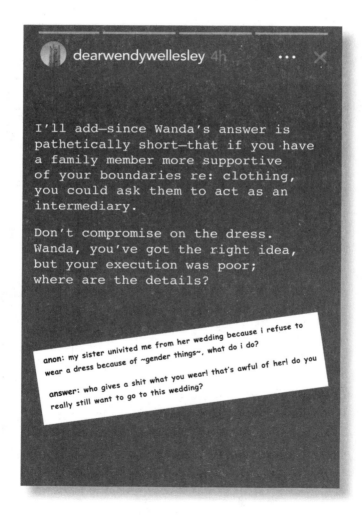

dearwendywellesley 4h    ···    ✕

I'll add—since Wanda's answer is pathetically short—that if you have a family member more supportive of your boundaries re: clothing, you could ask them to act as an intermediary.

Don't compromise on the dress. Wanda, you've got the right idea, but your execution was poor; where are the details?

anon: my sister univited me from her wedding because i refuse to wear a dress because of ~gender things~, what do i do?

answer: who gives a shit what you wear! that's awful of her! do you really still want to go to this wedding?

**wandawellesley69** 3m ··· ✕

hey wendy if anything this is a self-burn HAHAHA
the reason i'm giving such short answers is because
i've been getting so many questions!
how are you getting so few that you have
the time to write paragraphs upon
paragraphs for each??? or do you just
not have a personal life???

 **dearwendywellesley** 4h ··· ✕

I'll add—since Wanda's answer is
pathetically short—that if you have
a family member more supportive
of your boundaries re: clothing,
you could ask them to act as an
intermediary.

Don't compromise on the dress.
Wanda, you've got the right idea,
but your execution was poor;
where are the details?

 **dearwendywellesley** 4h ··· ✕

How amateur that Wanda can't handle an
influx of submissions. When people ask
me questions, they can trust I'll give
a thoughtful, honest answer regardless
of how much else I have to do, because
I put 100% effort into running this account.

 **wandawellesley69** 3m ··· ✕

hey wendy if anything this is a self-burn HAHAHA
the reason i'm giving such short answers is because
i've been getting so many questions!

# CHAPTER 37

## Not Over Yet

### JO

I swear, Wendy is going to be the death of me.

We've gone back and forth on this one post about five times. Wendy has now called me incompetent, incoherent, annoying, attention-seeking, and annoying again. I've called them nosy, soulless, vain, and also annoying twice because it's true.

If anybody called me any of these things for real, I would probably never get over it for the rest of my life, but I am not hurt at all that Wendy thinks these things about Wanda. Even if they were telling the truth—and I don't think they are because they like exaggerating—they don't think these things about me, Jo Ephron. These words are reserved for my fictional online personality, and my fictional online personality deserves it.

Unlike me, Katy and Lianne are starting to get concerned by Wendy's taunts. We're watching *You've Got Mail* (Katy's idea) and crocheting together.

"What if Wendy figures out who you are?" Katy asks me as she pieces together a halter top.

"How would they?" I ask, sticking out my tongue as I fumble through a granny square.

"Maybe from your voice?" Lianne asks. "It's very distinctive, even in writing. Oh, fuck," she adds, looking forlornly at her misshapen crocheted chain. Katy motions for Lianne to hand it to her to fix.

"Nobody here knows me that well except you guys," I say. "It's not that easy. I mean, do you have any idea who Wendy is?" I haven't really put any thought into who it might be. I barely know anyone, after all.

Katy says, "Well, actually, I've been able to narrow it down."

"What?" Lianne and I both say.

She shrugs and hands Lianne her yarn and hook, the chain redone neatly. "I was bored, okay? I read some of their old posts one day. I think they used to be a little less careful of revealing their identity."

"What did you find out?" Lianne asks.

Katy reaches out and pauses the movie. "They had a post back in December where someone asked about fighting with their parents about their thesis topic, and Wendy said as an introduction to their response that they haven't even begun to think about a thesis, which means they can't be a senior."

"Gee, that narrows it down," I say. "Instead of it being one of our twenty-four hundred students, it's one of the eighteen hundred non-seniors."

After considering if Sophie's big was Wendy, I decided Wendy couldn't be a senior. I feel like I shouldn't be having this kind of banter with someone at least three years older than me. They're probably a sophomore or first year; what kind of upperclassman has time to just start a random Instagram anyway?

"That's not all," Katy says. "They also answered a question about immigrant family expectations where they said that they relate. So they probably have an immigrant family."

"I feel like that still leaves us with hundreds of options," Lianne says.

"Well, that's fine, then," I say, and I reach over to Katy's computer and hit play on *You've Got Mail*. My crochet hook falls out of the loop it's in. Oops.

"Geez, Jo," Lianne says. "Don't you want to know?"

"I just don't really care," I say. "I think it's better that I don't know."

But also—and I don't tell this to Katy and Lianne—I don't want to figure out who Wendy is because that means it's possible that Wendy has figured out who I am. And I am not ready for that.

"Suit yourself," Katy says, returning to her halter top. She starts making a chain for the tie.

I look at Lianne, who's looking at Katy with a deep concentration. Not at Katy's hands, which are deftly forming the same kind of chain that Lianne's been struggling with this whole time, but at her face.

Right. That. I guess it's not over yet.

# CHAPTER 38

## Guidelines

### SOPHIE

*Your Story Goes Against Our Community Guidelines.*

It's the first thing I see when I open Instagram in the morning, and immediately, I am alarmed and keep reading. It doesn't say why I've violated guidelines, just that I have, and that my story has been removed. It was the last one I posted yesterday, where I said Wanda was an "attention-seeking loser." I guess that goes too far for Instagram.

Oh my god. I have never violated any social media app's guidelines before.

What have I done?

An hour later, Priya finally wakes up. I didn't go on my run. I just sat on my floor, thinking. (And also doing a bit of stretching. My calves feel almost tingly.)

Immediately, I shove my phone in her face. "Look."

"Huh?" Priya blinks and squints. "Is that a picture of your math homework?"

"What? Oh." I'm on the wrong file in my camera roll. I swipe to the screenshot of Instagram's notification. "Look."

She reads it over, mouthing the words, and when she finishes, she starts laughing.

"That's incredible," Priya says. "You actually got a community guidelines violation?"

"Stop laughing!" I say. "This is very serious."

"How is it serious? You didn't even get your account suspended."

"Nobody can *ever* know about this, Priya," I say. "Nobody, got it?"

"You know I'm already telling Izzy as soon as this conversation's over."

"Not even Izzy. This is humiliating."

"Then why did you tell me?" Priya asks. "You could've kept it to yourself, saved the humiliation."

I guess I could have.

"Okay, never mind!" I say. "Go tell Izzy. No one else knows I'm Wendy, anyway."

"Fantastic," Priya says, already typing on her phone.

At first, I don't want to say anything to Wanda, but if my account can get a community guidelines violation, then theirs can too. I think I should warn them somehow without making it clear that I've actually received a violation, so I write them a DM.

> Hey Wanda! You know how yesterday we kind of tore each other into shreds? Well, today's a new day, and with a clear mind, I've realized this can't continue.

No, I can't send that. That doesn't even sound like me. I delete the text and try again.

> Hey Wanda! So . . . yesterday got a little out of hand. Maybe we should lay off on the insults? This is supposed to be fun, and if it continues like this, I don't think it will be anymore.

No, this doesn't work either. It sounds *too* genuine.

Hey Wanda! Yesterday was fun, but can we agree not to take things too far in the future? I don't want to get our accounts suspended lol!!

Okay, yeah, that's the one. I'm serious, but I can't look too serious; the "lol!!" helps.

I send the message, and it only takes a few minutes for me to get a response.

**@wandawellesley69:**
lol i admire your optimism for thinking instagram actually cares enough to ban us for this
but fair enough, you're probably right

**@dearwendywellesley:**
Of course I'm right! I'm Wendy Wellesley

# CHAPTER 39

# Pretend that It Will Happen

## JO

Oh my god.

I was rude enough to Wendy yesterday that they actually asked me to stop. Like, genuinely.

What have I done?

When I was younger, before I knew that my lack of attraction to others would be permanent, I was always afraid of being too mean for people to like me. It's probably because of those report cards that said I wasn't nice enough to my peers, prompting a number of discussions with my moms about how to decide what stays inside my head and what's kind and good to say.

"People will love you more if you show them your love," Mom would tell me, again and again.

And I tried to. And I still try. But time and time again, I grew apart from my friends. I was never able to hang on to those connections, and I think it is because at my core, I am not always a nice person.

But I want to be nice. And I want to love and to be loved. And yet, the only way people seem to want to do that is in a way that I can't. And so, people will leave me, and I will be alone. Forever.

I know it shouldn't be that scary. But can you imagine that being your reality, every single day of every month of every year, for your entire adult life? Every day, you come home, and it's silent. Completely barren.

And okay, maybe I'll have a pet. Or multiple pets. Or a roommate! Plenty of young adults have roommates. But . . . older adults don't. Have you ever heard of a person over thirty-five with a non-spousal roommate? Besides Matthew and Marilla from *Anne of Green Gables*? (And no, I don't want to live with my brother for the rest of my life.) Queerplatonic partners are a thing, of course, but what are the odds I'll have one when almost everyone wants a romantic partner?

Sometimes, when I can't sleep at night, I pretend I'm in bed with someone I love. I make up a fake scenario, or I pretend I'm some fictional character, and I cuddle up next to the imaginary love of my life, pretend they've kissed me on the forehead, that they've wrapped their arms around me.

It's not real. None of it's real. I wake up every day knowing that I don't truly want to fall in love, and I never will.

But it's nice to pretend that it will happen. Even though it won't, and I'll be alone forever, and I'll live a sad boring life with nobody in my life who loves me more than they love anybody else because everybody has The One that they love.

Hell, maybe even Wendy is in a committed relationship. There's no way for me to know. They're such an expert on relationships that it's quite possible.

Isn't it pathetic that I could be fully feuding about whether I'm better at giving relationship advice than someone *in a relationship*?

I should probably call my parents before this spiraling gets worse.

Mama picks up my FaceTime call after a couple seconds. "Oh, hi, Jonie! Everything okay?"

I breathe out, trying not to show my mother how close I am to crying. "Can I come home for dinner?"

It's so sad. I'm literally going home for spring break this weekend.

"Aw, honey, of course you can. What's going on?"

"I . . . I just really miss you and Mom. I don't know."

Mama's expression softens. "Is this the whole 'I don't want to grow up because being an adult is lonely and terrifying' thing?"

Shit, she knows me well. I nod and squeeze my eyes shut. "Yeah . . ."

"Oh, baby, I know. Yes, you can come home. Do you want me to pick you up, or would you rather bike?"

What does she think? I can't bike like this. Nor do I want to; it's late March, so it's still a little cold outside.

"Can you pick me up?" I ask.

"Of course. Mom's making dinner right now. Can I come get you in about twenty minutes?"

I sniffle. "Yeah. Thanks."

"All right. Love you, sweetie."

"Love you too."

So now I have twenty minutes to kill before I can cry in a car with the woman who birthed me. Out of habit, I open Instagram.

Here's a post from Meghana, a high school friend, at a family wedding. Here's a picture of Alicia Flores, posing on the Tower courtyard steps. Here's a photo of the sunrise on Lake Waban from Sophie, undoubtedly taken on a morning run.

Shit. Sophie.

We're supposed to get dinner tonight. To plan our next Dianas meeting.

I could cancel on my parents. I could cancel on Sophie.

I text Mama.

Me (5:28 PM)

i just realized i was going to get dinner with a friend to work on something

what do i do

becky ephron my hero (5:29 PM)

You could invite them over!

There's enough food for another person

That . . . is . . . certainly an option.

Yeah, I guess I can do that. We can work on stuff at my house. I hope Sophie doesn't think this is super weird. I open up my messages with her.

Me (5:30 PM)

hey this is like really last minute but how would you feel about dinner at my family home

No need to explain the reason why. She can infer whatever she wants. Maybe that my parents insisted I come home, maybe that I'm a poor planner. Better than her knowing one emotional breakdown is enough for me to want to go home.

Sophie (5:32 PM)

Oh sure! Lol did your parents make you come home or something

Mine would definitely do that if they lived nearby

Me (5:32 PM)

lol something like that

my mom will be here in like 10 mins? could you walk to stone-d in that time

i'm sorry this is extremely last-minute

Sophie (5:33 PM)

I'm at the science center right now so yes that's completely feasible

I'll be there in 5!

# CHAPTER 40

## *Voice*

### SOPHIE

It is not as weird as I thought it would be, going to Jo's home for dinner.

I feel like I'm in middle school, being picked up and brought to my friend's house for dinner. I used to eat dinner all the time with my next-door neighbors, and I'm sure Abby still does. But there's not really a way to do this in college. Except in the case of Jo Ephron, who lives a seven-minute drive away from the edge of campus.

One of her moms, who tells me to call her Becky, picks us up from Stone-Davis, and I barely have time to introduce myself and talk about how I met Jo before we're already here, at a cute little two-story house with a front yard decorated with so many plants and garden gnomes that I can barely see the lawn. Once we get inside, I meet Jo's other mom, Melissa, and her brother, Theo, who seems like he couldn't care less about Jo's and my presence.

"Sophie, dear," Becky says after all introductions have been made, "how about you go up to Jo's room and put your things down? I want to talk to Jo for a moment."

I hope she's not in trouble or anything. It was very sudden for her to switch plans; if I did that, my parents would definitely be mad at me.

Jo's brother, an absurdly short twelve-year-old with Jo's greenish eyes but lighter hair, shows me the way to her room. It's at the top of the steps, and when I walk in, I am not surprised at all that this is Jo's childhood bedroom. The walls are covered in posters and artwork. She has a small bookshelf nailed to the wall, which I immediately gravitate toward, and the books here are all so distinctly *middle school reader phase*: lots of contemporary novels about dramatic straight white teens, stuff I absolutely devoured as a preteen.

I'd feel awkward disturbing anything here, so I end up sitting cross-legged on the carpeted floor, checking the notifications on my phone. I have a bunch of texts from my sister, a few messages from the Slack group I'm in for the *Wellesley News*, and a mention in my Instagram story from Wanda that I've already seen on Priya's phone. It's not long before Jo comes up, and I immediately sit up straight and put my phone down.

"Hey," I say. "Everything okay?"

Jo gives a hint of a nod. "Uh. Yeah. I'm fine."

She does not seem fine at all. "Um . . . just know that you can always talk to me."

In response, Jo collapses backward on her bed and groans loudly.

I wait a little for her to collect her thoughts. I have absolutely no clue what she and her mom talked about. Maybe Mrs. Ephron—Becky—is upset that Jo double-booked herself, or maybe Jo had to come here in the first place because they needed to talk about something else.

Finally, Jo sits back up. "Do you ever . . . get . . . really sad that you'll probably be forever alone?"

Not at all what I expected to hear. But I can help her with this. I think.

It never really bothers me that I'll likely be single for the rest of my life. Actually, it was a relief when I realized it would be a viable option. In eighth grade, my English teacher let me and my friends eat in her classroom during lunch. She told us about how she lived by herself with two cats and a lot of houseplants, and I immediately decided that this was the ultimate life goal. So far, I've got the houseplants, but no cats—unless you count stuffed animals.

Yes, there's a little voice in my head that tells me that I won't be happy, that I can't achieve a fulfilling life without a romantic partner, but I know that it's an intrusive little voice put there by society, or maybe my family.

I put it away in a little corner of my mind, and I don't let it bother me because it's not telling the truth.

I think if the right opportunity came along, yes, I would like to live with someone else, but I don't need that to be happy. But wanting to live alone, or even to be single, isn't a universal experience for a-spec people. I know this from the internet, from books, and from the small handful of a-spec people I've talked to.

I am keenly aware that I'm taking way too long to answer Jo's extremely simple question. She's looking at me, almost nervously, as if she knows my answer won't be the same as hers.

"A bit," I say. "Sometimes."

Jo sighs and picks at her nails. "I got all emo about it today, so I asked my parents if I could come home for dinner because being around them makes me feel better, and then I remembered that we already had plans, so that's why you're here now. Mama just wanted to make sure I'm okay."

She sounds oddly calm. Either talking to her mom really helped, or she's deliberately hiding how she feels.

"So, wait," I say. "You got so wound up about existential loneliness that you forgot we were getting dinner?"

Jo gasps dramatically. "Oh my *god*, Sophie, let me have my moment!"

"Did you not put it in your calendar or anything?"

"Do you think I check my calendar in the middle of a crisis? Also, who the fuck puts meals on their calendar?"

"Uh, I do!" I say.

"You're ridiculous."

"I'm organized."

As much as Jo is just pretending to be offended, I'm not going to nag her anymore. I can't dismiss the fact that, as she said, she had a crisis.

"Anyway," I say. "Are you feeling better now?"

She faintly smiles. "Yeah. A lot."

Wow. Imagine that.

If I mention being aroace (or anything queer) to my parents, it just becomes an argument. They're not like that with Abby, who came out last year. I guess they think lesbians are more valid, most likely because they've had more exposure to gay people in their lives—college friends, coworkers, and the like.

Thanks to my choice of college being a bigger point of contention between us, I didn't realize how frequently I was arguing with my family about queer stuff until I left for Wellesley and came home for winter break. Then I couldn't stop noticing the depth of my parents' micro-aggressions and subtle digs at my identity.

I know I should count myself lucky. My parents are immigrants from Communist China and *don't* think being gay is wrong? My dad went to a fundamentalist church in high school, the formative years of his life, and *doesn't* think Abby will burn in hell? That's so much better than what so many people my age have.

But it's the fact that they refuse to open their minds any more—how they think that they've done enough, that this is a matter of personal opinion, that opinions don't harm others.

That still hurts. It means I can't tell them a lot of things.

"You're lucky to have your moms," I say, and it comes out quiet, a bare whisper, a confession.

Jo frowns, and then she speaks slowly, calmly. "I know you've mentioned it before, but I guess I'm curious. You don't have to say if you don't want to, but . . . what *are* your parents like?"

And before I realize it, I start talking.

# CHAPTER 41

# Ephron Moms Interrogation

## JO

Whoa. Okay.

I let Sophie talk uninterrupted and it comes gushing out: how her parents accept her gay sister more than her, how she wishes they kept their minds open, how she feels like she *has* to be confident about her identity in order for them to believe her, but they still don't get it.

Maybe my life isn't that bad in comparison.

When Sophie's finished info-dumping, I am speechless.

She sighs, clears her throat, and tightens her ponytail; it came loose while she was talking.

"I had no idea," I murmur. Then I clear my throat and say, "I mean, I knew they weren't great. 'Cause you mentioned that a while back. But I . . . I didn't realize."

Sophie sighs. "I know I should feel lucky. Right? Like . . . they *technically* accept me."

"For the wrong reasons," I say. "Accepting you by saying you're picky isn't exactly the same as accepting that being aroace is a real thing that exists."

"I *know*," Sophie says. "But so many people don't even get that."

"So are you just going to let them walk all over you?"

"They're my parents, Jo."

"But—"

I'm about to counter Sophie's point again when I am suddenly reminded of something Mom tells me about.

Her parents—my grandparents—were devout Catholics, and they wouldn't acknowledge that she was gay for seven years after she first came out to them. But they didn't kick her out or send her to conversion camp. She knew that if she pushed any boundaries, that was a possibility. So she took what she could get.

Is it ridiculously unfair that there's sometimes no way to change people's minds? Of course. But is there anything we can do about that? No.

I concede. "You've got a point."

Sophie clicks her tongue. "It sucks, but there's really nothing I can do except wait. Maybe when I'm still single at, like, thirty, they'll finally get it. But is it wrong of me to want more from them?"

"No, of course not."

"Sometimes I wonder if it's only a matter of time before they start setting me up with people. You know, like in the movies."

"If you ever need someone to fake-date if they're being too pushy, I volunteer."

Sophie rolls her eyes. "Thank you for your help, but I think that won't be necessary."

Soon, Sophie and I creep downstairs to see if dinner is ready. My parents are just setting the table, so the two of us help out and then sit down to eat.

My parents give Sophie the same Ephron Moms Interrogation that they gave my roommates the first time they came over—intended major (psychology and/or women's and gender studies), favorite book (undecided, but her favorite recent read was a love story set in Chicago about two *very* mentally ill people), what her family's like (accountant mom, nurse practitioner dad, annoying sister).

"I think you'd get along great with Sophie's sister, Theo," Mom says.

My brother sighs and shovels more potatoes into his mouth.

"She actually hates boys with a burning passion," Sophie says. "No offense to you."

"None taken," he replies, not bothering to look up from his plate. "We suck."

Twelve years old, and Theodore Ephron already knows how to put himself in his place.

"And Sophie, dear, how did you meet our Jo?" Mom asks, even though I've probably told her, like, four times and she definitely knows by now.

"Oh!" Sophie says. "We're classmates. We randomly ended up doing a group presentation together, and we started talking a lot."

"Very sweet," Mama says. "And, I'm sorry, where did you say you were from?"

"The Chicago suburbs," Sophie says. "Jo says one of you is from there?"

Mom smiles. "You've been paying attention. Yes, I'm from Schaumburg. What about you?"

The questions go on and on, one after the other. They keep on asking Sophie if she wants more potatoes or asparagus, and Sophie declines, which I don't blame her for because we get potatoes and asparagus all the time in the dining halls. I'm going to die of embarrassment. My moms will probably know more about Sophie than I do by the end of this conversation.

Once we finish eating, Sophie and I decide we'll work on planning the Dianas in the comfort of my childhood bedroom. And miraculously, we manage to stay on topic and get our next meeting figured out pretty quickly.

I'm feeling a lot better, and not just because of my parents—maybe it's just as much because of Sophie.

**anon:** apologies if this is a little hard-hitting, i'm looking for some humor right now. (wendy, if you're reading this, i am only a little sorry.) i'm queer, but i have a super traditional christian family. last summer, i came out to them, hoping they'd accept me, but they didn't. it's like my parents completely ignored what i said. how do i feel better about this?

**answer:** lol fuck 'em.
i mean, look, you're not alone. i know you wanted humor, but just wanted to get that out of the way. you've got to take what you can get. don't push it with them until it's safe to do so.
but anyway lol yeah. the way the church encourages homophobia really fucking sucks! jesus did not die from crucifixion for 21st-century bigots to still be using religion as an excuse for bigotry.
whoops i've lost track. ways to feel better uhhhh

- talk to your friends about it, if you haven't
- tbh have a dance party in your room?? idk this always helps me
- write an angry letter about your family's homophobia and then straight-up burn it. (outdoors. don't set off the smoke alarms it's so annoying.)
- have a good scream.

**dearwendywellesley 11m**
That all sounds right to me
Reply

**wandawellesley69 3m**
no rebuff? who are you and what have you done with wendy??
Reply

# CHAPTER 42

## Far Away from That Drama

### JO

Our third Dianas meeting is attended by the same three people who have been here. To be honest, I didn't expect any more to come. Sophie and I did little to promote the meeting besides messaging our email list, and it's also the first day of spring break; I'm heading home tonight, and Sophie's flight is tomorrow.

It's all right, though, because Charlie, Evelyn, and Hannah are plenty of company. Since there's nobody new, we forgo our conversations in the Penthouse and go for a walk in the Ville to visit some downtown shops.

Most of the places here are too overpriced for us and targeted toward wealthy, middle-aged white people, but at least we can go to the bookstore, where Sophie thumbs through a copy of a relationship self-help book, which I think is hilarious.

"You're never going to need that," I say.

"You can never be too prepared," Sophie says.

Sophie starts giving the others a massive amount of recommendations for books starring asexual and aromantic characters. I lose track of all the titles; there's a heist novel, a romance with a thirty-year-old stuck in a love triangle, a YA anthology, and a book about a girl who can raise the spirits of dead animals.

Once we leave the bookstore—I've purchased a copy of a book about amateur teenage spies that seems hilarious—we head to the ice cream shop. It's not warm enough yet for us to be eating ice cream, but there really isn't anything else to do.

Charlie and Hannah have gotten into a lively discussion about a TV show they both watch, and Sophie and Evelyn are talking about a book they couldn't find at the bookstore.

"I heard that the author wrote it to fulfill a desire to set Mitch McConnell on fire," Sophie says.

"Oh my god, yeah, it was so obvious," Evelyn says. "I support that agenda."

"Maybe I should've bought a copy for my mom," I say.

"You need to read it sometime!" Evelyn says. "The main character is aromantic and ends up in a queerplatonic relationship."

"That does sound like something I would enjoy," I admit.

Evelyn's phone, which is sitting face up on the table, lights up with a message. Evelyn glances at the screen, rolls her eyes, and turns her phone face down.

"Sorry, it's just my roommate," she says. "They started dating one of our friends recently, and they've been having drama and want me to mediate."

"And do you want to be mediating?" I ask.

"Hell no," Evelyn says. "I would like to stay as far away from that drama as I can. I am not about to choose sides and lose a friend because the two of them can't settle their arguments like adults."

Sophie starts suggesting ways that Evelyn can tell her roommate directly that she doesn't want to get involved. If that were me, I probably wouldn't have wanted the two of them to go out in the first place.

I mean, this is barely a hypothetical for me; I genuinely don't want Lianne to go out with Katy. Or anyone that we're both friends with. Which isn't really a lot of people besides Katy.

But she doesn't seem to be over Katy yet.

I should really talk to her about that.

"We need to work on recruitment," Sophie says once we've all gone our separate ways. She and I are at Bates Hall eating dinner, which for her is a rarity because it's on the opposite side of campus from her dorm.

"Isn't it good that we're at least getting consistent attendance?" I say. "Nobody has stopped coming."

"But a club can't be five people," Sophie says. "That's just a friend group."

"Well, why aren't the other people in our email list showing up?" I ask. "There's at least twenty of them in there now."

Sophie shrugs. "Darcy told me that that's normal. At least for the geese-watching club."

"Well, that's—I mean, who's actually going to go to that? The geese are terrifying."

"You'd be surprised," Sophie says.

In any case, we decide we're going to have a new flyer sent out in a few different email newsletters that reach the student body, and we'll also post flyers on the bulletin boards around campus. Sophie says she'll create a Dianas Instagram account so we can advertise there too—apparently, she's put it off until now.

"Can I be in charge of it?" I joke. "I'm, like, basically a social media expert."

"Ooh, yes," Sophie says, clearly not getting my sarcasm. "That would be great!"

"Wait, no—"

"I'll send you some ideas I have," Sophie continues. "It should be pretty straightforward, and—"

"Sophie, please, no, I didn't—"

"—it'll be really easy for you to put it all together! This'll be really helpful, thank you for offering!"

"I—okay," I say, accepting my fate.

I guess I'm running three Instagram accounts now.

# CHAPTER 43

## *W-2*

## SOPHIE

I'm working on math homework when my sister barges into my room. It's the middle of spring break, and I've been trying to mostly relax while I'm at home, but the pile of assignments I have to work on needs my attention.

"*Sophieeeeeeee*," she whines. "Help."

I roll my eyes. "Help with what?"

"Dad tried to explain *taxes*."

I know already that Abby has made some sort of mistake. Our dad tends to ramble, but only when prompted.

"Why was he trying to explain taxes?" I ask.

"Because," Abby continues whining, "I asked what a W-2 is because one of my friends was talking about it or something, and instead of just telling me what it is, he launched into this whole thing about all the forms you get and the ones you have to fill out and stuff. Why does he even know this? *Mom* does all our taxes."

Our mom is an accountant. Abby really should've asked her. When I tell her this, she shakes her head and complains that Mom is shopping for groceries.

"Let Dad let out his steam, and he'll be done mansplaining soon enough," I say.

"Yeah, I already did," Abby says.

"So why did you come up here?" I ask.

"Because I *still don't know* what a W-2 is."

"Google it, silly." I scoff. "It's a form that an employer sends you that tells you how much money they paid you this year."

Abby groans. "That's *it*?!" She sighs dramatically. "Why couldn't Dad just say that?"

"Because he loves to explain things."

Abby glares at me. "Ugh. Okay. That's it." She turns to leave.

"No!" I say, waving my hand around. "Wait! How was school today?"

"Ugh. Not this again." Abby pretends to hate catching me up on drama, but I know she loves it. "Madeleine almost ate a peanut cookie during lunch, but then she didn't, so she's not dead. Dylan and Ellie broke up *again*. Andrea made Mr. Tracy mad during math because she told him he has no friends, even though it's totally true. And Emily Wang left the group chat after Emily Kim insulted her new haircut or something. Oh, and Mrs. Thorne's grandkid was born."

It takes my mind a moment to catch up to everything Abby has said. Madeleine's name I recognize. The other names I don't know, although there are definitely many people named Emily in Abby's grade. And the final name—

"Wait, really? That's so exciting! I miss her so much."

Mrs. Thorne is an English teacher at my high school. I am forever grateful to her for helping me edit my college essays.

Abby glares at me. "You know, she's always calling me 'Sophie' by mistake."

"Because we look—"

"*Yes, I know, we look alike.* Do you know *how* many teachers have told me that? It's like *everybody* knows you. I can't do this for four years."

"You'd better not go to Wellesley."

"Obviously. It sounds so boring there."

"Uh, excuse me. It is not. I do many fun things that you don't know about."

"Yeah, right," she says, raising an eyebrow. "I bet all you do is read and study and eat bad food and go on runs."

Well . . . she's not totally wrong. That *is* how I spend about 80 percent of my waking hours. She doesn't keep track of the clubs I do, nor does she know about Dear Wendy. I only allow Wellesley students and alums to follow the account, so there's no way Abby could know that I'm behind it.

I don't think my parents would take me seriously if I did tell them about Dear Wendy. They wouldn't understand how important it's become to me, nor would they begin to comprehend the work it takes for me to scour the internet and check out books from the library to find the right answers. I can hear my mom's voice now: *You shouldn't be giving people love advice when you always say that you're not interested in romance! What makes you think you have the right to tell people what to do?*

It's not that I'm making people do things. I'm just being helpful. Because I like it.

Abby groans. "Ugh. Okay. I'm gonna go now. But in case you missed it, you're *really* boring."

This I won't take. "I am *not* boring. I do things. Like . . ." I look over at my windowsill. "Water my plants."

Abby groans loudly. "You're *kidding*. Being a plant mom can't be your entire identity."

"Well, I love them. Wait, look." I grab my new plant off my desk, a peace lily I got when I went to Lowe's yesterday out of sheer boredom. I'll get my dad to water it while I'm gone. "This is Taylor."

My sister narrows her eyes. "Did you seriously name a plant after Taylor Swift?" She loves to slander my taste in music.

"Who said it was Taylor Swift? Maybe I named it after . . . Taylor Lautner."

Her gaze only becomes more piercing. "No you didn't."

"I didn't. It's named after Taylor Swift."

"You're so uncool."

"I—but—you love Olivia Rodrigo just as much as I love Taylor Swift."

"Did Taylor Swift put out a masterpiece of a debut album at the age of eighteen?"

*"She did it when she was sixteen!"*

I hear a door shut.

"Mom's home!" Abby says, voice suddenly chipper and about two octaves higher. Our mom must be back from grocery shopping. In a flash, Abby leaves my room and thunders down the stairs. "Mom, what's a *W-2*?"

"What—I already explained it to you," I say, following her down.

My mom is in the kitchen, grocery bags in hand. "Hi, Yuányuan," she says to Abby, ignoring my comment. "A W-2 is a tax form." Abby mutters a thanks. "And hi, Lèle."

"Hey, Mom," I say.

"Yuányuan, nǐ zěnme yòu qù *bother* Lèle le?" Mom says, again to Abby, as she starts putting away the bags of fresh vegetables. "Tā hěn *busy*, nǐ zhīdao ma?"

"I'm not bothering her," Abby says. "And she's not busy."

"I was actually doing my math homework."

Abby sticks her tongue out at me. (Seriously?) "Well, you always answer my calls when you're at school, so why would you be busy while you're at home on break?"

"Lèle," Mom says, crossing her arms. "Shì zhēnde ma? Nà nǐ wèishénme bù *answer* wǒde *call*?"

"I'm sorry, Mom!" I say. "It's just, you always call when I'm busy."

It's a half-truth. My mom does tend to call at inconvenient times by chance. But sometimes, maybe I conveniently ignore her because I really don't want to talk to her.

I love my mom. But it's exhausting to be her daughter. Or, at least, to be her aroace daughter who goes to a liberal arts college, when what she wants is for me to marry, produce children, and graduate from an Ivy League university.

Not necessarily in that order.

My mom *tsks*. "I will have to find a better time to call. Yuányuan, come help me with groceries."

"Ughhhhhhhhhh," Abby groans, which makes me laugh. "Why doesn't Sophie have to?"

"Because she's busy with math homework."

I laugh at Abby and take this as my excuse to go back upstairs. No bad conversations with Mom today.

Maybe I worry about that a little more than I should. Not every conversation with my mom results in hurt feelings, but when I went home for winter break, it felt suffocating to be around her for too long, which is why this time, I've been holed up in my room or out of the house pretty much the whole time. It's actually kind of worked.

When she's around, there's always something. I love college too much. (You can't love college too much.) I don't know what I'm doing with my life. (I like psychology and gender studies, but my mom thinks the concepts of mental health and intersectional feminism are made up.) I disrespect boys my age. (Who wouldn't?)

Things are better with my dad. He isn't as argumentative. And he's lived in the US since high school—not *that* much longer than my mom, but enough that he spent some formative years here. But he still thinks I need to marry and that my school isn't good enough.

It's all very complicated. But I'm in college now, usually a thousand miles away from their nagging voices, so you know what? I'm perfectly fine.

They don't know how much I've done. I've started a club! I've made one of our most popular Instagram accounts! I've written half a dozen articles for the *Wellesley News*!

But they don't care about any of that.

I can't wait to go back to school.

Dear Wendy,

My roommate is a nightmare.

My first-semester roommate was fantastic, but this semester, they're on a leave of absence, so I got assigned a new one for the spring who just got placed in my room a few weeks ago.

I can already see why they moved out of their old room.

Here are some things that my roommate has done while living in our room for the past couple of weeks. (Weeks!)

- hung up her dirty underwear on one of my hangers (why???)
- laid down in MY bed. WHILE STILL DAMP FROM THE SHOWER.
- ate my food that I brought from home after spring break without asking
- had a screaming match over the phone with her on-again off-again boyfriend while I was studying for an exam
- spilled a bunch of cosmetic glitter on my desk and left it for me to clean up

And this isn't even all of it.

What do I do? She never listens to what I say, and she's friends with our RA. Is it too late in the semester for her to move out? Who would I even ask about that since our RA would be no help?

Sincerely,
Sick of This

P.S. I know this is specific enough that my roommate might see this, but honestly, I don't care at this point.

Dear Sick,

Oh my goodness. Any one of those things would be enough for most people to complain to their RAs, and the fact that you've put up with this and more is commendable. But you shouldn't have to.

I am not a reslife expert, so I can't provide specific guidance. What I can say is that you have other options besides your RA. Try talking to your house president or your dorm neighborhood's community director. This sounds like an unlivable situation, and even if it's only for the last month of school that one of you moves, it might be worth it for your mental (and possibly physical?? what with the dirty underwear) health.

You do not have to put up with this kind of behavior.

All best,
Wendy

**dearwendywellesley 9h**
Comments on this post will be locked and any comments deleted if I see anybody speculating about Sick of This's identity (or the identity of their roommate). Wrongful speculation is hurtful, and even if you are correct, this is a private matter.
Reply

**wandawellesley69 5h**
holy shit this one was a lot . . . godspeed to you, sick of this
Reply

**dearwendywellesley 4h**
Thank you for being respectful in my comments, Wanda!
Reply

**wandawellesley69 3h**
don't push it, wendy
Reply

# CHAPTER 44

## The Wellesley Main Character

### JO

"Did you fucking see that Dear Wendy post?" Lianne asks as we line up for dinner.

It's the first day back from spring break, and Katy, Lianne, and I are getting a meal together for the first time since before break. We even took a trip to the Tower dining hall because they have make-your-own burgers today, which is one of the only consistently good meals our dining halls have to offer.

Since it is consistently good, apparently the whole school has decided to get dinner at Tower, so the line is massive. Which means we have a lot of time to chat.

"Of course I did," Katy says. "Can you imagine if that was us?"

"Really puts into perspective our argument about alarm clock noise last September," I say.

"I'm so sorry," says a voice behind me, "but are you guys talking about that horrific roommate situation on Dear Wendy?"

I turn around to see Sophie's roommate, Priya, standing behind us with a tote bag over her shoulder.

Her brows shoot up in recognition. "Oh, hey, Jo!"

"Hey!" I say.

I make quick introductions between Priya, Lianne, and Katy—Priya compliments Katy's crochet bucket hat—and then we get right back to that post.

"I couldn't believe it was real," Priya says. "I mean, I thought it was an April Fool's joke because it was that severe."

"What I want to know," Lianne says, "is what some of the other stories are that the original person omitted."

We all nod emphatically. Priya says she's dying to know the extent of it.

"This person is already the Wellesley main character for the week," Lianne says. "Look at this."

She holds up her phone; someone has taken a screenshot of the post and put it on Twitter, writing, "oh. my. god." It has over a hundred likes. I would guess many of those likes aren't Wellesley students.

Once we've had enough of talking about the Wendy post—without revealing to Priya that I'm Wanda—Priya asks Lianne and Katy to tell her more about themselves. Katy launches into a detailed self-introduction; she's from New York, she's an only child, she played a few different instruments in high school band, she loves cooking but oddly loves cleaning up even more.

I glance at Lianne; Lianne's brows are ever so slightly raised, the corner of her lips just barely lifting into an amused smile. Her gaze seems faraway.

Okay. No. I'm not going to do or say anything. I am not going to become a nightmare roommate. That is not what this is.

Or maybe I could do a little prying. Just to see.

It's a few hours later when I'm alone with Katy and decide I'll talk to her about it, just as a hypothetical. Not even about Lianne specifically. Just dating at all.

The thing is, I don't know if Katy is open to dating anyone, let alone Lianne. So if I can just confirm that she's not interested in dating, then I can rest assured that nothing will happen.

"Do you think you're ready to start dating again?" I ask her while we're both working on assignments for class.

She turns from her spot at her desk to look at me. "What are you talking about?"

"Just—if the opportunity arose. If someone you liked asked you out. Would you say yes?"

Katy sighs. "I don't know."

The way she says it carries a shocking amount of weight to it, and I almost do a double take. She sounds weary. Exhausted, even.

"Oh. God. I didn't mean to—"

"No, you're fine," Katy says, waving a hand absently. "It's just complicated, that's all."

I don't want to pry, but I feel like I really need an answer. "Complicated how?"

She clicks her tongue and then says, "If I could guarantee the next person I date isn't going to fuck me up like Jason did—"

"Ooh, look at you, using adult words."

"—then yes, I would go out with them. But I can't guarantee that with, like, any stranger."

"What about a person you already know?" I ask.

"I guess that depends on the person. But I'm not going to bank on that being a possibility. Either way, with the point I'm at now, I think I'd just feel too anxious in any romantic relationship."

"That makes sense. You should take your time."

"Exactly."

Well, that solves it, then. She's not going to date Lianne, if Lianne ever even gets the courage to ask her out.

So why do I still feel so uneasy?

# CHAPTER 45

## Comfortable

### SOPHIE

Alicia and I are eating lunch today at Stone-Davis, in a circular room paneled with huge windows that look out at a bunch of trees. The reason we're here is because I saw on the @wellesleyicecream Instagram account that Stone-D has Graham Central Station ice cream today. It's a campus-wide favorite: ice cream with bits of graham crackers and chocolate-covered honeycomb candy.

As usual, the ice cream tastes terrific. I can't say the same for the peanut butter and jelly sandwich I'm eating—the bread is so dry. But food is food, and I've had worse here. I'll just finish up and go study in the library until I have my writing class later this afternoon.

"Uh, Sophie?" Alicia says. "Look outside."

I turn my head to look out of the massive floor-to-ceiling windows and . . . oh no. It is pouring rain. I hear a clap of thunder, and I groan. I don't have an umbrella with me; I *do* have a rented textbook and a laptop in my tote bag, neither of which can get wet.

"Oh, that's not good," I say. "Should we just study here?"

"I guess," Alicia says. "I haven't been through the residential space here since I hooked up with a sophomore last semester."

"Ew," I say automatically. "Well, I think there are a few living rooms we can go to."

We gather up our things, throw away our trash, and head upstairs from the ground floor. I spot it soon enough: a living room, shelves on the wall stacked high with board games and books. It's not quite as elaborate as the Claflin living room, but it'll do.

And who do I see but Jo Ephron, sitting on one of the couches with two other people whom I recognize as their roommates, the three of them all in extremely different states of dress: Jo, in a crew-neck sweater and jeans; a brunette who must be Katy, wearing a blazer over a striped jumpsuit not unlike the one I wore to homecoming my junior year; and Lianne, in pajamas patterned with brown paw prints.

"Oh, hey!" Jo says when we enter. "What are you two doing here?"

I wave. "Hey! We're sort of stuck here until it stops raining."

I notice Alicia looking intently in Lianne and Katy's direction. Their body language is a little close, but that's typical for college kids with no physical boundaries. I know they're not together, but Alicia probably doesn't.

"You're more than welcome to hang out with us!" Katy says, clearly not noticing anything. "You're Sophie, right?"

I nod. "Yep, that's me. And this is Alicia."

For a moment, Alicia pauses, her eyes trained on Lianne. And then she looks down and clears her throat. "Uh, yeah, hi. I'm Alicia. Um, Sophie said that already."

Katy, completely impervious to what's going on, waves and says, "I'm Katy! And this is Lianne and Jo."

She has a serene smile on her face, and it's kind of adorable. Meanwhile, Lianne has barely said a word. She looks like she wants nothing more than to melt into the floor.

We settle into seats, and I pull out my phone and text Jo.

Me (1:07 PM)

Does Katy know who Alicia is??

I can see Jo flinch as they feel their phone vibrate. They send a message back.

Jo (1:08 PM)

i don't think so????

"So!" Katy says, and I snap my head up. "Sophie, I've heard so much about you. It's really cool that you and Jo became friends."

"Yeah," I say, plastering a smile on my face. "I can't believe it took me this long to be friends with someone outside of an org or my dorm. Except now we made an org together." This makes everyone chuckle.

"Ooh, what other orgs are you in?" Katy asks.

"I write for the *Wellesley News*," I say. "I'm thinking about applying to be a Sexual Health Educator. And sometimes I take pictures for the *News* too."

"Oh, I did yearbook in high school!" Katy says. "It was my main extracurricular."

"Wait, so did I," I say. "I was editor-in-chief my senior year."

Katy's eyes widen. "Oh boy, that's a lot of work."

"Uh . . . yeah, you know, I managed."

High school yearbook was a little stressful. Lots of deadlines, a bit of drama. But I met a lot of my friends doing journalism, and there are far worse activities to do.

Jo is the perfect person to prove my point. "Yearbook is nothing compared to theater."

I hiss. "One of my friends was a show choir kid. It always sounded grueling."

"Oh, I couldn't imagine doing show choir." Jo shudders. "Tech rehearsals in nonmusical theater are bad enough as it is."

Lianne still hasn't said a single thing, and I must notice at the same time as Katy, because she says, "Hey, Lianne, did your high school have a show choir?"

"Huh?" Lianne says, looking incredibly out of it. "Um, no. I don't think show choir is really big in Texas."

"I only learned about it from Jo," Katy says to the rest of us. "There are almost none in New York."

"Wait, Lianne, you're from Texas?" Alicia says, eyebrows raised. "Which city?"

"Houston," Lianne says.

Alicia laughs. "I'm from San Antonio!"

"Oh!" Lianne says, smiling. "That's cool, I've barely met anyone else at Wellesley from Texas."

"Wait, is there *anyone* from Texas who actually has a southern accent?" Katy asks. "Because neither of you sound very southern."

"Ah, well," Lianne says. "In the big cities, uh, not—not as much."

"Being nonwhite probably also contributes to that," Alicia says nonchalantly, and I almost laugh because Alicia talks *all* the time about how if she ever wants to make it in broadcast news someday, she's going to have to speak the "neutral" (i.e., white) news anchor accent you hear on TV instead of her natural accent.

Jo's back on their phone, and pretty soon, mine pings with another text.

Jo (1:10 PM)

the tension in this room is astronomical

i'm going to pee myself

I have to hold my laughter as I type back that they should go use the restroom. I would be a little tired that we've defaulted to talking about high school, but I'm too busy trying to scope out what kind of dynamic is going on between Lianne, Katy, and Alicia. At some point, Lianne starts talking about speech and debate.

"I mean, it's bad enough no matter who you are, but as a queer Black girl?" Lianne says, and it sounds like she's finally comfortable enough to speak the way she normally does. "Jesus. Everybody hated me whenever I won."

I wince at the thought. I didn't really know anybody in speech or debate, but Priya and Izzy's politics club had some debate elements, and they've told me plenty about how much harder they had to work to be taken seriously.

"And she won a lot," Katy adds.

Lianne fights back a smile. "It wasn't that much."

Katy shakes her head. "You won the state competition three times. That's a *lot*."

"Well . . . I . . . it doesn't matter," Lianne says. "I'm in college. It's not like I can put that on my résumé anymore."

"You should still be proud of your accomplishments," Alicia says.

Lianne looks like she'll explode if the others say one more nice thing about her.

I glance at Jo. They raise their eyebrows at me, lips pressed tightly together, and look over at Lianne, which confirms my suspicions.

After talking a little bit longer, we all start doing our own work. I pull out my computer and start reading through an interview transcription to pull quotes for the news article I'm writing about a professor who just won a cool award, and then I start skimming some readings I'm doing for my sociology class.

Finally, the rain stops. When I notice, I save my work and close my computer. "Okay, I think I'm going to class now," I say.

"Where are you going?" Jo asks.

"Pendleton."

I have my writing class in half an hour. It doesn't take long at all to walk to Pendleton, a building in the Academic Quad, but I should leave now in case the rain picks up again.

"Oh," Jo says. "I was gonna go pick up a package. Want me to walk with you?"

Pendleton *is* on the way to Lulu. But Jo didn't even have to ask.

# CHAPTER 46

# Should I Splash in This Puddle?

## JO

As soon as we're out of earshot, Sophie wastes no time asking for the tea.

"So, Lianne," she says as we walk down the stairs that lead to the lobby.

I sigh. "It's that obvious, huh?"

"She's having a YA main character love triangle moment," Sophie says, and I burst into laughter.

"Never say that again," I say. "It sounds weird coming out of your mouth."

"Noted," Sophie says. "But, so, what is going on exactly? She's not dating Katy, is she?"

I shake my head. "No. She's not. I mean, you know as much as I do. Lianne has had a crush on Katy for months, and she's pretty sure she can't do anything about it, so now she's trying to meet new people, but then it gets awkward when those people interact with Katy."

I hold the door open for her as we walk out, down the outside steps toward the Academic Quad.

Sophie frowns. "Have she and Alicia . . ."

"Hooked up? I don't think so."

"Oh my god, no!" Sophie says. "Have they *met each other* before? Alicia's never mentioned . . ."

I shake my head. "They've texted. Sporadically. Ooh, should I splash in this puddle?"

"Please don't. So, then, is Lianne planning on telling Katy?"

I step in the puddle anyway. I'm wearing rain boots, and what's the point of wearing rain boots if you don't splash around? It makes Sophie squeal and complain that I'll get her jeans dirty, and I laugh and hop in the water again.

"Uh, sorry, what was your question?" I ask, feigning ignorance.

"Does Lianne want to tell Katy?"

"Uh . . . maybe? But Katy doesn't even want to be dating right now."

"Interesting," Sophie says. "Are you kind of caught in the middle?"

"Yeah." I sigh. "I don't know what to do."

Sophie shrugs. "Talk to Lianne about it. Does she know that you know?"

"No. Um. Maybe."

"There you go. Have a conversation about it. Maybe you'll be able to give her better advice after you figure out the specifics." She shrugs nonchalantly. "I don't know, I'm not a relationship expert or anything."

Since I'm Wanda, am I more of a relationship expert than Sophie?

"I didn't think you were," I say to deflect, "given your . . . condition."

Sophie bursts out laughing. "Are we calling our sexual orientations 'conditions' now?"

"I don't know, I was trying something! Stop laughing!"

"It just—" She wheezes. "It reminds me of how period dramas describe pregnancy."

"Oh my god. No. Shut up. Stop! No! I didn't mean that!"

By the time I return from Lulu with my package, the living room is empty. I'm pretty sure Katy has gone to meet up with a friend, and I guess Alicia has left, too, which means this might be my chance to confront Lianne.

When I enter our room, Lianne's sitting at her desk, staring at her phone.

"You okay?" I ask as I set down my stuff. "You're looking at that *very* intently."

Lianne sighs. "Look at this."

She hands me her phone, and on the screen are her text messages. She has one, unopened, from *alicia from bumble*.

> funny seeing you in the flesh! we should hang
> out sometime :)

"Oh my god," I say.

"What do I say?" Lianne says.

"Uh, does she want to hang out as friends?"

"I'm gonna guess no?" Lianne says. "Considering that, you know, we met on Bumble."

"Okay, well . . . reply!"

"With what, though?" She's looking increasingly panicked. "I don't even know if I want to hang out with her!"

*No you don't,* I think. She doesn't. She shouldn't. She shouldn't want to date anyone. She's going to use Alicia as a way to get over her feelings for Katy. Or she's going to actually fall in love with Alicia but then get her heart broken.

"Just—uh—say it was cool seeing her too? I guess?"

I pull out my phone and rapidly text Sophie, who responds almost immediately.

> Me (2:45 PM)
> help lianne and alicia are texting

Sophie (2:45 PM)
> OMG

> Alicia just texted me a screenshot

> It would be so funny if they ended up together lol!!

Right. Funny. It would be funny.

I look up from my messages. Lianne is smiling down at her phone. I don't want her to be.

In a split second, I make a choice.

"Hey, Lianne," I say, "So, uh . . . Sophie asked me what's going on with you and Katy." Not a lie. Entirely. "And sort of Alicia. Uh, I think she knows you and Alicia have . . . um . . . flirted?"

She looks up at me, the smile gone in an instant. I can't read the expression on Lianne's face. We sit in silence for some amount of time that's way too long to be comfortable for either of us.

"What does that mean?" Lianne finally asks.

"You tell me," I say, wringing my hands.

Her eyes widen. "Did she tell you why?"

"Why what?"

"Why she asked."

"You were obviously uncomfortable the entire time Sophie and Alicia were here."

Lianne sighs loudly and leans backward, rocking her chair back a little.

"Yeah, I know," I say.

If I tell her to confess to Katy, and Katy doesn't like her back, everything will be so awkward. But if Katy does like her back, then they might start dating, which . . . can't happen. Katy doesn't even want to date anyone right now. She shouldn't.

And if I tell Lianne to go with Alicia, she'll probably spend all her time with Alicia and leave me and Katy behind, or things will be ruined one way or another.

I just don't want my friends to date anyone. I don't really know why. But they can't.

"I just . . . I want to stop having all of these feelings," Lianne says. "You know?"

And before I can stop it from slipping out: "No."

No, I don't know. I wish I had this problem. I would give anything to live through a foolish teenage love triangle. It sure beats being fucking lonely all the time.

Lianne sighs. "Okay, yeah, you don't know. But it's . . . exhausting."

I don't reply to this. She can talk it out herself.

"I mean . . . you're right, I like Katy. I've been liking her. But I feel like I can usually tell when someone likes me, and I don't think she does. But, then, what if she's open to it? But *then*, also, this new girl comes along, and she's fucking hilarious, and we have so much in common? And I can't believe it took me this long to meet her in person, and it was literally by accident. And I . . . I don't know. I don't know anything. Maybe I shouldn't even think about either of them."

Shit, does she expect me to have an answer for this? "That's not fun."

Lianne glares at me. "Very helpful, Jo."

"I'm sorry! I . . . I'm not Dear Wendy. I don't know what you should do."

"Well, what would you say if I sent all of that in your DMs?"

"I don't know, probably . . . I don't know."

I know what I want to say. I want her to stop liking Katy and not date anybody so the three of us can be the fun single friends we deserve to be. But she can't just stop liking someone. And I can't tell her that.

"I'll ask Dear Wendy myself," Lianne determines. "Sorry to betray you."

"What? No. You can't do that." That is more of a betrayal than anything else she could possibly do. This is worse than dating Katy. She can't—

"I can, and I will," Lianne says. "This is a last-ditch effort."

"But—"

"No buts. I'm doing it. You can't stop me."

I groan. "Fine. Do it. Whatever."

It's just a silly Instagram rivalry. It's not a big deal.

Dear Wendy,

I am having a bit of a crisis. I have a crush on someone I'm very close with, but I don't think there's a chance they like me back, so I've been trying to forget about it by trying to meet other people. And I met this girl who's super cool, but I'm afraid that if I ask her out, I might miss out on a chance with the first person, because maybe that person does like me back after all. What should I do?

Sincerely,
Yearning Lesbian

# CHAPTER 47

## *Objective*

### SOPHIE

I have a question from Lianne.

In my months of running Dear Wendy, I've never gotten a submission that I can easily determine is from someone I know. I've had a few that could *potentially* be from people I knew in real life, but I never knew outright, and I didn't make assumptions. Except this time, I'm not making assumptions. The timing, the whole situation: I know it's her.

But I'll treat this the way I treat all my Dear Wendy questions. To be honest, I don't know what to suggest to Lianne. There aren't any good relationship theories I can pull from. Attachment styles won't help; the four horsemen of the marital apocalypse are obviously no use; love languages were invented by a homophobe.

Lianne has a few different options. Tell Katy, or don't tell her. Ask out Alicia, or don't. She could just not tell anyone. Or . . . tell Katy and then ask out Alicia? No, wait, that makes no sense. Or maybe it would, if Katy doesn't like her back, but then wouldn't it be super weird for them?

The whole point of being Wendy is that I am objective. A third-party observer. Someone who isn't connected to the situation. And in this case, I am very much connected to this situation. I was really hoping that Jo would be able to talk to Lianne about it, and they'd come up with a solution on their own.

"Priya," I say, interrupting her two-hour-long FaceTime call with Izzy. "What do I do?"

"Get a second opinion," Priya says. "From someone who doesn't know any of the people involved."

"You don't know them."

"I know Jo and Alicia."

"Izzy, can you help?" I say.

"Sophie, come on," Izzy says. "I know Alicia too."

"This is hopeless," I say. "I can't tell anyone I'm Wendy. And you two are the only people who know."

Priya hums. "Can you message someone *from* your Wendy account?"

"I mean, sure, but it's not like I routinely talk to anyone on there—"

But then I think of who to ask.

**@dearwendywellesley:**
Hi
I don't usually like to admit defeat, but i have a question that
I don't know how to answer for reasons I cannot disclose
Would you be willing to help?

**@wandawellesley69:**
omg
i never thought you'd ask
hit me with it

**@dearwendywellesley:**
Don't make me regret this
Basically the situation is that the person who wrote to
me kind of likes two people
One is a close friend, the other is someone they just met
And they're not sure who to pursue

# CHAPTER 48

## Do You Need a Serious Answer?

### JO

God fucking damn it.

I didn't want to have to be the one giving Lianne advice. And in a roundabout way that would be hilarious if it weren't so infuriating, I now have to. Because Wendy doesn't know that I'm me, or that I'm in any way involved with this.

Maybe Wendy knows Lianne or something. And it's a conflict of interest for them or whatever. It wouldn't be hard; Lianne knows a lot of people at this school, way more people than I do.

The longer I wait, the longer I leave Wendy on read.

> **@wandawellesley69:**
> i think
> uh wait do you need a serious answer

> **@dearwendywellesley:**
> Yes

> **@wandawellesley69:**
> okay

is "pursue neither of them until you fucking figure yourself
out" an option?

**@dearwendywellesley:**
Oh!
I guess so
Minus the expletive
Thank you

**@wandawellesley69:**
happy to help

# CHAPTER 49

## Gets to the Point

### JO

"**W**ell, that's disappointing." Lianne frowns at her phone.

I look up at her from my spot on the couch in the common room. "What?"

"Look at Dear Wendy," she says.

I open up Instagram. The post is the first one on my feed.

Dear Yearning,

This isn't going to sound fun, but I think the best solution for you at the moment is to sit with it for a while. Figure out what you would really prefer before you decide what to do; there are so many possibilities for what could happen to you that I don't think you should make a move right away toward anyone. Try not to get yourself stuck in an awkward situation!

Best of luck,
Wendy

"It doesn't seem on brand for them," Lianne says. "This is such a short answer."

"Oh. Well . . . it—it gets to the point."

Lianne sighs. "It's just . . . usually there's so much more nuance. This is so little."

Yeah. Usually there is. When Wendy isn't asking *me* for the answer. I thought their answer would elaborate. Give Lianne a better explanation for why she shouldn't say anything.

"Maybe if you DM them, they'll explain further," I say.

"Hmm. Maybe."

# CHAPTER 50

## Appropriate

### SOPHIE

**@butler.lianne:**
hi! i hope this isn't super rude of me but
i'm the one who sent in the question in your last post
and i just felt like it was a little??? simple???
it seems like your usual advice is that things are complicated and there are many courses of action and i was
wondering if there was any way you could elaborate a
little
because i'm kind of feeling like i didn't get the full picture

Shit.

This is my fault. I really should've spent more time thinking about it. But I've been busy with coursework and all my other Dear Wendy posts, and the answer that Wanda gave seemed to be appropriate, so I went with it.

**@dearwendywellesley:**
Hi! I'm sorry that you're not feeling good about my answer, it
happens
Is there something specific you wanted more clarification
on?

**@butler.lianne:**
idk i guess i felt like there should be more?
sorry if that makes no sense

**@dearwendywellesley:**
Not a problem
Yeah so I do have a confession: I asked someone else for
help with your question
Which is why it might seem kind of brief
But I can elaborate more!
I think the main issue is that I don't necessarily know how
either of these other people feel about you, so that makes
it harder for me to know what the right choice for you to
make is
Like if you're certain your close friend doesn't feel the
same way (say, for example, they're a straight girl)
Then obviously you don't say anything because nothing
good could come of it
Does that make sense?

**@butler.lianne:**
yeah that does
wait uh
who did you ask for help? if you don't mind me asking

I stare at my phone screen for a moment. There can be no harm in
telling her, right?

**@dearwendywellesley:**
Don't let this get out to the public but
I asked Wanda
Sometimes you've got to consort with the enemy :/

**@butler.lianne:**
uh

        **@dearwendywellesley:**
I'm so sorry, I would've asked your permission to get outside
help, but you submitted anonymously and all

**@butler.lianne:**
no no it's just
that account is my roommate
uh. not the person i like. i live in a triple

Oh.
*Oh.*
"Priya?" I say, my voice eerily calm.
"Yes?"
"We have a problem."

I've been pacing around our room for at least five minutes now, rambling to Priya about how much I just can't believe Jo would keep up this charade for so long. It's not like her. She wouldn't. My friend would not do this to me, even if she didn't know it was me. There's no way.

"Call her," Priya says. "Maybe it's a mistake."

"How could it be a mistake?" I stop pacing and look at Priya. "Lianne messaged me."

"Well . . . I mean, maybe it's a joke? On Lianne's part?"

I shake my head. "I highly doubt that it's a joke."

What if it's not Jo? What if Lianne actually has a crush on Jo and it's Katy who's Wanda? At least that would be less humiliating. But Katy would not be the type to make an account like Wanda. And Lianne would know that Jo can't possibly like her back. And now that I think about it, the posts do sound like Jo.

How did I not see this earlier?

"You should call Jo," Priya repeats.

I know she's right, but . . .

"But then she'll know I'm Wendy!" I say.

"You already know she's Wanda!"

"Fine," I snap as I pull out my phone. "I'm calling her."

# CHAPTER 51

## I Fucked Up

### JO

"Jo, what the fuck?" Lianne says.

I look in her direction. "Huh? What's going on—"

At this moment, my phone rings, Sophie's contact appearing on the screen. My stomach drops—Sophie's never called me before.

"Lianne, sorry, I'm getting a call—" I go out into the hallway and answer the phone. "Hey, what's up?"

Sophie's voice comes through my phone, panicked. "Are you Sincerely, Wanda?"

My heart sinks to my stomach. "What—how—"

*"I'm Dear Wendy."*

And, well, now my heart drops approximately to my ankles. Am I hearing her right?

I look at my door, and I look at my feet, and I stand there, frozen.

Faintly, vaguely, I hear a tinny voice from my phone speaker.

"Jo? Jo, are you there? Hello?"

"Yeah. Um. How . . . how did you . . ."

Sophie starts explaining to me while I pace up and down my hallway. She got a question from Lianne. She thought knowing her would be a conflict of interest, so she decided to ask a neutral party. Lianne messaged her a few minutes ago asking for elaboration, and inadvertently told her who I was.

"And I just . . . why didn't you *tell me*?" Sophie says. "When I asked you for help? I—if *I* thought I was a conflict of interest, then *you*—"

"I didn't know you were you!" I say. "I thought you were just . . . some stranger! So why would I tell you who I am?"

"Why would it matter who I was? You shouldn't have given me any of that advice, given that you were now *clearly* acting in your *own* interest, complicating the efficacy of the response I was giving—"

I groan loudly. "How can you use *so many big words* while you're *arguing*?!"

"Oh, am I being pretentious now? What does that have to do with what we're talking about?"

"Why can't you answer a single question with an actual answer instead of another question?"

"You're doing the *same thing*, Jo!"

I take a breath and lean against the wall and slide down to sit on the floor and take another breath.

"I'm sorry for yelling," I mutter.

A pause. And then: "Yeah, sorry."

"But . . . so, you're Wendy."

"And you're Wanda."

"Why didn't you say anything?" I ask.

"Nobody knows except Priya and her girlfriend. The point is to keep it as confidential as possible."

"Well—but—I thought we were friends."

"Then why didn't *you* say anything?"

"Because it's embarrassing!" I say. "You were so cool, and smart, and you knew everything, and if you knew I ran this account where I make these *weird jokes* . . ." I trail off, not wanting to finish that sentence: *I thought you wouldn't want to be friends with me anymore.*

"You could've said something when I asked you to help me answer Lianne's question."

I squeeze my eyes shut. "And *you* could've answered the question a little better in your post so we wouldn't be in this situation to begin with."

"I wouldn't have answered it that way if you hadn't told me to."

"I didn't know that you would take my word so literally!"

I hear Sophie sigh loudly. For a minute, neither of us speak.

"I'm gonna need a bit," Sophie says. "Can we talk later?"

"Yeah."

"Okay. Bye."

"Bye."

I hang up, and I feel like I'm about to throw up. Sophie's mad at me, and this is not good.

When I go back inside, Lianne is sitting at the edge of the mattress, hands folded in her lap.

She looks at me and says, "I heard your call."

Shit. The walls in the Wellesley dorms are unbelievably thin. If Lianne heard everything on my side of the conversation, then she knows basically everything that just went down.

"I'm not mad," Lianne says. "But I just want to know something."

My response is meek, scared, exhausted. "Yeah?"

Lianne exhales, a shaky sound that threatens to destroy my entire sense of composure. "Why don't you want me to tell Katy?"

I have to own up to it.

"Because . . . because if you start dating each other, you—you'll start to ignore me. And hate me."

Lianne looks me up and down. For a split second, I think she's going to comfort me. *No, Jo, we'd never do that to you, you know us.*

But instead, Lianne says, "I can't believe you would be this selfish."

And then she stands up, pushes past me, and walks out the door. I hear a single sob echoing down the hall.

All I can do is lie on the wooden floor of my room and stare up at the ceiling, thinking about the many ways in which I fucked up.

# CHAPTER 52

## Lied

### SOPHIE

I don't know what to think. I don't know what to say. I didn't want it to be true, but it is: Jo lied to me. Or, well, maybe not lied, but she definitely didn't tell the whole truth.

My thoughts, or lack thereof, are interrupted by the sound of Priya's voice.

"Sophie, are you good there? I heard the whole call."

In response, I whine, flip over, and stuff my face in my pillow.

"Maybe you should've answered Lianne's question without consulting anyone."

I immediately flip back around and look at her. "You were the one who told me to ask for another opinion."

Priya raises her eyebrows. "Right. Yes. Apologies."

"I should not have taken your advice."

"You should not have. I'm sorry. Hey, what would you have said if you hadn't asked Wanda?"

I hum and sigh. "I don't know. Usually with crush things I say to suck it up and tell them, and if it ruins the friendship, then it wasn't a very strong friendship to begin with."

"And you didn't think this would apply to Lianne?"

"Well—I don't know! Knowing who she is made it so much harder! This is why my form is anonymous!"

"You answer non-anonymous messages in your DMs all the time," Priya says.

"And I've never *gotten* a DM from someone I know."

Priya rolls her eyes. "In any case, you kind of messed up."

"And it's kind of your fault too."

"I will only take . . ." She considers for a moment. "Twenty-eight percent of the blame."

I groan.

"Sophie, this is all for you to figure out, not me."

She's right. I don't like it, but she is.

I take down the post. I can't stand to even see it up now. And it's probably for the better. Otherwise Katy or Alicia might see it, and the idea of that makes me want to tear my hair out of my skull.

What do I do now?

# CHAPTER 53

## Chat

### SOPHIE

WGST 110 is excruciating the next day. I haven't talked to Jo; we sit next to each other, though, and I spend the whole class avoiding eye contact. Luckily, most of our class time is Professor Fineman giving us a lecture, but as soon as class is over, Jo leaves in a rush without so much as giving me a glance. I start gathering my things, and by the time I'm finished slowly sorting through all my notes, everyone is gone except Professor Fineman. She looks at me and smiles.

"No rush," she says. "Slow day?"

"A little bit," I say. "I don't know, I have a lot to think about."

"That's perfectly fine. Is there something we went over during class that I can clarify for you?"

"Oh, no. Um . . . no, it's just some personal things."

Professor Fineman nods. "Understandable." She pauses. "If you ever need to talk, you know where my office is."

The gesture is simple, but I could cry. "Thank you."

I'm about to step out of the classroom when I stop in my tracks. "Actually, do you have anything you need to do right now?"

Fineman shakes her head. "No, not for a while. Do you want to walk back to my office with me, and we can chat?"

I nod. "That would be great."

We start out the door, and she starts talking about how warm it is outside all of a sudden. I mention how the weather is just as unpredictable in the Midwest, and Professor Fineman tells me how she lived in Chicago for a few years in between getting her bachelor's and PhD.

"So," she says once we're seated in her office. "What is it you wanted to talk about?"

I sigh loudly, and it's so not worth her time, but I came all the way here, so I can't turn back now. "This is totally unrelated to school or WGST or anything, but I'm having a fight with a friend."

"Is it Jo?" she says. "I noticed how quickly they left class today."

I knew she was observant, but not *this* observant. "Um . . . yeah. Wow."

She chuckles at my surprise. "Professors notice more than you think. Do you just need a place to vent?"

"I guess. I mean—" How do I explain the entire situation to her?

It's a split-second choice. I've gone so long not telling almost any-one I'm Dear Wendy, but now that Jo knows, and Lianne probably knows too . . . and it's not like Professor Fineman would tell anyone, especially not any students. I bet she doesn't even know what Dear Wendy is.

"How much do you know about Wellesley's social media culture?" I ask her.

"I probably don't know nearly as much as you and your peers," she says. "But I am aware that Twitter is very important."

"So, there's also a considerable subculture on Instagram . . ."

Before long, I've explained way too much about Wellesley social media. Fineman thinks the ice cream account is pretty great, and she's perplexed by the one that posts random patches of grass. I save the Dear Wendy stuff for last.

"Oh my goodness," she says as she scrolls through the posts on my phone. "You've posted all this on your own?"

"I've asked my roommate for help a few times," I say, tugging on my ponytail to keep it in place.

"How long have you been running this account again?"

"Since November."

"Oh my goodness," she says again. "This really takes commitment. How much time do you put into this?"

"Does that include the time I spend reading self-help books?"

"You do research for this?"

"Well, yeah!" I say. "It's so cool."

Fineman laughs. "Are you, by any chance, thinking of majoring in psychology or WGST?"

"I want to double major in those two," I say, blushing. "But . . . I feel like that doesn't have much to do with Dear Wendy." Based on Fineman's expression, I can tell she thinks I'm wrong, but I keep going. "I mean, I can't tell people my opinion without having information to back it up, right? That's Wanda's thing."

She frowns. "Wanda?"

"Oh. Right. Uh, could I just ask that you not tell anyone about anything I'm going to say?"

"Of course," Fineman says. "Unless someone is directly in harm or you're clearly violating the college's honor code."

"Oh, no, it's nothing like that," I say.

So then I start explaining it to her, how I found out about the account and immediately started a somewhat-ironic feud with them, and I get through everything up to what happened last weekend. For a split second, I consider not telling her that Jo is Wanda, but I trust that she's not going to say anything to anyone.

As I'm talking, I realize how childish this all sounds, and I hope Professor Fineman isn't judging me too badly. It's literally been one day since we fought, but I already miss Jo and my Wendy account. I miss how fun it is to comment on each other's posts. I miss texting her my random thoughts instead of broadcasting them on Twitter. I miss the way she mocks me for my type A Wendy-like tendencies. It's funny how she calls me a Wendy so much; almost like she knew all along.

"And I guess . . . I guess I'm worried that I've completely screwed up everything," I say, my voice catching. "What if—what if she never wants to talk to me again? I just . . . I feel like I've been such a bad friend. I should've told her I'm Wendy, I should've been more helpful with my answer, and I generally should've been more honest with her, and I definitely shouldn't have gotten so mad at her on the phone. I mean, I've told her so much stuff. She even knows about my 'mommy issues,' as she calls it."

I can barely see through the tears welling up in my eyes and the hair falling in my face. I blink hard and tuck my stray hairs back.

The way Fineman is looking at me, it's not exactly a look of pity, but it's not judgmental either. I can't possibly predict what she's going to say.

Her eventual response is pretty much the last thing I'd expect: "Mommy issues?"

"Oh. Uh. That's a whole other thing."

She presses her lips together. "We can get to that some other time. Sophie, it sounds like you already know what you need to do now. You know what you did wrong, and you want to apologize to your friends, right?"

"No," I say with my arms crossed.

Professor Fineman laughs. "You *don't* want to apologize?"

"Well, I want Jo to apologize first."

"So you gave me this explanation of everything you did wrong, but you want Jo to apologize first?"

The way she says it, it sounds really bad. "Well, I just—I feel like I need some time."

"That's understandable," she says. "You can give it some time. But don't wait for her to talk first. Talk when you're ready."

I suppose she's right. "Okay."

"Anyway," Fineman says, "is there anything else you haven't had the chance to talk about yet?"

I shake my head.

"How about we talk about something else to take your mind off of things for a little bit? I'm very curious to hear more about your Dear Wendy Instagram."

I leave Fineman's office with her cell phone number saved into my contacts. She tells me it's nothing special, that she always puts it on the syllabus in case students have any emergencies, but I think this is an invitation to talk to her again if I ever need to.

I don't know if I'm going to talk to Jo yet. I'm not sure I'm ready to forgive her. But at least I have Professor Fineman to talk to.

# CHAPTER 54

## That's So Long

### JO

It takes just over one day of me and Lianne being mad at each other for Katy to finally say something. I'm surprised she noticed so soon; it's not hard for us to avoid each other when we have such different schedules. At least she hasn't seen Wendy's post. It's not on the account anymore.

I come back to our room with my dinner in hand. I grabbed a salad to go from the dining hall, thinking I could eat in peace since Lianne has Ultimate Frisbee practice and Katy likes to paint in Jewett, the arts center, but Katy is actually in our room, picking at a plate of rigatoni.

"Oh, hey, Jo!" she says when I come in. "Didn't think you'd be back so soon."

"Ah, yeah," I say. "Um, I left class pretty quickly."

She tilts her head, lips pressed together. "Is everything okay? I've noticed you've been a little out of it these last few days."

I really, *really* don't want to explain what's been going on to Katy. I start putting down my things and sit cross-legged on the floor next to her.

"I'm fine," I reply.

She rolls her eyes. "You're obviously not. Are you and Lianne fighting? I can tell you haven't been talking much."

Katy and her mom friend tendencies.

I sigh and lie down on the ground. "I messed up."

It's worse than Lianne being mad at me. Sophie's mad at me too. All because I didn't want things to change.

All because I don't want to be alone.

I'm aware Katy's staring at me, waiting for an answer. But I can't explain it.

"I . . ." I take a labored breath. "I hate it."

"Hate what?"

"I hate . . . this little voice in my head. Telling me that . . . that I won't be happy without a relationship. That I'll be forever alone, and I'll have to do life by myself, without anyone to help me. And all my friends will forget about me."

And yeah, I know it makes no sense to Katy why I'm talking about this. This fear can't possibly be a disagreement between me and Lianne.

But she doesn't question it. She gives me a pitying look and says, "Even if all of your friends find their *literal soulmate*, Jo, I promise they won't forget about you. I won't."

I swallow hard, tears welling up in my eyes. "But what if—" *What if you and Lianne do get together, and you do forget about me? What if Sophie never forgives me, and I lose the one friend I have who's like me?* "What if that *does* happen?"

Katy smiles sadly, watching as the tears start falling down my cheeks.

She reaches out and puts a hand on mine, coaxing me to sit up. "Hey. That's just what your brain's telling you. But it's wrong. We *do* care about you. We love you."

I press my face against her shoulder and start sobbing.

"What if—what if she stays mad at me forever?"

"Lianne? Come on, Jo, she forgives so easily."

"N-no," I choke out. "Sophie."

I feel Katy's grip loosen for a moment in her confusion.

"Well," Katy says, "I don't know why Sophie is mad at you. But . . . she seems nice. I don't think she'd hold a grudge."

"Oh, she would."

"Then . . . I don't know, give her a couple of weeks."

A couple of *weeks*?

"That's so long!" I wail. And I return to sobbing on Katy's shoulder.

Needless to say, I take an unannounced break from posting on Sincerely, Wanda. If anyone asks—which I'm sure nobody will—I can blame it on midterms. Perpetual midterms season and all that.

Wendy—well, Sophie—isn't posting much either. According to Katy, who's been checking Dear Wendy while I'm in a perpetually shitty mood, Wendy's story said that they'll be on a brief hiatus. One Wellesley student tweeted that it's probably because of the drama from the roommate post; "just look at how banal their last post was," they said.

Sophie will probably just let them believe that. I would.

It's ironic, isn't it? The whole school blew up over a huge dramatic Dear Wendy post, but what silenced Wendy and Wanda was an unrelated, boring question about having a crush.

# CHAPTER 55

## *Over*

### SOPHIE

'm still mad at Jo, and Jo is still mad at me, so we cancel our Dianas meeting for the week. Nobody was going to show up for it anyway.

Priya tries to comfort me and get me to let go of everything, but I shrug her off every time. I elect instead to immerse myself in the rest of my life. I finish a short essay for my writing class in one sitting. I go on extra runs, which is easy now that the weather is getting warmer. I borrow a camera from the technology center to help take some photos of the library for a story in the *Wellesley News*.

"At some point, you're going to have to talk about it," Priya tells me one morning.

"Not yet," I insist.

"You can't be mad at Jo forever."

"I can."

"Well, you can't just stop posting on Dear Wendy."

"I can."

"Oh, come on. You know you don't want to end Dear Wendy."

"Maybe I do."

But she's right. I don't. I love being Wendy. I just need some time.

Time to do what, I'm not sure. But I can't confront this right now.

About a week after finding out Jo is Wanda, I run out of things to busy myself with. I've finished all my assignments, studied for my math exam, written and edited an article for the *Wellesley News* about a queer BIPOC professor attaining tenure, and even gone on an extra run.

I look at my calendar app, hoping for something—anything—I need to do, and I spot an entry for our next Dianas meeting.

We can't cancel it again. And we can't have it with just three people again.

Jo and I never made that new flyer and Instagram account. We got so caught up in other things, it just fell out of our minds. So I guess I should do that now.

I play some music—Taylor Swift's *folklore*, unshuffled—and open Canva to design the flyer from a template. I use lots of earthy tones to make it warm and inviting, and I swap out the existing clip art on it with a picture of a few people talking. Before "my tears ricochet" ends, I'm all done.

I make the Instagram account for the Dianas. Nothing fancy in the name, just @wellesleydianas. I want to post it now, but . . . yeah, I should show this to Jo first.

Reluctantly, I pull up my text messages and send the JPEG file to Jo.

She replies almost instantly, *it looks fine you can post it,* and that's it.

Maybe I should ask how she's doing. Or if she wants to talk. But I don't want to do that because that means we'll have to actually talk to each other, and at the moment, I would rather eat dirt.

I thumbs-up-react to her text and post the graphic, then repost it to my own story. And now I think I'll turn off my phone and go to bed early because I just want the day to be over.

# CHAPTER 56

## Or, You Know, Whatever

### JO

should repost it, shouldn't I?

I don't have a lot of Instagram followers. Most of them are people from high school. So I don't know if it'll really do anything. But I don't want Sophie madder at me than she already is.

Maybe I should post it as Wanda? I have a lot more followers there. And they're all Wellesley people.

Before I can tell myself not to do it, I open the Wanda account. It can't look too suspicious that I'm only sharing this one post, so maybe I'll just go on a sharing frenzy.

I type out a quick little blurb to include in my first story post:

```
hello everybody. it has come to my
attention that there is a world outside
of me giving questionable relationship
advice. turns out you might have other
    interests too. so i'm going to boost
      a few orgs that i think would
          benefit some of you.
```

I share posts from our Office of LGBTQ+ Services, the Sexual Health Educators, the queer South Asian org, the queer Latinx/e org, the trans and nonbinary org, and, finally, the Dianas.

```
as an a-spec person myself it
means a lot to see an org that
puts together people like me!
   or. you know. whatever.
```

Check for typos, post to story.
Done.

# CHAPTER 57

## Back to Square One

### JO

"Jo?" Katy says. "You're going to want to see this."

That's never a good sign.

I've just woken up, and I'm still feeling a little groggy, but what Katy said makes me shoot up and out of bed. I walk over to her bunk, where she turns her phone and shows me Sidechat.

Sidechat is this anonymous app where college students can all post things for everyone else at their college to see. I don't use it because it's kind of boring most of the time. I rub my eyes and read the post on Katy's phone.

---

### wait wanda's ace??? lol????

---

"People are talking about you," Katy says. "This one is very mild, and most of the posts are just people saying 'Oh, wow, that's cool,' but there's one that's just, like, awful. I didn't want to show it to you."

"Oh no."

"It already has a ton of downvotes—" she tries to explain, but I'm already opening Instagram. I have ten DM notifications. I feel my pulse pounding in my ears as I tap the screen to see them all.

This isn't so bad. I have a question from someone, as usual. And an org saying thanks for promoting them. And a person saying another org sounds cool. And a couple of people saying it makes a ton of sense that an a-spec person would be able to be snarky like this.

And a message request from an account I recognize from our second Dianas meeting. One of the people that Hannah told us to block.

This is not good.

**@tracy_campbell_:**
"as an a-spec person"?
why have you been giving us love/sex advice this whole time?

"Hey, Jo," Katy says. "Don't go on Twitter right now. They're kind of fighting about you."

No. This can't be happening. Please, no.

Everyone's talking about me? Well, not me, but Wanda, and Wanda is me. No, no, no, no, no. No.

I think I'm going to be sick.

I never should have started this account. Now all the attention is on me. And some people are mad.

Maybe they're right. Maybe I shouldn't be doing any Wanda stuff at all, and I should sit alone and be sad that I'll never understand anything that anyone is talking about. I mean, I do get it, but I don't get why they feel the things they do. Because I don't know what that feels like. And I never will. I will grow up and get a job and buy a house and get old and never know what it's like to be in love.

I hate it. I can't be in love, and I'm so pathetically lonely all the time. I shouldn't pretend I know what I'm saying or doing. And now Lianne is mad at me, and Sophie hates me, and it's all because I thought it would be funny to start this account.

I'm back to square one. No ace friends. No support. Nothing.

My thumb hovers over the keyboard on Instagram. I squeeze my eyes shut and lock my phone. There's nothing I can say right now.

Katy says, "Hey, are you okay?"

"Yeah," I find myself saying even as I'm fighting back tears. "I'm fine. Don't worry about me."

# CHAPTER 58

## Response

### SOPHIE

When Priya tells me that Jo has become this week's Wellesley social media main character, I have no idea what she's talking about. I've barely touched my phone lately, and I definitely haven't been on social media. But as soon as she explains—Wanda casually mentioned that they're a-spec, and now the whole school is talking about it—I grow panicked.

"Why did you tell me this?" I say, almost yelling. "I was having a perfectly good day! This is terrible!"

"First of all, it's nine in the morning," Priya says. "The day has barely begun. But also, wait, are you mad at me right now?"

"No!" I yell, and then I will my voice to soften. "Sorry. No. I'm—god, why? Why would she do that?"

"I think a better question," Priya says, "is why so many people are talking about it."

She's right. "No, yeah, that's—that's awful. Holy shit. Should I say something?"

I kind of want to say something. If I, as Wendy, show Wanda my support, maybe people will back down. And maybe they'll find something else to talk about.

"I thought you were still mad at Jo," Priya says, lifting an eyebrow.

"Well, yeah, for keeping being Wanda a secret, not for being Wanda. This is just—" I break off into a sigh. "I need to say something."

"To Jo? Or just in general?"

"Um . . . in general?"

Priya looks visibly disappointed in me, but she says, "Then you should go and do that."

I start drafting a post saying that people should leave Wanda alone, but no, that's too dramatic, isn't it? Maybe I can find a Dear Wendy question and then just casually slip in that people should stop taking internet discourse so seriously. Yeah, okay. I can do that. Except as I scroll through my submissions, which have been accumulating since I haven't been keeping up with them, I don't find any that I can possibly use to talk about internet drama.

But there is one about being aromantic. How fortuitous.

Before I know it, I'm typing up a response. And then I read it over. And post.

Dear Wendy,

I know this is usually a romance account, but I was hoping you'd be able to answer my question. I'm aromantic, and I've come to accept this after years of wondering why I didn't understand so much about other people, but now I'm feeling lost. How do I exist in a world with so few people like me?

Thanks,
Lonely

Dear Lonely,

I can tell you this for sure: You're not the only one who's scared of being alone. Plenty of people, allo or a-spec alike, worry about the ramifications of singledom every day.

That being said, being aromantic doesn't mean you have to spend your life alone. You didn't disclose whether you're also asexual, but whether or not that's the case, romantic partners are not the only kind of life partners. There are many, *many* options for how to live your life with at least one other human being. A roommate, a family member, a kid, a platonic partner, a friend with benefits (if that's what you're looking for)—you're not limited to either living with a romantic partner or living alone.

If you're looking for more support, there's a new org for a-spec students that just started—I've tagged them in this post. There's been a lot of chatter about it with regard to Wanda, and all I'll say is that as an a-spec person myself, I'm glad some students have taken the initiative to provide a space for those of us who might want it, especially when aphobia still runs rampant even in the Wellesley community.

Lots of love,
Wendy

# CHAPTER 59
## Comments

### SOPHIE

At first, the comments aren't so bad. They're pretty supportive, and I'm not mad that my page is getting a bit more engagement than usual.

**maisielenort546 14m**
lol did dear wendy just come out?
2 likes Reply

> **mcnolty.talia.19 9m**
> ^ we love you wendy!
> 1 like Reply

**wellesleygsa 47m**
We love to see support for our a-spec sibs!
4 likes Reply

**e.vie.dawson 26m**
Yesssss shoutout to the Dianas for being a super welcoming space!
Reply

The comment from Evelyn is especially nice. I'm glad she's been enjoying our meetings so far. But, as expected, soon after I post my response, this happens:

**carlystewart01 12m**
uhh have we all been trusting an aromantic/asexual person to give us love advice?
Reply

> **briannapeterson12 9m**
> and the timing of this announcement . . . when wanda just pulled the same shit . . . yikes
> Reply

> **saoirseflanagan 5m**
> Hey Wendy never specified their specific identity, maybe don't assume?
> 1 like Reply

> **lilyreyes.jpg 2m**
> **@saoirseflanagan** ^^ and even if they were aroace that shouldn't invalidate their work, this shit takes tons of research,, like i'd like to see you try to tell someone how to break up with their long term partner
> Reply

I'm glad that Saoirse Flanagan and Lily Reyes have come to my defense—even if I don't know who they are—but . . . these other comments. They sort of makes sense: Why *would* I be the person who should be doling out this kind of life advice? What does it say about me that I'm telling so many people what to do with their love lives when I don't have or want one for myself?

I work so hard at being Wendy. I've read self-help books to be a better Wendy. I've been considering taking WGST 205, a class on love and intimacy, to be a better Wendy. I do so much work learning about stuff that will *never* apply to my life, just for this Instagram account. And yet, two little comments like that are still enough to bother me.

It's fine. I've gotten through worse emotional turmoil before, and I did it on my own, and I was fine. A few Instagram comments are nothing.

Right?

At the worst possible moment, my mom calls.

I've been lying in bed all morning, trying not to think about the comments. It hasn't been going well. Answering this call will probably just make it worse. Or maybe it won't.

I slide the bar to answer her WeChat video call, and she comes up on screen, dyed-dark hair tied in a low ponytail that looks as neat and tidy as mine, free of flyaways.

"Hey, Mom," I say.

"Hi, sweetie!" she says. She turns the camera, and there's my dad, too, sitting next to her on the couch.

She only calls me "sweetie" when she's being nice and doting and there's nothing wrong. In other words, she called me because she misses me, which would be nice if I weren't absolutely exhausted at the moment.

"Is everything all right?" I ask anyway.

"Yes, we just miss you."

I mean, I do miss them too. I think a lot about how much I wish they accepted me better, but on pretty much all counts except for my sexuality and my choice of schooling, my parents are the ideal parents. They provide for me, they care about me, and they're generally supportive of most things I do.

"Are you okay?" Dad asks, seeing that I haven't said anything in return.

I try to come up with something significant enough to talk about, but not *too* dire, but not something that'll make them mad, but not something I'll have to explain a lot, and—

I've got nothing.

A lump forms in my throat as I remember my fight with Jo. That is dire. It might make her mad. I might have to do a lot of explaining.

"Uh, Mama, can I just talk to you for a bit?" I say.

"Wow," Dad teases. "No appreciation for me?"

"Um . . . it's girl stuff?"

It's not girl stuff. But my dad has the emotional intelligence of a house-plant, so he's going to be no help with this. Mom witnessed the entire downfall of my friendship with Oliver. I don't think she was actually that helpful, but she's better than nothing, and I really, *really* don't want to talk to anyone else about it.

My dad says goodbye to me and leaves my mom in the living room.

"Okay," I say. "So. I had a fight with my friend."

"Which friend?" Mom asks.

"You, um, don't know about her."

I tell my mom that I met Jo in WGST and became friends with her. I leave out the Dianas and the Wendy accounts; it's all a bit too complicated for me to explain to her, even if I wanted to. But I tell her we got into a fight about "something I posted on Instagram," and my mom immediately says, "Oh, that so silly, Lèle."

"What?" *Is she saying I'm being silly, or Jo?*

"Abby show me your Instagram sometimes. Nothing to fight about."

"Uh—wait, she?—okay. Um." I'm not going to bother saying that it wasn't on my personal account. "Yeah. It was all kind of a big misunder-standing. And then we kind of started yelling at each other. And now we haven't talked since then."

"Do you want to talk to her?" she asks. "Or do you want to be mad?"

Of all the things she could've asked me, this is not what I expected. "I . . . kind of want to be mad. I don't know."

"You can be mad for a little. I am mad a lot."

"But isn't it kind of bad to be mad?" I ask.

She sighs. "That is what a lot of people think. But being mad is good sometimes. If you hold it in, you will be more mad later. Same with when you are sad or tired."

"I know. You tell me that sometimes."

"Like when Oliver stop talking to you," Mom says. Oh no, I knew she'd bring him up. "You hold in being sad for a long time. And then what? You sad for a long time! And now you still a little sad!"

"What? No! I've moved on from that!" I've told her so many times.

"You can move on and be sad," Mom says. Then she switches to Mandarin, saying: "It's true, you don't want to be friends with him anymore, but you might always be a little sad about that, and also a little angry. He was your best friend, and now you only talk when we eat dinner at his house. I saw the last time we went. You looked miserable that he seemed not to like you at all."

As much as I don't want it to be true, I think she's right. It really sucked, over spring break, to be eating his family's food—his mom is Taiwanese, and his dad is Mexican, so the food is amazing—and watching our parents and sisters enjoy each other's company, knowing that the two of us resented each other so much. I left as soon as I finished my dinner.

"I don't care if he doesn't like me," I say.

"You care a lot." Mom scoffs.

"What? I don't care if anyone likes me. That was, like, my whole thing in high school."

"You pretend you don't care," Mom says. "But you care a lot."

Oh.

Oh my god.

Jo hates me right now. The *whole school* hates me right now.

Spontaneously, I burst into tears.

"Aiya, Lèle, bié kū!" Mom says, trying to stem my sobs. "It is okay to care if people like you! Everybody cares!"

"But—but I—" I don't even know what I'm trying to say. "But it's better if I don't care! Because then I'm happier!"

Mom clicks her tongue. "You have to learn to be happy even though some people don't like you. That is just life."

"Then I hate life!" I wail.

My mom just looks more exasperated than anything else, which is pretty much what always happens if anyone starts crying around her. She hates watching people cry.

"Not everybody has to like you," she says, returning to Chinese. "Just the people you like. And if they don't like you, you don't like them either."

"What if everyone hates me?" I ask.

"No!" Mama says with a groan. "Everybody does not hate you. Shǎ háizi."

She finally gets me to calm down after this. I've pretty much cried out all my tears. All Mom can really do is sit there and watch, which is a little pathetic now that I think about it, but it's not like she can physically send hugs.

"I leave you alone now, okay?" Mom says. "Take a nap. You are tired."

"I'm not tired." I am tired. "Okay, fine, I'm a little tired."

"Okay. Bye, Lèle."

"Oh. Bye."

And that's it.

Phone calls with my family always end a bit abruptly; it's just who we are, with no time to waste, no willingness to dawdle.

So I am left alone once more.

Priya has Izzy over in the evening. I can hear them talking and laughing from down the hall as soon as the elevator comes up. But when Priya opens the door and the two of them step in, they both pause.

"Are you okay?" Izzy asks.

I realize that I am fully cocooned in my blankets, and that's how the two of them are seeing me. I probably look like I'm sick, and I might as well be. I've spent much of the day avoiding the outside world after my call with my mom. I even skipped class. I never do that.

Being holed up in my room is actually pretty nice. There's lots to do all by yourself. This afternoon, I read a sapphic romance novel in one sitting, ate half a bag of microwave popcorn, took a nap like my mom told me to, and staged a wedding and then a funeral with the stuffed animals on my bed. (I have a series of pictures on my phone to commemorate the occasions.)

"I'm fine," I mutter, and then I turn and face the wall.

The two of them whisper something to each other that I can't hear, and then I feel my mattress sink down with someone's weight.

"Are you sure you're okay?" Izzy asks again.

I don't respond. I want to make them go away. I just don't want to talk about this right now. Or about anything.

"She's definitely not," Priya says.

I finally turn around and look at them. Sure enough, Izzy's sitting on the edge of my bed, looking at me with a concerned expression.

"There you are. What's going on?" she asks, even though she's probably heard the whole story from Priya already.

I don't want to tell her. Izzy will leave me alone if I tell her to.

But Priya's not going to let it go, even if Izzy would.

"Jo and I are fighting," I admit. "And now people are fighting about Wendy and Wanda. And I called my mom, and she was, like, kind of helpful? But also, she dug way too deep into the recesses of my mind and told me how I *actually* feel, and now I feel worse."

Izzy gapes at me. "You're fighting with Jo?"

Okay, so maybe Priya didn't tell her the whole story.

The two of them manage to coax me to sit up and explain everything to Izzy. I run through it all, and Izzy sits there, nodding and listening. Priya is on her bed and plays a game on her phone, which I don't blame her for since she's already heard this from me so many times, but Izzy gives her a sharp look, and Priya puts the phone away. Once I get through everything—call with Mom included—Izzy looks off into the distance for a moment.

"I think your mom was right," Izzy says.

"I hate that," I say.

"Like it or not, she is right about a lot of things," Izzy says. "You may fight with her sometimes about being aroace or going to Wellesley, but those are, like, the only things you really disagree about, right?"

"She also thinks we shouldn't tax the rich," I say.

"That's not what I meant," Izzy says, chuckling. "But, yeah, she is right that you need to feel liked. Even in high school when everyone thought you were a bitch because all you cared about was getting good grades and making the yearbook, I know you pretended it didn't affect you, but I think it did."

I grimace. "Yeah. Maybe."

"Also, regarding the Wendy stuff," Izzy says, "it's all going to blow over in a few days. It always does."

"Are you sure?" I say.

"That's just how internet drama works," she says.

"But this is different!" I say. "This time, people don't know it's me! So it's more interesting, and they'll keep on talking about it for longer because they don't care about whose feelings are getting hurt!"

"Counterpoint," Priya says. "Because they don't have a real person's name attached to the drama, you're completely safe from rumors about you. Nobody knows that they're talking about Sophie Chi when they're talking about Dear Wendy. Wendy is just a disembodied figure. Didn't someone figure out who that nightmare roommate was, like, two hours after that post went up? That's not going to be you."

"Yeah, that was kind of bad," I admit. "I probably shouldn't have posted it, but even I wanted to see where the drama would go."

"We are all susceptible to the drama," Izzy solemnly says.

"The point is," Priya says, "you're going to be fine. You can wait for it to blow over, and since nobody even knows that you're Wendy, you're not going to get a bunch of weird stares and whatnot wherever you go. To the whole school, Sophie Chi is just some random first year, or if they're *really* in tune with campus culture, they *might* recognize you from the *Wellesley News*."

As much as I want to disagree with them, I know Priya and Izzy are right. Nobody knows that Wendy is me. People will stop talking about Wendy and Wanda soon, and I will get out of it, reputation undamaged. I just need to wait it out.

"But that doesn't fix my thing with Jo," I say.

Izzy and Priya give each other a look. They seem to communicate a lot just from a couple of facial expressions; they've always been scarily good at that. Priya shrugs; Izzy turns back around.

"So from what I understand," Izzy says, "you and Jo are mad at each other because . . . you didn't tell each other you were Wendy and Wanda?"

"Sort of," I say. "I don't know. I'm kind of mad about other stuff."

"About what exactly?" Izzy asks.

I think for a moment. "Well, Jo gave me that really bad advice about her roommate's whole situation. And I'm kind of mad about all the times Jo was so rude to me as Wanda because I don't think they would ever do that to my face in real life. And . . . I guess I'm a little mad I spent so long hating Wanda when it was really just Jo having a bit of fun."

"Hmm," Izzy says. "That last one is interesting."

It is a bit interesting, isn't it? But as soon as I said it, it made sense. I'm mad at Jo, sure, but I'm also mad at myself. Why did I take all of this so seriously? Why did I think that everything Wanda said to me was a personal attack? Why couldn't I just focus on what I actually run this account for: to give people advice about their lives?

"Sophie, have you considered that maybe it's time for you and Jo to just talk to each other?" Priya says. "It sounds like it was all a bit of a misunderstanding. I mean, you're always going on about how communication is important."

"I—but—" I stammer. Except I don't really have anything to say to that either.

"You can't keep ignoring each other forever," Izzy says. "Or else you'll end up like you and Oliver."

I get what she's trying to say—Oliver and I stopped being friends because he stopped talking to me, and then I refused to talk to him. But I am not in the same situation right now.

"This isn't like that," I say. "Oliver was clearly in the wrong there."

"He probably doesn't see it that way," Izzy says.

"You're not even friends with him. Don't play devil's advocate with me."

"Don't bring up devil's advocate in my presence," Priya says. "I've had enough of that from those annoying moderates who are really just conservatives who don't want to admit their opinions to you."

Oh, the things being into politics in high school will do to you.

"Anyway," Izzy says, "you and Jo can't ignore each other forever. Even if it's for no other reason, you have a club to run. So you should at least gain closure on this. But really, you should just apologize because you are partly in the wrong for exploding on her so much."

She's right. "God, why do you have to be so right about everything?"

Izzy smiles serenely. "It's payback for all the times you knocked some sense into me whenever I panicked about something insignificant in high school."

"This is not insignificant," I insist.

"It is to everyone else except you and Jo," Priya says, which earns her a glare from Izzy. "Sorry, but it's true!"

If nothing else, I at least feel better now that I've hashed this out with my friends. I'm not sure what to do next, but I'm out of my funk.

After we eat dinner, and now that I'm on a full stomach, I come to my senses and apologize to the two of them for taking up their time. They visit each other to spend quality time together, not to help me with my silly problems.

"It's okay," Izzy says. "You've done the same for me."

"Yeah, but it's different."

"I don't think it's that different," she says, and then she and Priya look at each other in that cute way that they do.

"If we were really that bothered by your presence, we would have left you alone all afternoon," Priya adds.

"No," Izzy says, eyebrows shooting up. "We wouldn't have."

"No, we wouldn't have," Priya immediately repeats.

I chuckle. "Thanks, guys."

I go to bed early, leaving the two of them to hang out and chat in the common room.

I don't know when I'll be ready to do anything about this whole situation. For tonight, I'm going to take three milligrams of melatonin and go to sleep.

# CHAPTER 60

## That Scene in Little Women

### JO

I saw Sophie's post yesterday. I wanted to talk to her about it right away. She didn't have to do that, you know? She must have seen how people were talking about Wanda. And instead of letting me take all the hate, she put herself into the mix.

But I don't even know what to say.

It probably doesn't help that Lianne still isn't talking to me and Katy still doesn't know what's going on. I haven't even told my parents any of it. Everyone's going to tell me that I should suck it up and apologize, but I can't.

Because what if Sophie doesn't want to hear it?

What if she's already moved on?

Just like everybody else who used to be in my life.

It's only been, like, a week or two, but I'm sure that's enough time to go on without me. She's already started making Wendy posts again. Just that one, but still.

It's fine. I'm fine. I'll just keep on doing what I was doing before Wanda, before everything exploded in my face. I was perfectly happy then: no Sophie, no Dianas, no Wendy/Wanda rivalry.

But at least then, I had Lianne and Katy.

It's been so painful living in the same room as Lianne. Even more painful than back in September when we were arguing about her alarm clock being too loud or my computer screen being too bright at night. Right now I can barely stand to be in the same room as her.

Katy has tried talking to me about it, and she's probably tried to talk to Lianne, too, but neither of us have told her anything. So now she's been a little pissed at me too.

I want to go home.

Luckily, I'm able to go home whenever I want.

On the drive back, Mom wastes no time, immediately asking me what's wrong as soon as my seat belt is buckled. Sometimes, I really like this about her, how she gets to the point so quickly instead of dawdling like Mama tends to, but today, I can't be quick with my answer.

She doesn't know about my Wanda account. Neither of my parents do. I never really got around to telling them because they're definitely too old to understand Instagram. But at this point, I think it's time.

So I explain it to her: Wellesley's many Instagrams, Dear Wendy, the thing with Katy's ex. The feud Sophie and I had that now feels very short-lived.

When I finally catch up to the present—my fight with Sophie and Lianne, the Dianas post, Sophie's subsequent post—Mom hums and nods, and I know that she knows what's really bothering me.

"Is this about being 'forever alone' again?" Mom says.

I close my eyes and press my lips together. It is, isn't it?

As soon as Lianne and Sophie got mad at me, I convinced myself that they didn't want to be friends with me anymore. When I started seeing all those tweets and DMs, I was brought back to the realities of my lonesome life.

I hear the thunks of my mom switching the gear shift, and I open my eyes. We're home.

"You know that scene in *Little Women*?" I ask. "The Greta Gerwig one. Where Jo's in the attic with Marmee talking about how sick she is of feeling like her only purpose is to be in love."

"You always cry when we get to that scene," Mom says. "I knew we shouldn't have called you Jo, it made you too attached to her." She shakes her head. "Anyway, what about that scene?"

I take a breath. "I just . . . I just feel like, that's how I feel, all the time. Every day. There's that . . . nagging feeling, you know? It's . . . it's there when I wake up, it's there when I go to bed. It's there when I'm with my friends, or by myself, or watching a romcom on Netflix. That . . . that my life doesn't matter as much. That once we're all grown up, I won't be relevant. That everybody actually hates me. Because I can't love people the way everyone else does. So they won't love me at all."

Mom doesn't say anything for a moment. She looks at me in a way I can't dissect, maybe a little comforting, a little sad. She places her hand on top of mine.

"Jonie, sweetheart," she finally says. "Your life is just as important as anybody else's in this world."

"So . . . very unimportant?" There are billions of people in the world. I'm just one.

She chuckles. "No. *Extremely* important. Because there are so many people who hold *so much* love for you. Not everyone is so foolish as to believe that the only important form of love is romantic." *Foolish.* That's a new one. "And your friends don't hate you. That's why they're your friends."

I don't know what it is about the way she says that, but it absolutely wrecks me.

I've never had a stable group of friends before. I've had no reason to believe that people like me.

"I know it's hard to think about your future," Mom continues. "When I was your age, I wasn't even sure if I *had* a future. A future that I wanted, in any case. I thought I'd meet a guy and have an unhappy marriage and have to cook and clean and whatnot, all day, every day, for the rest of my life, because that was all I knew I could do."

"And then you met Mama. I know." I've heard this spiel from Mom a gazillion times: After she properly fell in love, all the things she couldn't imagine doing were now her goals, her aspirations, her dreams, because she wanted to do them with Mama.

"No, no, Jonie, you're skipping a few steps." She clicks her tongue and unbuckles her seat belt. "Before I could fall in love with a woman, I had to *accept* that I would someday fall in love with a woman. That that wasn't wrong of me, that that was my reality. I had to find people like me, to show me that that was who I really was, and it wasn't something I could just hide or suppress or hope would go away."

"So what are you saying?" I ask, even though I think I know where she's going with this.

"Honey, I know you've identified as aroace for nearly three years now, but I think that maybe, you're still not comfortable with it yet. And that you've decided that your singledom means you're not as deserving of love, not as *human* as those around you. And Jonie, you *need* to let go of that." She puts a hand over mine. "Because it's holding you back. You are worthy of love." I think there are tears in her eyes. "Everyone is."

Oh.

"But how—how am I supposed to get past that?" I ask. "Literally everybody thinks that the only way to be happy and find companionship is to fall in love."

"Not everybody is telling you that," Mom says. "Yes, the media and pop culture and everything have yet to catch up, but haven't you been telling me all about that club you and Sophie started? Don't you think maybe those people have something in common with you?"

Right. They do.

In our few meetings, we haven't talked that extensively about existing in the wider world, but there must be people who feel the same as me. There have to be.

"So," Mom continues, "just like how my college friends showed me how I could live authentically and happily, yours can too. They can probably give you better advice than I can, if I'm being honest."

I nod, looking down at my lap.

"Now," Mom says, "let's go inside. Mama made matzah ball soup." My comfort meal.

I love my parents.

"Jonie?" whispers a voice outside my door.

I'm lying down in my bed after dinner. My parents are taking me back to school tomorrow morning because Mama thinks I need a good night's sleep, and "that dorm bed will do you no good at helping you relax."

"Yeah, Theo?" I say at normal volume.

"Can I come in?"

"Yeah."

The door opens, and he walks in and stands awkwardly by my bed.

"What's up?" I ask.

He rocks back and forth on his feet, looking down at the floor, or maybe at the holey socks he's wearing. I've never seen him this nervous before.

"Can I tell you something?" he says quietly. "And you can't tell Mom and Mama."

My brain jumps to the worst. He's in trouble at school, isn't he? Or maybe he broke something expensive? Or maybe he did weed and has regrets. Where would he even get weed? He's twelve.

"Uh, sure," I say.

He bites his lip and squeezes his eyes shut. This isn't going to end well. He takes a deep breath and lets it out.

"I'm straight," he mutters.

What?

"You're . . . straight?" I ask, not sure that I heard him right. "Like . . . heterosexual?"

"Is it really that hard to believe?!" he wails, and oh no, I am in trouble.

"Oh my god, no, Theo!" I say, reaching over, waving toward my bed.

He plops down next to me and groans. "I'm so sorry, I just thought I didn't hear you right!"

I manage to get him to calm down after a minute or two. He sniffles and hugs the large stuffed animal I've given him.

"Were you very scared about telling me you were straight?" I ask, trying my absolute best not to laugh at this reverse coming-out situation.

"Well, it's just—nobody else in this family is straight!" he says, hugging the stuffed animal tighter. "I thought you might think I'm super uncool and boring. Who wants a straight white boy for a brother?"

At this, I can't hold back my laugh anymore. This is just hilarious. "Theo, I am *honored* that a straight white boy as kind and funny and self-aware as you could be my brother. There aren't a lot of people like you."

"Oh."

We sit there for a moment. I really don't know how to deal with this situation. So I do what any good older sister does.

"So . . . does this mean that you have a crush on a girl?" I ask.

"Stop!!!!!!" he whines, and he hits me with the stuffed animal, which makes me shriek and duck. "I don't wanna talk about it."

"Okay, okay," I say, holding my hands up. "Uh, just know that, um, I accept you for who you are, and I'm, uh . . . proud of you? And you, um, don't have to tell Mom and Mama until you're ready? But also, they're not heterophobic, that's not a thing, so—"

"Look, I'm just really scared, okay?" Theo asks. He sighs. "I know they won't care, but if they find out I like—well—they're gonna start lecturing me about *dating* and *being safe* and, like, I don't know! It's embarrassing! I don't want to talk about my *crush* with my *moms*. Especially if it's on a girl. They know what it's like to like a girl, so honestly, it makes it worse."

If this is the most pressing issue in Theo's life right now, I envy him an unbelievable amount.

I tell him a few things to try to calm his nerves. He really doesn't have to tell Mom and Mama right now. Like, yeah, it is probably embarrassing.

They get *really* excited seeing us grow up. Mom cried more than I did when they moved me into Wellesley.

Finally satisfied, Theo leaves my room, closing the door behind him. I chuckle one more time. Scared about being straight. Wow.

This really puts my problems into perspective, doesn't it? Theo is freaking out about being straight; I'm freaking out about being lonely. We are being equally ridiculous. Sophie and Lianne don't hate me. Wellesley Twitter and Sidechat will move on. My life is not ruined.

I think it's time for an apology tour.

Mama drives me back to campus after breakfast. Katy's gone, doing a day in Boston with one of her friends from home who goes to Northeastern. I sit quietly in my room, working on a couple of assignments. Lianne wakes up pretty late on Sundays, even later than me, so by the time she gets out of bed, I ask her if she wants to grab lunch before they stop serving hot food.

"I just want to talk," I say. "About everything. It's okay if you don't want to, but I do."

She presses her lips together. "Yeah, okay."

We head downstairs to the dining hall and get what's left of the scrambled eggs and pancakes that are always served during weekend brunch. They're actually kind of gross, but I'd rather eat this than a salad.

For a moment, we're quiet, both picking at our food. Then Lianne says, "So, what did you bring me here to tell me?"

"Um." Oh no. I should've prepared what I was going to say. I don't even know what I want to say, just—

"I'm sorry," I say. "I feel like shit for what I did. You were just looking for a real solution to your problem, and I just—I blew right past you."

I can't read her facial expression. If I were her, I'd be feeling a million things all at once right now, so I can understand that look. But I want to know what she's thinking.

"Thank you," she finally says. "I wish you had just told the truth. I

mean, you could've showed me Wendy's message to you before saying anything back. At least then all the rest of the stuff wouldn't have happened."

"It's not just that," I say. "I should've been more supportive to you
before that even happened. I mean, I let it get to the point where you had
to ask Wendy for help."

She grimaces. "That's not just on you. I need to move on. Like, obviously, nothing's gonna happen between me and Katy. I don't need you or
Wendy to tell me that."

I want to comfort her and say that you never know, but in this case . . .
I know. Katy doesn't want to date anyone right now. She told me herself.

"So . . . what are you going to do now?" I ask.

Lianne sighs. "I guess . . . I should text Alicia back."

"Oh."

"I never responded to her after she and Sophie hung out with us that
one time."

"Oh my god."

"She probably hates me now, right? This is the second time I've
ghosted her."

"Uh. I think you still have a chance?"

"Speaking of Sophie," Lianne says, clearly unimpressed by my answer,
"what happened there?"

I feel a pit of dread settle in my stomach. I really haven't talked about
it to anyone besides my parents. I've sort of been hoping I'll just get over
it. But Lianne wants to know, and she deserves to hear my side of everything, so I guess I'll have to tell her.

"Well, she's Dear Wendy."

"Right."

"And she's mad that I didn't tell her I was Wanda, and I'm mad that she
didn't tell me she was Wendy."

Lianne frowns. "Is that it?"

"Well, yeah, when you put it that way, it does sound pretty . . . minus-
cule," I say.

Lianne tries and fails to hold back a laugh. It comes out as a snort, hidden behind her hand. She looks at me, wide-eyed. "Sorry."

And then, all of a sudden, we both burst into laughter.

It's loud enough to make heads turn to look at us, but in this moment, I don't particularly care. This whole situation is so silly. I can finally see that. Sophie and I are mad at each other for keeping one secret that nobody else cares about.

We are ridiculous.

"God, I am so sorry for giving you the silent treatment," Lianne says after our last giggles subside. "You've seemed so miserable lately."

"I was fine," I say, which is such a blatant lie that nobody would possibly believe it.

"One thing about you, Jo," Lianne says, "is that when you say you're fine, you're almost definitely the opposite of fine."

"Would you believe me if I said I'm feeling fine now?" I ask, even as my stomach churns knowing I still have yet to make up with Sophie.

She shakes her head so emphatically that I think her head might fall right off her torso.

"Thanks a lot," I say.

We finish our food and head back upstairs. Lianne gets ready for Ultimate Frisbee practice, and I sit down and craft a message to Sophie.

dear wendy,

i love my best friend.

to be clear, my best friend probably doesn't even know that she's my best friend. we haven't exactly talked about that.

it's not what it sounds like. i don't love her the way the sun and moon love each other. okay wait that sounds weird. the way those two swans on lake waban love each other? idk if swans can experience love. the way my moms love each other?? i mean i guess that's the best approximation.

i love my best friend the way best friends always love each other. except . . . more.

at least, it feels like so much more. i've always thought we needed more words for "love" and "friend." words to describe every possible kind of love, every kind of friendship. other languages have so many words for love, and they all convey these tiny differences between the way you feel, and they make things so much clearer.

but in english, we're stuck with "love." so why not use it to its full potential?

i love my best friend. i love the way she speaks to you and immediately figures out your entire life story. i love the way she gives such perfect advice for every possible situation—or if she doesn't, she trusts you to help, even if she shouldn't. i love the way she casually walks up the hill from lulu like it's just another smooth path. i love how much she cares about little things.

i love her, and i messed up.

she asked me a question, and i didn't tell her the whole truth.

because i was scared. because i was selfish. because i didn't know
how to answer her without saying too much.
   and that was wrong, and i'm sorry.

sincerely,<br>
joanna ephron

(please don't print my name if you post this but i
wanted you to know it was me)
(you can post it if you want to. it's kinda embarrassing
but i'll live.)
(wait please don't post it)
(i'm really sorry)
(i miss your texts)

# CHAPTER 61

## Sorry

### SOPHIE

I stare at Jo's message for a solid three minutes.

I expected that I would need to say a lot to Jo for her to forgive me. I never imagined that she would want to say sorry too. But here it is, right in front of me: Jo still likes me—no, she *loves* me—and she's sorry.

I'm sorry too. For so many things.

I need to tell her.

I cross my fingers, hoping she isn't in class right now, and call her.

She picks up on the second ring. "Hello?"

"I got your message."

Silence. Then: "So . . . did you read it?"

I laugh. "Yeah, I read it."

"I really am sorry," Jo says.

"No," I say. "*I'm* sorry. I shouldn't have blamed you for my mistake. I should have given Lianne the same advice I give everyone else who asks about a crush."

"I shouldn't have given you such shitty advice when you asked," Jo says. "It was completely in my own self-interest. I was just scared of—of being alone, I guess."

We really need to have a conversation about this fear that Jo has held for so long, but I can't get into it right now.

"But then," I say, "when you gave me that answer, I should've thought about it more. I could've written a better explanation. Or considered whether that was the right advice to give."

"I shouldn't have yelled at you afterward."

"I shouldn't have been so rude." I exhale. We could go on like this forever. "What I meant to say is . . . I'm sorry. I was wrong."

"Me too."

"I miss you."

"It's been, like, a week, Sophie."

"You said you missed me in your letter."

Jo whines. "That doesn't count, it was for dramatic effect!"

"So you *don't* miss me?" I ask.

Jo sighs. "No. I mean—yes. I mean—you know what I mean! I do miss you."

"So can we go back to being friends, then?" I ask.

A pause.

"Yes," Jo whispers. "Please."

I wish I were with her right now. I wish I could give her a massive hug, and tell her that I regretted everything I'd said as soon as we hung up after that argument, and tell her that everything will be okay.

Wait, I definitely can do that. We live on the same campus, after all.

"Are you in your dorm right now?" I ask.

"No, I'm at the library."

Even better. It's closer to me. "What floor?"

"Fourth. Sophie, what are you—"

I hang up. A little dramatic, yes. A little rude, also yes.

But I have no time to waste.

# CHAPTER 62

## It Was Nice While It Lasted

### JO

She isn't coming here.

No way. It's pouring rain, and the clouds are so heavy that it's completely dark out, and she . . . no, there's no possible way.

But there's no other reason she'd ask those questions and then hang up like that.

I know it'll be a few minutes, so I turn back and look down at my table at the assignment I'm working on, trying to forget that Sophie is probably attempting some grand, dramatic gesture right now. But I can't take in a single word or number of the code I'm supposed to be writing.

About five minutes later, I hear squeaky footsteps approaching. I lift my head and turn around, and there she is, in a yellow raincoat and bright pink rubber boots, positively drenched, her hair dripping and coming loose around her face, her glasses covered in little droplets of water.

She sees me, and she breaks out in a smile.

"Hey," she says, not even wheezing or panting. Damn runners.

"Sophie, why—"

She steps forward and pulls me into a hug. I'm so stunned that I barely notice how damp I'm getting, unable to do anything else but awkwardly wrap my arms around her waist and put my head against her stomach.

"Uh . . . hey," I say, practically gasping in surprise.

"I love you too," Sophie murmurs.

I'm not a stranger to hearing "I love you" from people. My parents shower me with the phrase. My friends from high school throw it around everywhere in our conversations.

But I've never heard it spoken to me so deliberately, with such intention, such weight behind it.

I never thought I would.

I feel Sophie shift.

"Hey, are you okay?" she asks.

"What?"

"You're crying."

I pull back and touch my hand to my face. Huh. Yeah. I am.

"I'm sorry," I say. "I'm . . . I'm really glad you're here."

Sophie looks at me, her brow creased in concern. She reaches out and tucks a stray curl behind my ear.

She smiles. "Me too."

I need to say it again. "I love you."

"Love you too."

"No romo." It slips out, the term coined by the a-spec community making fun of straight boys who say *no homo* after showing even a morsel of affection.

Sophie glares at me. "Never say that again."

"Say what, 'I love you'? Okay, it was nice while it lasted."

"You know full well what I mean."

We both laugh for a moment, and then I look down at my shoes, not wanting to look in her eyes. "I should've told you I'm Wanda."

"You had no reason to."

"But we're friends. And it's just an Instagram."

Sophie kneels down, forcing me to meet her gaze. "Jo, you're not *required* to tell me everything about your life."

"It's not like your account. You give actual advice. Nobody would care if they found out I was me."

"I'm sure many people would care," Sophie says. "I certainly do."

I exhale a shaky breath. "Which is why I should've told you."

Sophie shakes her head and stands back up. "In any case," she says, "I'm glad we know now. Even if it took . . . all of that." She waves her hand around.

Sophie sits down at my table, and we catch up with each other over all the things that have happened in the last couple of weeks. She tells me her mom gave her helpful advice, which I'm thoroughly shocked by, and when I tell her about Theo coming out to me as straight, she laughs so hard we get shushed by others in the library.

I know I already told her this, but I really, *really* missed her.

Sophie ends up coming with me to my dorm, saying she owes Lianne an apology. We walk back as the rain starts to slow down. When Sophie and I enter my room, with Lianne fortunately there and Katy away in class, Lianne takes one look at us from her spot on the beanbag and sighs.

I bite my lip and brace myself. "You probably know what this is about."

Lianne doesn't say a word, just nods, the corner of her mouth quirked upward.

"I am so unbelievably sorry," Sophie says. "I totally screwed up with that answer I gave you. Seriously, so many things went wrong for that to have happened, and it never should've. I can't imagine how terrible that made you feel."

"I've been worse," Lianne says. "But continue."

"Yeah, I'm just—I'm really, really sorry," Sophie says. "If there's anything you need me to do, I'll do it."

Lianne stares at us for what feels like an eternity. And then she wrinkles her nose. "Even kill someone?"

It takes a moment for that to sink in, but then, the three of us are all laughing.

"Okay, anything *legal* I can do, I'll do it," Sophie says.

Lianne rolls her eyes. "All right. Consider yourself forgiven."

Oh, thank god.

"But," Lianne says, "I would like something."

"Go for it," I say.

Lianne turns toward Sophie. "What is your *real* advice to me?"

Sophie counters, "What's your *real* situation? In detail."

We sit down on the ground next to her, and she starts to explain.

"I guess I've kind of always thought she was cute?" Lianne says. "Like, when we met online over the summer during housing selection, I really liked her. But, like, realistically, I know there's no chance she likes me back. I'm not totally clueless—I can tell when someone's feelings for me are purely platonic."

"Okay," Sophie says. "That's valid. So then what?"

"So then, I guess around the start of this semester, I decided to get on a dating app to see what happens. And I ended up meeting—uh, so, Jo's probably already told you—I met Alicia on Bumble, and, I don't know, we texted, we exchanged Instagrams, and it was . . . fun? She's so cool and so nice, and we have a ton in common.

"But the more I talked to Alicia, the more I was like, oh, shit, wait, I still like Katy. Like I was still getting really on edge when she was around, and I can't let go of her in my head. So now I'm like, wait, am I using Alicia to get over Katy? 'Cause that's kind of problematic. I should like Alicia for her, not to get over someone else. But then, I *do* like her for her, and it's just—it's a mess. I totally ghosted Alicia because I got all in my head about whether I actually liked her or if I was just using her. And I'm just so tired of it all."

Sophie seems to sit with it for a minute. I look between the two of them.

"That's a lot," I say.

"I've never had to deal with anything like this before," Lianne says. "Where I went to high school, there were only, like, two sapphics out of the closet in my whole grade, and I was *not* one of them, even if some people suspected. I have never had to experience anything but hopelessly unrequited and often deeply suppressed crushes until now, when all of a sudden, I'm lowkey in a queer utopia."

"Okay, Wellesley is *not* a utopia," I say.

Lianne rolls her eyes. "Right, right, wrong word choice, but you know what I mean."

I do. For most people, it's much easier to be out here—where the vast majority of those you're around are accepting and welcoming and often queer as well—than at home. It's even been easier for me—I literally have gay parents, but even then, high school wasn't like what Wellesley is.

Sophie clears her throat. "So I think it sounds like you know what you want, Lianne."

"Do I?"

"You tell me," Sophie says. "What do you want your relationship status and situation to be?"

Lianne sighs, blinks, and then twists her mouth into a frown. "Yeah, okay, I want to make up with Alicia and see if she's still into me."

"There you go," Sophie says. "I think you're afraid of the side effects. You're right, it is hard to let go of your feelings. Katy might have been the first person you ever liked who had a chance of liking you back, right?"

Lianne's eyes widen. "Oh my god. Yeah. I didn't think about that."

I had no idea.

"Do I tell Katy anything?" Lianne continues.

"Up to you," I say. "I mean, personally, I wouldn't even want to know, but she might feel differently."

"I feel like I *would* want to know," Sophie says. "But then again, I kind of want to know everything."

I roll my eyes. "You're literally the worst."

Lianne leans back in her seat and groans. "I guess I'll have to figure it out."

"What do you even like about Katy, anyway?" I ask, almost by accident. It kind of slips out without me realizing. I clap my hand over my mouth. "Don't answer that if you don't want to."

She clicks her tongue and sighs. "I don't know. She's . . . nice. She makes me laugh."

"*I* make you laugh," I say.

"Oh, shut up, you don't want me to like you, too, do you?" Lianne says, glaring at me.

"No, of course not! Ew."

"And what do you like about Alicia?" Sophie asks gently.

And there it is—a soft smile, the one that shows up on your face when you think nobody's looking. Lianne doesn't even need to say anything for me to know exactly how she feels.

"She gets me," Lianne says. "She's just really easy to talk to. I don't know. She makes me not hate talking to a stranger."

Oh my god, this is so gay. I love it.

"You know, her family's a lot like mine," Lianne continues. "They expect her to marry some guy right out of college and give them a ton of grandchildren."

"Oh, yeah, she complains about that," Sophie says.

"I . . . you're right, I really like her. I don't know. I guess that's my answer, huh?" She chuckles.

And the look on Lianne's face—something has changed. She seems ready. For something. I'm not quite sure what.

Sophie smiles, and I know she's seeing the same thing I am. "My work here is done."

# CHAPTER 63

## A Creepy Weirdo

### JO

**lianne not-a-butler (11:03 PM)**

jo

help

okay i know you're probably asleep but

so i bumped into katy in the living room

and

i sucked it up and told her

basically i said i liked her like all of this year but that i think i'm finally getting over it and that if being around me makes her uncomfortable then i totally get it

slkdfjljskdflkjsdf this was SO AWKWARD

HELP

i think she went to study in another room LMAO?????

Me (11:34 PM)

omg i'm awake

i was watching the bachelorette lmao

come back to our room we can talk

it'll be okay

# CHAPTER 64

## Reactions

### SOPHIE

It's long overdue, but when Alicia comes over so we can pretend to do homework while actually chatting with each other about mindless things, I end up telling her everything (with Jo's permission).

Her reactions range from shock (that Dear Wendy is me and not an overenthusiastic upperclassman) to confusion (that Lianne would possibly ask Dear Wendy about her) to frustration (that none of us thought to tell her about the situation until now).

"I understand not telling me initially," Alicia says. "I wouldn't want me to be involved in this drama either. But considering that I sort of got dragged into it, I'm a little shocked you didn't say anything sooner."

"I would have, I swear," I say. "But I had so much going on, and it was never the right time to tell you I was Wendy, and I would've had to do that to tell you about anything else, and I didn't want to get involved in your love life, and—"

"—and one thing led to another," Alicia finishes. "It happens."

"Do you hate me now?" I ask timidly.

"Of course not," Alicia says, scoffing. "I mean, I haven't had any secrets quite like this, but I have accidentally meddled in a relationship before."

"When?"

"I accidentally got my brother dumped by his girlfriend when I was twelve because I told her that he had a small penis." She says it completely nonchalantly, no emotion on her face.

"I . . . I don't even want to know what led to that conversation."

"Yeah, you really don't."

"She really broke up with him because of his penis?"

"No, of course not," Alicia says. "But it was the last straw for her. He was an asshole when he was sixteen. Still is sometimes."

"I hope he stops being an asshole. And that he finds someone who doesn't care about his penis size."

"Thank you. I actually don't know how big his penis is. I don't ever want to know."

We dissolve into giggles, and I know everything will be okay.

"So, anyway," I say. "What are you going to do about Lianne?"

Alicia looks at me and frowns slightly. "I'll see where it goes."

"Do you like her?"

She looks down now and smiles, more to herself than to me, and I can't help but think that Lianne had that same smile on her face yesterday. "Yeah. But she still ghosted me."

"I hope it works out."

"So do I."

It would be nice, wouldn't it? For the two of them to work out after all this?

Dear Wendy,

So I've been seeing someone for a while now. It's been a few months. But I'm constantly worried that they're going to dump me. And I know it's unrealistic, I know that I shouldn't be worried, but how do I stop myself from seeing a period in a text and being like "omg they're going to break up with me"?

Sincerely,
anxious bb

Dear Anxious,

I think it's fitting that you signed your name as "anxious bb," seeing as you seem to be a textbook example of an anxious attachment style! (Check out my post from March 21 for more on attachment theory.)

As for ways to combat this, I have a few suggestions. Talk to your partner about how you're feeling! The end of many relationships is miscommunication, so by communicating properly, you'll have a better chance at working through any issues. And practice being conscious of your thoughts and emotions; I think you probably do a good amount of that already, but definitely keep it up. If all else fails, I definitely suggest trying a therapist; individual or couples' counseling can do wonders.

Best wishes,
Wendy Wellesley

**wandawellesley69** 30m

love how wendy's advice is "go to therapy" and "communicate" like 90% of the time

2 likes Reply

> **dearwendywellesley** 11m
>
> Love how wanda's advice is "break up with them" like 90% of the time
>
> 1 like Reply

**wandawellesley69** 30m

also it's good to have you back lol

Reply

> **dearwendywellesley** 10m
>
> You too :)
>
> Reply

# CHAPTER 65

## Discourse

### SOPHIE

As soon as Wendy and Wanda started getting harassed on Instagram, I disabled the comments on the Dianas' account to avoid me and Jo being personally attacked. As a side effect, though, we don't really know the interest level in our next meeting aside from the number of likes on our posts. Which has gone up. But that could be because we've gained followers—followers that may never come to any of our meetings.

I'm a little nervous about our next meeting, which is happening in fifteen minutes. Like usual, we're in the Penthouse, and I've taken the liberty of arranging the couches and chairs in a circle. As soon as Jo walks in, they curse loudly.

"What?" I ask.

"I forgot to bring food," Jo says.

"Is that really going to be an issue?" I ask about the cookies.

Jo looks at me like I've said something positively incomprehensible. "This is a discussion group, Sophie. What are we without unhealthy snacks?"

I sigh and shake my head. "I really don't think this'll impact—"

In response, Jo groans. "You don't get it, you hated the cookies."

"As much as I'd love to keep on talking about snacks," I say, "we do need to discuss what's going to happen in our meeting. Specifically, the Wendy and Wanda stuff?"

"Ugh, right," Jo says. "Are we gonna tell them?"

"Tell them what?"

"That we're Wendy and Wanda."

I shake my head rapidly. "I was not planning on doing that."

"Good, me neither," Jo says. "So, then, how do we talk about it without giving ourselves away?"

I stare at them, mouth slightly agape. "Good question."

We don't have time to ponder this any longer, though, because Charlie and Hannah come in, chatting about some TV show that I haven't heard of before. Nice to see they're already talking after having only met recently. They're closely followed by two people I don't recognize: a lanky redhead with light skin and freckles and a petite person with warm brown skin and box braids.

"Hey!" Jo says, in a way that's so enthusiastic that I know they're purposefully trying to be welcoming. "Are you here for Dianas?"

The taller one nods. "Yeah, is this where the meeting is?"

"You've come to the right place," Jo says.

As the two of them sit down, I lean over and whisper in Jo's ear.

"How have you suddenly become perkier than a kindergarten teacher?" I ask.

"Easy," Jo whispers back. "I just channel your energy."

I have no time to be offended, though, because a *third* new person walks in, an East Asian with long pink hair and round wire-rimmed glasses. And just before we're about to start introductions, Evelyn shows up and takes a seat next to Charlie.

I soon find out the two who came here together are juniors Saoirse Flanagan and Lily Reyes, who I remember came to my defense on my sort-of-coming-out-post on Dear Wendy. Saoirse is extremely adamant that we say her name right—*SEER-shuh*, not *SUR-shuh*. I like her already. The third stranger is Ashley Jeong, a sophomore who found out about us from Evelyn. She doesn't even have Instagram.

"Well then, you missed a lot this past week," Charlie says.

"You can say that again," Jo says.

"Uh . . ." Ashley says. "Does anyone want to explain what happened?"

"I can do it," Hannah says. "If that's okay?"

That is more than okay, especially since it means Jo and I won't have a chance to accidentally use the first person when referring to the accounts. Hannah gives an explanation of everything that went down—Jo's post, the comments, my subsequent post—and at the end, Ashley looks pissed off.

"Gosh, what is wrong with some people?" Ashley says. "I thought they had all this ace discourse, like, five, ten years ago."

"They literally did," Jo says. "But it keeps on happening. I mean, really, any sort of exclusion in the community still exists, right? Like there are still people who don't believe bi people exist, and there are literally TERFs who identify as queer, stuff like that."

"It's so exhausting," Evelyn says. "Like, I would assume that nobody knows how Wendy and Wanda identify, right? So why did those people assume they were aromantic?"

"And even if they are," Saoirse says, "that doesn't mean they can't, you know, run these accounts anyway. Wendy gives *intense* advice. They're really read up on this. And Wanda isn't exactly there to give super serious advice all the time."

I feel a little proud of the fact that I have this image.

"On the bright side," Hannah says, "it looks like most people were pretty supportive."

"Yeah," I say. "I think I saw some comments from Saoirse and Lily, actually."

"You'd be right." Lily grimaces. "I was fucking pissed at some of the comments on Dear Wendy."

Saoirse smiles bashfully. "I was the one who sent in the question. I kind of thought something like this might happen."

"I'm so sorry," Jo says. "You did not deserve that."

"Wendy took most of the heat," Saoirse says. "It's okay."

Oh, she has no idea.

Our conversation eventually turns to social media in general—how it can fuel hatred while at the same time bringing together communities. It really gets me thinking about Dear Wendy, what kind of impact I'm having on students, why I'm doing this in the first place. Turns out we almost all learned about asexuality and aromanticism from social media. The one exception is Jo, which is to be expected—they learned from their parents—but even they did more research online and became involved with the community that way.

It makes me angry, this acute knowledge that we are firmly not in the mainstream. That occasional side characters are our only representation in TV and movies, and we normally have to seek them out specifically.

"I've definitely watched an entire show because one ace character had a storyline in one episode," Charlie says. "And it wasn't even a good storyline."

Before everyone leaves, we all go around and share some of our favorite a-spec media. I type up titles of books, songs, short films, and more, all to send in an email to everybody here. And I couldn't be happier.

"Why do we even do the Wendy-Wanda accounts, anyway?" Jo asks after everyone leaves. We're still lingering, sitting on the couch and talking.

"What?" I say, frowning.

"Like, why?" Jo says. "I mean, it's fun and all, but . . . I don't know, I guess I'm still thinking about our conversation."

"Well, I guess this a little cheesy," I say, "but I really do enjoy being able to help people with this account. But I've been thinking about it recently, and I do think a big part of it is just wanting to be liked by everyone. And people really do consider what I have to say. Like . . . I don't know, I never really got that back when I had all these questions about identity and stuff. And so I learned everything on my own, and now I'm, like, a repository of dating advice."

Jo sighs. "I guess I also like helping people. I don't know. I never really felt like I needed advice from a peer. Maybe it's because I had my parents for that." That would make sense. "How did you learn everything on your own, exactly?"

"Well, I told you most of my high school friends were queer, right?" I say.

"You might have mentioned it. Your neighbor, right?"

I nod, lips pressed firmly together, and tuck a strand of hair behind my ear. "Besides him, I had others. My yearbook co-editor, Cassie. I catch up with her, like, once a month. And Izzy, of course."

"Cool. You should introduce us sometime."

"I keep forgetting to do that. She knows about you. Only good things, of course." Well, and a few of the bad things, but Jo doesn't need to know that. "Anyway, we were all figuring things out on our own, and I had to fumble through helping Cassie with her dating life and dealing with Oliver and even witnessing Izzy and Priya's relationship beginning, and I think that because of that and because of who I am as a person, I'd like to pass on that knowledge to other people."

Jo stares at me, eyebrows raised. "That is . . . a lot." I laugh, and Jo continues. "I mean, I guess I did have to knock some common sense into my high school friends pretty often. You know my high school friends were all theater people, right?"

"I sure do."

"Yeah. So. Lots of drama."

"Give me an example."

"Where do I even begin?" Jo sighs and scratches their scalp absent-mindedly. "My friend Courtney had an on-and-off relationship with this guy Luke who was tangentially connected to our theater friend group because he was, like, cousins-in-law or something with my friend Raquel. And Luke is a total asshole, right? Like, the classic jock who doesn't give a shit about your feelings. But anyway, so, Courtney and Luke were in off-mode, and long story short, at the after-party for our junior year spring play, *A Midsummer Night's Dream*, which is hilarious because it's also about ridiculous drama, Courtney gets, like, super drunk and makes out with Raquel *in front of Luke*. And the thing is, at the time, both Courtney and Raquel thought they were straight. So that morning, I had to break the news to them that, hey, maybe you need to unpack this, and also Luke is super mad and jealous, and like, you don't just make out with your sort-of-boyfriend's cousin, you know? Especially not in front of him. So then—"

"Wait, wait, wait, I'm gonna stop you right there," I say, feeling entirely overwhelmed by this barrage of information. "You said 'long story short' and then proceeded to tell the bulk of the story."

"Oh. Whoops. Sorry."

"It's okay! Just wanted to keep things on track."

"The point of the story is that I had to meddle and make Courtney break up with Luke for good. And I guess I've had to do that for a lot of people. I mean, that's how Wanda started, right? I was encouraging Katy to break up with her ex."

"Wait, what?" I say. "I don't think you ever explained that to me in full."

And as Jo explains that whole thing to me, I can't help but laugh.

# CHAPTER 66

## Historically Women's College

### JO

Between the Dianas, my sociology class, and WGST 110, I've gotten myself into way too many deep conversations lately. Our class is starting to wind down now that it's near the end of the semester, so Fineman's lecture today is about Wellesley and historically women's colleges as a whole. I know everybody will have a hot take.

I really do appreciate that this is today's topic. I love talking about stuff I understand.

Sophie has raised her hand after less than a minute of our lecture, when Fineman asks our class what they feel Wellesley has taught them about gender and sexuality and how we've interacted differently with the world since we got here.

"Yes, Sophie?" Fineman says.

"It's really interesting to think about how Wellesley is perceived by the majority of society versus how we see ourselves," Sophie says. "Like, to most people, Wellesley is kind of a relic of the past, from before the Ivy League really started admitting women, so when I told people I was going here, I'd usually get a response like, 'Oh, really? An all-girls school? You're never going to learn how to assert yourself to men.' And that always bothered me."

"It's funny you say that, Sophie," says a classmate named Nichole, "because I've taken a few classes at MIT, and I feel like Wellesley students talk during discussions more than female MIT students do. Because we exist in this environment where there are no cis men to dominate a conversation, so we have no choice but to speak up, and we feel more empowered to do so."

That sounds like the exact opposite of something that happened to me a few months ago. I hung out with some high school theater friends during break, and as soon as a boy arrived, my whole body seized up for a minute. I had to remind myself that (1) he was a very trustworthy friend and (2) he was definitely not going to harm me. I've never even been physically harmed by a man; it was just paranoia.

"Actually, when I was home during winter break, I had almost forgotten how to interact with cis men," I say. "Like, besides my little brother, being around cis male teenagers and young adults started to feel kind of weird and unfamiliar."

"Oh, I totally get that," Nichole says. "But once I shake off that initial shock, my personality goes full-force."

Good to note if I ever cross-register at MIT.

"Circling back to what Sophie said earlier," a classmate named Julie says, "I heard a lot of the same few ignorant comments about Wellesley as I was telling people where I committed to college. Like, did everybody else get told they'd find a boyfriend at Harvard?"

And literally the entire class snaps and nods. It's such a universal experience.

People keep listing off the worst reactions to their choice of college, and eventually, this leads us to make a physical list on the board at the front of the room of what are basically microaggressions related to historically women's colleges. It's a very familiar list.

"Isn't that a girls' school? How will you find anyone to date?"
"Oh, I could never go to an all-girls school, it would be so catty and dramatic."
"Mm, I bet your dad is happy about that. [Wink.]"
"What's that?" "It's where Hillary Clinton went." "Ohhhhhhhhhhhhhh."

"I prefer having guy friends, though."

"Oh, I know someone at Wesleyan!"

"Won't that school turn you into a lesbian?"

"Be careful of all the pink-haired liberals!"

"At least you can take classes at MIT."

"Aren't you afraid you'll miss the male perspective?"

"I think we can agree," Fineman says as we finish compiling this list, and I can tell she's trying not to laugh, "you've all faced some pretty misogynistic, cisheteronormative comments about your choice of college. Um, let's see . . ." She starts reading off the responses. "It looks like a lot of you hear the term 'all-girls school.' Anyone want to comment on that?"

"Uh, it's terrible," a classmate named Ria says. "I mean, besides the fact that it infantilizes us by calling us girls instead of women, it's also a massive erasure of trans and nonbinary identities. But our student population is probably a lot more accepting of trans, nonbinary, and gender-nonconforming people than the average college in America."

"But the thing is," Julie says, "even though we're more liberal than other colleges, there's still so much work we have to do. Like, every month, there's another incident that blows up, whether it's a student or a member of our faculty or administration who says or does something harmful."

That is . . . a very fair point. One person called bi people selfish on Twitter a few weeks ago; another time, a student government ballot measure caused the whole school to argue about who's the most oppressed.

As I've been thinking, Fineman has been poking around with other things we wrote on the board. It's really upsetting seeing it all laid out in front of me. I've heard a version of most of those things, and it's especially upsetting when a woman says those things to you—internalized misogyny runs deep.

We finish class by talking about Wellesley's role in the world and a bit of our history. Fineman spends a good chunk of time talking about the years it took for most historically women's colleges to adopt trans-inclusive admissions policies.

"Today, when higher education is largely not segregated by gender, historically women's colleges serve different purposes, one of which is to serve as a safe space of sorts for those of marginalized genders," Fineman says. "And the growing opinion is that that should include trans people regardless of their biological sex."

Our college's policy right now still needs work, as it excludes transmasculine people from applying (you won't get kicked out if you come out and/or transition later in your time here). I've met many transmasc students at Wellesley, and I can't imagine how it would be without them, if they'd realized it just a few years earlier and been barred from applying.

"So?" Sophie asks when class finally wraps up. "How are you feeling?"

I've had discussions like this with friends, in informal settings, but I never realized this was something you could talk about in class. And I guess that fits this class as a whole; we've talked about a lot of things I only knew from the internet.

"Holy shit," I say. "Fineman made sense. The whole time."

Sophie bursts into laughter. "Yeah, you see this side of her more in office hours."

"Do you go to her office hours?"

"All the time," Sophie says. "I think I'm going to ask her to be my major advisor."

"Oh, wow." I say. "Are you declaring this early?" I wasn't planning on declaring my major until next October at least. I'm really liking my sociology class, even more than the one I took first semester, so I'm planning on majoring in that, but my major really isn't that important to me.

"No, no, no," Sophie rushes to say. "If I decide to major in WGST—or minor, I guess—then I will ask her. That is not happening right now."

"Oh, good," I say. "I was going to call you a Wendy."

Sophie rolls her eyes. "It was funnier before you knew I was Dear Wendy."

# CHAPTER 67

## Literally What Does That Mean?

### JO

It didn't take long for us to tell Katy everything. Lianne's crush was the tip of the iceberg, really. She now knows that Sophie is Dear Wendy and about the whole drama that happened with us over the past week or so. Thank god she isn't mad, but then again, I don't think Katy could be mad at anyone.

It's the weekend again, but not just any weekend: Lianne and Alicia are *finally* talking again, and they are officially going on a date. And the hubbub of trying to get Lianne ready for it has consumed my entire morning.

"Does my eye shadow look okay?" Lianne asks. "I haven't done it in months."

"Oh my god, it looks fine!" I say. "I don't think Alicia will even notice. She'll be too busy staring at your lips or whatever."

"Stop, wait, my lipstick is going to smudge!" Lianne says. "Fuck!"

"Are we saying no to the lipstick, then?" Katy says. "I can go get a wipe."

"No, no, it's fine. I'll be fine. I just . . . won't kiss her."

"Oh, no, that's not gonna do," Katy says. "This needs to be the perfect date."

"Are you saying the perfect date has to result in a kiss?" I say. "That's kind of a high bar."

"Or a really low bar, depending on who you ask," Lianne adds.

"Maybe she'll think it's hot if you get lipstick on her," I say, entirely unhelpfully.

"Jo, I say this in the kindest way possible, you have no idea what's considered 'hot,'" Katy says.

"Anything can be hot if someone likes you enough," I argue.

"Fair point," Lianne says. "But—oh my god, no, we don't have time to talk about this. She's gonna be here in, like, two seconds."

"Are you ready?" I say.

"Physically or emotionally?"

"Both!" Katy and I scream.

And then a knock sounds at our door.

This is the most unnecessarily harrowing experience I have ever had. All of us freeze and turn to the door.

"One second!" Lianne calls out, and then, under her breath, she mutters a string of swears. "Okay. I'm ready."

Katy swings open the door to reveal Alicia, dressed super casually in a T-shirt and jeans. She has two cups of coffee that are clearly from the convenience store in Lulu.

"Hello," Alicia says. "Just so you know, I did stand outside your door for approximately thirty seconds because I didn't want to interrupt the chaos."

So she heard everything.

I glance at Lianne, who is absolutely mortified. She clears her throat. "Uh. Hi."

"Hi yourself. Coffee?" Alicia offers one of the cups.

Lianne reaches out and takes it, flinching when her hand brushes Alicia's, and I stifle a laugh.

"Thank you," she murmurs.

"Are you ready to go?" I ask.

"Wow, very eager to get rid of us," Alicia says. "I'm ready when Lianne is ready."

"I'm ready too," Lianne shoots back.

We all stand there for a moment, and I'm not sure what to say now. I don't know how much longer I can take this without losing my mind. In a good way.

"Don't just stand there!" Katy says. "Go! Have fun!"

It catalyzes us to finally start moving again. With a whirlwind of goodbyes and *we'll be back soon*s and a *not too soon, though!* from Katy that nearly causes Lianne to spit out her coffee, Alicia and Lianne are off.

As soon as the door is closed, Katy and I look at each other, and we immediately burst out laughing.

"That was the most painful thing I've ever experienced," Katy says, struggling to catch her breath. "It's like Lianne's never been on a date before."

"Do you think Alicia went through a similar process with Sophie and Priya?"

"Absolutely not," Katy says. "She's too cool for that."

"Maybe her coolness can rub off on Lianne."

Lianne texts us at 9:30 P.M. that she is not going to be back tonight.

And to my own surprise, I'm not freaking out about it. I'm happy for her. Actually, it's kind of cool that Lianne is finally having a lesbian U-Haul moment after a whole year of lamenting her singledom.

"I'm glad you're not freaking out too hard this time," Katy says. "Let's keep it that way."

"Got it."

"No Wanda business."

"None of that."

"Although . . ." Katy taps her foot on the ground. "I think it'd be funny if you made fun of her for this."

Hmm. Yeah. I haven't made a post about the gays moving too fast yet. And I haven't posted anything that I fully made up myself since those first two posts mocking Katy and Lianne all the way back when I started the account. Could be a fun evening activity.

Katy flops onto her bed and pulls out her phone, and I sit on our beanbag. For a minute, I think we're both about to go back to doing our own thing. But one thing still nags at me. Something I really should've asked by now, but I've been too scared to.

"Katy?" I say.

"Hmm?"

"Would you have gone on a date with Lianne? If she had asked?"

Her eyes move up toward me, but otherwise, she doesn't move. There's something in her gaze. Not annoyance, but maybe something resembling it.

"No," Katy says.

"Why not?"

"I may be attracted to women, Jo, but I don't like all women. Lianne is great, but she's more like a sister to me, you know?"

"Oh. Yeah, that makes sense."

That's enough of an answer for me, and I've pulled out my phone when Katy sits up and starts talking again.

"You know, I think a part of me isn't ready to be in a relationship at all, no matter who it's with. Even if I knew it would go well."

Whoa. Okay. That's a bit of a shift from the last time we talked about this. Really? Even if she knew it would go well?

There are a lot of things I could say in response to that—a joke that I'm not either, a question of why, a curt nod. I'm not sure what's appropriate.

"How long have you felt like that?" I ask.

She looks up at the ceiling, then back down. "I don't know. Awhile."

Katy is . . . very complicated. She's quiet, but she has so much to say to you. She's usually observant, but she couldn't even tell Lianne had feelings for her. She's sure of how to help you, but she doesn't seem to know how to interpret her own thoughts and emotions.

I don't know how to help her.

"Do you still . . . like people?" I ask. "Just, you know, find people attractive."

There's a fraction of a second where something deep inside of me wonders if she's ace.

"Well, yeah," Katy says with a smirk. "Can't really help that."

Never mind.

I wonder what that's like. Being attracted to people but not wanting to be with anyone.

"But I think," Katy continues, "that I've really needed this break from trying to find The One. Like, I made such a big deal of trying to get with people last semester. I think my Rice Purity score went down like twenty points." Damn. Mine's in the nineties. Maybe the eighties if I push the technicalities. "But it wasn't that fulfilling. And you saw what happened with Jason."

"Pretty standard bad boyfriend, right?"

"Yes, in retrospect. But . . . you didn't see this at the time, but I really put a lot of pressure on myself to be the perfect girlfriend. Like, thinking that if I did everything right, he'd put in the effort. And then he didn't, and it kind of fucked me up for a bit. You saw how long I went to therapy before and after the breakup."

"The right person isn't going to need your constant attention to pay an ounce of attention to you," I say. Sophie said that recently, in one of her posts.

"I know that now," Katy says, smiling. "But not at the time. I spent so much time thinking I'd find my soulmate in college when that's not what this is about. Like, duh, I'm here to get an education. So I've spent most of this semester single, and I'm a lot happier."

It's funny how so many people still think of college as the place to find The One. Even a lot of Wellesley students think this. A lot of us *do* find The One here, or at a neighboring college.

This is probably something Katy has spent a lot of time thinking about. I never noticed it enough to bring it up to her, but I've spilled all my insecurities on her in the meantime. God, I should've paid her more attention.

"Do you think you'll eventually be ready to go back into the dating world?" I ask. "I mean, if you aren't, that's obviously fine—"

Katy laughs. "I know you know it's fine, Jo, you're literally aroace." She chuckles again, then sighs. "I don't know. I think that right now, if the right person comes along, then sure, I'll give it a shot, but otherwise, I'm not going to date for the foreseeable future. I don't need to."

Huh. Would you look at that. Some good old inner peace.

"That sounds fantastic to me," I say.

# CHAPTER 68

# You're Twelve Years Old

## JO

Sophie and I have made plans to get Starbucks this morning. She made me wake up at 8:30 for this so we can be at Starbucks during what she calls "normal breakfast hours."

As soon as I've taken a shower and put on my clothes, I hop right back onto my bed and open up my laptop, telling myself to get some work done before I need to go even though I know I'll probably just be scrolling through Twitter. Everyone was right. Twitter forgot about the Wendy/Wanda drama, like, three days after it happened.

I'm laughing at a comedian's tweet when Lianne walks inside, wearing the same clothes she was wearing yesterday, a white turtleneck under a black T-shirt and ripped jeans.

"Good morning," I say, dangling my feet as I sit on the edge of my mattress. "How was your night?"

Lianne narrows her eyes and stares at me as she puts down her phone and keys. "Why . . . are you up?"

That was not a proper answer to my question, but I'll continue. It's early for me to be awake, but I can get up before 10:00. Geez.

"Sophie and I are getting breakfast. Why are *you* up?"

Lianne groans. "Alicia wakes up ridiculously early."

I can't possibly hide my grin. "So, what, are you together now?"

"No!" Lianne says. "God! I mean, it's more complicated than that!"

"So what are you, then?"

"Um. Well. We're not . . . putting labels on anything. Yet. So."

Lianne looks ridiculously embarrassed, her eyes wide, her eyebrows raised. I guess I am being a little mean, but what's the point of being friends with me if you don't want to be interrogated about all aspects of your life?

"So you're . . . two people who kind of like each other and know you like each other and have gone on a date but for some wild reason aren't dating?" I smirk.

"I fucking hate you," Lianne says.

"Love you too," I say as I slip on a thin cardigan over my T-shirt. "Anyway, see you!"

"What—where are you going?"

"Breakfast, remember?" I start to open the door.

"Ugh. Okay. Tell Sophie I said hi."

"Will do."

When I get to the archway in front of the Ville, I see Sophie already standing there in a sage-green T-shirt and black leggings, her glasses falling down her face slightly, her hair in a messy ponytail.

Always early to everything.

I wave at her, and she looks up from her phone. Her face brightens.

"You're late," she says as I approach.

"A queen is never late," I say. "Also, Lianne says hi, and apparently, she 'accidentally' fell asleep at Alicia's last night."

"Oh, yeah, I saw her leave Claflin this morning," Sophie says with a smirk. "Looks like the thing with Katy was over pretty quickly."

"I think she already liked Alicia a lot to begin with, so that probably helped."

When we get to Starbucks and a barista with big glasses and curly auburn hair takes our order, I immediately begin to make fun of Sophie for her drink of choice. You'd expect her to get something a bit more classy—an iced latte, a London Fog, maybe a black coffee. But no, she orders a strawberry Frappuccino with extra whipped cream.

"Jesus," I say. "What are you, twelve?"

"Shut up, it's what my sister gets."

"Uh, you guys get the same order?"

"No," she admits. "But I always steal some of hers. Besides, it's too hot for me to get a caramel apple spice." She says it the way my mom says it, CAR-mul.

"What the hell is that?"

"Hot apple cider with cinnamon syrup, whipped cream, and a caramel drizzle." She looks way too proud of herself for someone who orders glorified apple juice at Starbucks.

"Oh my fucking god, you're twelve years old. Also, it's pronounced CARE-a-mel."

"Car-mul."

"Care-a-mel."

"Car-mul."

"Care-a-mel."

"Car-mul."

"I hate you."

She smirks. "Good."

It's not a bad breakfast, if you forget that it cost me almost eight dollars to get an iced coffee and a chocolate croissant. Sophie and I spend a good hour talking about mindless things that I'll forget about, which is oftentimes the best way you can spend an hour. We bicker about how to pronounce things; we gush over our favorite queer media. We plan our last Dianas meeting, which is happening next week, and make a group chat for current members.

I love her so much.

It's nearly 11:00 when both Sophie and I feel our phones buzz several times in a row and end up checking them. The group chat is already full of commentary thanks to a question from Hannah on how to dress more queer.

Charlie (10:54 AM)

idk man i just wear a lot of flannels

Evelyn (10:54 AM)

GRAPHIC TEES

also!! thrift store finds

if you can cobble together a bunch of things from goodwill that don't match at all, congrats, you're one of us

Sophie and I both laugh, and she says, "You know, I was wondering the same thing. How do you make yourself look like you aren't straight?"

"I don't know, honestly," I say. "It's about owning your terrible outfits. Also, no black leggings unless you've got a *really* weird shirt to balance it out."

Sophie balks. "What's wrong with black leggings?"

"They're tacky!"

"They're comfortable!"

"Is it more important to you to look queer or to be comfortable? Also, there are other comfortable pants."

"I know that," Sophie says. "I mean . . . I get it in my head that I look like a straight girl, and I don't want to."

"You don't look straight to me," I say. "If that helps. I don't know, it's more of your general aura that matters. Clothing is just a part of it."

In the group chat, Evelyn is saying something similar, and I can't help but smile. We're really doing something here.

"At the end of the day, you wear what you want to wear," I say. "If you want me to help you find gayer clothes to wear, though, let me know. We still have a couple weekends here before we have to go home. I can make my mom drive us to the mall, or we can take the shuttle."

The college has a van that takes students to the mall and a few other places in the area. It always fills up too fast, so I always ask my parents to take me places whenever I need something. Perks of living in Natick.

Sophie narrows her eyes. "I'll let you know about that."

That's, like, definitely a yes.

# CHAPTER 69

## Gesture

### SOPHIE

Priya tells me, when I come back from Starbucks, that I need to let Izzy into the building while she's out; I think she's planning some sort of surprise. But half an hour after Priya leaves, I hear a knock at my door, and Izzy's right there. Her hair falls in gentle waves; the pink ends are fading a little.

"Oh, hey!" I say. "Who let you in?"

"Alicia," Izzy says. "She happened to be in the lobby. Do you know where Priya is? This is the first time she hasn't been there to open the door for me."

"Uh . . ." I don't know. "I think she's running errands."

Izzy frowns. "That doesn't sound like her."

I shrug. "I don't know, that's all she told me."

"Oh well. I'm sure she'll be back soon." She shrugs. "How have you been?"

"Well, you know Jo and I made up," I say.

"Yes," she says, smiling. "I'm very glad."

"How have you been?"

She starts telling me about a linguistics professor at Brown that she's trying to get research work with. The lab employs a few students, and she didn't get in for the summer, but she wants to see if she can do it in the fall. Before I can tell her my suggestions on how to get hired for it, I hear the click of the door opening, and in walks Priya holding a large brown paper bag and a potted succulent.

"Sorry I took so long," Priya says, smiling. "But I wanted to do something cute." She turns toward me, as if just noticing my presence. "Hi, Sophie."

She gives Izzy the plant.

"This is for you," Priya continues. "I know you told me you wanted a plant, and this was on the Free and For Sale Facebook group, so I went and picked it up."

Izzy gazes at Priya adoringly. "This is the best thing you've ever gotten me."

"And this," Priya says, brandishing the bag, "is Chinese takeout. Because I had a Grubhub coupon, and I really didn't want dining hall food, and I didn't think you would either. But the driver took forever to find Claflin, so that's why I've been gone so long."

She exhales dramatically.

Izzy reaches out and takes Priya's hand. "Have I ever mentioned how much I adore you?"

Priya smiles. "Maybe a few times."

The way they're looking at each other, it's like I'm not even here. I think Izzy mouths the words *I love you*. I almost need to look away.

Priya raises Izzy's hand to her lips and kisses her knuckles like a Victorian gentleman. "You want to eat up here or in the common room?"

I'm sure Izzy says something in response, but I don't process anything they're saying. I'm not sure why, but at this moment, I get an overwhelming sense that the two of them are perfect together. If this is what love looks like, no wonder everyone craves it all the time.

I look up, about to say something, and my friends are gone. They must have decided to eat somewhere else.

It was a tiny gesture, really, just food and a small potted plant, but it's so sweet how people who love each other will do these little things for each other. I wish I had someone I could do that with.

Wait.

I do.

# CHAPTER 70

# No, I'm Not Going to Cry

## JO

I have an evening alone. Katy is at a painting night at the arts center, and Lianne's doing a horror movie marathon with a few other people in our dorm. I don't want to participate in that because the last time I watched a horror movie, I had trouble sleeping for three days.

I've decided to have a bit of a spa day, so after taking a shower, I lie on my bed in my bathrobe with a sheet mask on my face, turning on a fiction podcast that my brother and I have listened to since I was sixteen. Theo was pissed when I went home this afternoon and told him that I'm a few episodes behind; he's threatening to text me spoilers.

The podcast's host is talking about the mysterious disappearance of her pet lizard into a parallel universe when a knock sounds at my door.

*Now? Really?*

I call out, "Just a minute!" and hastily pause the podcast, peel off my mask, and wipe my face. No time to change into more presentable clothes.

I pull open the door. Standing in the hallway is Sophie, clenching something in her fist, wearing a Taylor Swift cardigan over her outfit from earlier today. Her hair is, once again, coming loose; I think she ran here.

I'm not at all surprised that she's randomly here, given that I can't remember the last time she texted me if I was here before coming over. She's very lucky that she always finds me.

"Hi," she says, looking me up and down. "Bad time?"

"Oh! No, no, you're fine. I've been, uh, lying on my bed."

I feel extremely exposed right now. And to be fair, I'm wearing absolutely nothing but a robe. But why is Sophie here? What does she have to say that can't be said in a text?

"Ah." She nods, eyebrows raised. "Um, can I come in?"

"Yes! Yes. Uh, give me a sec to put on some real clothes."

Once I've thrown on a T-shirt and shorts, I let Sophie in. I don't think I've ever looked this terrible in front of her, my hair damp and tangled, my face free of makeup and bespeckled with angry red pimples.

"So," Sophie finally says, "this afternoon, I went back to Claflin fully thinking I'd turn in, spend the rest of the day doing nothing, right? But then Izzy was here, and Priya did something for her that was really cute, and I couldn't stop thinking about how I feel like you deserve cute things like that. So . . . I made you this."

She opens her hand and reveals a friendship bracelet, patterned in candy stripes of green, purple, black, white, and gray. It's crumpled from being held in her hand.

It looks adorable.

I stare at it, dumbfounded. "What's this?"

"Um . . . I did Girl Scouts for a year before my mom pulled me out of it saying it was some white people garbage, and honestly, it is, but also no, it teaches kids valuable skills, but anyway, I learned there how to make friendship bracelets, and I saw Priya and her girlfriend being cute today, and—okay, basically, I wanted to give you this because I really appreciate you and everything you've done for me, and I think you should be proud of who you are, and wearing the colors of your flags is a really good way to be subtle but also extremely loud about it, so . . . uh . . . yeah."

Holy shit.

No, I'm not going to cry. No. Stop. It's just a bracelet. It's a crumpled-up little bracelet that might not even fit my wrist.

But . . . "Did you make this? Today?"

"This afternoon, yeah."

". . . How long did it take you?"

"Um . . . like, a few hours. I don't know. I was rewatching a recorded calculus lecture. Actually, uh, several recorded calculus lectures."

"Nerd."

"I made one for myself too," she says, ignoring my comment. She pulls up the sleeve of her cardigan. It's another candy-striped bracelet in white, yellow, orange, and two shades of blue. "Uh, it's the aroace flag. Less common, but I, uh, didn't have enough green."

"Yes, I know that flag. Oh my god, that's not how friendship bracelets work, I'm supposed to give you one in return."

"Well . . . do you have one?"

"No. Not right now."

"Okay, then . . . anyway, here, I'll tie this one to your wrist."

Wordlessly, I hold out my right hand, and she neatly secures it onto my wrist. From her pants pocket, she pulls out a small pair of scissors and cuts the extra thread.

"There you go!" she says.

"Why did you do this?" I ask, even though I think she's already explained that.

She looks at me like I've asked the most ridiculous question ever. "Because I love you. And I love all the stuff we do. And I wanted to show you that with a little token of appreciation."

I stand there, mouth agape.

I never thought anything like this would happen to me.

And like any moment where I can't process what's happening, I ruin it with a joke.

"Wait," I say, narrowing my eyes. "Are we about to kiss right now?"

Sophie raises her eyebrows, staring in awe for about two seconds before bursting into laughter. "You're the *worst*."

It isn't that funny. It really isn't. But we can't stop laughing.

"God," I say between giggles. "I'm so glad we met. And did this weird Instagram thing."

Sophie shakes her head, grinning. "I need to catch up on posts. I might have to close submissions for a bit if I don't get my act together."

"Oh, I need to look at mine too."

So naturally, we end up sitting on my bed, going through each other's submissions and helping pick out what to respond to and how to word our answers. Sophie is surprisingly good at coming up with snarky responses. And I manage a serious answer or two.

"You know," Sophie says, "you're really good at this. When it's not your roommates."

I chuckle. "Thanks, but . . . I don't know. It's like those commenters told us. Why do we have any authority over romance?"

Sophie sighs. "I've been thinking about it, and . . . if anything, we have plenty of authority. Because we don't have feelings attached to things—uh, usually—we can boil things down to their basics, analyze things without overanalyzing them. You know what I mean?"

"Huh. I guess I never thought about it that way before." I sigh. "I mean, half the time, I'm still on the other end of that, wondering if I actually do have a crush on this or that person, if I've been lying to myself this whole time."

I say it as a joke, but we both know that that sentence is deeply rooted in truth. It's what my mom told me I should stop feeling and let go of.

Sophie looks at me sympathetically.

I brace myself, ready to hear that I'm being silly, that I should stop thinking like that, that I have better things to worry about.

And then she speaks, slowly, but firmly.

"You know . . . something I once heard that I still think about sometimes is that . . . when you're asexual or aromantic or both, to accept your sexuality, you have to accept that you're probably going to question it for a really long time, and possibly the rest of your life.

"Because there's that part of your brain that goes, like, who's to say it can *never* happen, right? What if that person made me nervous because

I like them, what if liking romcoms makes me—sorry, what if it *means* I want that for myself. Or . . . or what if I'm an *extremely* late bloomer? It's so hard to prove a *lack* of something, much harder than to prove something exists.

"So those thoughts might never go away. They haven't for me, and I've identified as aroace for almost five years. But you know yourself. And you know the way you feel. So . . . let those thoughts run their course. They're not real unless you make them real, but they'll happen, and you just need to accept that they'll be a part of you, but they don't define you."

Whoa.

I was not ready to hear a whole speech from Sophie Chi today.

It sounds so counterintuitive. To accept my sexuality, I have to be okay with constantly questioning it?

"But how do I do that?" I ask. "How do I . . . allow the thoughts to happen?"

Sophie shrugs. "I got used to it. I'm not a therapist, so I can't give you much insight into *how* to make things happen. But it's possible, and it's kind of the key to loving yourself."

Well, shit.

Something to think about.

"You really feel like that?" I ask.

"Of course."

"You seem so sure about everything to me. I honestly don't understand how anyone could possibly think you're anything but aroace."

Sophie frowns. She looks like she wants to say something but doesn't know what.

"What is it?" I ask.

She sighs. "Nothing. I . . . I guess I'm just remembering that my mom and dad still don't really get it."

"Oh. Right."

I've talked with Sophie so many times now about our families. Her parents seem totally unwavering, still.

"I mean, they have to know, right?" Sophie says. "Somewhere, deep down, my parents know that I'm never going to get married, and that terrifies them because it's totally against everything they've ever been taught to believe."

I nod. "But they don't get how you can't be attracted to anyone."

"Right. They think I'll change my mind."

"Yes. We've been over this."

"Well, yeah. But I was just thinking, and I think I'm fine with that. Like, I think I'm going to live my life and let them believe what they want to believe, and that'll be okay because at least they still love me, and at least they aren't trying to marry me off to some misogynistic creep who works at Facebook."

"Does that actually happen?"

"Sometimes. Chinese parents are intense."

"Wow. Love that for you."

It comes off as a bit of a joke, but it's true. I look at Sophie, and the expression on her face, the way her eyes are just a little more lit up than before, and I know she's at peace with how her mom and dad feel about her. And I'm at peace with how I feel about myself. At least in this moment.

Look at us.

Sophie decides to stay over for a few hours, and we obviously have to queue up a movie. Sophie suggests *The Half of It*, a movie I've heard about a million times but haven't sat down to watch. She says she's seen it so many times that she practically has the script memorized. It's a love story of sorts, but there are so many different kinds of love being shown here. And at the center is a friendship.

Sometimes, love isn't between two people falling *in* love. Sometimes, love is between a himbo football player with a great sausage recipe and a lesbian who writes love songs and wears long underwear to stay warm.

When the credits start playing, tears are streaming down my face.

"Hey, are you okay?" Sophie asks. "This is the second time this has happened."

"What?" I say, sniffling.

"The second time you've cried while watching a movie with me."

I wipe at my eyes. "Fuck you."

Sophie laughs and pulls me in for a hug, and we haven't even hugged that many times, but it feels so very familiar to be in her arms. Safe. Comforting.

"I feel like such a mom right now," Sophie says after a minute.

Way to ruin the moment.

"Well, I already have two of those," I say. "Plus Katy a lot of the time. I don't think I need another."

"Fair point." Sophie lets go.

"Nooooooo," I whine. "Come back."

She rolls her eyes and wraps her arms around me once more.

I don't know if Sophie showed me *The Half of It* specifically because of the friendship story, but I have a feeling it's why she likes it so much. There are a lot of things to like about it—the sapphic representation, the small-town aesthetic, the immigrant experience—but I don't know the last time I watched a movie where the main relationship was platonic.

It's so refreshing.

"Would you run after a train for me?" Sophie asks me.

She's referring to the last scene in the movie, where Ellie's leaving town, and Paul runs by her train until it picks up too much speed.

"Uh, no. You're the runner here, not me."

"Damn. I guess we can't be friends anymore, Jo." She shakes her head. "I thought you cared."

"You're the worst," I respond.

We look at each other, and then, all of a sudden, the two of us both burst into laughter. It's the kind of laughter that's contagious to an inconvenient point, a laughter that subsides soon enough but then immediately starts back up as soon as you make eye contact again. Peals of laughter probably ring through the thin walls into the hallway.

I don't know what it is about this moment, right now, but something in me clicks. This is what I want. In my life, in my future. Someone who gets me. Someone I can banter with, someone I can trust, someone who loves me in the same way that I love them.

And the last piece of the puzzle slots itself in. Suddenly, I can see my future, clear as day. I'm a law clerk, or a teacher, or working in a nonprofit, and Sophie's a journalist, or a clinical psychologist, or a social media manager, and we have two cats or maybe a dog, and we live in a big city in a tiny apartment with walls completely lined with books and plants, almost all of which are Sophie's, and we absolutely don't have our lives figured out, but at least we have each other.

Holy shit.

I look over at Sophie, and I cannot figure out the expression on her face. A few seconds pass, or maybe it's more than a few, maybe it's several minutes, but all I know is that we stare at each other in this liminal moment, and then I blurt something out.

"Do you want to be roommates?"

Sophie raises her eyebrows. "What?"

"Like, next year. I mean, if you don't already have one planned. But, I don't know, I thought maybe it'd be cool for us to hang out, like, all the time."

Sophie looks at me incredulously, and for a moment, I think I've completely fucked this all up, and my stomach drops and I completely stop breathing and I'm about to spontaneously combust, but then she laughs.

"Absolutely," she says, grinning. "Oh my god, I almost forgot about housing selection! Wait, yes, that would be terrific."

I finally exhale. "Sophie, that was the most stressful moment of my entire life."

And now we're both laughing again, blabbering about how exciting this is. Sophie manages to tell me she needed a new roommate anyway since Priya's living in a single dorm next year as an RA. I straight up haven't thought about housing at all, and now I guess I need to break the news to Katy and Lianne that I won't be joining them next year.

But yeah.

It's happening.

# CHAPTER 71

# Partners

## SOPHIE

I wake up about two minutes before my alarm is supposed to go off.

I stayed over at Jo's last night on an air mattress on her floor, which was probably a bad idea since we have class today, but oh well. I don't have any morning classes on Mondays. Maybe this is silly, but I can really see this being my life next year: staying up late talking about guilty pleasure TV shows and middle school fandom phases and fourth-wave feminism. Waking up absurdly early, trying not to wake Jo as she dozes at the other side of the room.

I think Jo might be the best thing to ever happen to me.

Last night, we talked for hours. About Dianas. About a weird person in our WGST class. About my plants. My sister called and gave Jo a million reasons to make fun of me, one of which was that my Spotify Wrapped from last year was almost entirely Taylor Swift. I can't believe Abby's almost done with freshman year.

After Abby hung up, we started talking about our families. At some point, Jo mentioned she might like to have a queerplatonic partner someday.

"Not right now," she said. "But, you know, maybe, if the stars align or whatever. It'd be nice to have someone around."

"You know," I replied, "there was a thing for a few decades in the 1800s and 1900s called the Wellesley Marriage. Two female academics teaching at Wellesley would live together because married women couldn't teach here. Most of those were probably sapphic relationships, but it's possible some were purely platonic. So it's been done before. A long time ago."

"That's fucking iconic," Jo said, and then I told her about Katharine Lee Bates and her probable lesbian lover who was also named Katharine, and we laughed and moved on.

But now I'm thinking about it again.

I've never had a platonic partner. Honestly, I don't really know what it entails. But now I'm thinking about all the kinds of partners you can have. Romantic partners are just one; there are also business partners, group project partners, co-writers of books. Co-presidents of school clubs. Jo and I might as well be partners with our Wendy and Wanda accounts, at this rate.

Partners with our Wendy and Wanda accounts . . .

That makes a lot of sense. We could easily do something together. Something more than our petty, silly disagreements. We could give advice together! Or compile helpful (or unhelpful) resources! Or maybe we can even ask our followers to give their own takes! Jo mentioned matchmaking yesterday—we could literally do that!

It is taking every ounce of self-control in my system not to shake Jo awake and tell her about this immediately. It's almost 8:00. Or just past 7:30. That's late enough to wake her, right? Katy's already up and out of the room. We went to bed around midnight. We're adults, we only need seven hours of sleep.

I'm doing it. I'm waking her up. I go over and gently poke Jo in the arm. Nothing.

"Jo?" I whisper. "Jo. Joanna. Joooooooooooooo."

I reach over and pat her shoulder a couple of times. She suddenly gasps and opens her eyes and jumps, which makes me jump.

"What the *fuck*, Sophie?" she cries. "Holy shit!"

"I'm sorry!" I say. "But I had the *best* idea, and I needed to tell you!"

Jo shakes her head rapidly and rubs at her eyes. "What time is it?"

"Seven thirty-eight."

"What the *fuck*," she repeats. "What was so important that you had to wake me up now?"

"Sorry," I squeak again. "But hear me out. What if . . . we combined Wendy and Wanda?"

Jo stares at me, face completely devoid of emotion. She is not blinking. Staring me down. Unmoving. This is getting scary.

Finally, she closes her eyes and chuckles. "Sorry, what?"

I explain the concept to her. The two accounts stay the same as always, but we make a new third account for posts that can't neatly fit onto one of ours. Basically, bonus content for people who enjoy what we make.

When I'm finished talking, Jo's back to staring at me.

"You think it's a bad idea, don't you?" I say.

"No, no," Jo says, looking off to the side. "I just think it's silly that you woke me up for *this*."

"I—wh—it's a *great idea*, Jo!"

"And it couldn't have waited another hour?" She laughs and rolls her eyes. "You're ridiculous."

"Well . . . I . . . it's not that early!"

"It's not even 8:00 yet."

I sigh. "You can go back to sleep now if you want."

"Oh, no, I'm staying awake," Jo says. "I don't have class until the afternoon. Let's make this account."

hey guess what?

i have a new account!!!!
or rather, *we* have a new account
introducing: wendy.wanda, an extra place for me and dear wendy (ugh)
to post any stuff that doesn't quite fit onto our usual accounts.
need to crowdsource some advice?
want our takes on viral reddit relationship posts?
want book or tv recs about anything and everything love-related?
just want another place to appreciate my talent? (and i guess dear
wendy's too?)
consider following @wendy.wanda, coming to an instagram feed near
you!

---

Hi, everyone! Fun little surprise for all of you: Wanda and I have
made a new account! Don't worry, I'll still be posting here as
much as always, but we'll also be sharing bits of non-love-related
advice, talking about resources that we find helpful, and (shockingly) being friendly with each other. Come give us a follow if you
want to see more from us, but if you don't, Dear Wendy will still
be doing business as usual.

Love,
Wendy Wellesley

# CHAPTER 72

## Is This a Dorm?!

### JO

Our last Dianas meeting of the semester goes very smoothly. Everyone who came last time shows up again, and we sit on the couches in the Penthouse and watch a Studio Ghibli movie that Sophie picked out. It's a nice way to end the year.

Afterward, Sophie and I pack up one last time, heading out the door. It's a beautiful day out, though unusually cool for May in Massachusetts. As soon as we get out the door, though, we hear a shrill voice.

"Is this a dorm?!" says the voice.

I look around and realize it's coming from a girl holding a map. She's with another girl and an older woman, all three of them East Asian. Map Girl and the woman have long, stick-straight hair; the other girl's short hair is tied in a tiny ponytail, and she looks very unenthusiastic. I'd guess that they're a family touring campus.

"It's not a dorm," I hear Sophie say, which makes the whole family turn around. "This is an administrative building, for the most part, though our college radio and LGBTQ+ office are both here too."

Map Girl comes up to us, looking very excited about this place. "You guys have an LGBTQ+ office?"

"Yeah," I say. "It's pretty small, but it's a good meeting space. Are you touring campus?"

She nods and then points over to the others. "That's my sister and my mom. Are you two current students?"

"Yeah, we're both first-years," Sophie says. "I'm Sophie, she/her, and this is Jo, she/they."

"I'm Nora," the girl says. "She/her pronouns." She seems to even think it's cool that we share our personal pronouns. "What were you doing in this building?"

"We actually just came from the LGBTQ+ office," I say.

"Okay, I already committed to going to Wellesley, but this really cements it," Nora says. "What were you doing there?"

"Holding an org meeting," Sophie says. "Jo and I are co-presidents of Dianas, an asexual and aromantic discussion club."

I swear, Nora's eyes bug out of her head. "You have one for that?"

Sophie chuckles. "We just started it up this year. Are you interested in joining?"

"I would love that," Nora says. "How can I stay updated?"

Sophie adds her to our email list, using her personal email since she doesn't have a school-issued one yet. When we're done, Nora smiles and thanks us.

"Is your sister in college yet?" Sophie asks.

"She's in the same year as me," Nora says. "We're not twins, though, it's just how our birthdays work out. I feel like I need to clarify that to everyone."

"That's cool," I say. "Is she coming to Wellesley?"

"Yep!" Nora says. "But she isn't as excited about it as me. She wanted to go out of state, but this was how college apps worked out for her."

I get a sense that Nora overshares a lot.

"Well, we're looking forward to seeing you two around next year!" Sophie says. "Thank you so much for your interest!"

"Thank you!" Nora says. "I'm really excited!"

The whole family walks off, and not two minutes later, Sophie and I both get Instagram follow requests from @noradeng13. It's honestly impressive.

"She was so sweet," Sophie says. "Did you see the way her eyes lit up when we told her about Dianas?"

"Oh my god, yeah," I say. "I feel like that just became, like, a core memory for her."

"Holy shit," Sophie says, startling me with the exclamation. "Our club made this soon-to-be student *that* excited? We did that?"

"That is . . . wow," I say. "That's so weird to think about."

Sophie laughs incredulously. "We're, like, actually making a difference. Oh my god."

Before we can walk any farther, my phone, which I'm still holding, buzzes. It's an email from the WZLY group: Someone's dropping their show, which is happening in twenty minutes.

And there's only one thing I can think to do now.

"Hey, Sophie?" I say. "Do you want to be on the radio?"

# CHAPTER 73

## *Love*

### SOPHIE

Being in the WZLY studios isn't as scary as I thought it'd be. The soundboard has too many buttons, and the whole back area with a mess of CDs and records is horrifying to look at—Jo called me a "Marie Kondo–ass bitch" when I remarked on it—but the place is pretty nice. The writing on the walls has a lot of personality.

"I promise it's not that scary," Jo says. "Talk to me like you'd normally talk, except a few random people might be listening in." Like all our friends.

After texting them to listen to the show, Jo makes me sit down in front of a microphone, right across from her. She fiddles around with the computer and the soundboard, explaining all the things to me as if understanding it will make it less intimidating, and then she goes on the air.

"You're listening to WZLY Wellesley, 91.5 FM. My name is Jo, and this is my show where I play whatever the heck I want, except today, I won't be. Because I have a special guest with me here."

She gestures at me. I lean uncomfortably closely into the microphone.

"Hi," I say. "My name is Sophie."

"And who are you, Sophie?"

Who *am* I? "I'm, uh . . . I'm your friend. Your future roommate. Your co-president."

"Co-president is right," Jo says. "So, Sophie and I are the co-presidents and founders of the Wellesley Dianas, a discussion group for a-spec students, and literally, like, fifteen minutes ago, we just made a touring prospie's day by telling her about this club."

"It was honestly magical," I say.

"So to celebrate the fact that we are now making a difference in people's lives," Jo says, "we're going to be playing some fun music for you. Music that we, as two aroace people, can relate to. Sophie, what are we starting with?"

"We're listening to one of my favorite songs," I say. "This is 'Solo' by Carly Rae Jepsen, from *Dedicated Side B*."

Jo presses play on the playlist and turns off our mics.

"See, that wasn't so scary!" she says. "Right?"

"No, yeah, that was pretty good," I say, nodding.

"I can't believe you listen to Carly Rae Jepsen, though." Jo rolls her eyes.

"She's an *icon*."

Jo frowns. "Is she? Is she really?"

"She's no Taylor Swift, but—"

"Oh my god, can you give it a rest with Taylor Swift?"

"She's the greatest artist of this generation!"

We're laughing, and it feels so normal and so weird to be here with her. Taking up a little more space in this pocket of her life. It's very intimate to be sharing your niche hobbies with somebody else. Your music, your thoughts, your words.

I get a text from Priya that says she's not surprised at all by the track I chose, and then I get another one from her saying Izzy agrees. Alicia sends me a text saying she wants to listen to Carly Rae Jepsen more now. Texts start coming in from the Dianas group chat, and they're lauding my choice in music and suggesting more songs and telling Jo her mic is way too loud, but it's not actually loud, she's just a loud person.

The next song plays—Sylvan Esso's cover of "There Are Many Ways to Say I Love You" from *Mister Rogers' Neighborhood*—and I look over at Jo, her eyes closed, leaning back, taking the music in.

And I do the same.

**anon:** Hey there! Quick question for you: How do I deal with the fact that my roommate for this fall is way cooler than I am? If you don't believe me, listen to this: they listen to indie bedroom pop, they wear Doc Martens and they enjoy polisci classes here. Plus, they play on the radio, and as we all know, anyone who DJs for WZLY is an absolute icon.

**answer:** lmao.
okay. here's a step-by-step list of ways you can be as cool as your roommate

- stop capitalizing your letters this isn't 2005
- use the fucking oxford comma. unless you're writing for the news, there is no reason why you shouldn't.
- listen to more indie bedroom pop?? i love this school but y'all are way too obsessed with taylor swift
- or . . . don't change anything at all. they probably think you're pretty cool too

happy first week of class or whatever!

---

**dearwendywellesley 1h**
What kind of advice is that? You should be kinder than this
Reply

> **wandawellesley69 42m**
> i literally said "they probably think you're pretty cool too" though???
> Reply

dear wendy,

my best friend thinks i'm cooler than her, but that's completely untrue. or, at least, i think her idea of "cool" is pretty different from mine. but i think she's cool. she actually has a normal sleeping schedule. she eats three meals a day. she tells me all the things i need to hear. that's extremely cool. and i guess sometimes i feel like i'm not. frankly, i can be a bit of a disaster sometimes.

how do i be more like her?

from,
the other one

Dear Other,

I think in your situation, you're fine just the way you are. At least, that's the kind of advice *my* friends would give me. People can be cool in different ways, and friends are meant to complement each other, not be each other's mirrors. Besides, everyone's a bit of a disaster. Your image of yourself isn't necessarily how other people see you.

I've found that approaching friendships isn't all too different from approaching romantic relationships. Maybe you know that already, since you did ask me, of all people, for advice. When two people work well together—whether that's platonically or romantically—all you need to do is enjoy that fact.

People choose, every day, to be lovers, to be friends, to be family. You seem to love your best friend a lot.

Bottom line: You don't need to change a thing.

Love,
Wendy Wellesley

P.S. Your friend sounds like quite the Wendy.

---

**wandawellesley69 31m**
she is.
1 like Reply

# Acknowledgments

First, I must thank the asexual and aromantic communities, as well as all the ace and aro people who've picked up this book, because without you, *Dear Wendy* wouldn't exist at all. Particularly, I am unbelievably thankful for all the a-spec people of color who exist boldly and remind me that we are not alone—that our voices matter. One novel by one person can't possibly represent the wide range and depths of our experiences, but I hope I've written a story we can be proud of.

My thanks must also go to the increasing number of YA authors who have written about characters on the asexual and/or aromantic spectrums in their own books, the books I yearned so desperately for as a young teen. In particular, I must thank Alechia Dow, Alice Oseman, Akemi Dawn Bowman, Chloe Gong, Emma K. Ohland, Racquel Marie, and Rosiee Thor for being inspirations for my own writing (and just for writing some really great books).

Thank you, thank you, thank you to my literary agent, Jennifer March Soloway. Way back in 2021, Jennifer saw a little book about an internet rivalry in her inbox from a nineteen-year-old fan of one of her other clients, and somehow, she decided this was the next book she wanted to take on. Thank you, Jennifer, for our endlessly delightful phone conversations and for always having my best interests in mind; your support truly means everything to me. Many thanks must also go to Andrea Brown and the entire ABLA team for their support and for being an absolute powerhouse of an agency. And thank you so much to Taryn Fagerness for your work bringing *Dear Wendy* to readers around the world.

Of course, all of my thanks to Foyinsi Adegbonmire, my amazing editor, fellow Taylor Swift enthusiast, and subject of my dead-fangirl squeals during a murder mystery game we participated in before *Dear Wendy* was even on sub. I still have you saved in my phone as "Foyinsi (Nicky Rook)." Your enthusiasm for and championing of this novel means the world to me. Thank you also to Jean Feiwel and the entire team at Feiwel & Friends, whose books are genuinely some of the best books of this generation. I can't believe I'm being published by the person responsible for bringing the Baby-Sitters Club to Scholastic; those books were my whole life as a kid.

Thank you to my copyeditor, Jackie Dever, and my proofreaders, Jessica White and Marinda Valenti for fixing my embarrassing typos and creating a style guide that both amused and humbled me. Thank you to my production editors, Ilana Worrell and Kelly Markus, and to my book designer, Julia Bianchi, for making my book look so pretty on the inside. Thank you also to my production managers, Kim Waymer and Jie Yang. Thank you to contracts, marketing, publicity, sales, managing editorial, and the ebook team. Thank you to Betsy Cola for illustrating the most amazing cover I have ever seen in my life, and to Julia Bianchi (again) for the cover design. Thank you to Miles Mikaya, Alice Gorelick, and Annabella Correa-Maynard for your insightful comments on the portrayals of characters in *Dear Wendy* whose identities I do not share.

Thank you to all the people who read early versions of *Dear Wendy* and gave me notes or cheered me on. Famke Halma, Sydney Langford, and Christen Randall read the very first draft of this book, before Alicia was even a character in it—thank you for being willing to read such a mess of a version of this. Thank you as well to Kalie Holford, Abbie Brown, Victoria Wlosok, Katya Ivanenko, Abby Knudsen, GiannaMarie Dobson, Jill Stebelton, and Bria Fournier for giving me feedback on subsequent iterations. Ananya Devarajan, Cindy Chen, and Layla Noor, you read an old version of this book purely to love it and not even to give me feedback, and I love you so much for that (though you really should've given me feedback because wow, it was messy back then). To Kyra Nelson, thank you for your notes on my *Dear Wendy* query way back when. Moreover, many of my friends in my personal life also read this book and gave me more love than I could possibly know what to do with. Thank you so much.

Thank you to the writer groups and individuals who keep me sane. Famke, Layla, Tori, and Sydney, I love you all to death, and I can't believe they actually let me put cameos of all your books or characters into my book. To those in WMC, the AAPI Writing Community Discord, the 2024 debut Slack, and literally anybody who's in my Twitter Circle, thank you for all of your support and love and camaraderie. Thank you to Birukti Tsige for all of the advice and commiseration,

---

and for becoming my agent sibling (I can't believe Jennifer would take on *two* college students in the Boston area as clients). Thank you to Abbie Brown for all our talks on Utah culture and fandom toxicity (completely unrelated to each other, and only one of which I know anything about). Thank you to the other 2024 publishing children for breaking into the industry with me at such a young age.

Many people have made a small but significant impact on me throughout these last few years, and I cannot possibly thank you all, but a blanket thank-you to all the authors and publishing folks who spoke with me in person or online, gave me advice, connected me with other authors, or even simply responded when I swiped up on your Instagram story or tagged you in a review of your book. Publishing is scary, and you made it a little less so.

Thank you very much to Adiba Jaigirdar, Aiden Thomas, Alechia Dow, Ann Liang, Becky Albertalli, Chloe Gong, and Racquel Marie, who all wrote the kindest words of support for *Dear Wendy*. It's incredibly heartwarming to get blurbs from writers I've been reading for so many years.

My many thanks to the educators who supported my love for (i.e., obsession with) reading and writing when I was a little kiddo. I don't know how many of you will find this book and see this paragraph, but you truly made a difference in my life, and it is in part because of you that I'm sitting here writing these acknowledgments. To my preschool teacher who introduced me to the first book I'd read with a Chinese protagonist, to my middle school teachers whose classroom libraries were stacked high with YA novels that would someday inspire this one, and to the high school teachers who taught me how to write with my own voice: thank you so much.

To Angela Carpenter, Sabriya Fisher, Jennifer Musto, Jeannine Johnson, Yoolim Kim, Irene Mata, and Matt Kaliner, for teaching my favorite classes at Wellesley and (at least for some of you) putting up with me when I missed class to do book things. Is it possible to schedule office hours with you after I've graduated? And to the current and past e-boards of the *Wellesley News* and WZLY—I'm sorry I left e-board to focus on my writing, but it had to be done. To E. B. Bartels, thank you for supporting my writing even though you're over a decade removed from my graduating class and you write nonfiction books about animals.

Izzy and Cheryl, I can't believe you put up with living with me for as long as you did. Tazrean and Riya, I can understand fully why you did *not* live with me.

Elaine, Adrianne, Vân An, Eugenie, Genie, Yuling, Claire, Elizabeth, and Elyse, thank you for the many dinners we have had, including the one where Elaine got COVID (I still think it was a false positive) and caused many of us to have to isolate until Christmas. Fun fact, I wrote a big chunk of DW's first draft during that week. And to Anna K.! We now have another oddly specific thing in common: being mentioned in a YA book's acknowledgments.

To everyone on Wellesley Twitter. Y'all are weird.

And to the actual anonymous Instagram accounts of Wellesley College, especially Wellesley Crushes, for inspiring this whole book. I'd be remiss if I didn't also mention Wellesley Crunches. I think I technically predicted your existence.

Thank you, now, to the rest of my friends and family for making my life as good as it is.

To the friends with whom I braved hours on Ticketmaster to see Taylor Swift for the first time. (Absolutely no thanks to Ticketmaster. Some thanks to Taylor Swift for making the music that got me through the writing of this book.) To everyone with whom I made it through the cursed politics club that shall not be named. Katie, if you have Zuzu when you read this, give him back; if I have him, I promise I'll return him to you soon.

To my little cousins in Massachusetts, you are definitely not old enough to read this book, but hopefully you can enjoy it one day. To my aunt and uncle there, thank you for the food, the summer basement storage, and all the rides to and from the airport. To my aunt, uncle, and cousins in Georgia, thank you for all of your support even though you barely know what this book is about, and thank you especially to Emily for putting up with all the weird posts I send you when I'm on an internet doomscroll.

Thank you to my siblings, Kate and Elliot, for humbling me all the time. You guys are growing up too fast. Mom and Dad, thank you for getting me this far in life and for supporting my career endeavors even though writing and academia are both incredibly underpaid and unstable fields of work. 我还要感谢我的姥姥和姥爷。虽然你们现在不能读这本书，但是我希望你们知道我多爱你。

And thank you, the person reading this, for, well, reading this. If you seriously read through all of these acknowledgments, you're *such* a Wendy. (If you skipped to the end to see who was thanked last, you're a Wanda.)

Thank you for reading this FEIWEL & FRIENDS book.
The friends who made

*Dear Wendy*

possible are:

Jean Feiwel, Publisher
Liz Szabla, VP, Associate Publisher
Rich Deas, Senior Creative Director
Anna Roberto, Executive Editor
Holly West, Senior Editor
Kat Brzozowski, Senior Editor
Dawn Ryan, Executive Managing Editor
Kim Waymer, Senior Production Manager
Emily Settle, Editor
Rachel Diebel, Editor
Foyinsi Adegbonmire, Editor
Brittany Groves, Assistant Editor
Julia Bianchi, Junior Designer
Ilana Worrell, Senior Production Editor
Kelly Markus, Production Editorial Assistant

Follow us on Facebook or visit us online at **mackids.com.**
Our books are friends for life.